ANARCHIST
UNDERGROUND
NICOLE ROWLES

Contents

To the fighters.
In you, they've met their match.
So fight.

One

Hot blood sprayed across her face, spattering bitterly into her mouth.

The thunderous cry at her back was afire with furious glory.

"Victory! Victory against Nielle! Hail to Dunwyn! Hail to King Saban!"

Each cry was like a knife, driving dread and fear into her heart. She had no idea who she was without the war.

And now the war was over.

★★★

"First thing I'm going to do when I get home is kiss the prettiest girl I can find."

Aela Rinn rolled her eyes. Landon Holland's tragic romanticism was adorable … and annoyingly resilient. He'd seen enough of the world by now to know better.

Chase Fenner snorted beside Landon. "After a year at war, *I'd* tumble a man with the face of a crag and the personality of a boulder."

"Let's not act like that's a choice for you," Aela said, shifting restlessly in the saddle, aching from the days-long ride on her stallion.

Laughter rumbled through the soldiers riding nearby. A company of seven thousand stretched out behind them, moving in perfect formation along the uneven pine forest road. More than ten thousand Dunwyan fighters had set out from the capital over the course of the four-year-long Border War.

Aela was thankful her closest friends had survived to ride home beside her. She knew them all like family. Chase, with his intentionally sloppy riding style that transformed in a heartbeat to speed and technical perfection when he was called to fight. Landon's flawless, upright posture, the concentration on his face, like he was checking off a list of everything he'd ever learned in training. Mason, with one strong hand resting on her horse's neck, occasionally speaking to the animal in her melodic voice, insistent that horses could understand her.

After more than a year in their company, Aela could identify each of them blindfolded, by hearing them laugh or spur their mounts forward with an easy click of the tongue.

"Be fair, Commander Rinn. We don't all have a good country boy sitting at home, dreaming about us."

Dimples dented Landon's face and he cracked a tentative grin, wanting to be included but afraid of ending up in hot water. At nineteen, he was only two years younger than Aela, but as the third son of a nobleman he'd lived a more sheltered life than most soldiers. He hadn't quite perfected the art of casual banter between comrades.

"Oh, yes." Chase seized upon Landon's words gleefully. "I have to say, stopping over in your hometown was worth it to see that poor boy fumble for your attention." He fluttered his long eyelashes coquettishly at Aela. "'You don't need the army! You're the commander of my heart!'"

He broke formation, dodging when Aela hoisted herself from the saddle and aimed a punch at his shoulder.

"You know, I never imagined you in a relationship with anyone, Commander," Landon said thoughtfully, flushing furiously red as he realised the implication. "Not that you're not … For a Borderlander, you're really quite … I mean the, ah, the darker hair and the blue eyes … It looks –"

"Landon?" Aela interrupted sweetly.

"Yes, Commander?"

"Shut up."

Aela wasn't particularly sensitive to comments about her appearance. As a Dunwyan soldier with Niellan blood, questions were inevitable. Curious remarks about her short brown waves, sun-streaked with caramel, and her Niellan blue eyes had followed her ever since she'd arrived in the capital. Aela scratched a hand through her hair, avoiding the band of brown fabric pulling the front strands off her face. Curiosity was preferable to some people's frankly insulting surprise that someone built like a twig could fight as well as she did. That she was weak was a dangerous assumption. She was all muscle, tempered in combat since childhood.

Captain Mason Tanner shook out her short curls, flexing her tattooed arms and neck stiffly, a mature woman preparing to school her young companions with sage wisdom. Not that she was old, but living to forty as a soldier of Dunwyn had become an impressive feat in recent years. At twenty-one, Aela was already older than many of the fighters she commanded. Mason captained the unit Aela had come up in as a cadet. She'd been an invaluable advisor over the past grim months.

Mason hadn't taken being passed over for the role of commander personally. Aela made up for her youth with her experience fighting in Borderland terrain, and Mason had celebrated Aela's victories, a constant source of support. Aela didn't know what she would have done without Mason at her side on the front line.

"A man wants a woman he can feel equal to," Mason told them solemnly, her rich voice commanding attention. "Must be hard to feel equal to the Reaper of Dunwyn." She winked at Aela. "I'm sure that lad will soon realise the error of his ways. If not, you can always wait until he experiences more of your charming personality."

More laughter. Aela flipped her middle finger. "Fuck off, Captain."

"Thanks for making my point."

Aela made a face at Mason, her thoughts wandering back to her tiny village with its red soil and proud people. When she'd received the order to make for Dunwald, the residents of Hiver hadn't begged the army to stay. They'd done what they always did, assigned a rotation of their own to watch for emerging threats across the border. They knew well that the uneasy peace between Dunwyn and Nielle wouldn't last. Aela knew it too. When she and the rest of the army had ridden out towards the capital, she couldn't bear to look back. Leaving them unprotected was a grievous betrayal.

The guilt hadn't faded. Each day of travel took them further from the battlefield where Aela had secured victory against the Niellan enemy on land that had once been the very heart of the One Kingdom. Despite the growing distance, thoughts of her hometown occupied her mind.

Aela thought of Amory, who despite his youth had raised her like his own child. She thought of Amory's husband, Ewan, and their small, cosy home that had always felt impervious to the dangers of the outside world. She thought of Tamas – the impulsive night they'd spent lost in each other haunted her memory. She'd ignored her better judgement, seeking desperately, selfishly for any feeling akin to the euphoria of battle. When it sank in how much more that night had meant to Tamas, how terribly she'd used him, it was already far too late.

Ever since they were children playing together barefoot, she'd hoped he would outgrow his feelings for her, or that her own feelings for him would become clearer. Apparently, it had all been for nothing … as if Aela needed further confirmation that hope was a useless thing to feel.

Her thoughts of Hiver fell away as the forest opened into a green valley, and a familiar, breathtaking formation rose up on the horizon.

Coming home after a year at war, it felt like Aela was seeing the city of Dunwald for the first time. She was awestruck by the enormous white brick walls and red-tiled roofs cascading down the craggy hills. Like the whitewash of the Great Ocean's waves, the flood of structures seemed to crash onto the rocks by the sea. The greenery of the forest curved along the eastern side of the valley, hugging the coastline in the shape of a crescent moon, sweeping in to meet the southern edge of the city. On the northern side of the hill, a familiar line of darker structures, the city's slum, was dappled with makeshift materials.

Aela's eyes were drawn upwards to a single, striking building, standing apart from the rest at the top of the hill. King Saban's marble castle balanced upon its own precarious tower of rock, connected to the mainland only by a drawbridge that spanned a sheer drop. After she'd been named commander, she'd followed Saban across the treacherous, slippery path over the rock pools at the base of the two cliff sides. She'd committed the classified escape route from the castle to memory as the roiling ocean threatened to swallow the entire area on the incoming tide.

The castle's walls and roof stood out against the blue-green ocean that stretched to the horizon, so bright that they reflected the sun, glinting during the day like a beacon. Reaching it was a slow trek upwards through streets, weaving past homes and shopfronts that jutted out of the hillside. Hooves clattered against stone as they entered Dunwald through the white wall that stretched around the city at the foot of the hills, meeting the rocky coast on either side.

"I dreamed of home," Mason said to Aela, her soft voice passing unnoticed by the rest of the group. "Those eight months we were cut off by the enemy, I thought dreaming was the closest I'd ever get to returning. You're the reason we're back here."

Technically, Mason hailed from Jahli, in Dunwyn's south. Her dark brown skin was clear evidence of that. She'd lived in Dunwald's army barracks for longer than Aela had been alive, but she still had a distinct southern accent, dropping her h's and dulling her th's.

Her grey eyes mirrored Aela's dark memories of the days when they'd been besieged on every side, impossibly outnumbered. All that time, with an entire army's welfare to consider, Aela hadn't once rested easily. The feeling of being safe was still foreign and disconcerting.

Slightly ahead of them, Landon turned in his saddle. "Do you think the king will –"

His horse violently shied, forcing him to whirl and tug hard on the reins. Landon struggled to stay mounted as a man darted suddenly from their left, almost throwing himself directly into their path.

The man reached out, desperation etched on his grimy face. As he opened his toothless mouth to issue a frantic plea, an arrow sailed in from the left and hit him in the side of his throat. Two more thudded into his temple and cheek, and he collapsed with a horrible gurgling sound.

Aela's sword sang from its sheath before he hit the ground, and she wrenched her horse hard in the direction from which the shots were fired. She dug her heels in, spurring forward, but someone grabbed the reins and pulled her up short.

"Commander, no." It was Mason.

Furiously, Aela turned on her. "What are you —"

"Look." Mason pointed beyond the dead man's body. Aela looked down. About eight feet away, a demarcation line was drawn in blue paint across the street they were about to turn down.

"We can't." Mason released Aela's reins. "It's Underground."

Chase muttered a curse. "That's not possible. How many times have we ridden up here before?" He pointed at the blue paint. "How the fuck did a main road to the castle become part of Anarchist Underground?"

Aela shook her head. King Saban relinquished control of Dunwald's massive criminal slum more than ten years ago, naming it a separate, unofficial city within the capital. In all that time, the anarchists had never encroached on the blue border that marked out their sliver of territory along the city's northern side. Saban had never allowed it.

"The anarchists aren't protected or governed by the rule of law," Mason said harshly. "They make their own rules. That was the deal. The king ordered that no officer of his army would interfere with their crimes, as long as they don't mess with us." She gestured at the blue line on the stones, her mouth twisting bitterly. "This sure feels like they're messing with us. How could His Highness let this happen?"

Mason's question echoed Aela's thoughts. Saban hadn't been able to resist offering the occasional covert bounty to locate particularly troublesome anarchists and transport them across the blue line to justice, although that had rarely been effective. Anarchists didn't turn on their own.

Righteous as he was, the king would have preferred to properly police the anarchists' trade of drugs, weapons, and drink, but too many innocent bystanders had been accidental casualties of the enforcement operations. The anarchists had no compunction about collateral damage. Saban's decision to leave the anarchists to their business was widely popular amongst law-abiding citizens who didn't want to be caught in the crossfire of a military crackdown. Everyone knew that if you left the anarchists alone, they left you alone.

That was supposed to be the agreement.

"He wouldn't." As Aela said it, she realised how true it was. "He wouldn't let this happen."

Oppressive foreboding seized her heart. She spurred her horse past Landon's, steering around the dead man's body in the street. No one could help him now.

She kept her blade out of its sheath as they rode away from the blue line to find another route to the castle.

Growing up in the Borderlands, Aela had never been present for a military homecoming. She'd heard stories of thunderous applause, flowers and confetti tossed at victorious soldiers. She'd imagined people lining the streets to welcome them with hands shaken and backs slapped. She'd pictured family members crying with joy as they were reunited with wives, husbands, brothers, sisters, children …

The streets weren't empty, but they certainly weren't lined with adoring crowds, and there was no fanfare. Drawn, sombre faces watched silently as the army rode through the streets. No one made eye contact. Every time Aela sought the gaze of one of the townsfolk, they looked away or hurried out of sight.

Almost a hundred feet across, the wooden drawbridge didn't so much as creak under the weight of dozens of soldiers and their mounts. Surrounded by other riders, Aela couldn't see the exposed edges where the bridge opened out to a forbidding drop.

"Commander?" Landon came up beside her as they rode across.

Pale-faced, he looked younger than usual, and he was trembling the way one did after a long ride, muscles aching from prolonged use. He'd never witnessed a military return either. But they all knew it wasn't supposed to be like this. Ahead, the portcullis was open, and the bridge was down. Beyond it, the enormous circular courtyard and the long, narrow front gardens that separated the main castle from the outbuildings housing soldiers and servants were utterly devoid of people.

Aela shook her head. "Don't worry," she told Landon. "The king will be pleased to see us." It didn't sound as convincing as she'd intended.

"About that," Mason said, looking around grimly as they passed over the bridge. "I was at least expecting him to have a herald here to greet us."

Aela tried not to look troubled, but she'd been thinking the same thing. The *least* King Saban could have done was send someone to welcome them after they'd spent eight months surrounded by enemy fighters, unable to advance or retreat. They had overcome desperate odds to emerge victorious from a bloody conflict, ending four years of war. *Especially* after what Aela had done to secure their victory, she'd been expecting the king himself to greet them.

She raised her voice. "Tend to the horses, take your weapons to the armoury, then go to the barracks and get some rest."

Dismounting, she handed her horse off to Landon, who gave a weary nod and trudged towards the barracks as more soldiers continued to trickle into the courtyard. Aela went straight ahead into the castle. Saban must be in the great hall, waiting to receive her.

The castle felt as much like home to Aela as Hiver did. She'd walked this route countless times, heading through the long main corridor to the great hall. It was a large and windowless path. Sconces lined the walls, casting flickering shadows across the floor.

For a moment, she stopped. Closing her eyes, she drew and in a long, slow breath. It was quiet. After a year of war cries and bloody fighting, the silence was unnerving. Everything around her felt softened and blurred, as ineffectual as a dulled blade. The sights, sounds, and smells of her surroundings barely penetrated her senses. If she stayed here forever, she could lose track of all time.

She quickened her pace towards the hall.

Outside the room, she paused again, this time because the heavy wooden doors were shut. They were never shut.

Four men stood in front of them, heavily armed and wearing, not the familiar purple robes bearing King Saban's arc of gold stars, but unfamiliar burnt-orange cloaks over their armour. Aela couldn't tell if she recognised the guards. They wore helmets, which was unusual off the field of combat. She supposed it spoke to how high tensions were running since the war. As she approached, they silently pushed the doors open, allowing her to enter.

Compared to musty dark corridor, the vast brightness of the great hall was overwhelming. Like the rest of the castle, it was built in pristine white marble, a breathtakingly airy space with a hundred foot vaulted ceiling. A row of windows almost as tall lined the raised dais at the back of the room, looking out on the endless blue of the Great Ocean.

Habit drew Aela's gaze to Saban's throne atop the dais. Carved in matching white marble and swathed in purple velvet, it was bathed in the golden light of the Dunwyan sun. She stepped forward and froze, wrongness jarring her certainty.

It wasn't Saban sitting on the throne. It was Huntley Bartome.

Aela had been in awe of Huntley ever since arriving in Dunwald as a sixteen-year-old Borderlander a few months before the start of the Border War. A full two decades younger than Saban, the woman was so intelligent, so capable, that she'd secured the role of ambassador to Nielle at the impressive age of twenty-one. She'd held the fraught position for more than twenty years, until war had broken out.

Huntley had always looked older than she was. It was probably a miracle she wasn't wholly grey considering the prolonged and precarious nature of her job dealing with the warmongering Niellan king and his antagonistic court. Still, something about her looked different now.

Her blonde hair was raked back into a characteristic severe bun and in the unforgiving light, Aela could clearly see new lines on her face. She looked frailer than a forty-five-year-old should, with dark circles under her intent hazel eyes that were over-bright. Even the way she sat made her look like an old woman. She was tall, but her usually straight posture was slouched, like she bore an exhausting weight.

Aela stood before the throne and gave a deep bow. If it was the king, she would go to her knees.

"Commander Rinn." Huntley inclined her head.

"Your Excellency, where is His Highness?" Aela asked.

Huntley bowed her head. "King Saban is dead. The council has appointed me steward of Dunwyn."

Aela's stomach dropped. Her world tilted, her throat closing up. She swallowed convulsively, trying to fight down the wave of grief that threatened to drive her to her knees.

On the eve of her departure to the front lines of the Border War, Saban had summoned her to his private garden. He'd always preferred to take his informal meetings outdoors. They'd sat together through the night, talking about how Dunwyn's forces at the border were severely depleted. The commander in charge was dead, and the Dunwyan army was rudderless. Aela would be sent with reinforcements to bring them relief.

She hadn't said it, but she was terrified, a twenty-one-year-old riding out to fill the shoes of a battle-seasoned commander who was cut down on the field. Before she left, Saban embraced her. His golden-brown eyes softening as he looked down at her, slipping the ring off his finger and onto Aela's. The gold ring's purple base was shot through with a curve of glinting gold stars, the Ryland family insignia. The symbol of the Dunwyan throne.

Saban had spoken to her in a soft voice.

"I love you like my own daughter, but that's not why you have risen through the ranks faster than others. It's because you are an exceptional fighter and an unrivalled strategist. You've fought hard for everything you have. I wish I didn't have to thrust such responsibility on someone so young. I wish you had more time to stay here and train, but we are losing this war. Commander Pollack is dead and no one knows how to fight in the Borderlands better than you. No one will fight harder than you to win victory for Dunwyn."

Now, Aela felt so alone, standing in the throne room, the pain of loss hanging oppressively heavy in the air. She squeezed the king's insignia in her pocket, running her finger over the raised gold stars to steady herself. The dark mood over the city and its people all made sense now.

"When?" she managed to say.

"Seven months ago," Huntley replied. Her voice cracked, and she slumped back against the throne. She ran her hand over her mouth and a flash of silver on her finger told Aela she was wearing the ring bearing the Dunwyan steward's insignia. Aela's heart ached for Huntley; Saban was one of her oldest friends. "Stabbed in the heart. His Highness always said Prince Bryn was excellent with a blade."

"*Prince Bryn* killed him?"

Saban's only son was indeed excellent with a blade. Aela had seen him in training – the only time he focused on anything other than infuriating his father and tormenting the servants and councillors. Rumour had it, Bryn only ever used his fighting prowess when he snuck out of the castle to earn a few coins in illegal fighting rings, coins he frittered on drink and women. Aela had never quite understood that. The way he looked, Bryn wasn't someone who needed to pay for sex.

"Yes, and then he fled like a coward. No one has seen him since." Huntley's voice was hard.

Aela shook her head. "I can't believe it."

She couldn't believe a lot of things. *Seven months*. It must have happened right after the Niellan ambush that had left the Dunwyan army surrounded, cut off so that no messenger could get in or out. But it felt impossible that she could have carried on without knowing, without feeling *something*, all this time. How did the world feel the same when the only father she'd ever known was no longer in it?

Fury crashed down over her grief. This explained the disturbing attack they'd witnessed on the street, at least. The death of the king and the disappearance of his only heir was certainly enough to embolden the anarchists to expand their grasp on Dunwald.

"The people are calling for the prince's arrest," Huntley said. "They're calling for his execution."

Execution. The word was jarring, as if spoken in a different language. Saban hadn't ordered the execution of a criminal in Aela's lifetime. But Huntley and Saban had been close friends for more than two decades, bearing the weight of the country's most difficult decisions together. The malice in Huntley's voice matched the feeling in Aela's heart. If there was any crime that warranted death…

Swallowing hard, Aela shook her head, pushing the ugly thought from her mind. "He needs to be brought to trial. With your permission, I'll assemble a small team to find him discreetly."

Backlit against the windows, Huntley's shadow stretched down the dais steps as she leaned forward and shook her head.

"No."

Aela was sure she'd misheard. "Your Excellency?" She stumbled slightly over the unfamiliar honorific reserved for the steward's position.

"You weren't here to witness it. The prince's treachery runs deep. Commander Rinn, Bryn Ryland is an anarchist."

"An *anarchist?*" Aela repeated. Her thoughts scattered as she scrambled to make sense of it, like trying to solve a puzzle with pieces missing. Prince Bryn had a reputation for being wilful, but it was impossible for Aela to believe that the son Saban had raised could align with those who were the antithesis of all he stood for. "How do you know?"

Huntley's grief-stricken expression showed a hint of surprise, and Aela's face grew hot. She was forgetting herself. She'd admired Huntley from afar, and they'd occasionally shared passing conversation, but her station was too far below Huntley's to demand answers.

Huntley rose from the throne, descending the steps of the dais to place a hand on Aela's shoulder. Under the crushing weight of desolation was a distant sense of relief. For more than a year, Aela alone had been responsible for making decisions that impacted the lives of all those around her. Knowing that Huntley, with all her wisdom, experience and courage, would lead them out of this dark place was immense comfort.

"My guard saw the prince with blood on his hands, kneeling over his father's body," Huntley said gently. "He fled before they could apprehend him."

"Your guard? Where was the king's guard?"

"Oh, Aela," Huntley began, the informal address not as startling as the steward's look of utter devastation. "They died with honour protecting the king."

This terrible blow took the last of Aela's remaining strength. The four men who'd guarded Saban were exceptional fighters. They'd trained with Aela ... and with Bryn, sharing their tactics and techniques, never believing for a moment he would turn on them.

Huntley watched Aela with concern, one hand still resting on her shoulder. "I regret that this is the nature of your homecoming. It isn't fair. All of Dunwald should be rejoicing at the Reaper of Dunwyn's return. We should be celebrating your single combat victory against Nielle's finest warrior, thanking you for saving the entire army from more bloodshed. You've given so much for our king, his council, and our people." She gave a small smile, but her eyes remained troubled. "You can rest now. I want you to take some time, not as a punishment but as a reward, for delivering peace to your country."

It took a moment to sink in, then horror washed over Aela.

"You're … discharging me from the army?"

A reward, Huntley said, but it wasn't right. Saban would have consulted her before bestowing this manner of reward. Saban would have known it wasn't a reward at all.

"Your Excellency," Aela said desperately, "the Niellans can't be trusted to honour the truce we won in the Border War. Even if they hold to it officially, King Marcus has no compunction about hiring mercenaries to raid our Borderland towns. He still seeks retribution for the death of his son. Our victory may have bloodied his nose, but I don't believe he'll be deterred for long, especially without a Dunwyan military presence on the border."

Something flashed in Huntley's eyes, and her voice turned hard. "Dunwyn did not kill King Marcus's son, Commander Rinn."

Aela bit her lip. Huntley knew better than anyone of the terrible tragedy that had started the Border War. It was unspeakably disrespectful to suggest she wasn't taking the threat of Nielle seriously. Still … "The boy is dead though. You witnessed the search for his body before the Niellans cast you out of their country. You know King Marcus believes Dunwyn is responsible, and he won't stop coming for us. Your Excellency, we can't fight a war on two fronts. We have to get the anarchists under control at home and send soldiers back to defend the border. I can help!"

Huntley sighed. "You've always been so determined." She let out a breathy laugh. "I give you my word that I'll do everything in my power to bring the prince to justice and keep our country at peace. You must trust me."

"I do trust you, but —"

"Then go. Please. I have much to do." She gestured towards the door. Numbly, Aela obeyed, pausing only when Huntley called out to her again. "Aela?"

She turned.

"Keep your sword close," Huntley said. "These are dangerous times."

There was a solid thud as the door shut behind her. Aela stood there, raw disbelief chasing all the thoughts from her mind. Dunwyn's troubles weren't over, but there was nothing she could do to help. Everything she'd worked for was on the other side of the door that had been slammed in her face. For four years, the rhythm of war had beaten in her chest, pumped life through her veins and given her purpose. Now, she was completely lost.

Emboldened by despair, she stole into King Saban's bedchambers. It was something she would never have been able to do, unchecked, if he was alive. His guard should be monitoring the rooms for unauthorised entries, but they couldn't do that. They were dead too.

Thin slivers of light peeked through the drawn curtains, slashing golden lines across the dark surface of Saban's bed. The sheets had been removed, but nothing could erase the dark stain on the mattress. Aela leaned down and splayed her hand across the mark. It looked black in the shadows.

But it wasn't black. It was dark red, the blood of a man who was knifed in his bed by his only son.

Two

Insouciantly, Aela ducked the sloppy blow of her opponent, grinning because she knew it would madden him. The momentum of his poorly-aimed punch sent him staggering into the jeering crowd, who shoved him back into the sawdust ring. As he lurched towards her, Aela planted a powerful uppercut into his jaw, and he went down hard. The spectators erupted in euphoric pandemonium.

Someone grabbed Aela's wrist, thrusting her arm in the air, declaring her victorious, and a shower of coins rained onto the floor, payment for her win. She barely noticed any of it. The fight had lasted all of two minutes, a disappointment. Scanning the crowd, she searched for her next opponent, wishing she could queue them up like goods on a warehouse production line, the next one stepping in as soon as she vanquished the last.

The moments between the fights were the worst. That was when she started to think.

It was five days since Huntley had removed her from the castle, from the home and life that had made her who she was. She'd never felt so numb. Her unwashed waves hung loose around her face, a risk in a fight that should have bothered her. She couldn't bring herself to care about anything anymore.

Maybe this was what the Reaper of Dunwyn deserved. After banishing so many souls to eternal purgatory, perhaps her own soul had been destroyed. It seemed fitting.

She gave the roaring crowd a cursory glance. Amongst the clamouring strangers, a familiar, disappointed face was focussed entirely on her. It was the first time Aela had seen Mason out of her military uniform. She wore typical civilian attire, a laced-up white shirt and functional brown pants, but she looked out of place here. Her curls were slicked back, her clothes too neat. She stood upright like a soldier at attention, incongruous in the rowdy mess of hollering drunkards. As their eyes met, Mason turned away and elbowed through the crowd. Swearing, Aela followed her outside, coins crunching under her feet.

"This is no place for a soldier of Dunwyn," she called to Mason when they were clear of the tavern.

Mason's sharp, frustrated grunt echoed off the grimy walls of the alleyway. The sky was dark. When Aela had gone into the establishment looking for a fight, the sun had still been up.

"Then what the hell are *you* doing here? Bare knuckle fights are illegal." Mason jerked her head down the alleyway. "And the boundary to Anarchist Underground's right there."

The blue line was only a few steps behind Aela.

"I'm not a soldier anymore," she said, unable to conceal the bitterness in her voice. "I'm a civilian now. I can go where I please."

"And what about your duties?"

"What do you mean?"

Mason gave her an appraising look. "Where've you been, Aela?"

Aela held up her hand demonstratively. The cuts and bruises on her knuckles from tonight's fighting overlaid older markings, a week's worth of blows from constant victories that were endlessly unsatisfying.

Mason raised her brows at Aela, unimpressed. "A fine fucking use of your time."

Aela spread her arms wide. "What do you want from me, Mason? I'm a fighter. I need to *fight*."

"That's funny," she said. "I thought you were a commander with principles." Mason waved her hand dismissively. "Coming here was a mistake. Damn the rest of us, Aela Rinn. You do whatever you want."

"Mason …"

The words she needed to call her friend back died in her throat. She didn't need the burden of Mason's criticisms or expectations. She didn't need to be compared to what she had been. Her whole life had been upended. Facing her friends like this was shameful. As a soldier, she'd always known exactly who she was, what she cared about, and what she valued. Right now, she was drifting untethered from the principles that usually grounded her, like she was falling through the sky at a nauseating speed. It was more terrifying than fighting in battle.

Mason paused then looked back at Aela. "I expected more from you," she said, before striding off down the alley without a backwards glance.

Aela backed away unsteadily. She closed her eyes, but the disappointment burning in Mason's expression lingered in her mind. Although she'd been fighting for days, this felt like the first time she'd actually been hit. She dropped her head, suddenly exhausted. When she opened her eyes again, she was staring at her boots and under them, a single line of bright blue paint.

Slowly, experimentally, she took another step backwards,

inside the boundary of Anarchist Underground.

Gripped by a mad, desolate impulse, she pulled the king's insignia off her finger, felt the scrape of the rough gold against her skin before tucking it inside her jacket. She took another step, then another, then turned and plunged into the darkness.

She was so consumed by her own thoughts that it took far longer than usual to realise she was being followed.

Aela took a hard right, ducking into an alleyway as the footsteps behind her quickened in pace. Silently, she pressed herself against the cool stone wall, waiting. A man whose face was concealed beneath a hooded cloak walked past Aela, pausing at the mouth of the alleyway. Aela wasn't sure if he moved first or if she did. Their blades rose almost in unison, meeting with shuddering force.

Circling her blade, Aela shoved him backwards. In the dim light, she could see his eyes fixed on her face. This time, he attacked first, advancing directly. Aela feinted left, and he moved to parry, leaving his own left side unguarded. Aela brought her sword down like a dagger, stabbing straight into his heart. The gruesomely satisfying resistance of flesh and muscle tugged at her blade as she drove it inside his body.

She was suddenly back on the battlefield. Red banners bearing King Marcus's golden eagle symbol flickered like flames on the horizon. Cries of pain and death mingled with the clashing of steel, and visceral savagery unified her mind and body into a single, deadly force. Her blade was an extension of her own arm, as if she was reaching inside the bodies of her enemies and ripping out their lives with her bare hands …

The man's rattling gasp whipped her back to the present. With a horrible gurgling sound, he thudded to the ground, dead.

Aela clenched her fists, trying to eliminate the tremor in her hands as she crouched down before him. Pulling back his hood, she gasped, recoiling.

She knew him, not well, but they'd crossed paths in training at the barracks. He was a soldier, a young and talented fighter only a year or two younger than Aela, on the path to becoming a member of the king's guard. Her head swam. He'd seen her face yet still attacked her.

Every soldier knew Aela Rinn, Dunwyn's half-Niellan commander, the king's favourite. It wasn't as if he'd mistaken her for some unknown anarchist, and even if he had, what reason was there to attack? It felt targeted, but that was impossible. It made no sense. Aela reached out, pressing against the wound at his chest, as if stemming the blood flow now would undo the fatal damage she'd already inflicted.

Aela staggered to her feet, bracing herself against the wall. Her legs almost gave out beneath her.

What have I done?

Blood dripped from her fingers, falling like rain onto the blue paint beneath her feet as a cry echoed from the other side of the demarcation line.

"Murderer!" someone screamed, pointing straight at her. "Murderer!"

Aela staggered backwards as two more dark figures joined the woman yelling at the mouth of the alleyway. Her desperate hope that they might hear her out evaporated with a single glint of steel. One of them began to advance towards the blue line. It wasn't too late to turn and run — they wouldn't follow her deep into Anarchist Underground — but her legs felt heavy as lead.

"That's a Niellan!" one of them said, panicked, as he drew

close enough to make out her features.

The other's tense whisper echoed off the alley, its walls suddenly oppressive. "No, that's the Reaper of Dunwyn!"

The figures shifted, and Aela heard the unmistakable sound of more weapons being drawn. Her own blade still in her hand, she tightened her fingers around the weapon until they hurt. If it came to a fight, she would kill these people, and she couldn't stomach the thought of killing more of her own countrymen tonight.

As if from a distance, she heard her sword clatter to the ground, felt hands close firmly around her arms.

"Killing one of your own, ay? The steward'll pay a pretty penny to have you brought back over the blue line."

Three

At sixteen, Aela had burst onto the Dunwyan military stage, a baby-faced, skinny teenager from the middle of nowhere, her natural talent and unprecedented combat experience silencing anyone who said she was too young or too weak to join the ranks. But fighting had never been about proving anything to anyone; it was what made Aela come alive. It was her purpose.

She would never forget the honour of being called up to fight Huntley Bartome, a true testament of her skill to be considered worthy. King Saban had insisted that Huntley train with the military so she could protect herself during her dangerous visits to the volatile Niellan court. Huntley had spent decades honing her swordsmanship with a soldier's dedication.

The fight tested them both, an almost equal match that went on for over thirty minutes, until Aela's arms were shaking, her body drenched in sweat. Finally, exhausted and unfocused, she made a critical error. In a single, effortless motion, Huntley disarmed Aela, bringing the tip of her blade to Aela's throat. From that moment, Aela was utterly in awe.

Facing Huntley now wasn't supposed to feel like this.

She hadn't put up a fight against the civilians who'd caught her in the alley, but she'd almost lost her nerve when the soldiers arrived. Chase and Landon had shown up, looking grim, along with another man and woman, Ricard and Cora, both familiar from the front lines of the Border War. The soldier's body was pulled out of the alley and back over the blue line. Chase had examined it and risen, pale-faced, announcing that they needed to see the steward.

It wasn't how she'd ever imagined herself entering the pristine white great hall, dirty and bloodied, her short hair unkempt and her clothes messy. She couldn't help wondering what Saban would say if he saw her like this.

Huntley's presence on the throne looked as incongruous as Aela felt, entirely out of step with the picture of this room she'd built in her mind over the years. Now, two guards in dark orange cloaks stood on either side of her, their faces shrouded by helmets. Aela felt rather than saw their gazes tracking her as she approached the throne. Flanking Aela, Chase and Landon avoided eye contact. Landon's boyish face was fearful.

His consternation made sense. He was young and hailed from nobility, not yet familiar with the way of things. But Chase's disquiet was baffling. However misplaced, Huntley's decision to stand Aela down from the army had been intended as a reward. Aela had saved the country, saved thousands of lives. Killing this man was awful but necessary. It was self-defence. The audience with the steward was a formality, an opportunity for her to explain what happened.

"Commander Rinn," Huntley said, softly furious, "you've done a terrible thing."

"I ..." Aela stopped as she fully processed the steward's accusation. "There was an attempt on my life, Your Excellency."

It came out wrong. Her tone was defensive, verging on disrespectful.

Huntley straightened on the throne. Her sharp features looked more severe than usual. "Is that so?" She sounded displeased, certainly, but there was an edge of something else behind it. Haste, perhaps, as if she was rushing to get to the end of this conversation.

"Yes, Your Excellency." With unease spidering across her heart, Aela reached compulsively for the king's insignia in her pocket, pulling it free and turning it over in her fingers. "It was self-defence. I think we need to discuss what drove this man to —"

"Commander Rinn, do you expect us to believe that this had nothing to do with Anarchist Underground?" Huntley interrupted.

"Steward, with your permission, I'd like to investigate … *What?*" She shut her mouth before any more unchecked words slipped out and got her into trouble. Aela redirected her incredulity by clenching her fist tightly around Saban's heavy gold insignia until her hand shook. Navigating the landscape of the Dunwyan court was second-nature. She always knew what was going to happen and how she was going to respond. She'd never felt out of control in this environment. But she did now.

Huntley clasped her hands under her chin, examining Aela through blazing eyes. Her lips were pursed with stern displeasure. "Commander Rinn, I understand you were participating in illegal fights for days before you committed this murder. Surely you don't think anyone in this room is stupid enough to buy that tonight was your first time in Underground."

Aela's stomach dropped. *"Murder?"* she repeated

incredulously.

Desperately, she looked from Chase to Landon. Their heads were bowed in deference, but Aela saw Chase's eyes flick towards her for a brief moment. His jaw was tight. Had they known that Huntley was going to accuse her of this?

Did *they* believe she'd committed murder?

It felt like the blood in her veins was on fire. Losing her career was one thing, but losing the respect of Huntley, along with that of her comrades and friends, was so much worse. She shook her head.

"Your Excellency, I did *not* commit a murder. I was attacked. I defended myself with reasonable force. I —"

Huntley raised her hand and Aela broke off, panicked. The look on Huntley's face was terrible, mingled disappointment and fury. "I would never have expected this from you, Commander Rinn. Your connections with the anarchists have directly resulted in the brutal murder of one of your own." She shook her head. "Because of your status, I'm compelled to be merciful. Life imprisonment instead of execution."

Aela's gut clenched. She wasn't a soldier anymore. She hadn't been on official duty when she had killed that man. And when you killed someone, a *soldier*, as a civilian in Dunwyn, you were arrested for it. With no witnesses to corroborate her version of the attack, it simply looked like a former soldier killing a serving military man, an unforgivable crime. Still …

"*Life?* With no trial? Steward —"

"I will not give a voice to an anarchist in this court," Huntley interrupted sharply. "You relinquished any right to be protected by the laws of Dunwyn the moment you set foot over that blue line. These are your actions, and you must face the consequences."

It sounded like she didn't want to make this decision. But Saban *wouldn't* make this decision. Aela was about to open her mouth with another protestation, but Chase stepped forward.

"Your Excellency, I respect the law, as we all do," he said, "but surely there should be a *trial.*"

"A soldier is dead," Huntley replied sharply. "Anarchy has run rampant in Dunwald for far too long. Anarchists are the reason our king is dead." Her eyes narrowed as she regarded Aela. "You have dishonoured that ring in your hands. Take her to the cells."

"Your Excellency —" Chase attempted.

"You're either with us or you're one of *them,* soldier," Huntley warned him coldly. "Which is it?"

Harsh silence stretched out across the room. Tension clear in every line of his body, Chase gave a short bow and turned. Landon followed his lead, still looking anxious. Unable to believe this was happening, Aela distantly allowed them to escort her from the room.

Their footsteps echoed as they walked down the hall, a familiar route to the cells, and each step was galvanising. Aela took stock of the soldiers guarding her. Chase, Ricard, and Cora had standard-issue swords at their belts. The long dagger Landon's father had given him when he'd been recruited hung at his right hip.

Moving before she could second-guess herself, she pulled Landon's dagger from its sheath and kicked out. Her boot made contact with the side of Landon's knee, not hard enough to break or dislocate, but Aela knew when he crumpled to the ground that he wasn't getting up in a hurry.

Hearing footsteps, she drove her elbow up and backwards, heard Cora cry out as the bones in her nose broke. Aela swung around, the dagger's blunt steel hilt driving between Cora's eyes. The soldier dropped like a rock.

She had two blades. Aela grabbed Cora's sword and whirled to face Chase and Ricard, whose weapons were drawn. They eyed her nervously. Smart to be nervous. Aela wasn't in the mood to fuck around.

"I don't want to hurt you," she warned them. "Walk away."

"You heard what the steward said, Commander," Ricard replied tersely. He adjusted his grip on his sword. A bead of sweat trickled down his hairline. "I'm with Dunwyn, not the anarchists."

I'm not an anarchist! Aela wanted to scream, but she knew it wouldn't do any good. Huntley's hardline stance in the wake of Saban's death made it abundantly clear that there was no grey area when it came to Underground. She was a fool. She'd thrown away her good name for a few cheap fights in a backwater bar and a nighttime stroll into Dunwald's criminal underbelly.

But she wasn't about to spend the rest of her life in a cell.

Aela was good at fighting multiple opponents, and unlike Ricard and Chase, her experience predated her military training. She stepped backwards, Cora's sword in her right hand and Landon's dagger in her left.

Chase swung at her left side, a notably noncommittal attack from one of Dunwyn's best fighters. Aela shoved him back easily. It felt wrong, fighting her friend without the safety net of a blunted blade. As Ricard advanced from the right, she swung Chase's blade clear, sweeping up her weapon again, feeling the clash of steel shudder through her arm at Ricard's two-handed swing.

She parried low and pushed back against Ricard's blade, forcing him in a half-circle towards Chase, hitting Chase's exposed side so that he staggered and dropped to one knee. Aela thrust Ricard's blade downwards, forcing him to the floor too, driving her knee up to connect with his forehead. Ricard fell backwards, moaning, barely clinging to consciousness.

A loud groan made Aela turn to see Chase pulling himself to his feet. He grimaced, and Aela almost smiled out of familiar affection. He did everything with a dramatic flourish.

"You're pulling your blows, Commander," he said breathlessly.

Aela dodged Chase's swing, catching his arm and using her foot to sweep his legs out from under him. He gave another groan and thudded back onto the marble, completely spent.

"Yeah, I was pulling my blows." She stood over him. "I don't want to hurt you, Chase. You're still my friend."

Chase's chest was rising and falling rapidly as he tried to catch his breath. Despite everything, there was still humour on his face when he looked up at her.

"You've no idea how much I needed to hear that," he said.

Aela swallowed the ache in her throat, dropped Landon's blade down beside him, and ran from the room before Chase or any of the others could see the tears in her eyes.

★★★

Footsteps alerted her to a new presence a moment before the familiar figure stepped around the corner of the corridor. Aela's heart plummeted. Having reached the limit of what she could take today, it was all she could do not to fall to her knees.

"Oh no, Mason," Aela said in dismay. "Not you too."

Mason's knuckles strained where she gripped the blade at

her belt. She stopped, no longer advancing but deliberately blocking the way forward. Her eyes reflected Aela's fears. They weren't evenly matched with a sword; Mason was good, but Aela was better, which had never been consequential when they'd sparred in training. Aela's hands shook so hard she almost dropped her weapon. If Mason really wanted to stop Aela, neither of them would walk away from this fight unscathed.

If Mason *didn't* want to stop Aela, she was committing a crime.

Mason shook her head. "Damn you, Commander. Don't make me do this."

That eroded the last of Aela's resolve. With her eyes on Mason, she lowered her weapon to the ground and kicked it across the room, raising her hands in surrender.

"I need you to know." Aela's voice shook. "I didn't want to kill him. You know me. I'd *never* kill one of my own soldiers unprovoked. He tried to kill me. I don't know why. I wish I did. Whatever comes next, I forgive you."

Mason swore. There was turmoil in her eyes.

Aela's sword clattered as Mason skidded it back across the floor to collide with Aela's boot.

"You did *not* see me," Mason said firmly. "There are only four soldiers in the king's garden. It's the cleanest route out, but you'll need to move fast before they raise the drawbridge."

Aela hesitated, terrified for her friend. This was treason. "Mason —"

"Go, damn it. I've lost my king. I won't lose my friend too."

Aela picked up her sword, and Mason stepped aside, offering a clear path down the corridor into the garden. From there, she could skirt the castle in the shadows towards the bridge. Until they locked down the citadel, there'd be enough people going in and out that she'd make it undetected.

As she turned her back, Mason called after her. "Aela."

Aela turned. Mason's eyes were blazing with conviction, her greatest strength, Aela had always thought. Betraying the Dunwyan throne and letting Aela go went against everything Mason believed in. Even if no one else found out, Mason might never forgive herself for this, but she was doing it anyway.

"I don't believe it," Mason told her. "You could never be one of them."

Four

The sprawling mass of dilapidated structures spanning the eastern slope of Dunwald looked like any other slum. But beyond the squalid streets stalked by drug-addled beggars was a king's wealth of dirty money. It was Anarchist Underground.

Before the blue line was drawn, King Saban had only ever succeeded in catching low-level criminals. Whatever he'd threatened them with to divulge their information was nothing compared to being branded a rat by every anarchist on the streets. On top of that, the king's soldiers were forbidden from setting foot in Underground since before Aela joined the army. With nothing concrete to go on, the picture she'd formed in her mind of this place was based on stories that ranged from exaggerated to downright fantastical.

The tavern she sat in was she'd pictured. Giggling, scantily-clad girls, slick-painted male prostitutes, a din of yelling punters jostling each other to get the best view of the fighting ring. Most importantly, there was a dark corner where she could sit in peace with her first ever tankard of liquor.

She stared down at the clear liquid. Drunkenness had always sounded like more of an inconvenience than the pleasure other soldiers made it out to be. Her decision to ban alcohol in the army during the war hadn't been popular, but she didn't like the idea of herself or her fighters being in any way altered whilst on the front lines. Tonight, she didn't give a damn if she wasn't in control of her body or her mind. She couldn't control anything else, so what was the point?

Aela took a deep draught from her tankard. Instant regret followed. Her eyes and throat burned and she gagged, bitterness filling her mouth. Chase would have laughed at her, but he wasn't here.

Smaller sips were better. Once the drink began to blur her senses, relax her muscles, and dull her taste buds, she understood the appeal. Drinking had nothing at all to do with enjoying the taste. Her troubles were gradually muted, as if a glass wall materialised between her and all the thoughts playing havoc with her mind. She could still see them, but she felt strangely detached.

She needed to fight.

Aela jerked to her feet, the legs of the chair scraping noisily against the floor. Haphazardly twisting the short, front wisps of hair off her face, she elbowed through the crowd of shouting patrons and towards the weathered old man who was taking ringside bets. A little clumsily, she grabbed his arm.

"I want in."

One of his eyes was half-closed, as if he'd taken too many punches there. He had pockmarks all over his face. His good eye widened as he took her in.

Here we go. He looked skeptical; they always did. To him, she was a wide-eyed, willowy woman with a heart-shaped face and western looks that told the world she wasn't from here. She looked younger than twenty-one.

"*You* want to fight?" he clarified.

"Yes."

The man gestured over to the ring, where a bald beast of a man, shirtless and pasted with sweat, drove his opponent face-first into the sawdust. "Dagny's champion. He won't have any hesitation smashing your pretty face."

"Dagny can try his very best to beat me," Aela replied without inflection.

The man's eyebrows shot up further. She could tell what he was thinking.

Your funeral.

"Buy in's two gold."

She thumped the coins onto his outstretched palm. Before she jumped the barrier into the ring, she reached into her pocket, closing her hand around the king's insignia for a moment before letting it go again. She didn't need it here.

Aela was used to winning a fight quickly and decisively with a few well-placed blows, conserving time and energy for the next onslaught. This crowd wanted something else. They were yelling for a slow, drawn-out show to sate their bloodlust. Aela gave them little more than a cursory thought. She also didn't care about Dagny, who stirred ominously before her. Closing her eyes, her heart swelled with adrenaline. This feeling was what she cared about.

Aela shifted her feet in the sawdust. Her senses were no longer dulled by the alcohol. Her mind felt sharp as a blade. She picked a spot on his built chest, tracking his hands and feet. She didn't raise her own hands, simply stood with one foot in front of the other, arms lazily at her sides.

Well over six feet tall, Dagny was the kind of fighter who used his imposing physique to intimidate an opponent, winning before trading a single blow. Nonchalance on Aela's part would make him angry. And an angry opponent was easy.

She waited.

Dagny's first swing was a knockout blow driving towards Aela's face. She dropped to one knee, propelling herself across the sand, rising to stand behind him.

"Lost something?" she asked him pleasantly.

Dagny whirled and came at her again, but she was ready, faking right, whirling to the left, jamming an elbow hard into his kidney as she moved to his back.

Dagny gaped and turned, his eyes blazing, furious that she'd managed to land a blow before him. She was used to winning fights efficiently, but she could hear the incensed roar of the crowd, greedy for a show. Aela raised her eyebrows questioningly.

"If you want to dance, you'll need a ball gown. Otherwise, you should actually fight me."

It felt good seeing the fury in his eyes, feeling the danger. She was so close to the precipice, on the cusp of the familiar tumult of battle that always sent her falling through the sky like a star on fire.

Dagny was stronger, but Aela was faster, hitting him progressively harder every time she struck. Dagny's swings became sloppy, unplanned, and he spiralled into rage without landing a single blow. Finally, Aela launched herself at him from behind, a flying jump, driving her fist directly into the back of Dagny's bald head. He crashed to the floor and didn't get up.

The crowd erupted.

Something flicked in Aela's mind, and she found herself looking out over the battlefield on the day she'd arrived at the Border War. Dagny's body became one of Dunwyn's soldiers, cut down right in front of her. Blood pooled around him. It sprayed onto her face and body, too hot, like it was burning her flesh. The grass underfoot wasn't green anymore — it was red. There were bodies everywhere…

A hard slap on Aela's back brought her back to herself. The man who'd put her in the ring pressed a bag of coins into her hand, taking her other wrist and driving her arm victoriously into the air. She couldn't see the battlefield anymore. Dagny scrambled to his feet, pupils dilated from repeated blows to the head, but he managed to focus on her long enough to draw his thumb viciously across his own throat.

Aela's blood sang. She smiled.

She was one of the last patrons left in the tavern, sitting back at the small, dark table, sipping whatever potent concoction she'd ordered without thought. The bag of coins, now strapped to her belt, was significantly lighter. The world tilted, dizzy and unbalanced but pleasantly so, as she gulped the last mouthful of her drink.

"Want another one?" The barkeeper strolled up and leaned against the table. She did, but shook her head anyway, her thoughts lingering on Dagny's threat in the ring. If he was waiting for her outside, she needed to be good enough to defend herself.

She looked about the tavern. Business during times of conflict was challenging for merchants who traded in non-essential items like liquor. "Aren't you rationed?"

The barkeeper snorted indelicately. "Taverns in Underground ain't rationed, not since the anarchists started brewing their own concoctions and selling them. They're not bad, if you don't mind the cheap stuff. The anarchists run this whole city. The nobles can say all they want about bringing prosperity to Dunwald, but the anarchists are the ones who make it happen. The war brought lean times for honest traders. The only business that's flourished over the past four years is the business of pleasure – drugs, whores, and drink. If the big man hadn't stepped up to provide, this entire city would've gone to shit."

All the attention on border fighting, all the misery and poverty that had gripped those who'd been left behind, it was a perfect storm, empowering the anarchists to expand their grasp on the city. Still, one thing *was* surprising, the way the barman was talking like there was someone in charge here. "The *big man?*"

The barman winked at her. "When you've got gangs fighting each other for power, someone's always gonna come out on top. If you ever meet him, you'll know about it."

"Boss!" A harried-looking teenage boy ran up to the table. "They're at it again."

A chorus of laughter rang out across the room. Aela turned to see a group of five young men by the wall, four of them circled around a skinny redhead whose eyes were fixed dully on a point above their heads.

"Five gold says he stays up longer than the last one," one of the men said.

To Aela's horror, another man stepped in and punched the redhead square in the cheek. He staggered backwards but maintained his footing. There was a fresh shout of laughter. The redhead barely straightened up when a second man stepped in and dealt another brutal punch. The redhead was still standing, but blood began to drip from his nose.

"Oi!" The barkeeper started towards the group of men threateningly. "Get out of here, the lot of you! I'll not have that grey dream shit in my tavern!"

Laughing louder, the four men ran, leaving the redhead to slump back against the wall. Aela heard their mirth echoing off the walls in the street outside as they retreated into the night.

"Fucking idiots," the barkeeper muttered. He gestured to the teenage boy beside Aela. "Get that kid out of here."

"What was that about?" Aela asked as the teenager guided the stumbling redhead to the door.

"Little bastard's a grey dream addict," the barkeeper replied. "City's full of them. There's one in here every other night. Kids like those pick them off the streets and make them do all sorts of stupid shit. One of these days, they'll cross a line and someone'll be killed."

"Grey dream?"

The barkeeper raised his eyebrows. "How green are you? That bloody drug's been everywhere in Underground since the war started. Gives you one hell of a high, but you'd never catch me taking it. Turns you into a right mess, and most can't function at all without it after a couple of hits. Besides, one mouthful of the stuff and anyone can make you do whatever they like. Someone tells you to stand there and take punch after punch until you fall over, you'll do it."

Aela felt sick, remembering the redhead's glazed-over stare and bloody nose. A buzz from liquor was one thing, but she couldn't imagine leaving herself entirely vulnerable to compulsion for the sake of a high.

"That's fucked up," she muttered.

"Tell me about it," the barkeeper agreed. He eyed her thoughtfully. "You know, fighting skills like yours don't belong in no bar brawl. And girls who look like you don't belong in a dodgy place like this."

"All right," Aela said, crossing her arms and leaning back. "Where do I belong?"

The bartender leaned forward conspiratorially, his fetid breath brushing across her sweaty cheeks. "I think there's someone waiting outside who wants to answer that."

It didn't take the barman's warning or any great stroke of genius to predict that Dagny would be waiting when she walked out of the tavern some time later, or that he wouldn't be alone. What Aela hadn't predicted was that her ambushers would be closer to a military unit than a disorganised rabble of thugs.

Four of them circled her, closing in with confidence. She could tell by the way they moved that they had the advantage of experience working together. Aela figured she could at least put up a good fight, but what was the point? She sized them up, three men and one woman, and discarded the idea of resisting. Wherever the bartender thought she belonged, these four clearly intended to take her there, and she had nowhere else to go.

Cloths and hoods covered their faces, leaving only their eyes visible. She picked Dagny immediately by his size, and the woman by her body. She levelled a crossbow on Aela, an arrow nocked in place. Dagny now carried a brutal-looking broadsword, which he rested against her collarbone as he approached. Another sword pricked her neck from the side.

Aela's heart pounded gloriously. They could drive their weapons straight through her throat. If she made one sudden move…

The fourth member of the company grabbed her from behind, arresting the impulse before she could act on it. One of his arms wound around her waist, pinning her arms to her sides. With his free hand, he brought a sickly-sweet smelling cloth up to her face, holding it over her mouth and nose. The world dipped and tilted. She couldn't feel the road under her feet anymore.

"Don't move," her captor said. His voice was oddly familiar. "We don't want you dead. Not yet."

Five

Aela's head pounded. The room tilted unsteadily when her eyes flickered open. She wondered for a confused moment if she was back in the castle. Her surroundings were exquisite, all dark wood, thick curtains, and plush carpet. A stained glass window threw rainbow light across the room, the rising sun shining through a symbol depicted in the coloured glass — a green snake contorted into the letter S, writhing in dancing flames of orange and red. The walls were adorned intermittently with the same image, artfully carved in the wood panelling. A fire crackled in the hearth directly in front of the comfortable four-poster bed she lay on, filling the room with musty warmth.

The coolness of metal sank into the sensitive skin at her wrists. Alarmed, Aela jerked instinctively and found that chains restrained her arms. They were long enough that she could sit up, but she couldn't move off the bed.

"Welcome back, sweetheart."

Aela started a second time as someone stepped inside a door by the dresser on her right. He must have been just outside, called in by the clanking of the chains.

She knew him.

It wasn't only that she recognised his voice and build from when he'd grabbed her and drugged her in the street.

He was around her age, about six feet tall, only a few inches more than Aela herself. His built upper body immediately marked him as a fighter. He raised his chin, regarding Aela with arrogant disinterest. The look was like a shard of ice driving through her chest, stalling her breath.

The last time she'd seen this man was when she'd knelt before the king in the great hall. This man had lounged sullenly against the wall, called in against his will to observe the king, because one day Saban's work would be his.

That was before he'd murdered his own father — a treacherous, bloodthirsty killing that had the people of Dunwyn calling for his execution.

Bryn, the crown prince of Dunwyn, the wanted king–killer, stood before her in Anarchist Underground.

Fury.

It exploded inside Aela like a ball of fire, bursting to escape. It was all she could do not to jerk against the cuffs. This man had ended Saban's life and he would pay for it with his own.

A sharp pain grabbed her attention, and she realised she'd balled her hand so tightly into a fist that her fingernails were biting into her skin. The pain stilled her racing thoughts long enough to think reasonably.

Saban was not a proponent of execution and certainly not of vigilante justice. He would want Prince Bryn brought before the Dunwyan council and tried for his crimes fairly. She wouldn't allow him to flee like the coward he was. She needed to get him back to Saban's court, *Huntley's* court, to face judgment. There, he would surely be crushed by the weight of the terrible thing he'd done. He had to feel *something*. He would pay, but not with his life.

Aela focused on slowing her breath as she looked at Bryn. He was the very picture of Dunwyan nobility, sun-bronzed skin, light hair, and dark eyes, like everyone in the Ryland bloodline, like most people from the northeast. His tangled golden hair skimmed the stubble at his square jaw. His thick brows and long lashes were darker than his hair, standing out against his skin and the striking deep golden brown of his eyes. Superficially, he had his father's eyes, the same colour and shape, but they carried none of Saban's warmth.

Aela had expected Bryn to appear fundamentally altered by the act of murdering his father, to look guilty or regretful or grief-stricken. It was a mistake. His posture was as untouchably imperious as the day she'd last seen him at the periphery of the great hall.

Watching her, the prince moved away from the door to lean against the post at the foot of the bed. The distance was carefully planned, out of her reach. Misreading the tension in Aela's posture, he said, "Relax. Your virtue's safe."

He didn't recognise her. Although Aela had trained alongside Bryn since they were teenagers, they had never so much as spoken on the exercise field. Bryn had given all of the soldiers the same cursory, impersonal treatment of a royal who didn't have the time or inclination to become acquainted.

Aela's hair had come loose while she was out. She shook the short strands off her face and eyed him with a challenging glare. "Is that so, *sweetheart?*"

It was as if someone else said it. She was shocked at her own boldness. This was the crown prince. But wearing a simple white shirt and brown pants, Bryn didn't look like royalty. His feet were bare, and his collar was untied at the neck, sloppily trailing laces. Facing him here didn't feel the same as in the castle. There, he was his father's son. Here, he was a killer in a city of killers.

He cocked his head, ignoring the question. "You murdered that soldier everyone's talking about."

His eyes glinted eagerly, searching for a reaction. Aela forced herself not to react.

"It was self-defence."

He folded his arms across his chest and gave her a conspiratorial wink. "You're protesting a bit too much. We're all murderers here."

Another white-hot flash of fury erupted in Aela. In a burst of bloodthirsty fantasy, she imagined how good it would feel to drive her blade through the heart of this wretched king-killer. "If you're going to kill me, you should at least unchain me first. Make it a fair fight."

"Kill you?" Bryn repeated coolly. "What would be the use in killing someone who fights as well as you do?"

Aela willed herself not to flinch. Perhaps Bryn actually *did* recognise her … Then it clicked. "You were in the tavern."

He shrugged. "You wouldn't have seen me. Besides, even if I wanted to kill you, I can't."

"I thought this was anarchy. You can do whatever you want."

"Nobody can do whatever they want. Not even an anarchist," said a silhouetted figure in the doorway. Aela whipped around, her instincts flagging danger.

This man hadn't been part of the group accosting her in the street. He had to be in his fifties, over six feet tall and with the muscular build of a fighter, although not as broad as Dagny. His eyes were grey-blue, and his silver-streaked hair was dark blond, the characteristic colouring of a Borderlander,

Aela noted with surprise.

There was an air of calculated malice about him, an intelligence both unnerving and captivating in his eyes, like he was sizing Aela up, cataloguing her every weakness. Bryn reacted immediately to the man's presence, pushing himself off the bedpost to stand up straight. His posture reminded Aela of a soldier at attention.

The man remained in the doorway, smoothing back his already flawlessly slick hair. His black clothes and boots were simple but well-made, expensive. He looked Aela up and down with an approving smile that made her feel unclean.

"The cuffs suit you." His voice was quiet, and he stood with reptilian stillness, arms casually at his sides.

Aela narrowed her eyes, outwardly calm as her heart punched a violent rhythm against her chest. "I think I look better without them."

He took a moment to consider this. With a decisive nod, he said, "Slate."

Bryn looked over at him, and Aela was startled by the alias. It seemed Huntley had been correct in her belief that Bryn was an anarchist, but the question remained: had Saban's murder been orchestrated with their support?

The anarchists either didn't know who Bryn was, or were colluding with him to protect his identity.

Bryn fished a key from his pocket and came forward to kneel beside the bed. He didn't touch Aela, sliding the key into the lock of the cuff on her right wrist. A moment later, her hand sprang free. Once he'd applied the key to the left cuff, Aela scrambled off the bed. By the door, the man gave her a small, gracious bow. "As the lady wishes."

"What do you want?" Aela couldn't hold the question in any

longer.

"You have military training."

Aela nodded. "I was in the king's army. I fought at Bayeau in the Border War." The small sliver of her brain still locked on self-preservation insisted that a soldier with little influence would be considered a minimal danger, while accounting for her proficiency in the fighting ring. "Until I was discharged by the steward."

She could almost taste the bitterness on her tongue as she said it. Apparently, her captor — or whatever he was — heard it too.

"Hence your presence in the ring. A therapeutic pursuit, no doubt."

Aela shrugged. "It did feel good, beating the shit out of your man."

He chuckled. Aela was aware that Bryn held himself very still. The cool, shuttered expression on his handsome face hadn't changed.

"What's your name?' the man in the doorway asked.

"Anna." Her sense of self-preservation told her to lie about that too. "And yours?"

He stepped towards her. His movement probably wasn't intended as an outward threat, but it was implicit in his size, along with his softly ominous composure, like he could burst into violence at the slightest provocation. Aela's pulse pounded as he extended a hand. "Splinter."

She could feel Bryn's eyes on her as she took it.

"What do you want, Splinter?" she asked steadily, not moving her eyes from his. It seemed the thing to do, the way one would stare down a predator in order to assert strength. Splinter's lips curled up. His smile made him look more dangerous as his gaze tracked down her body.

"I want a fighter," he said.

Six

It wasn't a great surprise that Splinter was rich, but following him through the lavish halls was a fast lesson in exactly how lucrative being an anarchist truly was. It was more a manor than a house, the pristine interior incongruous with the squalor Aela had seen on the streets of Anarchist Underground. She wondered how many other palatial residences were disguised by rundown facades in Dunwald's supposed *slums*.

Splinter led her down a hallway with soft red carpet on the floor and the same carving intricately engraved in wood panelling on the walls — a serpent curved into the shape of an S, engulfed in flames. The hallway widened into a landing, overlooking a breathtaking marble hall with a high ceiling. Descending the grand staircase, the entrance hall on the ground level was a complete sensory overload. Above them, an enormous chandelier winked like a sky full of stars. The marble walls bore the serpentine symbol, which also snaked across the centre of the stone floor in a meticulously-tiled mosaic.

Aela's mind flicked back to the memory of the simplistic grandeur of Saban's white stone castle and wondered if the wealth Splinter had amassed through his illicit dealings surpassed even the king's. It wasn't until she tore her eyes away from the overwhelming decor that she realised Bryn had silently disappeared.

Across the hall, Splinter pulled open a thick oak door and waited. Aela took his meaning and entered, stepping into a beautiful dining room. It bore none of the ostentatious opulence on display in the marble hall, but it was undeniably luxurious nonetheless. In the centre of the room was a heavy oak table surrounded by eight comfortable oak and red-upholstered chairs. Aela noticed a silky golden cord hanging in the corner, an arm's length from the head of the table. Emblazoned on the wall at the back of the room was an enormous replica of the symbol she'd seen outside. The serpent was as imposing as Splinter himself, who moved with surprising grace across the room to stand at the head of the table.

"Alone at last," he said with a smooth smile. Sitting at the head of the table, Splinter rested his elbows on the shiny wood, apexing his long fingers. He examined Aela with mingled amusement and curiosity. "Good. I'm *dying* to know what business the Reaper of Dunwyn has in Anarchist Underground."

Aela felt the bottom drop out of her stomach, too stunned to bury her shock. The smile on Splinter's face widened, the warning from the tavern shuddering through her mind.

Believe me, if you ever meet him, you'll know about it.

Splinter raised a brow acerbically. "Your surprise is insulting. I *own* Dunwald." His soft tone carried a clear threat. "There's nothing about this city that I don't know. Commander Aela Rinn was dismissed from the army and stands accused of murder. And then a mysteriously skilled fighter shows up in Anarchist Underground. A shocking coincidence, wouldn't you say, *Anna?*"

Surely Splinter could hear her heart hammering against her chest. Drowning her sorrows in that Underground tavern had been a mistake. She'd never considered that the anarchists would be organised enough to identify her so quickly. Her carelessness felt galling now. Even when the barman had warned her, she hadn't taken him as seriously as she should have. She never usually threw herself into danger without thinking. She always had a plan. She wasn't acting like herself.

Aela lifted her chin. "So you mean to kill me."

Splinter lounged back in his chair, examining her. "What an unimaginative assumption."

"You didn't answer the question."

Splinter scoffed. "And spill your blood all over my dining room?" He spread his arms wide to indicate the plush surroundings. "Tell me, Commander Rinn, do you really think that is the best use for you? Your rotting corpse fertilising my garden?"

Aela narrowed her eyes. "Why would you let me live?"

His sharp, steel-blue eyes bore into hers. "I'm not much of a betting man, but I have a feeling you're not here to report my secrets back to the steward of Dunwyn."

"My word isn't worth much in the halls of power." That same, bitter edge crept into her voice.

"Ah yes, the dead soldier." Splinter folded his arms over his chest, watching her intently. "An accident?"

"Self-defence." She didn't want to linger too long on her memory of the soldier's lifeless eyes staring up at her as his blood flowed freely across the stone street.

Splinter leaned forward, dangerously interested. "He attacked you?"

"I suppose he didn't recognise me."

"No, I suppose not." Splinter sounded amused. "I can't say that we in Anarchist Underground are in the habit of mourning dead soldiers. Tell me, how do *you* feel about having killed a comrade?"

It was a loaded question, and Aela knew that wasn't really the answer Splinter wanted. Killing in battle as part of an army was one thing. Splinter was trying to figure out if Aela would kill on the streets of Dunwald, for him. Categorically, Aela knew she wouldn't. She also knew telling Splinter that would mean her death. If she was obliging, she was an asset. If she wasn't …

Suddenly realising the danger of her position, Aela felt a twinge of anxiety and frustration. She'd allowed herself to be abducted by Splinter's gang on impulse, expecting some sort of initiation, a test that might give her time to figure out what she was doing here and if this was what she wanted.

Instead, what she'd encountered was a trap. Splinter's immediate welcome wasn't trust; it was clear-eyed confidence in his ability to destroy anyone who betrayed him without ever facing the consequences. Sweat pricked her palms. Her body was cold with creeping dread. Mason had told Aela she'd never be an anarchist, but her only other choice was death.

Aela wasn't used to playing by the rules of Underground, and she'd been outmanoeuvred because of it. It was like betraying her friend all over again. She tried and failed to wrestle Mason's disappointment from her mind.

Time. That was what she needed, at least enough to figure out what she was going to do about Bryn, how she was going to escape with him in her custody.

"I want to fight," she said. The best cover stories were truthful, but she wasn't so desperate to fight that she'd agree to work for an anarchist. Commander Aela Rinn was better than that.

She almost had herself convinced.

"My people won't be pleased that King Saban's most favoured warrior is living under my roof."

"Perhaps that can remain our secret," Aela suggested, trying not to think of Saban. "I doubt infighting is good for business."

Splinter chuckled appreciatively. "Already thinking like an anarchist. I'm not like the steward of Dunwyn, Commander Rinn. There is no dismissal from this job that you walk away from."

"I understand," Aela told him.

"Do you?" Splinter told her with quiet intensity. "You may be the Reaper of Dunwyn, but this is my city. I'll be watching you. Betray me and there's nowhere you can run where I won't find you."

"I know."

"Good," Splinter said. He reached over to the gilded rope hanging from the ceiling. With his icy gaze steady on Aela, he pulled it, and a resounding toll echoed through the house. "We have work to do. If you impress me tonight, we can discuss your payment. You say you want to fight? Let's see what you can do."

Splinter's people arrived one by one, and for the first time Aela had the opportunity to assess the group who'd ambushed her outside the tavern.

Dagny's distinctively enormous figure made the dining room feel smaller and more dangerous. He gave her an acidulous look as he circled the table and threw himself down at Splinter's right.

The next arrival was the woman who'd held the crossbow. In her late thirties, she had the same brown skin as Mason, an obvious clue to her southern heritage. Black lines like flames were inked into the skin on her hands, snaking up her forearms and under her shirtsleeves. Her hair was close-shaven, her deep-brown eyes framed with long lashes. She appraised Aela with a small, pleased smile and sat beside Dagny.

The third person to come through the door was a young man in his mid-twenties with the black hair and blue eyes of a Niellan. Well, *eye*. Aela tried not to stare. His face was scarred, his right eye socket nothing but an empty cavity. There were white, ridged scars on his hands, arms, and neck, vanishing beneath his collar. On his left hand, his middle and ring fingers were missing. Aela averted her eyes before he noticed her staring.

As the Niellan man sat down beside the woman, Splinter sat up straight in his chair, tapping a restless, staccato beat on the table with his fingertips. Of course this was a man who didn't like to be kept waiting. Dagny slumped in his chair, frowning. The other two were tense. Aela felt palpable unrest in the room.

Moments later, unhurried footsteps preceded Bryn's sauntering arrival, either blithely unaware or utterly unperturbed by his tardiness.

Splinter was very still, dormant. "Well?" he said dangerously. "Am I keeping you from an important engagement?"

Bryn's lip quirked upwards. "Now you mention it —"

"Careful, boy," Splinter said quietly. Bryn didn't take his seat. Splinter was looking at him expectantly. "Have you seen him?"

Bryn snorted. "You know what he's like."

"If you see him, send him to me."

Bryn said nothing but took his seat, carrying a slight tension in his shoulders.

Turning away from Bryn, Splinter said, "We have a new addition to our company."

The scarred young man was looking at her hard, unblinking. Murderous.

It was the woman who spoke up. "So we see," she said, nodding at Aela. "I'm Nula." She pointed to the scarred Niellan man. "That's Laz. And you already know Slate and Dagny."

"I'm Anna," Aela said. "I'm … I *was* a soldier in King Saban's army."

Dagny leaned forward, elbows on the table, eyes glittering maliciously. "Yeah, we saw you in the ring. All the king's little puppets fight prissy like that."

Aela gave Dagny a sweet smile. "I suppose you're referring to the prissy fighting techniques I beat you with."

Dagny's hands fisted on the table. "Any time you want a rematch —"

"There will be no rematch," Splinter interrupted firmly. "Anna has to prove herself to me now." His grey-blue eyes turned to her steadily. "If you are to my satisfaction, I'll consider whether I'd like to keep you in my company."

Aela met Splinter's cold gaze. In her peripheral vision, Bryn's dark eyes burned into her. He leaned forward with his elbows on the table, his hands at his mouth. The scarred Niellan man was staring at her too. He hadn't moved.

"I want you to join us on a job." Splinter's eyes swept around the table at the rest of the group. "But first, I'll see everyone in the armoury for training this evening."

Splinter rose and strode from the room. Dagny, Nula, and Bryn followed, leaving Aela alone with the scarred Niellan. He was still looking at her, disconcertingly still. Sensing danger, Aela rose to her feet, making for the door.

A gnarled, three-fingered hand slammed it shut, and Aela turned, coming face-to-face with a single blue eye, glaring at her murderously.

Seven

Laz's fist barrelled towards Aela's face. Driven by deeply ingrained habit, she ducked in time and his knuckles collided hard with the wooden door.

"What are you doing?" she demanded.

"You fought for Dunwyn! You dishonour your blood!" he growled in Niellan.

Shit. This again. Aela held her hands up, a quelling gesture. "I'm not Niellan —"

"Yeah? You look pretty fucking Niellan to me."

He took another swing. Aela ducked again. She resisted the urge to hit him back. Laz probably wasn't trying to kill her, and she wouldn't have Splinter looking her way for causing trouble on her first day. Her position here was already precarious enough.

"I'm a Borderlander!"

"Never seen a Borderlander with hair that dark."

She ducked the third swing too, and Laz's momentum drove him stumbling forwards. Seizing her advantage, Aela kicked him in the back so that he collided with the table. With the wind knocked out of him, it was easier for Aela to tug his arms behind his back and push him down onto the polished tabletop.

"Exactly how many Dunwyan Borderlanders do you know, Laz?"

He paused in the midst of struggling.

"That's what I thought," Aela snapped. She pushed away from him. "Listen, I'm sorry for whatever happened to you in the war. It wasn't personal."

"It wasn't *personal*?" Laz straightened up. "It feels fucking personal. The scars, the violence, the nightmares. I'd *never* do it again!"

I would. It's all I want to do. Aela swallowed the thought. Shaking her head, she pushed away from him. "Try to hit me again, Laz, and I'll cut off your other fingers!"

Clearly not that concerned about the welfare of his remaining fingers, Laz shot her an obscene gesture with his good hand and stalked from the room.

There was no way she was going to sleep under Splinter's roof until she trusted the uneasy truce between them. Instead, to pass the time before training, Aela wandered upstairs, tracing her footsteps back to the room she'd woken up in. At the top of the staircase, a pleasant breeze chilled her skin, flowing from an open door at the end of the hallway. After the stifling warmth of the dining room, she was drawn towards the cool relief.

There was a smaller, narrow spiral staircase through the doorway, which Aela climbed, emerging through the open door at the top onto the roof of the manor. It was early. The frigid morning air stirred her hair as she stepped outside.

The roof was flat, a railing running around its perimeter. From here, the sprawling expanse of the city was visible, spilling down the hill to meet the forest. The blackness of the ocean stretched out to the east of the trees. Uphill, the castle glowed in the light of the rising sun, magnificent and imposing, and

Aela realised how close Splinter's home was to the citadel.

Breathing in the fresh air, she tried to ignore the pull in her chest as she looked up at the castle. She used to sleep there, in the barracks. She'd be sleeping there still, if Saban was still alive. Aela leaned against the railing.

Even before she heard his footsteps, his presence closed in around her like a vice.

"Enjoying the scenery?"

Her fighter's instinct kept her outwardly calm, pushing down the warning in her thundering heart. She was on the same side as Splinter — for the moment, at least — but he was not a trustworthy man.

"For all the talk, I was rather expecting a place that was, you know … underground."

Splinter's smile widened. "One of many misconceptions about us."

He stopped at her side, inches from the edge of the building. Aela tensed reflexively. He'd been nothing but cordial to her, but her gut told her he was a mercurial man. There was every chance he might suddenly decide to throw her from the roof.

She took a moment to steady her breath before asking, "One of many?"

Splinter raised his eyebrows. "Why the questions?"

There was suspicion in his voice. If Splinter had any indication that Aela would betray him, she was dead.

"I want to be an asset. I can't be, if you tell me nothing."

For a tense moment, he made no reply, then he leaned against the railing and gazed out over the crowded mess of ramshackle buildings. "They call us anarchists. That's the biggest misconception of all."

"You're not an anarchist?"

"I have strict rules in this house, and my people are extensively trained. We're as regimented and disciplined as any military unit. Does that sound like anarchy to you?"

Aela shook her head. "Why do they call you anarchists then?"

Splinter gave a soft, rumbling laugh. "People don't understand us. Perhaps it's our fault for being so secretive, but why should outsiders know our business? Saban called us criminals. He blamed us for all the disorder and crime in his kingdom because it was easy that way. He didn't have to take responsibility for his failures, going to war with enemies across the country instead of looking after his people at home. And look where that got him."

Aela forced herself to inhale slowly, steadying her temper.

"Saban said we were demons incarnate," Splinter said, "that no amount of rehabilitation would do us any good. He told his people that we would keep peddling drink and sex and drugs until we destroyed the lives of his precious people."

Her mind still on King Saban, Aela said thoughtlessly, "Well, don't you do that?"

She bit her tongue as Splinter turned.

"Careful, girl," he warned darkly. "We supply for a demand. If people didn't want what we have, we'd find another job. And if we didn't do this, someone else would. Nothing I do is personal. It's all business. And my goal is to ensure my business is carried out in the most profitable way. Saban could have learned a lot from us. We take care of our own, and we settle our scores definitively, none of these messy battles and centuries-long feuds. You're either with us or you're not. So now," he drew himself up, turning to Aela, "you need to prove yourself before you can fight as an anarchist. Are you ready?"

It was odd the way "anarchist" felt akin to "soldier." It was the weight with which Splinter said it, as if he was thrusting upon her the same power, responsibility and hefty expectation she'd borne when taking up arms for the king. She couldn't ignore the way her heart began pounding with thrilled anticipation at Splinter's mention of a fight. She looked up, meeting Splinter's grey-blue eyes steadily.

"I'm ready."

★★★

The subterranean armory and training room was spacious and silent. Descending the stairs that evening, Aela stared in awe. Swords, daggers, crossbows, spears, and maces covered every inch of the stone walls like a terrifying wallpaper. Her hands itched to pick up a weapon, to push her body, feel violence ignite her blood again.

A sword caught her eye, hanging blade-down at the very centre of the wall opposite the stairs. It was exactly the type of weapon she loved to fight with, thin and feather-light so she could move freely with it in her hand. Without making a conscious decision to do so, she rounded the stairway and started across the room, her hand yearning to close around the familiar weight of a blade.

Then she stopped.

There was a small boy sitting in the far corner of the room with his back turned.

"And who are you?" Aela asked in surprise.

He moved so quickly that she didn't have time to make sense of what was happening. All she knew was that a knife thudded to the ground behind her, staining the sawdust underfoot with red. Blood dripped from a shallow, lancing cut in her right arm. Confused, Aela stared at the weapon then looked up. The boy was on his feet, one hand still outstretched after he'd let the knife fly, a wickedly accurate warning shot that had sliced through Aela's shirt and flesh.

She stared. He was small and skinny, no older than eight or nine. His stained white shirt was rumpled and untucked, haphazardly laced at the collar. Obviously Niellan, he had fair skin and messy raven-black hair that hung in a curled halo around his face. Even with tired, bruise-purple shadows beneath them, his big, solemn eyes were striking. Aela had seen lots of Niellans in her life, but never one with eyes such a deep, dark blue, the colour of the Great Ocean on a sunny day. As angelic as he looked, his presence was unsettling. He examined her with a disconcertingly adult look, penetrating and analytical.

There was something at his feet, a flat metallic spring and small screwdriver, whatever he'd been tinkering with before realising he had company.

"Nice shot," Aela remarked, too bewildered to think of anything else. She chanced a step forward, but the boy's hand jumped to his belt, to a row of small throwing knives, identical to the bloodied one at her feet. She froze.

"No need for that," she assured him, lifting her hands cautiously. "I'm ... a friend of Splinter's."

Warily, he cocked his head to the side, eyeing her like a wild animal. The look on his face told her he knew very well that Splinter didn't have *friends*. His free hand had jumped to his neck, his fingers scratching vigorously at his throat, leaving angry red lines on the delicate skin. It was a jerky, unstable movement that he didn't seem entirely aware or in control of.

Disappearing down the neck of his shirt was a glinting silver chain.

"I'm … Anna," Aela offered, stumbling over her alias. "What's your name?"

Silence.

"Oh, come on," she said lightly. "Am I that scary?"

The mistrust and guardedness telegraphed by his expression and posture were beyond his years. Unsurprising, Splinter wouldn't keep a child this young out of charity. This boy was capable, an asset.

Keeping her hands outstretched, she moved again, slowly closing the distance between them. As she drew closer, Aela saw him react then check himself, schooling his expression so that it was carefully neutral. His eyes never left her face. There was jittery tension in his posture, fear that he was determinedly trying to hide. His hand hadn't moved from the weapons at his belt. Out of self-preservation, Aela stopped a few feet away from him.

Making her tone and posture as non threatening as possible, she switched to Niellan. "Aren't you going to tell me your name?"

His eyes went wide, then darkened dangerously, the first hint of uninhibited emotion. For a quick moment, he looked as if he was going to say something.

The bell tolled, loud and low, echoing through the manor, and the boy whipped around as footsteps rang out on the stairs.

Splinter strode into the training room, wearing the same leathers as he had this morning. There was an immense broadsword thrust through his belt. He stopped a few feet away from the Niellan boy, glaring down at him.

"Nice to see you've decided to show up this time," Splinter

said pointedly.

For a tense moment, the boy watched Splinter warily, as if waiting for something to happen. Splinter jerked his head towards the side of the room, and the boy shrank back to the periphery as the others filed in, lining up along the wall. There was hungry anticipation in the air, and Aela knew what was coming.

Splinter's cool gaze fell onto Aela. "Let's see how our new girl fares."

Aela chose two weapons from the wall. The light sword and a dagger about the length of her forearm. The sword would probably be considered too small for her, but fighting with a feather-light weapon had certain advantages.

She took up her place before Splinter in the centre of the room, feeling six sets of eyes upon her. Even Bryn's apathetic posture was a little more upright at the corner of her vision. Everyone wanted to see what she could do against Splinter.

"Before I send you out," Splinter said. "I want to know that you can fight."

Aela frowned. "You saw me fight last night in the tavern."

"My *people* saw you fight, and they reported back. My standards are a little more exacting."

Aela, who was known for having high standards of her own, was supremely unconcerned. "You want me to show you what I can do?"

"I want you to impress me."

Aela smiled.

With no warning, she drove both her weapons towards him, felt the shuddering force of his parry, knocking her backwards. Aela was immediately engaged by the quality of his fighting, his certainty and the way his blade moved as if it was an extension of his arm. It wasn't military training, but rather the crude skill of a man who'd probably picked up a blade at an early age to amuse himself, thoughtlessly hacking and sawing into anything or anyone he could find and getting frighteningly good as a result.

Splinter's strength was twice Aela's, but her technique and reflexes kept him from driving her back. She whirled, dodging his blows rather than parrying them, conserving her strength and allowing Splinter's to deteriorate.

He caught on, changing tactics. Instead of trying to knock her down, he focussed on disarming. With a deft flick of his wrist, his sword swivelled in his hand, rotating Aela's dagger awkwardly in her hand. No time to adjust her grip. His blade knocked the weapon from her hand.

He grabbed her unarmed left hand, pulling her towards him so that she felt the heat of his breath against her face. Aela brought the butt of her sword down to hit him over the head, but he reached up and caught her other wrist. She kicked out, catching him between the legs. He grunted and threw her backwards. The air left her body in a rush when she thudded onto her back in the sawdust. Shuffling backwards, still gripping her sword she judged the distance of Splinter's approach. Then she went to her knees, shifted her grip on the weapon, and threw it like a spear at Splinter's chest.

He wasn't prepared for it. People never expected someone to *throw* a sword, but that was the appeal of fighting with a light weapon – versatility.

The sword hurtled through the air, bouncing off the thick leather of Splinter's jacket, leaving a dent right above his heart.

Aela rose, her blood singing. The slightly inebriated fight with Dagny last night had felt good, but sparring with Splinter was like a drug. He exuded danger, every manoeuvre a genuine threat.

It felt good to know she could beat him, even though beating him was probably unwise. Her limbs trembled with adrenaline that begged her to take up arms again. She wanted to drag out the fight with Splinter, continuing to bait him until his anger overcame him, until he forgot it was a friendly fight and put everything he had into coming after her.

For a moment, she closed her eyes and allowed herself the fantasy of facing Splinter on the battlefield. Taking on his brutal style with real, life-or-death stakes. She would beat him then too.

Aela opened her eyes. "In a real fight," she said, "I would've aimed at your throat. You'd be dead. No need to yield."

The room had gone very still. Near the wall, the rest of Splinter's company was staring, in various states of shock. Her performance in the fighting ring hadn't been truly indicative of her capability. Dagny's skills weren't a match for Aela's, but clearly they'd all assumed she had given that fight everything. She turned her attention back to Splinter. Slowly, he looked down at her sword, lying in the sawdust after colliding with his chest, then back up at Aela.

The expression on his face made her skin crawl. He was smiling. Outwardly, he looked pleased, but it overlaid something ominously hard-edged, a threat.

"I'll have to watch my back," he said lightly.

Aela shrugged. "I don't know," she said, matching his casual tone. Now he understood that she was not going to stay in Underground on anybody's terms but her own. "I'm only a danger to my enemies."

For a moment, Splinter's eyes darkened, then he barked,

"Training's over. Arm up, all of you. Rumours abound — a new faction has arrived in Dunwald."

A soft, murmured laugh trickled around the occupants of the room, and Aela realised that she was looking at Splinter's gang in its entirety. Six of them, if you counted the Niellan boy. Seven, if you also counted Aela. It wasn't the army she'd been expecting from Anarchist Underground's apparent kingpin.

"They'll create more competition for us, if they're allowed to operate in the city unchecked," Splinter explained to Aela. "More competition means buyers have more bargaining power over our wares. They don't care that our drink is the best, only that they're paying the best price. This new faction means to undercut us."

Nula laughed. "Everyone thinks they've got the balls to try it … until they make our acquaintance."

"Indeed," Splinter said quietly. "Like the rest, these people will regret their decision before the night is over."

This small group, whose skill and efficiency she had sampled last night, wasn't meant to be an army. They were a team of silent murderers.

"You mean to kill them," Aela said.

"Not all of them. Just all those unfortunate enough to come to the Devil's Tongue this evening. Well, all but one. This is how negotiations occur in Anarchist Underground."

It wasn't going to be a negotiation; it was going to be a bloodbath, a killing intended to run the remaining members of this new faction out of Dunwald. Aela's blood thrummed at the thought, even as her conscience nudged at her. Murderous infighting between two illegal factions was at the very heart of what Saban had despised about Anarchist Underground.

Splinter called it anarchists taking care of their own problems.

Saban was a different sort of man.

But Saban wasn't here anymore, and Aela needed this. No one would mourn dead anarchists, anyway.

She crossed the room to pick up her thin sword. The slight weight was natural in her hand. It was right. The Reaper of Dunwyn would rip through this tavern like a storm surge battering the rock walls of Dunwald, and the dulled edges of her world would sharpen like the blade she'd use to run these enemies through.

Splinter swept from the room without looking again at Aela. Nula, Laz, Dagny, and the Niellan boy armed up before departing in his wake. It wasn't until they were gone that Bryn crossed the room with a low whistle.

"So, you've got a death wish then," he said with a malicious smile. "No one beats Splinter."

Aela refused to be rattled. "He told me to impress him, so I did."

Bryn's dark smile widened. "You really don't know how things are done around here. You should have thrown the fight."

Aela raised her eyebrows. "Why would I do that?"

"Like I said." Bryn took a step closer. "*No one* beats Splinter. When he said he would have to watch his back, what he really meant was that you'll need to watch yours. You're not going to enjoy having him as your enemy, but I think I'll enjoy watching."

★★★

"I 've never seen someone fight the way you do." Nula held a crossbow on Aela less than twenty-four hours ago, but she seemed to expect there would be no hard feelings about it tonight. She fell into step with Aela as they followed Splinter and Dagny down the poorly-lit street towards the Devil's Tongue. Her voice was deeper than Mason's, but her familiar southern accent made Aela ache for her old mentor.

"I was trained as a soldier," Aela reiterated evasively.

"Trained?" The woman waved a hand dismissively. "What are you? Eighteen? Nineteen?"

"Twenty-one."

"Hmm. No one so young gets as good as you by training. No, you've got a gift. It'll be a pleasure to fight with you."

"Likewise —" Aela broke off as someone rammed hard into her shoulder. Laz jostled her as he passed, and Aela rolled her eyes. The street was wide enough for them to walk abreast. "He's a barrel of laughs," she muttered to Nula.

"Laz is Niellan," Nula replied, as if that explained everything.

"If he hates Dunwyn so much, why is he in Dunwald working for Splinter?"

Nula snorted. "The Niellan army wouldn't keep him on after he lost an eye in battle, and he was ashamed to go home after being turned off. He was at the front line when the war began. The only thing he knows is fighting. He's been in Anarchist Underground almost two years now. Splinter ... made sense for him. To be fair, he's not a prick to *everyone* from Dunwyn."

The words were pointed. Aela understood. "Only soldiers."

"If it makes you feel better, he hates the king of Nielle even more."

"King Marcus?" Aela had never given much thought to how Niellans felt about their king. As a soldier, it wasn't particularly helpful to consider your enemy's feelings about anything. "Why?"

Nula beckoned Aela closer. She lowered her voice conspiratorially while Laz walked a few steps ahead of them. "He says the old man's lost his mind, that he started the Border War because the death of his son drove him mad." Nula gave a short laugh. "I disagree. I reckon the warmongering bastard knifed the kid himself so he had the excuse he needed to attack Dunwyn."

Aela wasn't sure about that. King Marcus never had a problem finding excuses to attack Dunwyn when his son was alive.

Nula shrugged. "Doesn't matter anyway. All kings are as bad as each other."

"Couldn't agree more," said a smooth voice behind them. Aela whirled. Bryn had been shadowing them, walking silently a few feet away, listening. "What do you think, Anna, would you rather pledge your loyalty to a king who killed his own son or to the future king who murdered his father?"

Bryn's tone was a bitter contradiction to his handsome face. His voice was like a shard of ice, cold and sharp. Aela recoiled and shoved past him, wondering how a man as infinitely good as King Saban had somehow raised a son who was a monster.

Eight

The Devil's Tongue was exactly the kind of place that Aela would have studiously avoided as a soldier. Not only was it beyond the blue-painted boundary of Anarchist Underground, but it was also a cesspit of disrepute.

Swaying patrons staggered from the venue, some accompanied by scarcely clothed men or women, looking for a place to spend the night. Although the tavern's front facade was windowless, little more than a grubby black wall with a single opening at the centre, light and cheerful music seeped into the street from side windows. Every time the doors at the building's front and sides opened, lively shouts and laughter burst from inside, incongruous with the slumped figures huddled on the roadside, rocking and muttering agitatedly. Grey dream addicts, Aela thought.

Despite her disgust with the establishment, Aela was pricked by curiosity about how Splinter and the leaders of other anarchist factions handled matters like this. When they went inside, the interior of the tavern was an overwhelming crush of bodies. Amidst the churning crowd, it was too easy to remember the claustrophobic chaos of battle. She could suddenly hear the clash of weapons all around her, horrible cries as soldiers fell, friend and foe indistinguishable in the pandemonium. Aela had known the war couldn't go on like that.

Out of habit, she scanned the room, committing the escape routes to memory. There were exits at the front and sides of the building and another door behind the drink-drenched tavern counter, which probably led to a washroom.

A man stumbled drunkenly into Aela, and her hand whipped reflexively to the light sword at her belt. Someone caught her wrist. Dagny stared down at her, grinning viciously.

"Don't like crowds?" he speculated. "Let's not draw any blood yet."

Ahead, Splinter encountered no trouble moving through the crowd. The tavern's patrons parted for him, while the rest of his gang had to muscle through. He led them to the best table in the tavern's far corner. It was taken, but apparently the occupants got the unspoken message of Splinter's approach, vacating instantly. Dagny jostled Aela's elbow as he sat down beside her, his large shoulders an inconvenience in the cramped space. Splinter sat at Aela's right.

"Bowie," he said, "go get us some food."

With his big Niellan blue eyes and tiny frame, the little boy looked entirely out of place amidst the inebriated rabble of Dunwyan criminals, but he appeared completely oblivious to the grinding bodies, turning and navigating his way back through the crowd efficiently. When he was gone, Splinter turned his attention to the table.

"I know some of you have personal disagreements. I also know they're petty and inconsequential, especially compared with what you have in common: you all work for me. My goals are your goals. Tonight, our goal is to fire a shot into the heart of this new faction and send them fleeing from Dunwald like frightened rats." He leaned in closer to the centre of the table and lowered his voice. Everything he said was perfectly enunciated, unmistakable. "If you are *ever* the reason we, collectively, do not achieve one of our goals, you will die a death so slow and so painful that you will wish you'd never set foot in Anarchist Underground."

Aela blinked. Evidently, it hadn't escaped Splinter that tension was brewing between her and Laz. It wasn't exactly the rousing battle speech Aela might have given her troops, but she had to hand it to Splinter. The sentiment was motivating.

Bowie announced his return by unsteadily transferring an enormous tray laden with food onto the table.

"Sit," Splinter ordered. Bryn and Nula shuffled sideways so Bowie could sit between them, facing Splinter. "Could you see their brand?"

"No, sir." Bowie shook his head, looking a little agitated. "I still don't know who they work for."

Hearing Bowie's voice for the first time, Aela thought that it didn't match his demeanour. He appeared guarded, nervy, and hard-edged beyond his years, but he sounded like what he was, a little boy. His clear voice was quietly confident, lilting with a very slight Niellan accent.

"How many men?"

"Fifteen," Bowie replied immediately.

"Weapons?"

"Fifteen swords, seven daggers, two knives, and a crossbow."

"How many bolts?"

"Twelve."

"Where are they?"

Bowie brought his finger up to subtly tap his right shoulder.

"Three smoking by the right side door," he said.

Aela glanced over, immediately finding a small cluster of men unsubtly carrying weapons beneath their jackets.

"Six at the table beside the third window." Bowie tapped his other shoulder, then the table. "Directly behind you, four more. The man in the grey shirt isn't one of them. He's not armed. He's sitting at their table because he's beating them at cards." He touched the table again, pointing right. "The other two are up at the counter."

"Good." Splinter looked pleased.

As he should. They'd been inside the tavern all of fifteen minutes, and Bowie had already observed enough to provide him with a briefing akin to that of a soldier with extensive experience at espionage. Aela raised her eyebrows. Leaning in towards Dagny, she murmured, "How old is he?"

"The little freak? He's nine, and he'll gut you when your back's turned if you don't watch out. He doesn't think like normal people."

Aela doubted that Dagny thought like a normal person either, but she didn't say it. Bowie's eyes were still darting about the room. Usually, the ability to observe and recall details the way he could was born from years of training, as well as the gift of an exceptional memory and a detail-oriented mind. Since Bowie was only nine, he had to be working with only two out of the three.

Splinter gestured to the food on the table. "Eat, all of you."

As they did, Splinter allocated each of them their targets, assigning Aela the three men by the side door, which she noted left her with the greatest number of opponents to fight alone. She knew by watching the group that she could easily take them, but it didn't escape her that this was clearly another test.

It was impossible to eat at the crowded table. The longer Aela sat there, the more restless she became. She needed to move, to give physical expression to all that she was feeling. She gripped the edge of the chair until her fingers hurt, silently willing Splinter to give the command. It felt as if the walls were drawing together, mashing the crowd of bodies closer by the second.

Unable to stand it, Aela lurched to her feet, quickly excusing herself to go to the washroom. It gave her the opportunity to walk past her three marks, clocking their unsubtly concealed swords. She also made out the knife and one of the daggers Bowie had observed. Shoving through the crowd felt good. It allowed her to release some of her jittery energy. When she emerged from the washroom, she barely even jumped as she came face to face with Dagny.

He leaned on the wall across from the washroom door, arms folded, wearing a domineering smirk. Suddenly, it made sense.

"You're following me," Aela accused.

To his credit, Dagny didn't deny it. "Anarchists always have insurance."

Aela looked at him steadily. "You think because I was in the king's army I have no love for the anarchists."

"Obviously."

"You're right," Aela replied truthfully. Mild surprise registered on Dagny's face. "But I also killed a soldier, which means that if I was to be caught here, I'd be arrested and charged as an anarchist, same as you. I'm not here for anyone but myself."

It wasn't a complete lie, but she also needed to figure out what she was going to do about a certain blond-haired, golden-eyed murderous prince before Splinter forced her into anything too illegal.

"And by the way," she said, her voice laced with barely contained violence, "if I were here as a spy, you wouldn't know until it was too late. You have no idea what I'm capable of."

She turned and began shoving her way back to the table.

Splinter's tall frame was more distinctive than the others'. He sat with his back to the table of anarchists playing cards. They were entirely engrossed in their game. Too much so, Aela thought uneasily as she watched them stare intently at the table. The hairs on the back of her neck pricked.

She reacted reflexively to the bright reflection of light off moving steel and lunged into the path of the dagger flying at Splinter's head, knocking the weapon aside with her own blade. The discordant sound of steel striking steel cut across the lively chatter, and the room froze.

Aela expected the anarchist who threw the dagger to flee or launch a second attack. Instead, he remained entirely still, his arm outstretched, eyes unfocussed, allowing Splinter plenty of time to turn, pull a knife from his belt, and fling it directly into his assailant's throat. The anarchist's eyes flew wide, suddenly focussing, terrified, on Splinter as his hand grappled weakly at the dagger protruding from his flesh. He collapsed, sprawled across the table.

Like a spark igniting an inferno, the anarchist's death jolted the entire tavern into action. The other men at the table lurched to their feet, weapons in hand, except for one who cowered screaming. Aela recalled one of them was apparently not an anarchist. More screams erupted as bystanders began clamouring for the exits. Behind Aela, the wooden bench on which Splinter sat screeched against the stone floor as he jerked to his feet.

"Kill them," he ordered.

Dagny reached Aela's side, his weapon already drawn, laughing in deranged delight. The fighting bore down upon them. It was immediately clear that it wasn't only the four anarchists at the table in front of them who had been waiting for this moment. Aela whirled in time to see another man vault over a table behind her, his sword driving straight towards her chest. She slashed through his throat with deadly accuracy, savouring the familiar finality of the kill, like some terrible drug that both sickened her and gave her life. Blood spattered across her face and shirt.

Splinter's people were holding their own. A dark head and small frame on the other side of the table momentarily pulled Aela's attention. Bowie was fighting with a sword that was slightly too big for him and technique that would have been envied by half the Dunwyan army. Every step was intentionally placed, every blow to his tactical advantage, as if he'd mapped out the fight for hours beforehand. Aela might have believed that, were it not clear that his opponent was trying to catch him off-guard. Bowie's reflexes were a head-spinning flash of movement.

The anarchist drove his sword down towards Bowie's left shoulder and the boy whirled and tossed his blade into his left hand, raising it to parry.

Aela's jaw dropped. She'd always wished she could fight with both hands.

Since his efforts to find holes in Bowie's tactical defence had proven fruitless, the anarchist was opting instead to bear down on the boy with brute strength. Bowie was parrying consistently now with two hands, and he was sweating. A child fighting a grown man could only end one way.

Aela moved around the table without thinking, but someone

else got there first.

As the anarchist's sword barrelled down towards Bowie, the boy was yanked out of the way. Bryn held a fistful of Bowie's shirt with one hand and a sword in the other. His weapon clashed with the anarchist's, and he drove the man stumbling back with a single burly shove. Before the anarchist could regain his balance, Bryn's sword connected hard with the man's head, and he crumpled to the floor. Bryn shoved Bowie towards the tavern door, then turned and plunged back into the melee.

Aela spurred herself back into motion. Pausing to watch Bowie and Bryn fight was something she would never normally do, but it was difficult to look away. Bryn was a naturally gifted swordsman, as his father had been, and it was more than a year since she'd seen the prince fight. Evidently, he'd spent much of that time training, because he was better now than he'd ever been. The precision of his movement was pleasing on a superficial level, but Aela also couldn't help wondering if he had used those same precise strokes to cut down his father.

It would be a fast victory, Aela thought, her thoughts still lingering on Bryn's swordsmanship as she pulled her blade free of another unworthy attacker. Even outnumbered, Splinter's fighters outclassed their opponents. The anarchists still on their feet rushed for the doors along with the rest of the tavern's patrons.

Bryn appeared at Aela's side, sheened with sweat but remarkably clean of blood. "You stepped in front of a flying dagger," he said accusingly.

"It was going to hit Splinter. I figured I could probably deflect it with my blade."

"Probably?" Bryn gave her a withering look. "So you want to die, is that it?"

The last anarchist left standing fled, and a stillness settled over the room. The floor was littered with a dozen unfortunate anarchists who hadn't escaped their own attack. A loud, rattling cough cut through the quiet. Aela and Bryn looked over at the same time to see the man Bryn had knocked to the ground roll, moaning painfully, onto his side.

"Well now, that won't do." Splinter skirted the table, pushing past Aela and Bryn. Aela turned away; she didn't need to see that.

Looking away didn't help with the sounds. The man cried out weakly, gurgled, then gasped a rattling breath, choking as blood pooled in his mouth. He was dead.

Splinter turned to Aela. "You saved my life."

"Does that mean you owe me?" she asked boldly.

Splinter hissed out a laugh. "My trust is a more than sufficient reward. Now come, I need another drink."

He turned. And froze. Aela felt it too, the wrongness, like a terrible, creeping dread.

"Drop!" Splinter yelled.

Aela flattened herself to the floor without question, hoping the others had done the same. Around them, the tavern's windows shattered. The familiar whoosh of crossbow bolts split the air and Aela raised her head in time to see a new hoard of attackers flood into the room.

There were more than fifteen this time. Aela lost count of how many attackers crashed through the tavern's front and side doors. This was not a dishevelled rabble of anarchists; they were clad in helmets and blood-orange cloaks and moving with purpose through the room. This was the steward's guard. For the first time in more than a decade, Dunwyan soldiers were in Anarchist Underground.

Forced to give all her attention to pushing back the soldiers, Aela barely registered how deeply unsettling it was to see military fighters here. She'd warned Huntley that they needed to get the anarchists under control, but at the time the steward hadn't demonstrated any inclination towards an offensive.

A soldier advanced on her, driving a knife towards her unprotected side. She blocked, caught his wrist with her hand, circled her sword, and forced her way inside his guard. Through the slit in his helmet, his eyes went wide as she ran him through.

Aela hefted her blade as more soldiers circled, dozens of them. Unworkable odds.

"Hey!" Nula stood on the bar, holding two glass bottles aloft.

Aela swore. Flames crept ominously up the fabric that hung out of each bottle neck. She threw herself onto the ground again as Nula hurled the bottles towards the far sides of the room, where they blossomed into great fireballs, hurling soldiers, debris and flames about the tavern like projectiles. Screams rose as flames engulfed soldiers, and burning figures fled blindly from the tavern amidst opaque shrouds of smoke. The rest followed in retreat.

The air was thick. Smoke made Aela's eyes water and her lungs burn. She pushed herself stiffly to her knees, taking stock of the room. Splinter was braced on his hands and knees, Dagny and Laz slumped on either side of him, covering their ears. Beside Aela, Bryn was unmoving, blood trickling from a cut on the side of his head where some flying object had hit him.

"Slate?"

Ears ringing from the blasts, Aela heard Bowie call out as if through a wall of water. She'd thought the boy would flee when Bryn had shoved him out of the fight earlier. Instead, he stood over by the door, staring at Bryn's unconscious form with pure panic.

Bowie broke into a run, sprinting towards Bryn, but he was intercepted. An anarchist who hadn't fled the carnage hauled himself upright, grabbed Bowie by his shirtfront, and slammed him down onto a table a few feet away. Bowie lashed out, driving the heel of his palm into the man's nose. The anarchist reeled back but maintained his grip on Bowie's shirt. Dizzily, Aela struggled to find her feet as the man drew Bowie close. Through the hollow pounding in her ears, she could barely hear the anarchist.

"Well, *well*," the man growled at Bowie with delighted surprise, "I thought I heard Araxa say this is where you'd ended up."

"*Araxa?* The rumours about some new faction were meant to bring us out here!" The quality of Bowie's voice changed. "That man who threw the knife was on grey dream."

The man sneered. "You really think anyone would be stupid enough to draw on Splinter *willingly*? Sometimes you have to sacrifice a pawn to corner a king."

He pulled a dagger from his belt, placing it at Bowie's throat.

Panic expelled the heaviness from Aela's limbs and she raised her sword, but the man was already staggering back with a pained yell. He turned and retreated through the tavern door, clutching his broken nose with one hand and his shoulder with the other. Blood spilled through his fingers from under his sleeve.

Aela turned back to Bowie, who sat on the table, a trail of blood inching from his hairline down his ashen face. His arm was raised, his sleeve pushed up over his elbow, revealing a flat metallic spring that extended the length of his forearm, attached with a strip of leather. At the wrist was a small clamp with a lever beside it, which Bowie had apparently flicked to release the dagger he'd stabbed his attacker with. Aela recognised the trinket he'd been fiddling with when she'd first met him in the training room.

"You made that?" she rasped in disbelief.

Bowie shrugged, his attention elsewhere. The wrecked room was visible again as the haze lifted, and Bryn limped towards them. His head wound was still bleeding, his lip split and swollen, and his jaw bore a mottled bruise. He didn't look at Aela. Bowie jumped down off the table and appraised him, head cocked to the side.

"You look like shit."

"I was in a fight. What's your excuse?"

Bowie raised his eyebrows. "A fight? Is that what you're calling it? You were out cold."

"Not my fault Nula decided to blow the whole damn place up."

"She saved your ass."

Aela blinked. Bowie was gazing up at Bryn with blue eyes full of teasing light. For the first time, he looked like a child. Bryn reached out, pushing back Bowie's dark curls to examine the cut on the boy's head in a gesture so tender and familiar it startled Aela. Bowie flinched and swatted his hand away. "Ow! Stop messing around! We need to get to the warehouse."

"What?" Bryn asked.

"The warehouse," Bowie repeated with more urgency. "This whole fight was a diversion!"

Splinter was across the room, holding the tavern's side door open as Dagny bodily threw a man out of it. Aela gestured to Splinter, and he strode towards them.

"That man was on grey dream when he drew on you," Bowie said as he approached. "The fight was planned. They're at our warehouse. Araxa Leren is stealing from us!"

Splinter reacted immediately to the name, turning to Bryn but raising his voice so it filled the room. "You, Dagny, and Nula, get to the warehouse *now*." Bryn dropped Splinter a nod and slipped out the front door with the others on his heels. "The rest of you, stay here and clean house."

"Splinter!" Laz called from across the room.

One of the anarchists who'd been knocked out by the blast had regained consciousness. He bolted across the room and threw himself out of a side door.

"Anna, go!" Splinter yelled.

She gave chase. Her boots pounded the stone as she followed the anarchist uphill. She could see the outline of the castle, a ghostly shadow on the skyline, growing larger. Aela vaguely noted that they had crossed back over the blue line, out of Anarchist Underground. The castle's silhouette was growing larger, and the ground grew rocky underfoot as they approached the chasm. The castle walls loomed across the forbidding gap. Instead of crossing the drawbridge, the man veered right, following the cliff until it dropped away to the open ocean, marble walls traded for a strong sea breeze. He ran straight for the cliff's edge.

"Stop!" Aela screamed.

The man came to a skidding halt a step from the abyss, his head whipping around to look at Aela.

She knew him.

Confusion followed the jolt of recognition. This was one of her soldiers. Barely nineteen, he was among the youngest to have survived the Border War, a fighter with a promising future. How had he ended up here, embroiled in anarchist gang warfare?

His eyes met Aela's, glittering with a familiar blend of exhilarated anticipation and relief. For a moment, Aela was trapped in his gaze. He looked exactly how she felt when she was fighting, like she'd found some essential, lost part of herself that she didn't fully understand but was driven to search for.

Then he spread his arms wide and fell backwards, plummeting off the ledge.

"No!" The wind gusting up the cliffside ripped the cry from Aela's mouth. Her hand grabbed at air as the soldier dropped out of reach. If he screamed while falling, it was drowned out by the roar of the ocean. Aela's arms flailed desperately as she teetered precariously for a moment on the cliffside, barely regaining her balance. She looked down. The dark water had consumed the soldier like a gaping mouth. She could see only tendrils of white foam.

The Reaper of Dunwyn. Her ability spoke for itself on the battlefield, so she'd never given much thought to the nickname, beyond liking that it was analogous with power. It didn't feel that way now.

Now, it felt if she really *was* a reaper, bringing death to anyone with the simple misfortune of being in her presence.

Or maybe she wasn't death itself. Maybe death was stalking her.

Nine

The deep, claw-footed bath in the washroom adjoining Aela's bedroom at Splinter's manor was behind a sturdy screen that was bolted to the floor. She hung a towel, her clothes and weapons belt on the screen, filled the tub with suds and got in, holding Saban's heavy gold insignia above the water, tracing the raised golden stars over and over. Her mind wandered, replaying the moment the soldier launched himself off the cliff.

Desperate to clear her head, she balled her fist around the ring and pushed herself down. Bathwater flooded over her head.

Underwater, Aela closed her eyes and wondered what had suddenly possessed Huntley to go against Saban's decision to keep soldiers out of Underground. Was she looking to bring Bryn to justice? Or perhaps she had decided she could do what the king could not, bring down the criminal operation definitively. Aela doubted it was possible, but if anyone was dogged enough to come close, it was Huntley.

Aela recalled the wide-eyed surprise of the soldier she'd killed in the tavern. With his face covered, she'd been unable to recognise him, but he had of course recognised her. Her colouring was too easily distinguished. Guilt seized her heart, a cold, constricting fist. He had been in the Devil's Tongue because he was following orders, something Aela understood well. He hadn't deserved what she'd done to him.

A firm hand closed around her arm, hauling her above the surface. Compared to the heat of the water, the humid air of the bathroom felt cool as it spread across her face. Pushing her short hair out of her eyes, she came face to face with a pair of anxious golden-brown eyes.

After years living in military quarters, Aela wasn't shy about her body or the way people reacted to it. Attractiveness could be as effective against an enemy as a sword. Still, she prised Bryn's hand off her, feeling as if the world had been rearranged.

"What the *fuck* are you doing?" she demanded.

The suds were piled high enough in the bath to cover anything of note. Bryn hadn't taken the time to roll up his shirt sleeve before he'd pulled her up, and the sopping fabric clung to his muscular forearm. His wide-eyed gaze had disappeared. Now, his lip curled as he stood, folding his arms and staring down at her like he was very much enjoying himself.

"You sure you want to do that?" he drawled. "Stick around, sweetheart. We've been having such a good time."

For a moment, Aela didn't understand, then she thought about it. "I wasn't trying to drown myself."

"Whatever you say," he replied dubiously.

He moved away from the tub, becoming a masculine silhouette on the other side of the bath screen. Even with the screen between them, his proximity was invasive. Bryn was so close that, without the barrier there, she could reach out and touch him. A small part of her itched to lunge for her belt, draw her blade, and slice straight through Bryn's chest.

This is for the king.

"What are you doing here?" she gritted out.

"Can't I stop by for a friendly chat?" Bryn's deliberately mild tone was incongruous with his oppressive proximity.

Steam kissed Aela's exposed skin, bathwater straightening her wavy hair so that it was slick against her neck, water dripping from the strands that fell to her shoulders. The water sloshed around Aela as she rose, wrapping herself in the towel she'd hung atop the screen.

"Not in my washroom," she snapped, thinking that Bryn's reputation as something of a deviant was quite accurate. "Bathing's not a spectator sport." She lifted the edge of the towel that was wrapped around her and passed it over her face. Deviant or not, Bryn likely hadn't come here of his own volition. "And you can tell Splinter I'm fine after the fight and I thank him for his concern."

Surely Bryn could hear her sarcasm. Splinter didn't care for Aela's welfare. He'd only sent Bryn to check up on her because it wasn't prudent to employ a soldier who fell apart after a fight.

"He's not happy. By the time Nula, Dagny, and I got to the warehouse, everything inside was gone. A dozen barrels of product, lost to Araxa Leren. They must be holding it somewhere in the city, but if Splinter's got a plan to find it, he sure as hell hasn't shared it with me."

Bryn's tone remained casual, but Aela could see that he was holding himself very still behind the screen. Tension infused every particle of moisture hanging in the air. Aela wondered if he was uncomfortable sharing the space with her while she was undressed, then dismissed the thought. Prince Bryn was a womaniser, not a gentleman.

"Still," he went on, "it could've been worse, if not for Nula's explosions in the tavern. She had good timing."

Aela paused, the words unlocking something in her mind.

The heat of the bath evaporated, turning her whole body ice cold.

"What did you say?" she whispered.

"Nula had good timing." Bryn's voice on the other side of the screen was confused.

Aela shook her head. No, Nula's timing hadn't been good, but someone else's had been. She replayed the moment the steward's guard had interrupted Araxa's attack, calling on her military experience to recall every detail from the moment they'd entered the tavern. It had felt *off* at the time, but Bryn had now rattled loose the reason why. She and the rest of Splinter's gang had been targeted by the soldiers. She couldn't recall seeing any of Araxa's people fighting Huntley's men.

Huntley had always commanded loyalty and respect, and Aela didn't believe that her guard would have betrayed her. But it was even more impossible to imagine that they hadn't, and if that was true then whatever sordid work those soldiers were doing in Anarchist Underground was being done at Huntley's behest.

Securing the towel around her chest to ensure that it covered anything Bryn might wish to ogle, Aela sidestepped the screen and faced the prince. He started and stepped backwards, his tanned skin flushing red. From the steam, Aela supposed.

"Move aside," she ordered.

Bryn's eyebrows shot up. "Going somewhere?"

Aela stepped towards Bryn, close enough that his breath ghosted across her bare shoulder as she reached up and yanked her clothes and weapons belt from the screen. Bryn went still as she pulled free her dagger, pressing the sharp tip into his shirt, pricking the delicate skin of his belly. His eyes were wary as their gazes met, and Aela felt a tug of longing. It would be so easy to drive the point through flesh and muscle and organs, leaving him to bleed out on the floor.

"Tell anyone I've left the house and I'll kill you," she said.

Her self-control won out, and she pulled the dagger away, jostling Bryn's shoulder as she walked out to change behind the screen in her bedroom.

There was something she needed to do.

★★★

Aela's boots barely made a sound against the stone as she kept a brisk pace, retracing her steps back to the Devil's Tongue. It was late, but the streets were busy as ever. People pushed past one another, moving through the darkness like sinister shadows. Aela felt on edge. She didn't like how difficult it would be to see a threat coming.

Araxa Leren's people would likely return to the tavern to dispose of their dead, to cover their tracks. It was probably foolish for her to come back alone. She wasn't used to working by herself and wished she had Mason or Chase or Landon at her back. Trustworthy options were seriously limited in Anarchist Underground. Seeking reassurance, she ran a hand over her belt, feeling the familiar cold hilt of her blade. Aela paused, drew a slow, steadying breath. Then she plunged into the darkness of the tavern.

The Devil's Tongue was still and empty. It was difficult to imagine this was the same space that had hosted a mass of churning bodies earlier that evening. Everything was scorched now, small tufts of charcoal still steaming on the floor.

A floorboard creaked underfoot, and Aela whirled, throwing

her knife with razor sharp accuracy across the room. There was a cry as the weapon found its target, embedding itself into the wall … through the shoulder of the stocky, tattooed anarchist who'd tried to sneak in through the side door.

Aela stalked across the room and punched the trapped man hard in the face. "Where is it?"

"Where's what, pretty girl?" The man licked his lips suggestively. She hit him again. He laughed, blood trickling through his teeth. "I like it rough."

"Then I think we'll get along." Aela hit him in the jaw, her knuckles colliding painfully with bone. "You can talk, or I can start removing pieces of you. It will be slow. Tell me where Splinter's merchandise is."

The man spat blood on the floor. Aela hit him again, this time in the gut. He coughed, winded. "You have no idea who you're messing with," he wheezed.

"Likewise." Aela drove her knee in between the man's legs, and he let out a guttural sound, sagging as much as he could with the knife pinning his shoulder to the wall.

"The … warehouse … with the red door … by the castle wall. That's where your wares are hidden. No point though. It's well guarded and it'll be gone by morning."

"All the better. I enjoy a challenge," Aela said, "I'm done with you."

She turned … and froze. Two more men stood before her, one terrifyingly tall, the other a wiry southerner, both heavily armed, having apparently followed their companion into the tavern.

The man behind her gave a thick, painful laugh. "Did you really think it would be that easy?"

A stifled grunt behind her and before Aela could act, her

captive's thick, muscular arm circled her throat painfully. She gasped for air, grabbing at the sleeve of the tattoed man. Icy panic stabbed directly into her veins as his lips brushed her ear, his low voice charged with lascivious violence.

"You might be done with me," he growled. "But we're not done with you."

Ten

It was an elementary mistake, not watching her back, getting distracted. Aela would never have slipped up like this in the army. But here she was inexplicably off her game and now she was going to pay for it.

"She's pretty."

The tall man stepped forward, his hand skimming up Aela's body to the neck of her shirt. He tore at the fabric, and his touch wandered downwards, gripping her breast painfully. Aela froze, the world tilting around her.

Why couldn't she move? She was Dunwyn's best fighter. Taking on three men in Anarchist Underground should be a breeze. But with the tattooed man holding her and the giant's hand on her body, her capacity to fight back was obliterated. She hadn't been in danger like this since the war, and the sudden weight of memories of death and bloody fighting was too heavy to shift, so heavy she couldn't move.

"Me first." The giant moved in, pressing his body against hers.

Then his oppressive weight was gone. He tumbled to the floor. A shadow moved behind his prone body, driving the butt of a sword into the southerner's temple. He collapsed onto the tavern floor beside his enormous friend.

The shadowed attacker turned and started menacingly towards the tattooed man.

"You have *very* poor manners," the stranger snarled. A streak of light danced across the flat of his blade as he swept it up.

Before she could place the familiar voice, the tattooed man pushed Aela away with a panicked sound. Suddenly unrestrained, savage anger washed over her and she turned on him as he backed towards the door. She pulled another knife from her belt, jamming it directly into the tattooed man's throat. He made a nauseating, gurgling sound, blood bubbling up around the silver edges of the blade embedded in his flesh. As Aela pulled the knife out, blood spurted, spattering her. She watched him fall, and it hit her with violent clarity what this man would have done to her.

The edges of her thoughts were fuzzy, and the forceful sounds of her shadowy rescuer fighting the other two men faded away. She loomed over the tattooed man whose gaping wound leaked blood onto the floor. She drove her knife into his chest once, twice, a third time. The knife was slick with blood. Made for throwing, it didn't have a hilt. Aela's hand slid down the sharp edge of the blade. She barely felt it slicing through her flesh.

When she raised her hand a fourth time, someone caught her wrist. She turned, poised to attack, pulling her punch as she came face-to-face with a familiar pair of golden-brown eyes.

"Easy there, sweetheart." Bryn's grip on her arm didn't hurt as he pulled her upright.

Aela's head swam dangerously, and for a moment she was glad of his hand holding her up. She felt strangely distant, light-headed. The part of her brain that was sharp enough to think clearly recognised that she was probably going into shock, which would almost be funny if she could stop thinking about the giant man's hands groping her body. Revulsion shuddered through her, and a fresh wave of vertigo threatened to drive her to the floor.

Bryn said something else, but his voice was muted to Aela's panic-deafened ears. It sounded as if he was shouting through a glass wall. It was the shock of his warm fingertips, gently touching her cheeks, sliding down the sensitive skin at her throat, that reached through the wall and pulled her back to herself. Her eyes snapped to meet his burning gaze, where she saw mingled concern and fury.

"I said, are you all right?" His voice was rough.

It was hard to distinguish Bryn's hands from the lingering sensation of the giant's touch. "Get the fuck off me!" she snapped.

Acquiescing, Bryn stepped back, raising his hands. His gaze remained intent on her. His dark eyes looked black in the poor light, and the bronzed skin on his face was paler than usual. Aela was suddenly aware that her shirtfront was torn and stained with blood. There was blood on her right hand, some of it her attacker's, some her own. Behind Bryn were the two men he'd fought and bested. As far as she could see, there were no sword wounds. The giant had a nasty-looking bruise at his hairline. They'd been knocked out.

Bryn's expression was impenetrable as he looked down at the tattooed man Aela had killed. Blood was rapidly pooling at their feet. Aela wondered for a ridiculous moment if Bryn was afraid of her.

"What are you doing here?" she demanded breathlessly.

Bryn pulled his eyes away from the dead man. "You said I couldn't tell anyone, not that I couldn't follow you. I'm glad I did."

Aela was glad too, but she wasn't about to tell him that. She pushed past him, shoving open the door and starting off down the street in the direction the tattooed attacker had indicated.

"Hey." Bryn caught up to her, grabbing her arm again. "Go back to the house. You're done for tonight."

"I'm done when I say I'm done. And I thought I told you to get the fuck off me." Aela pushed Bryn away and turned her back on him. Haste was necessary. She took off through the streets again. Bryn followed her, keeping pace. Aela shot him a glare. "You didn't need to step in," she said. "They weren't going to kill me."

"No." Bryn clenched his jaw hard. "They weren't."

"I would've killed them," Aela snapped.

"You were frozen. I thought you were a fighter."

"You want to fight?" Aela muttered irritably.

"Anger's unbecoming, sweetheart," Bryn drawled.

"So's a black eye, which is what you're courting if you don't shut the fuck up."

Bryn chuckled, a short, almost startled sound that was much more pleasant than the deliberately unsettling way he'd laughed at her back at Splinter's house earlier. The warmth of the sound triggered a reflex, and Aela laughed too. Her hands were shaking, and exhaustion threatened to drive her to her knees. But for a moment she hadn't been thinking about those men. She stopped, staring at him. Intentionally or not, he'd been distracting her.

Bryn stopped too. "What?"

She crossed her arms over her chest, trying to stop the shaking that had spread from her hands to the rest of her body. Nausea turned her stomach. She hadn't been in shock like this since her first day on the battlefield at Bayeau. She tried to breathe through it.

"You didn't kill those men." Now she thought about it, he hadn't killed the anarchists who'd attacked them at the tavern earlier tonight … or any of Huntley's soldiers. Fighting to incapacitate and not kill an opponent who wanted you dead required more than skill with a blade. It involved a level of strategic intelligence that Aela hadn't expected from Saban's delinquent son.

"I'm not stupid enough to make trouble with Araxa Leren's gang unless it's on Splinter's orders," Bryn replied.

There was that name again. Aela remembered Splinter's immediate reaction to it in the tavern. "Who's Araxa Leren?"

"An absolute snake. He showed up in the city right after the war, started stealing other people's wares and flipping them to the highest bidder. He's never messed with Splinter before though."

"Why doesn't Splinter find his base of operations and shut him down?"

"He's been trying for years. Araxa's not that easy to find. We never even see him around the city, which is half-assed, if you ask me. You can say a lot of things about our boss, but at least he's willing to dirty his own hands every once in a while."

They'd been moving uphill. Ahead, Aela could see the wall of the citadel and lights beyond it. Her gaze shifted downwards by a stripe of colour in the dim light. A small, red door to a decrepit-looking warehouse. It struck Aela anew how close the anarchists were to the castle, to the very heart of Dunwald.

She stopped and cast a sideways glance at Bryn. His brow was furrowed. As if sensing her gaze, his eyes flicked up to meet hers. "Further questions?" he asked, looking amused.

"I'd like to know why you're still here," Aela replied drily.

Instead of offering an answer, he said, "I have a question for you. You didn't *expose* yourself quite enough in the washroom, in my opinion."

Aela didn't dignify that with a response.

"Why do you think Huntley disbanded the army?" Bryn asked casually.

His question brought Aela up short. All the breath left her body in a rush, and it took her a moment to find her voice. "What are you talking about?"

Bryn frowned. "You didn't know? It happened two days ago."

Aela's mind reeled. She remembered Chase staying down when she'd knocked him on the floor, and Mason stepping aside for her in the castle corridor.

I've lost my king. I won't lose my friend too.

A fresh wave of nausea rose. It couldn't be a coincidence. She thought about the soldier who'd jumped from the cliff. Now it made sense. He'd come to Underground for the same reason as Aela. After sacrificing everything at war, Huntley had decided there was no future for him with the army. Him or any soldier like him. Aela pressed her palms into her eye sockets and experienced a burst of light and pressure. "How do you —"

Bryn shrugged. "Splinter always has Bowie out on the streets, listening. He hears everything."

"Bowie likes you."

Bryn snorted, looking straight ahead. "He's a waste of space."

"You saved his life in the tavern tonight," Aela countered.

"Splinter seems to think he's useful. If it was up to me, the kid would've disappeared from that house a long time ago."

Aela's skin crawled as Bryn drew a finger across his throat before setting off towards the ramshackle building before them.

The warehouse was barely a building at all. The ceiling was half caved in on one side, and the moonlight shone through the jagged bits of rotting wood, casting sharp shadows on the dusty floor. The interior was empty, except for scattered wooden boards, dead insects, and a lone rat scuttling across the far side of the room.

Bryn looked at Aela. "They lied to you," he said flatly.

Aela bristled. "I know how to interrogate a man."

"Clearly —" Without warning, his hand shot out, grabbing her arm.

"What are you —" The shock of Bryn's arm around her waist silenced her even before his large, calloused hand closed over her mouth. Instinctively, her hands sprang up to his wrist and she felt his forearm flex as he resisted her attempt to tear his hand away. It didn't move.

A tide of desperate frustration rose from her gut. Fuck. He was strong.

"Be quiet and I'll let you go." Bryn's whispered words brushed the shell of her ear as he hauled her into the shadows, flattening against the grimy warehouse wall. She felt his heart thundering where her back pressed flush against his chest. His thumb brushed across her cheek as he hesitantly lifted his hand from her mouth. His other hand dropped from her waist, moving to her shoulder to keep her still. She shoved him off. "Don't move! Someone's here."

Sure enough, Aela heard soft, careful footsteps moving towards them from the opposite side of the room. The figure was barely visible in the warehouse's near-darkness. Aela saw movement, heard the soft hiss of a blade being drawn slowly from its scabbard. She wrapped her fingers around the sword at her waist and moved with speed, her blade whistling through the air and clashing with another. Looking down, she saw a pair of wide blue eyes.

"Stop!" Bryn pushed Aela's sword away with his hand and seized Bowie's blade from him. "Give that here, you."

Bowie's head whipped from Bryn to Aela then back to Bryn. His jaw dropped. "*Slate*? What are you doing here?"

"Me?" Bryn grabbed the front of Bowie's jacket. "What the hell are *you* doing here? You're lucky this place is abandoned. You're going to get beaten bloody —"

"It's not." Bowie, who clearly hadn't retained a word Bryn said, was looking back to the other side of the room.

"Not *what*?" Bryn sounded annoyed.

Bowie pushed Bryn's hands off him, turning away. "It's not abandoned. I followed two of them from the tavern earlier. They came in through here and never came back out."

He raised a hand, pointing towards the rat, sniffing the floor at the back of the room. It scuttled down a short staircase and into the darkness beyond.

"Another room?" Aela muttered, stepping past Bowie.

Descending the stairs, she pushed the wall slowly, carefully. Disintegrating wood crumbled away in her hands. Her breath caught as a section of wall swung open like a door, revealing an expansive space.

Unlike the room they'd entered from the street, this space was in perfect working condition. Its walls and roof were stable. Sconces lined the walls, casting an orange glow about the room. Above them, a wooden gangway circled the perimeter. In a perfect row across the floor, three huge barrels stood, each with the serpentine letter S symbol seared into its side. Splinter's symbol. Beside the barrels, Aela counted nine circles of spotless floor, impressions made recently by other containers.

Aela looked back. Bryn and Bowie had followed her down the stairs and gazed across the room with identical expressions of awe.

"Now we know what's become of Splinter's stolen liquor," Aela said.

She approached the nearest barrel, cracking open the lid with the tip of her blade. The liquid inside glinted silvery-green in the dim light. It appeared to be steaming slightly. She breathed in, and the vapours hit her with all the force of a blow, a cloying, acrid scent that made her head spin. She stumbled.

A hand on her arm prevented her from falling. "It's not liquor," Bryn said grimly.

"What is it?" Her voice came out raw. Inhaling the stuff had scraped her throat dry.

Bryn drew his hand away. "It's grey dream."

Aela shuddered, remembering the redheaded man's hazy stare as he was punched repeatedly in the tavern last night. She recalled what the barkeeper had said: *One mouthful of the stuff, and anyone can make you do whatever they like.*

Bowie took a tentative step towards the same barrel Aela had inhaled from.

"Oi." Bryn caught his arm. "You keep away from that shit." He slammed the lid back onto the barrel.

Bowie's eyes flitted around the room distractedly. "Araxa's got a big haul," he murmured.

The clattering of wheels and the sound of voices on the stone road echoed through the warehouse's thin walls. Footsteps rang out behind them, as well as in front. The way they'd come in was blocked. Bryn swore. "We need to get out of here."

Aela pointed at the gangway. "Up there."

She led the way towards a ladder in the far corner of the

room. Bowie scaled it first, then Bryn and Aela. They flattened themselves against the wooden floor as the door creaked open. Aela clapped a hand over her mouth, stifling a gasp. Two figures entered through the door wearing helmets and the orange cloaks of Huntley's guard. In the centre of the room, they met a blond anarchist who had come in the secret door Aela, Bryn, and Bowie had used.

"I don't get why it's up to us to load this stuff onto the wagon," said one of the guards to the other. He turned to the anarchist. "Do you people ever do any work yourselves?"

"Suck it up," the anarchist replied. "There were only twelve, and these are the last ones anyway."

There were sounds of exertion as the two guards picked up the nearest barrels.

"Oh, only twelve? They weigh a bloody tonne."

They disappeared through the door.

"We have to stop them!" Bowie lifted his head.

Bryn pushed him down again as the men came back through the door and hefted another pair of barrels. "They've already got the drugs," he whispered furiously. "Let it go."

They remained silent as the last barrels were lifted out of the warehouse. Aela felt Bowie's jittery tension rising a few feet away from her.

"You don't understand," Bowie whispered urgently. "You don't know what it can do. If you have grey dream, you can control anyone you want." He looked at Bryn imploringly. "They're about to leave. We have to do *something*. If we light the barrels on fire, they'll explode. Did you know that?" He scrambled to his feet.

"Bowie, get *down*!" Bryn hissed. He reached out, but Bowie dodged his grasp. Swearing, Bryn pushed up and reached for the ladder. Aela and Bryn ran across the warehouse after Bowie. Bryn lunged to grab Bowie's wrist, pulling him up short before he ran headlong into a figure rounding the door.

Aela stopped. It wasn't the orange-cloaked guards, who were lying motionless on the street, or the anarchist, who was nowhere to be seen.

Dagny stood in front of the wagon containing the barrels of drugs. Beside it was a carriage with Splinter's symbol carved on the side.

Bowie barely broke stride. He squirmed from Bryn's grip and tried to shove Dagny out of the way.

"Where do you think you're going?" Dagny grabbed the collar of Bowie's shirt and jerked him backwards. "How dare you touch me, boy?"

"Lucky," Bowie said with an entirely straight face. "With a face like yours, you'd normally have to pay someone to touch you."

Fury flashed in Dagny's eyes. His hand closed around Bowie's throat, and Aela heard the boy choke. "Think you're funny?" Dagny spat viciously. "I'll belt the life out of you!"

Bryn muttered an oath under his breath and pulled Bowie out of Dagny's grasp. "You keep your mouth shut," he snapped at Bowie irritably. He turned to Dagny. "And you. Really so sensitive to insults from a boy? What are you doing here anyway?"

Dagny kicked the door wide open, and Aela's stomach dropped.

The anarchist hadn't disappeared after all. Standing over his motionless body, Splinter wiped his bloodstained knuckles on a handkerchief. "Dagny came here with me."

"Shit," Bryn murmured.

Aela was inclined to agree.

✝

Eleven

"**H**OW *DARE* YOU LEAVE THIS HOUSE WITHOUT MY PERMISSION?"

Angry didn't begin to describe Splinter. He was murderous, his booming voice reverberating off the plush, velvet walls of his study. His cold, grey-blue eyes were wide, his face thunderous, his hands clenched dangerously into fists as he towered over them.

Aela stood taut in the centre of the room, Bryn on her right. Bowie was beside him, staring at the floor. Aela kept her eyes on Splinter as he yelled. It was something she'd never have done if this were a military reprimand.

"WE ARE NOT COMMON THUGS. I GIVE YOU ORDERS AND YOU FOLLOW THEM!"

He advanced on Bryn, who was watching him warily. Admirably, he didn't look afraid, though he was surely smart enough to fear Splinter in a state like this. Splinter bent down, bringing his face very close to Bryn's.

"Any insubordination is utterly unacceptable," he said quietly. He waited. So did Aela, Bryn, and Bowie. The silence was deafening. "Well?" Splinter demanded. "I'm waiting for a *very* compelling explanation."

The silence dragged excruciatingly.

Splinter drove a mighty blow into Bryn's gut. Bryn clearly knew how to take a hit, but he was no match for Splinter's strength. He thudded onto his knees, gasping, one hand pressed against his belly. The other was curled into a fist, the only evidence that he was willing himself not to fight back.

"Stop." Bowie's voice was quiet but commanding. "They were following me. They were trying to bring me back to the house."

Aela whirled to stare at Bowie, shocked by the lie. For his part, Bryn didn't look at all surprised. He closed his eyes in frustration, as if witnessing the manifestation of an ineluctable event, but he didn't say anything in Bowie's defence.

"I was only looking for what Araxa stole from you," Bowie said softly.

Splinter's hand shot out, grabbing Bowie's chin in a painful grip. "You found it," he said in that ominous tone that chilled Aela to the bone, "by breaking orders. Have you forgotten that I put a roof over your head? You're going to have to do a lot of work to remind me why you were worth the trouble. You can start by reporting back here at dawn. I have a task for you."

Bowie's eyes flicked over to Bryn then back to Splinter. It was a fleeting glance, but Aela saw it. So did Splinter.

He hit Bowie across the face with the back of his hand. The force would have sent Bowie sprawling onto the floor, if not for Splinter's hard grip on his arm. He pointed one long finger in Bowie's face. "What have I told you," he said, enunciating slowly, "about looking at him when I give you an order? Go."

Bowie dropped his head, his dark curls falling across his face. He made for the door without a word or a backwards glance.

"You should've left him in the gutter where you found him,"

Bryn muttered.

Splinter moved close to Bryn, inches from his face. "Something to say?"

"Yes," Bryn said exasperatedly, "kick the little smart ass out into the street where he belongs. He might be useful, but he's more trouble than he's worth."

Splinter bristled as if considering hitting Bryn a second time.

"I will not have this conversation with you again. You know better than to question my judgement." He stepped away from Bryn, cupping a hand under Aela's chin. He ran his thumb across her lip, and Aela's skin crawled. Still, she held his gaze. "And you. I'm sure that pretty face of yours can be useful, but there's plenty I can do without damaging you permanently."

"Stop." Bryn was still on his knees. The force of the single, quiet word made Splinter pause.

He raised his eyebrows dangerously. "Think about what you're doing, Slate. It's my prerogative to punish transgressions."

"Fine," Bryn replied quickly, "then I'll take her punishment as well as my own."

Aela's jaw dropped. It felt like the world had tilted at an obscure angle. He had no reason …

"Slate –"

"SILENCE!" Splinter's ringing command drowned out Aela's protestation. He turned from them, walking towards the fire. "It doesn't work that way. This is about personal accountability."

Aela's stomach turned as Splinter pulled a poker from the flames. The glow of the searing-hot metal reflected in Splinter's pale eyes as they came to rest on Bryn. Splinter whipped the poker towards him threateningly as he moved to rise from the floor.

"You'd best stay on your knees, boy." Slowly, he prowled towards Aela. His eyes were on her, but he spoke to Bryn. "Since I now know it bothers you …" He reached out, grabbing Aela's right wrist, turning to give Bryn a slow smile. "You can watch."

He pressed the poker's burning end down onto the open knife wound at her palm.

The poker's burn felt freezing cold and immeasurably hot all at once, and nausea gripped her as it sizzled, melting her skin. She bit down on her lip until she tasted blood, refusing to cry out. Her vision wavered then went momentarily black. When Splinter released her, she barely managed to stay on her feet. He jerked his head at her dismissively.

"Now you don't need to worry about that cut. Get out of my sight."

Aela fumbled for the doorknob with her left hand. Her right throbbed, hanging uselessly at her side. She slammed the door behind her.

She was startled by the intensity of her guilt, the feeling that she should stay, try to do something for Bryn. He deserved a harsh sentence for what he'd done to his father, but cruelty was not the same as justice, and Aela could only imagine what Splinter was going to do to him behind that door.

She wavered, caught on the edge of turning back. Closing her eyes, she paused to clear her mind before crossing the ornate hall and starting up the grand staircase to her room. Given Splinter's retributive mood, reappearing now to advocate for Bryn would likely only end with more suffering for both of them.

Besides, one of the first lessons she'd learned in the army was to keep her mouth shut.

***

Aela woke at dawn gripped by the urge to fight. Her burned hand throbbed, and her mind was tangled up in complicated thoughts.

Last night's exploits had interwoven with older memories as she'd slept, becoming an endlessly complicated web. The blood soaking Saban's mattress, her hand driving a knife repeatedly into her tattooed attacker at the tavern, Bryn kneeling before Splinter and volunteering to take her punishment as his own …

She tugged on her clothes, shoving open the door to her room with too much force. She wanted to stop thinking, to become nothing but a body, moving intuitively, one with her weapon. She made her way, single-minded, to the training room, so lost in thought that she almost barreled straight into Bryn at the top of the training room stairs. He stepped away from her, wincing slightly. There was a fresh bruise on his cheek that hadn't been there before they'd stepped into Splinter's office last night. Aela bet there were more bruises beneath the creases of his unlaced shirt.

"Here for the show?" He nodded his head indicatively downwards. Voices rose from the subterranean space, and pulled by curiosity, Aela followed him downstairs.

At first, Aela didn't recognise the fourth person in the centre of the training room with Splinter, Bowie, and Dagny. It took a moment to remember him as the anarchist Splinter had knocked unconscious at the warehouse last night. Dagny must have transported him back to the house while the rest of them rode in the carriage. The anarchist looked dirtier in the light of day, his blond hair lank, greasy strands pasted to his forehead. His eyes were a sickly light brown, full of pure hatred as he looked up at Splinter.

Slowly, drawn forward by the tension in the room, Aela followed Bryn to stand near a wall of weapons. Splinter shot them a single, disinterested look. Bowie glanced over too, but his eyes flicked back as Splinter's captive struggled violently.

He struggled because he was tied to a chair, his wrists and ankles restrained. Splinter and Dagny loomed over him. A pace behind, Bowie looked slowly from the two men to their prisoner, his expression careful. Whatever this was, he didn't seem to be in on it.

Splinter reached out and clamped a hand down on the blond anarchist's shoulder.

"He's going to sing like a bird, aren't you, friend?" Splinter's tone was amicable enough but it carried a dark threat. The man spat at Splinter's boots. Dagny raised a hand to strike him across the face, but Splinter caught his arm. "No, Bowie will do this. Come here, boy."

Bowie took a halting step forward between Splinter and Dagny. Splinter pulled a dagger from his belt and pressed it into Bowie's trembling hand. Bowie looked down at it as if he didn't know what it was.

"Now," Splinter said to the man in the chair, "I want to know where my supply is being taken."

The man gave a low growl of a laugh. "I'm not about to piss my life away by ratting out Araxa Leren," he hissed, eyes blazing.

Splinter folded his arms. "I'll ask you one more time. Where is my supply?"

The man smiled up at him defiantly.

Splinter turned. "Bowie."

Bowie looked up and swallowed hard. "I already know where the barrels are." His voice was very quiet. "They're being taken to Nielle."

Splinter raised his eyebrows condescendingly. "How would *you* know that?"

"I ..." Bowie shifted his feet uncomfortably, clearly wishing he was anywhere else. "I just know."

Splinter made an impatient gesture. "Dagny."

Dagny grabbed Bowie by the wrist, forcing him to raise the dagger. He drove Bowie's hand down, shoving the weapon into the prisoner's shoulder. The man cried out, but over the noise Aela heard Bowie suck in a shaky gasp. He tried to release the dagger, but Dagny moved his grip over Bowie's hand, preventing him from pulling away. Dagny rotated his hand and Bowie's underneath it. The blade twisted in the man's shoulder, and the prisoner gave a guttural scream. Bowie's face was ashen, as if he was about to vomit.

"All right!" the anarchist gasped. "All *right!*"

"Stop," Splinter said calmly.

Dagny let go of the blade, releasing Bowie's hand. Bowie jerked away as if the weapon was white hot.

"Where is my grey dream?" Splinter demanded.

"Outside the city ... to be taken to Nielle ... tonight," the man managed to say through thick, gasping breaths. "It's the truth, I swear."

Aela blinked. That Araxa Leren might transport the drug west across the border had not occurred to her. Surely there were plenty of buyers available in Dunwyn. And the journey to Nielle was long and dangerous, gangs prowling the roads waiting to get their hands on the treasures of passing merchants.

For any of them, a haul of grey dream would mean riches beyond compare.

That meant Araxa Leren wasn't transporting the grey dream across the border simply to get it out of Dunwyn. How did *Bowie* know the drugs would be taken to Nielle?

"Has anyone tried to copy the recipe?" Splinter asked.

Blood trickled from the wound in the prisoner's shoulder. The dagger was still protruding from his flesh. He shook his head. "Araxa has no interest in copying the recipe."

"Why not?" Splinter pressed mildly.

"With all the coin we're getting paid, we'll retire long before we need to start producing this stuff ourselves." The man laughed. "Ours is a *very* lucrative job."

Splinter's expression betrayed little of how he felt, but the way he shifted his weight restlessly told Aela he was as confused as she was. "Who's paying you to do this lucrative job?"

The man was still laughing, somewhat maniacally. "I'll die before telling you that."

"Well, you can have your wish." Splinter turned to Bowie. "Kill him."

Bowie went rigid. His head whipped to the man in the chair then back to Splinter. He shook his head. "No," he said. Splinter was dangerously still. "I – I don't want to."

"I didn't ask what you *wanted*," Splinter replied. "I gave you an order."

Bowie took a step away from the prisoner. He swallowed convulsively, staring at the floor. "I'm not going to kill him," he murmured so softly that Aela could barely hear him.

"I beg your pardon?" Splinter's tone was light, but his posture was menacing as he took a step towards Bowie, whose chest rose and fell unsteadily as he sucked in a breath. Bowie didn't move away. He seemed rooted in place as Splinter leaned down, bringing his face close to Bowie's.

"I thought I heard you refuse an order. I thought that after last night we had an understanding." Splinter brought a hand down on Bowie's shoulder, and Bowie flinched as Splinter dug his fingers in. "Kill him."

Bowie said nothing, just shook his head. He was trembling.

Splinter straightened up, looked at Dagny, and gave him a nod. Dagny grabbed Bowie's hand, closing it around the dagger again. The prisoner gave a yell as they pulled it from his shoulder. Tightening his strong fingers around Bowie's so he couldn't drop the weapon, Dagny raised the dagger, placing it at the prisoner's throat.

"*No*! Stop!" Bowie tried to jerk away. "*Stop*, don't —"

The deep peal of a bell cut through the room. Splinter huffed irritably.

"I'm not expecting anyone today. Get that garbage out of here before he makes trouble for us," he ordered Dagny.

Dagny let go of Bowie, who stumbled then stared mutely as Dagny hit the prisoner over the head with the butt of the dagger, slung him over his shoulder, and carried him from the room. Splinter followed.

Aimlessly, as if he wasn't really aware of what he was doing, Bowie went towards the stairs and left the room. It was a pitiful thing. He seemed so alone, cradling his right hand delicately with his left as if it was injured. It was covered in blood. But the blood dripping through Bowie's fingers and onto the sawdust wasn't his own.

Aela had always believed killing was something you either had in your blood or didn't. She and Tamas lived almost identical childhoods, but he'd chosen to become a healer while she had pursued the life of a soldier. Their natures set them apart.

Bowie was more than proficient at defending himself. Aela recalled the accuracy with which he'd hurled the knife at her yesterday, inflicting minimal damage with a warning shot, not a cold-blooded attack.

Splinter had clearly put in a lot of work to cultivate Bowie's fighting skills, but it was difficult to train someone out of a natural aversion to lethal violence.

In Anarchist Underground, gentleness was a weakness to be methodically stripped away through the most brutal kinds of training. Aela's frustration flared as she realised how powerless she was to do anything for Bowie while Splinter used cruelty to mould him into a killer.

She turned. Bryn lounged against the wall, casually spinning a dagger in his fingers as if watching a nine-year-old almost murder a man was everyday fare.

"Like I said, more trouble than he's worth," Bryn drawled. "How's the hand?"

"Terrific. Why did you offer to take my punishment last night?" Aela couldn't stop herself from asking the question.

Bryn scratched the stubble along his chin with his blade and gave a cool smile that didn't touch his eyes. "I like the idea of you owing me a favour. Which, by the way, you still do." In response to her questioning look, he reminded her smoothly, "Those men who attacked you in the tavern."

It should have been no surprise that he would use even that against her, but it still felt obscene.

Aela must have failed to control her expression, because Bryn shrugged. "If you're good at something, never do it for free." He pushed himself off the wall and sauntered towards her with an appraising look. "I haven't quite decided what I want in return yet. But when I do …" He pointed the tip of his knife at her casually. "You'll be the first to know."

"You're a fucking monster." Aela bit into the words with more aggression than the conversation warranted. Behind them was the full force of an unspoken accusation. Bryn wasn't a rogue; he was a killer, not half the man his father was. Not even close. Aela missed Saban desperately, but part of her was bitterly glad he would never see his son like this.

His smile widening, Bryn opened his mouth to retort, breaking off at the sound of footsteps and voices above them. Aela left Bryn standing in the training room and crept back upstairs. She peered out the doorway and immediately jerked backwards. Strolling into the manor's grand entrance hall, looking perfectly at home in Anarchist Underground, was Huntley Bartome. She hadn't bothered to remove the steward's insignia from her finger and was flanked by a dozen of her guards wearing their usual burnt-orange cloaks and full, unnecessary battle armour, faces obscured by helmets.

Entirely consumed by the fear that Splinter might reveal her at any moment, it took a beat for the peculiarity of Huntley's presence here to hit home. Only then did Aela's heart begin slamming against her chest like a clanging alarm bell. She jumped as Bryn appeared silently beside her, trying to lean past her to get a glimpse outside. Aela shoved him back against the wall.

"Of all the people to show up in my home today, Steward, you are the last person I would have expected," Splinter said with careful composure. Aela wasn't the only one who had recognised the steward's guard in the tavern last night.

"I thought you'd enjoy a surprise," Huntley replied.

"Depends on the manner of the surprise," Splinter said. "I

thought we had a professional understanding. After last night, I'm not so sure."

"Neither am I," Huntley said. "Imagine *my* surprise when I was told that you are in possession of something that belongs to me. I would appreciate you allowing my soldiers to search for it."

She gave a gesture, and the nearest guard stepped forward. Splinter drew his blade, levelling it at the soldier's throat.

"You might be projecting, Steward," Splinter said. "Why, last night you had your soldiers attempt to kill me and my people, at great advantage to Araxa Leren, given the circumstances. It appears you only take issue with theft when you're the one being stolen from. Besides, you haven't even told me what it is of yours I'm supposed to have in my possession."

"You don't need to know," Huntley said airily.

The soldier took another step forward. So did Splinter. The tip of his sword pressed against the soldier's throat, breaking the skin. He flinched. Both Splinter and Huntley looked entirely undisturbed by the blood or the tension that hung thick and heavy in the air.

"This is my house," Splinter said. "You have no power here or anywhere in Anarchist Underground for that matter. You have to keep your hands clean. I believe that's why you came to me with that little assignment in the first place."

"Speaking of which," Huntley said smoothly. "I have a new task for you. Double the pay."

There was a long silence that sounded like Huntley waiting for Splinter to ask questions. Aela imagined him staring at her with that intimidating icy gaze. After a moment, Huntley spoke again.

"I want you to kill Prince Bryn."

There was a smile in Splinter's voice when he finally replied. "Consider it done."

Aela's fingers gripped the rough stone wall. It was lucky she was leaning against it. Her legs threatened to give out beneath her. She felt sick. In the castle, Huntley had called for Bryn's execution without so much as a trial. And now this. Aela tried to tell herself that Huntley could very well be executing an intelligent strategy here. Rumours had reached Huntley that Bryn was in Anarchist Underground, so hiring an anarchist as an inside man to find him wasn't an entirely shocking approach … but hiring an anarchist to *kill* Bryn?

A horrible voice inside Aela's head told her there was another reason why Huntley would want Bryn dead, rather than brought to justice for King Saban's murder, but it was impossible.

As impossible as Huntley being here in Splinter's home? She knows him. She gave him an assignment. *That's what he said.*

Aela felt like she was going to be sick.

Her fighter's instinct forced her to refocus. She turned, and Bryn's gaze stopped her in her tracks. His face was carefully expressionless. His posture mirrored the manner with which he had lounged against the wall down in the training room. He looked casual enough at a glance, but there was an edge to his manner, as if he was trying a little too hard to look nonchalant. Aela paused, the reality of Bryn's situation sinking in.

If Splinter was commissioned by Huntley to kill Bryn, his days were numbered in blood. It was entirely probable that Splinter didn't know what Bryn looked like, since Bryn had spent his entire life shirking any and all royal duties that would thrust him into the public eye. But Huntley was thorough. She would have handed Splinter a sketch and a dossier that would quickly erode Bryn's anonymity in Underground. It wouldn't take Splinter long to realise who his man, Slate, truly was, and it would take him even less time to carry out Huntley's order.

Torn, she hesitated. She knew what she wanted to do. Killer or not, she had an obligation now to keep Bryn alive. He needed to stand trial, to face proper justice — it was what Saban would want.

She grabbed his arm and pulled him down the stairs, back into the armoury, shoving him up against the wall. Surprise registered on his face for a moment before he locked the expression down, replacing it with that arrogant smirk.

"It doesn't count as a favour to me if you initiate it, sweetheart," he said, maddeningly suggestive.

It was enough to drive her over the edge. Nerves pulled taut from what she'd witnessed upstairs, and already at the very edge of what she would tolerate under normal circumstances, Aela did what she'd been wanting to do ever since she'd first laid eyes on Bryn in the doorway of her bedroom upstairs. She punched him in the face.

"If I have to break your jaw to shut you up, I will," she told him. "Keep pushing me, *Prince Bryn*."

The world seemed to reform around them, as if this revelation had altered time and space. The training room suddenly felt much smaller … and more dangerous. Aela felt like she was standing far closer to Bryn, and she was keenly aware of his physicality, tall with a fighter's build. She was alone, unarmed, with a man who had murdered his father and who'd just been presented with a very good reason to protect his identity in Anarchist Underground at any cost.

Something flashed in Bryn's golden-brown eyes, disappearing before Aela could name the emotion. There was no warmth in the slow smile that slid across his face. "So, you *do* know who I am," he said. "I'm surprised one of your daggers didn't stray into my back at the Devil's Tongue last night." He cocked a brow at her mockingly. "I remember you in training. I remember how much you loved learning to kill. What's happened? Has the Reaper of Dunwyn gone soft since the war?"

Aela moved without thinking. She took another swing at Bryn, a powerful right cross that would have caught him directly in his cheek, already carrying a bruise from Splinter last night. Suddenly, his hand was there, blocking the punch, forcing her arm down with brutal strength. His eyes glinted with infuriating triumph.

"Raising hands against your prince is treason."

"You're not anyone's prince," Aela ground out through clenched teeth. "Unless you're trying to tell me you didn't murder your father."

Her hopefulness evaporated at the dark amusement in Bryn's eyes. He didn't deny it. Instead, he stepped in closer to her, and she exercised a heroic amount of willpower to resist moving away.

"What are you going to do about it?" he whispered, his breath stirring the strands of hair that hung loose around her face.

She kicked out, catching him between the legs. He made a choked sound, doubling over. Bryn was a fighter and recovered quickly from the blow, but Aela was faster. As Bryn's hand flew to the dagger at his belt, Aela yanked the nearest sword from the wall and pressed the tip against his throat. He froze.

"Pull that dagger," she murmured. "I'm *begging* you."

Tension rose thick in the air as Bryn weighed up the risk of resisting. A muscle twitched in his jaw, and he raised his hands, an unwilling surrender.

Keeping her eyes and her blade on Bryn, she reached carefully for his belt, her fingers wrapping around the hilt of his weapon. Bryn's lip twitched.

"While you're down there…" he said.

Aela jerked the dagger out of his belt. She circled behind him and pushed the weapon into his back, feeling hard muscles tense beneath his jacket.

"Move," she ordered.

Forcing Bryn along at knifepoint, Aela rounded the back of Splinter's house, peering around the building to look out towards the street.

Dagny had led Huntley outside. They paused for a moment, speaking in hushed tones before Huntley shook Dagny's hand and climbed into a stout, unmarked carriage. A large trunk was strapped to the back. Huntley was heading somewhere for an extended stay. It wasn't unusual for a statesman to travel, but Aela suspected that if she was continuing her journey without the comfort of the castle's plush carriage, this visit might not be of an official nature. Either way, Huntley's mere presence in Anarchist Underground was troubling enough, and then there was her apparent business relationship with Splinter.

Suspicion compelled Aela to shove Bryn towards Splinter's carriage house. Evidently, between last night's chaos and this morning's interrogation, no one had been ordered to tend to the horses. They were still neatly tethered to the carriage.

Aela jerked her head towards the box seat. "You're driving."

"We're going to follow her?" Bryn looked at the carriage. "If I refuse, what will you do? Tie me up and throw me in the back?"

"If I have to." Aela grabbed Bryn's shoulder, pushing him

around to face her. "But I don't expect I will. You're not stupid enough to stay in a house with a man who's been commissioned to kill you. And I want to find out why the steward wants you dead so badly that she's willing to hire an anarchist to do it."

"Are you stupid?" Bryn took a step forward, coming up short when Aela pressed the tip of his dagger defensively against his chest. "She wants me dead because I'm the one who killed King Saban."

Twelve

The truth hung between them, almost a tangible thing as they drove out of the city. Aela kept the dagger on Bryn, whose knuckles were visibly white on the reins. It wasn't the threat of discovery that had him on edge. The people of Dunwald were unlikely to recognise their prince, who had spent the majority of his life avoiding them along with the rest of his responsibilities.

Aela suspected that Bryn's unease also wasn't due to the threat of being held at knifepoint. Despite the danger posed by Splinter, Bryn was inexplicably not wild about leaving Dunwald. He even seemed oddly reluctant to leave Splinter's house.

Keeping a careful distance from Huntley's carriage, it wasn't difficult to remain discreet. The roads were bustling with travellers. When Aela had returned from the Borderlands, merchants and traders were slowly beginning to venture back onto the roads. It was a concertina-like effect that had followed the army as it travelled east. Dunwyn's people were gradually regaining confidence that the country was secure again, stable enough to trade, to visit family, to pack up and move somewhere new for a fresh start.

Only an hour out of the city, Aela was already restless. The seat beneath her was too hard, her inactive body too heavy. They should have ridden horses. Bryn would be more difficult to contain, and she'd been concerned about being identified or exposed to the elements if this was to be a long journey, but now she was irritated by her own cautiousness. All she could hear was the monotonous creak of wood, the crunch of stones under the wheels. The occasional birdsong seemed louder and more grating than when she rode. She bounced her knee up and down impatiently.

"That's annoying." Bryn's hand came down hard on her thigh, stalling the restless movement. Instinctively, she slashed out with her blade, catching the bronze skin at his forearm. He hissed a breath through his teeth and jerked his hand away, staring at her in furious disbelief as a trickle of blood emerged from the shallow cut.

"Gods! You're out of your mind," he said irritably.

Embarrassed at the overreaction, Aela forced her gaze straight ahead, directing a large amount of focus into ignoring him. Her nervous system hadn't been wound this tightly in weeks, not since she'd walked alone onto the battlefield at Bayeau, facing Nielle's champion in single combat with the Dunwyan army at her back. Aela found herself irked that she was just as on edge as Bryn.

In her peripheral vision, she noticed him watching her. She adjusted her grip on the dagger.

"Don't you think this is a bit redundant?" he asked. "Investigating the steward's motives for ordering me killed?"

Aela gave him a narrow look. "While I'd imagine that everybody who has ever met you has a strong argument for wanting you dead, I'm not the one who's being stupid."

Bryn raised an eyebrow. "I'm sure you're going to enjoy enlightening me, since I'm a captive audience." He gestured to the blade in her hand.

"Huntley's the steward of Dunwyn. She should be trying to bring you to trial, not doing backstreet deals with anarchists to discreetly murder you. Besides, you heard that talk in there about some other assignment she's given Splinter. Something is … off."

Off didn't begin to describe it. Aela's unease was growing with every mile they covered in pursuit of the steward.

"The king gave you his insignia," Bryn said. "I saw it when you were in the bath the other night."

Aela's grip around the dagger's hilt was so tight it hurt. Cold metal bit into the raw skin at her burned palm. "Don't speak about the king," she gritted out.

Predictably, Bryn ignored that. "You were his most favoured warrior. You were the entire country's hero after the war. You could've retired anywhere and been treated like royalty. How the hell did you end up in Underground?"

"I didn't want to retire."

"What about going home? What about honouring your parents by returning to your village with a victory in battle?"

He had to be mocking her. Aela looked over at him. Recent experience had indicated that you could only have two kinds of conversations with Bryn Ryland, a frustrating exchange of bitchy remarks that achieved nothing or a full-blown argument. Although his expression was difficult to name, his face was open, his light-brown eyes searching her expression, as if he was trying to read her.

"My parents died in a raid at Hiver when I was a baby. My mother barely had time to tell my guardian my name before she died."

"What about a lover?" His tone was completely shameless.

"What the fuck did you say to me?" she demanded. Unbidden, her mind flashed on Tamas's strong, calloused hands tracing the lines of her body, the heat of his bare skin on hers. She'd made a lot of mistakes in her life; using her dearest friend in that way had to be among the worst. Familiar guilt stabbed at her, coalescing into rage at Bryn's malicious interest.

"Oh, come on. Don't be modest. You know what you look like." Bryn's gaze roved up and down her body approvingly, and Aela resisted the urge to stab him again.

"You're disgusting."

Bryn gave a short, unapologetic laugh. "So you're an orphaned Borderlander who joined the army. How cliché. It blows me away that you people still fancy yourselves my family's soldiers. What are you protecting out in that wasteland? The ruins of a castle no one's set foot in for two hundred years? The One Kingdom's gone."

"Don't flatter yourself," Aela said, her voice as hard as the steel in her hand. "No one on the border is fighting for *you*. We fight because if we don't then King Marcus's mercenaries will kill us and take everything we have."

"There's no proof that the Niellan throne sponsors the border raids."

Aela scoffed. "Please. Marcus wants to push every Dunwyan settlement as far east as possible so he can extend Nielle's border. Who else besides him would care to claim that land? You said it yourself — the only thing out there is a ruined castle that Marcus's own family razed to the ground two centuries ago. And look where the quest for Niellan independence from the One Kingdom got them. Neither Nielle nor Dunwyn is better off now than they were when all of this started. The only difference is that the body count gets higher every time a fight breaks out in the Borderlands."

She looked down at her blade. In the sunlight, its polished edge threw orange light across her hand, like the flames that had licked through her village after every attack by Marcus's ruthless swords-for-hire.

"You have no idea what it's like," she told him, "constantly living in fear of an attack on your home. I didn't want to be scared anymore, and I wanted to protect those who couldn't defend themselves. I was sixteen when I left home to train in Dunwald. I said I was eighteen."

She shook her head and gave a breathy laugh. She still couldn't believe anyone had bought it.

The king hadn't bought it; he'd understood why she lied. Unlike Amory and Ewan, who had grudgingly let her go because they loved her, Saban had *understood* her. He'd known that Aela needed to fight the way she needed air in her lungs.

"Do all Borderlanders look like you?" It would have been a tactful question if Bryn was a commoner. Most people from Dunwald assumed Aela was Niellan and were rightly suspicious. Given his station, Bryn should be better educated than most about Borderland history, but he'd never deigned to learn anything about his people.

"Back in the old days, more of us looked like me. My father was Niellan. Both of my parents were travelling merchants who worked across the border. They met on the road."

"I see." Bryn's voice was emotionless. "Did you ever face any resistance from the soldiers you commanded? You look pretty Niellan for a Dunwyan."

He was referring to her blue eyes but especially to her

shoulder-length brown waves, sun-streaked with light caramel. It had never grown long enough to pull back properly, so she took the precaution of tying the front strands off her face with fabric and moving fast enough that no one could grab the pieces that hung loose at the back. Her skin was tanned, darker than most Niellans', the only clear hint to her Borderland roots. Her appearance marked her out as an interloper this far east, where most Dunwyans had light-blonde hair and eyes the same colour as Bryn's. Resistance from the other soldiers hadn't been much of a problem. Given her youth, being underestimated had been the greater issue, but her life was none of his business. She didn't even know why he was bothering to ask.

She pulled her focus off the road and met his dark gaze. "I'm not the enemy here."

Thirteen

Several hours clear of the city, Huntley's carriage, visible a distance ahead of theirs, veered onto a bumpy road through the trees towards the western villages. The Borderlands tended to be poor, war and raid repairs eating away at their funds, so domestic merchants rarely traded in the west. But the road was littered with carts belonging to travellers who hadn't crossed the border since before the war. Unlike their respective kings, Dunwyan and Niellan traders bore no enmity for foreigners … as long as they offered up their coin. Aela was glad the crowds remained, drawing attention away from them.

A muffled cry rang out from inside their carriage. The horses whinnied in protest as Bryn tugged hard on the reins, steering them off the road. They jumped down.

"I need a weapon," Bryn murmured.

"Not likely." Silently, Aela pulled the sword from her belt, bringing her other hand up to the carriage's door handle. She jerked open the door …

Bowie was inside, curled up in a fitful sleep on the plush seat, murmuring something in Niellan.

Aela heard "please stop" and "don't" before Bryn said sharply, "Bowie!"

The boy jerked upright, his chest heaving. He looked more dishevelled than usual, his shirt cuffs and collar unlaced, creased brown jacket piled haphazardly on the seat as if he'd thrown it there in a hurry.

"I'm sorry!" Bowie blurted out. He said it in Niellan then shook his head, as if breaking himself from the stupor of sleep. His expression became more composed, his breathing evening out.

The silver chain had slipped out from beneath his shirt. Like last time she'd glimpsed it, Aela couldn't make out the shape of the shiny pendant on the end of it before Bowie hurriedly shoved it back under his collar.

Murderous anger passed over Bryn's face as he looked at Bowie – the boy's face was pricked with sweat. One trembling hand scratched at his throat.

"You. Out. *Now*," Bryn said dangerously.

Sensing trouble, Aela moved to stand in front of Bryn as Bowie dropped down onto the side of the road. "Back up," she ordered Bryn.

He looked confused for a moment before realisation changed his expression. "You think I'd hurt him? He's a kid."

"I really don't know what you'd do," Aela told him icily.

Bryn gave her a long, expressionless look then made an impatient noise and stepped around her. "What are you doing here?" he demanded of Bowie. "In a language I can understand."

It intrigued Aela that Bowie dreamed in Niellan but was also apparently fluent in Dunwyan. While the people of Hiver upheld the tradition of bilingualism two centuries after the fall of the One Kingdom, Aela rarely met anyone outside the Borderlands who spoke both Niellan and Dunwyan.

Bowie pulled a piece of paper from his jacket pocket, handing it to Bryn, who glanced at it then looked up exasperatedly. "This is written in Niellan, smart ass."

Living as far east as he had and the political climate with Nielle being what it was, King Saban's grasp of Niellan hadn't extended further than basic comprehension of essential enemy phrases. Bryn's was considerably poorer than that.

"Here." Aela snatched the paper from him. She looked at it then up at Bowie. "Did you lift this from Huntley's pocket?"

"Obviously not," Bowie answered, as if the suggestion was unspeakably stupid. "I took it from her carriage while she was inside with Splinter. Then I saw you preparing to follow her, so I decided to come with you. To help."

"To be a stowaway, you mean." Aela paused. Bowie was nine, a commoner, and a Niellan. "Wait, how do *you* know who Huntley is?"

Bowie frowned. "She rules Dunwyn. I'm not stupid."

"What does it say?" Bryn's tone was impatient.

"Directions," Aela explained, "to Eterre."

"Huntley was the ambassador to Nielle for more than two decades, until Marcus banished her at the start of the war," Bryn said.

Aela took his meaning. There was no way Huntley didn't know the way to Nielle's capital city, the place where King Marcus resided, where all of her diplomatic meetings had taken place.

"They're bad directions anyway." Bowie gestured at the paper. "All those back roads will take her ages. I can get us there just as fast without following right behind them."

"Back roads," Aela muttered. "Let's find out why she doesn't want anyone to know where she's going." She looked down at Bowie. "Come on."

"I don't fucking think so." This time, Bryn stepped between Aela and Bowie. "I'm taking him back to Dunwald."

"Stop." She shoved him as he tried to move towards the front of the carriage. "It's too late to go back. We'd never get to Nielle before Huntley. Besides, Bowie says he knows a discreet route."

Bryn shoved Aela back. "I don't care *what* he knows. It's none of my damn business what Huntley's doing in Eterre. You know what is my business?" He jerked his head at Bowie. "Getting him back to Dunwald before Splinter realises he's gone, or have you forgotten what happened last time?"

That brought Aela up short. Fury was blazing in Bryn's eyes. His sudden concern for Bowie's safety made no sense, but she didn't have time to analyse it any further. With every wasted second, Huntley progressed further towards Eterre, and Aela was gripped with the urgent need to know what she was doing there.

"You know why it's your business," she retorted in a low voice, conscious that Bowie was standing behind them.

"You do whatever you want," Bryn snapped at her. "I'm taking him home. Bowie, come."

"I'm not going back to Dunwald, Slate," Bowie said quietly. He wasn't trembling the way he had when he'd refused an order from Splinter back at the house and his tone left no room for uncertainty. "I'm going to Eterre."

Bryn froze, clenched his fists, turned. "You're going *home*," he said slowly, as if he was willing himself not to lose his cool. "That's an order."

Bowie rolled his eyes. "Kiss my ass, Slate. I don't have to take your orders. I don't work for you."

Horrified, Aela tensed, ready for Bryn to take a swing at Bowie for that. Instead, Bryn raised his hands in frustration.

"No, you work for *Splinter*," he snapped impatiently. "And what do you think he'll do when he discovers you've run away?"

"Some things are more important."

"Agree to disagree."

"Fine. Then *you* can go back to Dunwald, and we'll go without you." Bowie crossed his arms over his chest, unyielding. It stunned Aela that he clearly wasn't afraid of Bryn at all.

A furious silence stretched out between them, during which Bryn dropped his head, shoving his fingers through the blond wisps around his face. After a long moment, he looked up, his dark eyes meeting Bowie's blue ones. "How can you be so smart and so stupid all at the same time?"

"Get over it," Bowie said. "I'm going with Commander Rinn to Eterre."

It took a moment for the use of Aela's real name to sink in. When it did, her stomach dropped like a rock. "I —" Flabbergasted, she stared at the boy. "You *know?*"

Bowie rolled his eyes by way of an answer.

Aela whirled on Bryn. "Who else knows?"

It was Bowie who volunteered the information. "Splinter, Dagny, Nula, and Laz. And Slate and me, obviously. And also probably some of those soldiers we fought in the tavern last night." He walked towards the front of the carriage and hoisted himself up onto the box, calling back to her, "That ring of yours isn't exactly subtle. Neither's the way you fight."

Speechless, Aela closed her mouth and concentrated on controlling her shock.

Bryn was watching her, arms crossed, lips pressed firmly together. If he hadn't been ropable moments earlier, Aela might have believed he was trying not to laugh. "Think he's annoying now? Wait until you've spent a few days with him."

Aela raised her eyebrows. "And just like that you're coming with us? Have you finally discovered your sense of duty to Dunwyn? Better late than never."

"I don't give a shit about Dunwyn," Bryn spat. He drove his shoulder into Aela's as he walked back towards the carriage.

★★★

"How are you the *Reaper of Dunwyn*?" Bowie said in Niellan with disgust. "You're from Nielle."

Aela glanced away from the road. The boy was sitting between her and Bryn. He'd refused to ride inside the carriage, even though he clearly hated being squeezed so closely between them. Bryn looked displeased too. His frown deepened now that Bowie was deliberately excluding him by speaking in a language he couldn't understand.

"I'm Dunwyan," she corrected firmly. "I'm a Borderlander."

"I've seen plenty of Borderlanders. They don't look like you."

Aela raised her eyebrows. If Bowie had seen that many Borderlanders, he had to be from the centre himself, which didn't make sense given his quintessentially western features. "You're from the Niellan border?"

"No. Eterre."

"But you've met plenty of Borderlanders," Aela clarified sceptically. He was telling tall tales. Aela doubted there were any more Borderlanders in Nielle's west than there were along the coast of Dunwyn.

"Never said I'd *met* them."

Aela rolled her eyes. Definitely annoying, as Bryn promised.

"Do they hate you?" Bowie asked casually.

"Who?"

"The people in your village, on the border." Bowie said it like it was obvious. "Is that why you didn't go home after the war?"

"Why would they hate me?"

"You look like the raiders."

Aela went rigid.

"Bowie, that's enough," Bryn said in Dunwyan, his eyes warily on Aela. "Whatever the hell you're saying, it's pissing her off."

"Borderlanders are more open-minded than that," Aela gritted out in Niellan, ignoring Bryn. She was offended, but more than that she was annoyed that a child was so adept at antagonising her. "Most of us might look more Dunwyan now, but in the days of the One Kingdom, Borderlanders looked more like me. Dunwyans mixed with Niellans a lot more back then."

Bowie was silent for a moment, considering this. Then he said coolly, "Maybe they hate you because you love killing people so much. That's what everyone says about the Reaper of Dunwyn."

Aela jerked the reins hard, bringing the carriage to a lurching stop. She turned on Bowie. "What's your problem?"

He looked up at her through furious blue eyes. "*You're* my problem."

"Oi," Bryn snapped more forcefully. "I said *that's enough*, Bowie. Shut up or go sit in the back."

Bowie muttered a particularly vulgar Niellan curse and climbed over Bryn, deliberately stepping on both his feet before jumping down onto the road. He got into the back of the carriage and slammed the door.

"Little shit," Bryn muttered irritably, but Aela was struck once again that Bowie had done what Bryn told him to do, despite the absence of a clear threat.

You can't be both a murderer and a protector. She realised belatedly how ridiculous it was for her to think that, as a soldier. The only reason she'd ever wanted to raise a weapon was for the sake of those who couldn't fight for themselves.

Lost in thought, she clicked her tongue, coaxing the horses into motion. A realisation teased at the edge of her mind, not quite in reach.

Fourteen

A day later, as the sun dipped low on the horizon, casting long shadows across grassy fields, Bowie was back out front, free from his time-out in the carriage but no less prickly. In sullen silence, he pointed up the road. Lights were beginning to bloom from a building on the skyline.

Aela huffed out a long breath, expelling some of her tension. Having left on uncharacteristic impulse, she'd brought no provisions, and they hadn't eaten or slept since departing. This was the first sign of any civilised accommodation … although *civilised* was a relative term.

"No one will ask questions. That's why people come here," Bowie said. "But we should hide the carriage. It's too fancy."

It was immediately apparent why no one would ask questions. From the road, the two-storey inn they approached had all the aesthetic appeal of an outhouse, grimy rotting wood and a muddy threshold. The dirty, weathered men smoking outside reminded Aela of the clientele of the Devil's Tongue. They watched through bloodshot eyes as Bryn, Bowie, and Aela approached.

Bryn's unease was palpable. When one of the smoking men opened the door for Aela with an exaggerated genteel bow,

Bryn clenched his jaw, hand hovering near his belt, where he would usually carry a weapon.

The inside was marginally more pleasant. The tavern on the ground floor was dark and cramped but warm, lit by a pair of fires, one at each end of the room. The patronage was predominantly male, most of them huddled around gaming tables.

Bryn looked down at Bowie with narrowed eyes. "Nice," he said drily. "How do you know this place?"

The answer was averted eyes. "Go find a table," Bowie said. "There's something I need to do."

Aela frowned. "What do you need to do *here?*"

"As I live and breathe!" An enormous, muscular man with a blond ponytail and a spiderweb tattooed across his right cheek approached them. He wore a brown leather apron and rolled-up shirt sleeves, showing thick, muscular arms marked with what appeared to be another enormous spiderweb tattoo. He wiped his meaty hands on a grimy cloth. "Bowie? Is that you? Look at how much you've grown!" Grabbing the arm of a reluctant Bowie, he wrenched it up and squeezed the boy's bicep triumphantly. "Ha! So strong now!"

"I can only stay for one night, Walter," Bowie said. "The three of us, we need a room and some food." Bowie jerked his head at Bryn. "He can pay."

"Well, I'm pleased to hear it," Walter said. He gestured to the counter at the back of the room. "If your friends are paying gold, then go get them some food. You can eat once you're done for the night."

"Yes, sir." Bowie made off through the tables before he could be stopped.

Confused, Aela looked to Walter. "What's he doing?"

"Working," Walter said, as if it was obvious. "Given the size of his debt, I suppose one night's better than nothing."

Bryn's posture shifted slightly beside Aela as he watched Walter, but he remained silent.

"Debt," Aela repeated. "What for?"

Walter's brows shot up. "What's it to you?" he asked dangerously.

"Bowie's our … friend," Aela said.

It didn't feel like the right word while she was surrounded by enemies.

"You're them anarchists from Dunwald then." Walter's eyes narrowed. "I didn't want him to join you, you know. Not that there was much of a choice after your boss caught Bowie lifting coins out of his pocket." Walter chuckled then appeared to check himself. "Ahem. Not that I condone that sort of behaviour in my establishment."

"If you like Bowie so much, why are you holding a debt over his head?" Bryn cut in coldly.

Walter laughed again. "Where've you been the last four years, boy? The war's meant lean times for anyone who relies on business from travellers heading west to Nielle. If I could offer charity to every orphaned kid who appears out of the forest I would, but as it is I've barely been able to keep my doors open. All I'm asking from Bowie is that he repay me for services rendered."

"Did you say he came out of the *forest*?" Aela clarified.

Walter folded his arms across his chest, eyeing them suspiciously. "You have a lot of questions."

Aela ignored that. "How much does he owe you?"

"More than can be repaid in one night." Walter waved a hand at the haphazard rows of tables. "I have to get back to work. Go find yourselves a seat. Bowie will bring you some food."

They found a small table in the corner and watched Bowie move about the room, delivering food and drink to patrons with the air of someone using a very small percentage of their brain power. Aela watched his eyes flick about the room and knew he was taking everything in, as he had in the Devil's Tongue. Eventually, Bowie brought them a stew that smelled a lot better than Aela had expected. It dawned on her that the key to weathering the night in an establishment such as this was to have extremely low standards so that she was constantly pleasantly surprised.

Bryn, on the other hand, threw his spoon down in disgust without touching the meal. "I think perhaps Walter *should* have closed down his establishment. His menu is distinctly sub-par."

"We weren't all raised on food prepared by castle chefs," Aela shot back.

Bryn reached into his jacket, producing a red velvet drawstring bag. It looked expensive, something he might have taken with him when he fled the castle. Aela heard coins clinking inside. It was stuffed full of them.

"I think this night can be salvaged," Bryn said, nodding towards one of the gaming tables.

Aela wondered how many coins Bryn was carrying, probably more than anyone else here had seen in their life. "What are you doing?" she asked.

She'd had to force him out of the city at knifepoint, but now he seemed perfectly content to be along for the journey.

"Eating shit food," Bryn offered. "Gambling."

Aela gave him a flat, unimpressed stare. "I mean, why? I'm here because I'm afraid for Dunwyn. I believe Huntley means to do the kingdom harm. You've made it perfectly clear you don't care about your country, so *why are you still here?*"

"It's not *my country*," Bryn replied, a deliberately infuriating non-answer as he lounged back casually in his chair. "Dunwyn belonged to Saban, and now it belongs to Huntley Bartome."

Aela gripped the edge of the table to prevent herself from striking Bryn again. Saban had understood the heavy burden that came with the privilege of his birth. He had always taken seriously his responsibility to his people and his country.

Aela was ambushed by an unpleasant twinge of anger towards the king for failing to raise his son with the same sense of duty. She clamped down on the feeling, diverting it towards Bryn. He was an adult now and knew full well that he was the king's only successor. He had known it when he'd driven the knife into his father's heart.

Aela knew she should be careful, but she wasn't feeling careful right now. Bryn had been coddled enough in his life, and she shouldn't have to tiptoe around the subject. It wasn't like Bryn was being discreet.

"You don't want the throne. Then why did you kill him?" She gave voice to a thought that had been playing in her mind. "Did Splinter make you do it?"

There was a violent silence in which Aela allowed herself to internally play out the fantasy of driving her dagger slowly across his throat, watching him collapse forward onto the table, bleeding out onto the wood. As if he was pulling the brutal thought from Aela's mind, Bryn's expression shifted, becoming entirely unreadable for a moment. Then that horribly familiar arrogant smile stretched over his handsome features.

"Sweetheart," he drawled. "If I told you that, I'd have to kill you too." Bryn tilted his head, drinking in Aela's revulsion, his lip twitching when he was satisfied that he'd rattled her. He stood and sauntered over to one of the gaming tables, settling himself down without a backwards glance.

Resting her elbows on the table, Aela dropped her head into her hands. She wasn't going to get anything else out of Bryn tonight.

She sat alone for a while, watching Bowie weave about the room, delivering food and drink, cleaning, and deflecting any unwanted attention with a few choice words. Over at the gambling tables, a pretty woman with long, golden hair lounged in Bryn's lap, taking a clear fancy to the inn's handsome, wealthy patron. Bryn's hand slid to her curvy waist, and Aela gritted her teeth. If he attempted to bring some conquest into the room they were sharing, she'd punch him in the balls so hard it would cause lifelong damage.

★★★

It was late. The inn was clearing out as guests departed the tavern or found their way to the lodgings upstairs. Even Bryn had left the gaming tables, no longer carrying his red bag of coins. Aela hadn't seen which fortunate gambler had pocketed the prince's dazzling wealth.

Walter emerged from behind the counter and tapped Bowie on the shoulder. Together, they disappeared into the back room, and Aela rose. She followed them without drawing attention. Those left in the tavern were swaying drunkenly or distracted by prostitutes or cards.

Cautiously, she pushed open the swinging double doors leading to the back room, finding a short corridor that led to another door, which was slightly ajar. Peering through, Aela glimpsed Bowie sitting atop a bench as Walter stood beside him. They both stared intently into a cauldron perched atop a metallic tripod, an open flame dancing beneath it. Walter sprinkled something into the pot, his thick fingers surprisingly dexterous.

"It's been two years," Bowie said, drumming his heels impatiently against the bench. "You must have made *something* that works."

"A concoction like this could take an entire lifetime to perfect, Bowie," Walter said irritably.

"I don't have a lifetime," Bowie replied.

"It would be helpful if you shared more about exactly *how* you're planning to use it."

"You know enough."

Walter sighed with a level of frustration that was entirely relatable to Aela. Trying to have a substantive conversation with Bowie was impossible. Although, for his part, Bowie appeared to quite like Walter … in the mundane sense that he wasn't openly rude or completely terrified.

"Well," Walter said, "I suppose you can at least try this brew and see if it's in any way effective at reducing the symptoms. I make no guarantees though, mark me." Pulling on a thick glove, he removed the cauldron from the fire and poured clear liquid into a small glass vial. "And your supply is very limited."

"Two vials," Bowie said, unimpressed, as Walter began pouring into the second glass. "That's it?"

"If my theory's correct, two vials should be more than enough to know if it's effective. If it works, I can make more." He picked up one of the vials, examining it closely. "If it works, it might make me a small fortune."

Bowie snatched the vial off him. "You can't sell it. You

promised you wouldn't say anything. At least until we know it works."

"And when you take off again tomorrow with your little friends, how will I ever know that it works?"

"Believe me, you'll know." Bowie watched Walter for a moment. "Thank you."

He went to jump down from the bench, but Walter caught him, his big fingers wrapping all the way around Bowie's thin arm. "Listen to me. I like you a lot. You know I do. That's why I'm telling you — stay here. Work off your debt, learn some skills so you can grow up and make an honest living. I know that when you're little everything that happens seems like it matters a lot, but whatever you're mixed up in, it's not worth losing your life over. Stay here where you're safe."

Bowie shook his head, but there was a longing in his expression that pricked at Aela's heart. "I'm not safe anywhere," he said quietly.

He tucked the vials into his jacket, jumped down from the bench, and made for the door. Aela darted back into the tavern and made for the lodgings upstairs, wondering what on earth she'd witnessed.

⋆⋆⋆

Aela had never been good at sleeping in new places, and she hated the idea of closing her eyes and drifting into unconsciousness with Bowie and Bryn lying in the very same room. Bryn had at least done the courtesy of not attempting to get laid in their shared quarters, but he'd occupied the entirety of the room's only bed without consulting anyone. It was unchivalrous but also fine by Aela.

After months at war, she found familiar comfort in sleeping on the hard floor. She stared up at the ceiling, which was illuminated by the crackling fire, tracing the ridges and imperfections in the wood with her eyes.

A soft creak shattered the deep silence. She closed her eyes, feigning sleep, listening to light footsteps padding towards the door. It creaked open, and Aela opened her eyes in time to see Bowie slip outside. She rose, glancing at Bryn, who was fast asleep in the bed, hair splayed across the pillow. Sleep smoothed out his arrogant smirk, rendering his handsome features more captivating. It would be easy to get caught up in his beauty, to stand here and stare at him for hours, mapping the contours of his muscular arms, the strong line of his jaw, the softness of his slightly parted lips. Shaking her head, Aela followed Bowie out of the room, stopping at the top of the staircase and shrinking into the shadows.

The tavern was quiet now, mostly deserted in the early hours of the morning. Bowie stood by the fire at the foot of the stairs. There was a chair before him, and sitting in it was a figure obscured by a scantily clad woman astride her lap.

Hair shaven, wearing trousers and a man's leather riding jacket with cutoff sleeves, she was a hard woman of thirty or so with the calloused hands and muscled arms of a fighter. Her eyes were dark brown, almost black in the dim light with short lashes, narrow brows, and lips to match.

Bowie faced her, focused and steady, wholly oblivious to the half-naked woman draped all over her. They were speaking Niellan.

"I didn't think I would see you again," the woman said to

Bowie. Her voice was low and gravelly. She sat completely motionless, paying no attention to her escort's hands roaming over her body. Something about her watchful stillness reminded Aela of a bird of prey on the hunt. "You have some nerve crossing me."

Bowie's lip twitched, an attempt at Bryn's arrogance that was too forced. His shoulders were tense. "Do something about it … unless you're afraid."

The woman smiled slowly, but the expression didn't reach her eyes. They bored into Bowie, unblinking. "Careful now. We both know you're not in a position to be overconfident."

Bowie ignored this. In a quiet, fierce voice, he said, "I know what you're doing, Araxa."

Recognition jolted Aela. *This* was Araxa Leren? She'd suspected in Dunwyn that Bowie had some kind of history with Araxa. Watching them now, she believed it. If looks could kill, the tavern would be a war zone.

With the woman still hanging off her, Araxa kicked an empty chair towards Bowie. He flinched as it scraped loudly along the floor. "Have a seat, Bowie," she said lightly. "Warm up by the fire."

Bowie looked reluctant but did as he was told, positioning the chair so that there was a table between himself and Araxa before sitting down. He turned to face her. Even from far away, Aela could read the unease in Bowie's careful posture.

"Are you comfortable? Do you want a drink?" Araxa's tone was disconcertingly pleasant, incongruous with her predatory stillness.

"I want you to tell me how much of it they have." Bowie's voice was stony, giving nothing away.

"You've made a lot of trouble for us," said Araxa. There was an edge of something dark beneath her mild tone. "They're still looking for you."

"I'm not scared."

Araxa pursed her lips with mild surprise. "Aren't you?" she crooned. "I wonder if that makes you brave or stupid."

"I figured it out years ago. If I can put it together, how long do you think it'll take everyone else?"

Araxa murmured something in the ear of her escort, who immediately rose and made herself scarce. Appraising Bowie calmly, she pulled something from her belt, a short, thick dagger with a serrated edge. It glinted in the firelight as she twisted it in her hands. Bowie eyed the weapon warily.

Thud.

Araxa stabbed the blade's sharp tip into the table. The tension in Bowie's shoulders became more pronounced.

"You'd better watch yourself. There isn't a lot stopping me from tying you to the back of my horse."

Bowie gave the woman a long, challenging look. Still, no hint of feeling in Araxa's gaze. "Isn't there?" His light tone appeared untouched by the danger of his situation, but his posture was taut, as if it was taking everything he had not to flee. "I wonder how Splinter would feel about that. It's one thing to steal his drugs, but taking one of his people? You'd have to have a death wish."

Thud.

Bowie jolted, almost imperceptibly, as Araxa drove the blade into the wood again. "Always so clever," she said.

There was amusement in her face, but now her posture was tense too. Whatever game they'd been playing in this bloodless battle, Bowie had won. Although Araxa didn't like it, she clearly respected it. "One day, you're going to talk yourself into a bind you can't get out of."

"Show me."

"You really think I would leave evidence?"

Bowie stared her down. "I think you'd have insurance. Show me."

There was a long pause. Slowly, Araxa pulled a yellowed piece of folded paper from the breast pocket of her jacket. She pushed it across the table to Bowie, who reached out to hold it steady on the table, reading quickly. His brow furrowed as he progressed, and when he looked up at Araxa, he was trembling. Whatever he'd read on that page had frightened him.

Araxa smirked. "And finally I've managed to shut you up."

Thud.

Araxa's dagger skewered the paper and the wood beneath it, the deadly tip driving down between Bowie's fingers, a hair's breadth from piercing his flesh. Bowie sucked in a sharp breath, but impressively he didn't jerk his hand away.

"You might belong to Splinter now," Araxa said, "but if you jeopardise my business, I *will* come for you. And I'll take you back to where you *really* belong. How many people do you think you'll be able to convince before they cut your throat?"

Bowie recoiled. For the first time, something flashed in Araxa's eyes. Pleasure. At his fear.

"So you *are* scared," Araxa said smoothly. "I knew you were smart."

Bowie's chair scraped the floor again as he jerked to his feet. When he turned, Aela dashed back into their room. She settled down, closing her eyes as Bowie came through the door and went back to his bedding on the floor. In the darkness, his harsh, panicked breaths abraded against her mind as she found her way to sleep.

***

Apparently, they hadn't hidden the carriage well enough. It hadn't been stolen in its entirety, but it had been rendered undrivable by ambitious looters who'd hacked off pieces of the fine wood and upholstery and made off with them. Three of the wheels were missing, along with large chunks of wall, the curtains, and parts of the plush seating inside. Fortunately, the horses had fared better inside the inn's stables. Bowie suggested helpfully that they could simply borrow some tack from Walter's other guests and continue their journey without delay.

"Splinter's going to flog us for wrecking his carriage," he said matter-of-factly.

"We'll make better time riding anyway," Aela pointed out.

"There are only two horses." Bowie folded his arms across his chest. Aela recalled from their journey in the carriage that he didn't like close proximity.

"You can ride with me," Bryn said. He gave a slow smile. "Or Aela can."

"No thanks," Aela said coolly, not looking at him. "I don't want to catch something."

"Like Slate fever?" Bryn wiggled his thick eyebrows with juvenile suggestiveness.

"A venereal disease?" Aela replied sweetly.

"What's *venereal?*" Bowie asked, frowning.

There was no hint on his face of the interactions he'd had with Walter or Araxa overnight. He looked perfectly innocent. To be fair, he wasn't the only one hiding things. Earlier, she'd quietly paid Walter rather more than he deserved to select a cache of weapons from a trunk in his back room, where he stored possessions left behind or confiscated from his patronage. She'd also bartered for two packs to carry supplies, hiding the weapons inside the one strapped to her horse. She wasn't stupid enough to allow Bryn access to them. As for Bowie … he appeared unarmed, but Aela was willing to bet everything she owned that he had at least one weapon concealed on his person.

"Ah! Bowie." Walter had to duck his head to get through the stable door, raising a hand to greet them. "Glad I caught you before you left. I need a word."

Bowie stepped forward, looking uneasy. "What is it?"

"Listen, now that the border's open again, things are a lot better for the business." He clapped Bowie on the shoulder, jovially ignorant of his own strength as Bowie winced. "I'm calling off your debt."

Bowie's mouth fell open. Whatever he'd been expecting Walter to say, clearly that wasn't it.

Walter said cheerfully, "It won't take long for me to earn back the money. You don't need to come back here again … At least, not to work. I hope to have you visit." He glanced mischievously at Bryn and Aela. "As long as your friends are paying."

He squeezed Bowie's shoulder, seemingly oblivious to the boy's frozen shock. As Walter turned, a splash of red caught Aela's eye. The fine velvet fabric barely peeked out of his back pocket. Walter tucked it away as he strode from the stable.

Aela was caught off-guard by an unnamed but not entirely unpleasant feeling. A single bright flare in her heart she didn't understand.

✝

Fifteen

The morning was still and quiet, and a fine layer of mist drifted around them. Riding pillion on Bryn's horse, Bowie directed them towards a narrow path that veered off the main road, evaporating into the trees. If she'd been on her own, Aela would have ridden right past it without noticing it was there.

Bryn frowned, hesitating. "Are you sure you're not going to get us lost?"

Bowie turned to give him a scathing look. "Do you want to get to Eterre without being caught?"

"I hope you're not overrating your memory," Bryn replied.

After what she'd seen last night, Aela wondered if Bowie might cause bigger problems than navigational errors. She was used to being surrounded by trusted allies. That both Bryn and Bowie posed uniquely concerning threats gave her deep discomfort, but they couldn't be seen approaching Eterre on a main road. Aela had no choice but to follow Bryn as he spurred his horse forwards, and together they plunged into the forest.

On the ride, Bowie appeared increasingly anxious, his head whipping towards any slight noise. She was aware of how alone they were. The trees that stretched out on either side of the road were skeletal, having lost their leaves to the cold. Bare branches reached like gnarled tendrils out into the road, forcing Aela and Bryn to maneuver their horses constantly to avoid being scratched. The mist was growing heavier, impeding their vision. Reflexively, Aela felt at her hip for the reassuring presence of her blade. This wasn't a wise place to linger.

"Slate." There was the barest hint of a tremble in Bowie's voice. He raised his hand to point ahead.

Through the mist, Aela made out an odd shape in the middle of the road. They drew closer and a man came into focus, hunched over and ambling with an unusual gait. His clothing, tattered and filthy, drew her attention. Even in its sorry state, she recognised his Dunwyan military jacket.

"Defector?" Bryn murmured, looking back at her.

Aela doubted that. It didn't make sense for a defector to still be wearing his army's uniform. She dismounted, handing her reins up to Bowie, and approached the man.

"Hey there," she called out. "Are you all right?"

The man was mumbling incoherently to himself. He sounded agitated.

"We should go," Bowie said, that same tremor in his voice.

"Wait," Aela said without looking back.

Although she wasn't the commander anymore, she still felt responsible for the man. Since he was out here alone, still uniformed, such a short time after the army's return to Dunwald, Aela doubted he'd ever actually made it home. But that made no sense. Everyone who had survived the campaign at the border had been accounted for before they'd left the Borderlands.

Aela moved to stand in front of him, making certain she was in his line of sight. "Soldier," she said. "Are you all right?"

The man stopped directly in front of Aela, so close that she could reach out and touch him. His hand shot out, grabbing the front of her jacket. Slowly, he raised his head to look at her. His face was dirty and gaunt, his eyes sunken and hollow. When he smiled, Aela had to force herself not to draw back in horror. His teeth were broken shards, as if they had been chipped away, some down to stumps, others entirely missing. A wheezing laugh followed.

"They let me go!" he said, shaking Aela's jacket slightly. "Can you believe that? After months, they let me walk free!"

"Aela." Bryn's voice behind her was quiet. He and Bowie had dismounted, and Bryn put a hand on her shoulder, trying to pull her from the man's grasp. "He's not in his right mind."

"Wait," Aela said again. She looked back at the soldier. "*Who* let you walk free?"

The soldier's gaze flicked to Bryn when he spoke then slid away. His eyes went wide, his mouth opening in a silent, desperate scream of terror as he pointed a trembling hand at something. Aela whirled to see what had him so petrified.

"*Niellan!*" The soldier lunged at Bowie.

Reflexively, Bryn stepped in front of the boy. "Back off!"

The man staggered unsteadily backwards as if he'd been pushed, even though Bryn hadn't laid a hand on him. His eyes were unfocussed. Aela heard Bowie gasp.

"Slate," Bowie breathed, "tell him to do something else."

"What?" Bryn glanced back at him, confused.

Before anyone could stop him, Bowie stepped in front of Bryn, moving frighteningly close to the soldier.

"*Bowie.*" Bryn reached out to grab him.

Bowie dodged Bryn's outstretched hand, his careful gaze on the soldier. In a shaky voice, he said, "I want your jacket. Take it off and give it to me."

In another unsteady movement, the soldier shrugged off his jacket, bunching it up and offering it to Bowie.

Aela's insides seized as her mind caught up to what she was seeing. "He's on grey dream."

Bryn swore under his breath.

"I've changed my mind," Bowie said to the soldier. "Put your jacket back on."

Still disconcertingly unfocussed, the man obeyed. Bowie swayed where he stood. Like he was as unsteady as the drug-addled soldier, his legs seemed to give out and he sank onto the ground. The movement was like breaking an enchantment. The soldier looked up, his demeanour suddenly agitated, aggressive.

"Shit," Bryn muttered.

"Niellan!" the soldier screamed wildly, pointing at Bowie. "You did this to me! You did this to me! I'll kill you!"

He advanced on Bowie, who scrambled backwards. Bryn collided with the soldier. The man's arms flailed as he tried to shove Bryn aside. Bryn grunted, struggling to subdue him. Aela grabbed the soldier from behind. His strength seemed inhuman as he thrashed against them. Eventually, they pushed him to the ground.

"Sorry," Aela muttered, hitting him with the hilt of her blade.

His head lolled to the side, his eyes rolling closed as he lost consciousness. She and Bryn looked up at the same time. Bowie was still on the ground, breathing rapidly, looking over at the unconscious man. Bryn rounded on him. "What the *hell* were you thinking? He could've killed you!"

Bowie flinched at Bryn's raised voice. He was still staring at the soldier, no fear on his face, only pity. His eyes were red-rimmed.

Sighing, Bryn moved to kneel in front of him. With uncharacteristic gentleness, he said, "Hey, listen. That wasn't about you or that you're from Nielle. You haven't done anything wrong."

Bowie looked at the unconscious soldier despairingly. "Yes, I have," he breathed.

"No. Look at me." Bryn went to put a hand lightly on Bowie's shoulder, but the boy recoiled. "Bowie, he wasn't in his right mind. That isn't your fault. Stand up, little man. We need to keep moving."

Straightening, Bryn passed a hand over his face, pushing away the messy golden strands of hair that fell across his eyes. He gave Aela a searching look that reminded her of her soldiers, awaiting orders.

"He'll be fine when he comes to," she assured him.

Bryn hesitated, eyes lingering on the unconscious man, then he nodded like he'd come to a decision, and swung himself back onto his horse. Bowie had risen to his feet, but his gaze hadn't broken away from the soldier's motionless form.

"Bowie. Now," Bryn said firmly.

As he hauled the boy up behind him, Bryn dug his heels into his horse. Catching Aela's eye over Bowie's head, he mouthed, "What the hell was that?"

Aela looked away, equally troubled. She had no idea.

★★★

Despite Bowie's pleas that they continue riding through the night, they made camp off the road underneath a copse of bare trees near a shallow stream as the sun set. Travelling after dark would only get them lost. The forest was pitch black beyond the light of their small fire.

While Bryn went off to water the horses, Aela set about banking the fire and found herself alone with Bowie for the first time since they'd met. He still seemed rattled from their encounter with the soldier. He'd been quiet for most of the ride, and even now he kept anxiously looking out into the darkness, as if worried some deadly threat would suddenly burst forth from the shadows and attack.

"Are you all right?" Aela offered.

Without making eye contact, Bowie shrugged.

Aela tried a different tactic. "Slate was kind to you today. I didn't know he had it in him."

Staring intently into the darkness, Bowie scowled. "You're not better than anybody just because you were a soldier once. You're an anarchist now, like us."

"*Us?*" Aela repeated. "You're not an anarchist, Bowie. You're a kid."

For a moment, Bowie didn't say anything, and Aela was beginning to believe he'd decided to end the conversation. Then, very quietly, he murmured, "You don't know him."

Aela raised an eyebrow. "I suppose I don't," she conceded. "I'm curious. What should I know about Slate?"

Bowie's eyes flicked up to meet Aela's for a moment then returned to the fire. "He looks out for me."

"I know that," Aela said. After three days of travel with Bryn and Bowie, the complexities of their relationship were coming into focus. "But that's not enough to make him a good person."

"Better than you. You kill people." Bowie swallowed hard. "Niellans, like me."

Aela's gut clenched with guilt, and she looked away, unable to meet his eyes. Painfully obvious now, it had never occurred to her that her past might be the cause of Bowie's adversarial demeanour. The Reaper of Dunwyn had killed hundreds of people who looked and spoke like him, and she'd been celebrated for it.

She wasn't like Splinter, didn't thrive off others' fear, but was she really any better than him? She didn't regret saving her country, even though her victory had been bought with the blood of Niellans and Dunwyans alike. What she regretted was ending the war. All she yearned for was the feeling of being in a fight, the thrill that ripped through her at the clash of blades.

Restless, she reached out and pulled a burning stick from the fire, watching as the flame inched closer to her fingers. "I don't hate Niellans," she told Bowie. "And I don't *like* killing anyone." She threw the stick back onto the fire before it burned her. "I…" She broke off with a ragged breath.

She still longed for battle, even as her hands were drenched in blood. What was wrong with her?

"That's what Slate said."

Aela's head jerked up. "What?"

"When you first came to Splinter's house, Slate told me not to be afraid of you, even though you're a Dunwyan soldier. He said people aren't really themselves when they're fighting a war … or sometimes when they come back."

At first, Aela was struck by how surprisingly compassionate that was, but then her hands curled into fists. What right did Bryn have to be magnanimous to her, or to any Dunwyan soldier? Whatever horrors they had committed in the heat of battle were far outweighed by the atrocity Bryn had perpetrated against his own father.

She couldn't tell Bowie the truth of Bryn's identity, so instead she said, "You really think he's never killed anyone."

"I *know* he hasn't," Bowie said with utter certainty. "That was his condition to stay and work for Splinter, that he wouldn't kill anyone."

It couldn't be the truth. Bowie wasn't naive and trusting, but perhaps he was simply believing something he wanted to believe because he liked Bryn.

"Why would Splinter allow that?" she asked Bowie.

He shrugged. "He said Slate had other skills he needed."

Suspicion pricked at Aela. That didn't make any sense. There were plenty of good fighters who would kill for Splinter if he paid them to. She was unsure what set Bryn apart.

"You talking about me?" Bryn emerged from the darkness with the horses. He glanced at Aela. His dark eyes, glittering with amusement, looked molten in the firelight. "Let me guess. You asked him to give you an A-to-Z list of reasons why I'm a demon straight from hell itself."

Bowie's lip twitched as he looked up. Bryn's reappearance seemed to ease some of his nervous tension. "I can't remember if I was at O for obnoxious or P for piece of —"

"Perhaps you were at Q for questionable judgement, insulting someone who's bigger than you?" Bryn suggested, amusement barely concealed beneath his glare.

Bowie flipped his middle finger at Bryn, and the prince's face broke into an affectionate grin.

With her guard lowered, Aela felt the full force of it like a punch in the gut. The rare, genuine smile transformed his entire face. She knew Bryn was handsome, but like this he was ... breathtaking.

"Smart ass." Still smiling, Bryn pulled the saddle blanket off one of the horses and tossed it to Bowie. "Get some sleep."

"We need to take turns on watch," Bowie insisted.

"Sleep. I'll take the first shift. Aela, I'll wake you in a few hours." Bryn's grin lingered as he looked at her, and Aela ducked her head, forcing her gaze elsewhere.

She was off her game, her mind still half on visions of carnage at the Border War. That Bryn was attractive was not new information, and it didn't change what he was.

He's a murderer, she told herself firmly. As she settled down and stared up at the cloudy sky, a nasty voice wormed into her mind. *Yes, and so are you.*

$$\dagger$$

Sixteen

It was getting colder, especially at night. Five nights on the road, and this was the clearest sign yet that they were getting close to Eterre. Although it was still technically summer, the creeping chill of autumn descended faster inland than it did in the east.

The chill in the air made Aela wish the carriage hadn't been destroyed. It was difficult to stay warm, and she was furious with herself for not anticipating the need for more outer layers when leaving Dunwald. Acting on impulse wasn't something she'd ever done in the army, but apparently now it was a regular occurrence. The night before they were due to reach the Niellan capital, they built a large fire. Bowie huddled in front of it, trying not to shiver, looking as if he was about to crawl into the flames.

Bryn shrugged off his jacket and dropped it over Bowie's shoulders. Then he sat down by the fire, extending his hands towards the flames to warm them. "What's Nielle like?" he asked Bowie.

"Cold," Bowie replied.

"Do the Niellan people like King Marcus?" Aela asked, moving to sit beside Bryn.

She recalled that Laz, Splinter's Niellan soldier, had apparently hated him. Bowie gave Aela a peculiar look. "*Like* him?" he repeated, looking baffled. "He's the king."

"Did he really go mad," Bryn said. "After his son died? I mean, he lost the only one of his heirs who ever lived past infancy. Before the prince, the last baby Queen Ives conceived was born twelve years earlier, and it didn't even survive a day."

Saban had vehemently denied having a hand in the five-year-old prince of Nielle's death, but King Marcus hadn't believed that.

Aela remembered being in her first months of training, eager to impress the king as he stood atop the stands in the training arena, appraising his troops. Huntley had come galloping in, her face flushed and her mount flagging, pulling up beside Saban.

"Your Highness! King Marcus's son is dead. He claims the child was murdered by Dunwyn. His troops are marching to the border as we speak!"

Huntley had told them of Marcus's distress. He had ordered his soldiers on a relentless search for the boy, growing more furious and desperate, day after sleepless day, until suspicion had fallen on Dunwyn. Huntley had fled her ambassadorial duties, fearing for her life. The child's body had never been found.

"Ives died giving birth to the prince," Aela said. "After that, no other legitimate heir could be conceived, which is why he kept that boy so sheltered. Even Huntley only saw him a couple of times, and Nielle refused to tell Dunwyn anything about him, not even his name. Honestly, I don't know how Marcus could blame anyone from Dunwyn for the prince's death. We had so little intelligence on him that we wouldn't have known who to kidnap and murder even if we'd wanted to. But it didn't matter to Marcus. The loss destroyed him. That's why he declared war on us."

Marcus's heirs had sometimes survived a few days, sometimes weeks, but in the end they'd all died. There had been much speculation in Dunwyn that Prince Bryn's misbehaviour had been met with unreasonable lenience over the years because he was the reason King Saban had the winning hand against Nielle. Bryn symbolised what Marcus would never have, an heir.

Bryn shook his head. "Ives was from Dunwyn." The marriage had been a failed attempt at diplomacy between the Niellan crown and a high-ranking family from Dunwyn, carefully selected by Saban's father.

"Didn't he consider that he'd be attacking his wife's homeland? Killing her countrymen?"

Aela gave a humourless laugh. "He's a warmonger. He didn't care." She sighed. "Still, he didn't deserve to lose his child."

"So you don't believe the rumours that he killed his son to start the war?" Bryn asked.

"Of course he didn't," Bowie snapped. He glared at Bryn. "Those are stupid lies to make it easier for soldiers to kill each other in battle."

Bryn looked at him, rather surprised. "I'm sorry," he said sincerely. "I didn't realise —"

"That I know more about Nielle than you do?" Bowie interrupted bitterly. "King Marcus *didn't* kill the prince."

Staring into the flames, he picked up his water bladder and took a sip.

Bryn leaned towards Aela and said in a low voice, "Do you think Marcus ever tumbled another woman?"

"We'd never know. Bastards take the mother's family name

in Nielle." Aela snorted derisively. "I suppose it's their society's way of indicating that babies out of wedlock are entirely the woman's problem."

"Marcus must've been getting desperate for an heir," Bryn said. "And apparently he was a looker, back in his day. I'm sure he was well aware that every woman this side of the Borderlands would happily line up to ride his —"

Across the fire, Bowie choked on his water. He slammed the bladder down. Bryn's jacket fell off his shoulders as he snapped to his feet, scowling. "Shut your damn mouth! Don't you *ever* talk about the king like that!"

There was a stunned silence. Bryn opened his mouth then closed it again, apparently thinking better of whatever he was going to say. If you ignored his dark hair and those impossibly blue eyes, it was easy to forget Bowie's Niellan heritage when he was speaking Dunwyan with a near-perfect accent. But Bowie's patriotism confirmed what Aela had suspected. Bowie had not come to Dunwyn by choice. He loved Nielle and, despite Marcus's many failings, apparently loved the Niellan king.

Perhaps the rest of Nielle loved him too. It was difficult to accept that Niellans might feel about Marcus the way Aela and her soldiers had felt about Saban.

Bryn pulled a coin out of his pocket, fidgeting with it absent-mindedly to occupy his hands. It was a sleight-of-hand trick, rolling it across his knuckles one by one. Across the fire, Bowie watched him with interest. "What are you doing?" he asked quietly, breaking the tension.

"Magic," Bryn replied with a hesitant grin.

Bowie scoffed. "The only magic I've ever see you do is convince three women at once to —"

"Watch it, you," Bryn interrupted, but he looked as if he was fighting back laughter.

His gaze flicked to Aela's then away as he ducked his head. His face was flushed. From the warmth of the fire, probably.

Bowie skirted the fire to sit beside Bryn. "Teach me."

"So you can steal from me?"

"Steal what?" Bowie asked. "That one coin?"

Smirking, Bryn repeated the trick slowly, once then again. He closed his right hand around the coin.

"I shouldn't have disrespected King Marcus like that," he said to Bowie. He circled his left hand around his fist, fluttering his fingers as if performing a spell. The humour was gone from his face. "It was wrong. Forgive me?"

With his eyes on Bryn's hands, Bowie nodded, and Bryn gave a quick smile. When he reopened his right hand, the coin had vanished. Bryn tipped his hand down, giving his sleeve a shake. Nothing fell out. Bowie's eyes widened. "Fuck off," he muttered in admiration.

"Mind your language," Bryn said, his scolding entirely ineffectual since he was laughing.

He drew a second coin from his pocket, offering it to Bowie, who clumsily attempted to replicate the trick. Bryn watched with fond amusement as Bowie closed his own hand, fidgeting awkwardly for a moment before opening it, looking at Bryn proudly. "Good?"

Bryn tapped Bowie's wrist, where the edge of the coin peeked out from beneath his sleeve. "Subtle as a kick up the ass."

Bowie made a frustrated sound.

"You want to know the secret?" Bryn said. "You've got to make sure your audience is looking..." He reached out and prodded Bowie's chest with a finger. Bowie looked down and

Bryn flicked his finger up to catch Bowie's nose. Bowie gave a startled cry. "Somewhere else."

Bryn reached into his left sleeve and produced the coin. He winked at Bowie, who punched him in the arm. "That was *clever!*"

Bryn winked. "You're not the only genius."

★★★

As a child, Aela had known Nielle only as the home to her country's great enemy. She had always pictured its capital to be some sort of barren, hellish wasteland with winged demons circling the sky overhead. In actuality, Eterre looked in all ways like paradise. Stretching out from the city walls was an ocean of lush green meadow, speckled with colourful wildflowers. Striae of clear streams ran through the grass, snaking into dense forest a few miles beyond the walls. Like Dunwald, Nielle's capital city was built on a slope, but instead of backing onto an ocean, it was nestled into the formidable towering mountains of the Jaws Range, an impassable wall of inhospitable, snow-capped peaks that stretched southeast all the way to the Great Ocean.

It wasn't strategically located. Eterre was simply the capital because it had been home to the warlord who'd marched on Hiver back in the days of the One Kingdom. Once Nielle became its own country, King Marcus's ancestors had been too proud to leave their ancestral home.

Marcus's sprawling castle stretched from the foot of the mountains down to the northern side of the city wall. It was made entirely of expensive grey marble and stained-glass windows, a splash of colour against the craggy snow-covered slopes above. Dismounting Bryn's horse at the tree line, Bowie stared up at the enormous structure with an unreadable expression.

Aela said, "Did you spend much time here when you were younger?" She had a faint picture in her mind of a much smaller Bowie, trailing the streets of Eterre, tugging on the sleeve of a man who resembled him. She imagined Bowie looking at him with the kind of ardent admiration he usually reserved for Bryn.

"A bit." He didn't look at her.

Aela frowned. Perhaps now that they were here, the things Bowie was doing would start to make more sense. Although, since it was Bowie, she wasn't certain she would ever entirely make sense of him. "That chain you wear, did it belong to your father?"

Bowie's eyes were still fixed on the castle, but he clamped a hand over his chest, fabric bunching as he grasped the pendant beneath his shirt. "I don't have a father," he replied shortly. He drew in a long breath then said, "I can get us inside the castle."

"No, I'm going alone." Aela grabbed an extra dagger from her pack and shoved it through her belt.

Bryn made a disbelieving sound. "Proposing to go behind enemy lines without backup? I'd always heard you were a *good* strategist."

"Watching my back with you around will only split my focus," Aela replied bluntly. "Besides, you said that Huntley's none of your business. You're only here for him."

She jerked her head at Bowie. Bryn gave her an amused look. "And you think *he's* going to stay here?" He glanced at Bowie. "Are you going to stay here where it's safe?"

Bowie looked at him like he was insane, and Bryn gestured

at him demonstratively. Apparently that settled it.

Aela narrowed her eyes at Bowie. "Why do you care anyway?"

"Nielle's *my* country." His tone was furiously passionate. "The steward of Dunwyn shouldn't be coming here on a secret visit. Something's wrong. Besides, I used to live in Eterre. I can get us into the castle, so you need me."

Aela looked at him in surprise. He cared a lot for someone who hadn't lived in Nielle for years. "You're not a soldier, Bowie."

"Neither is Slate. Neither are you anymore, technically."

"All right," Bryn spoke up. "That's enough. If Bowie says he knows how to get into the castle, then he's coming."

Aela shot Bryn an unimpressed look before turning her back. A gently restraining hand on her arm stole the breath from her body. She turned to see Bryn's dark eyes flick to her parted lips then away, so quickly she'd have missed it if she wasn't entirely pinned by his gaze.

"Aela," he said in a low voice. His tone held a warning, like he was barely holding himself back from doing something dangerous. "I need a weapon."

She ripped her arm from him and her skin cooled in the absence of his touch. He was right, of course, it was a risk for both of them to have him walking through the enemy stronghold unarmed. That didn't mean she had to like it. She produced a sword from the pack and thrust it, hilt first, into his hands.

"I'll kill you if I have to," she cautioned.

Antagonistic amusement glittered in his eyes. "Don't worry sweetheart, I have no desire to stick it inside you."

Arrogant fucking prick. "You're a pig," she spat at him.

"We'll go in through the drain," Bowie said, calmly oblivious.

The drain was a channel for a shallow stream that flowed fast out of Eterre's northern wall, right below the castle. The thick undergrowth lining its banks concealed their path to the small, semi-circular opening. Bowie ducked under without difficulty, but it was harder for Aela and Bryn. They both had to squeeze through on all fours. The clear water from the icy mountains numbed Aela's hands.

"Do you realise how mad this is?" Aela whispered to Bryn as they moved. "He's Niellan, and we're following him into enemy territory. How is it that he even *knows* the way into the castle?"

"He used to live on the streets here," Bryn whispered back.

"And you think every street urchin knows how to break into the king's home?"

"He wouldn't do anything to put us in danger," Bryn replied confidently.

Bowie stopped at what looked like a dead end. The way was bricked off in front of them with the wall extending almost to the floor, water running through a smaller opening at the bottom.

Bryn straightened up, rubbing his own chilly hands together as he looked to Bowie. "Where now?"

Bowie pointed upwards at the ceiling. Aela and Bryn both looked to see a circular piece of wood covering a hole in the stone above their heads. "The kitchens," Bowie said.

Bryn gave Aela a boost. She gritted her teeth, exerted a hard push and dislodged the covering, hoisting herself up into a food store full of wooden barrels and crates. She peered down at Bryn and Bowie.

"I'll go next and pull you up," Bryn told Bowie.

Bryn jumped, grabbing the stone edges of the hole. His jacket and shirt were pushed up past his elbows, and Aela saw his forearms flex as he pulled himself up. She found somewhere else to look.

Bryn leaned down to Bowie without extending a hand. "Go back to the horses. We'll find you once we've followed Huntley."

Bowie's eyes went wide as he realised he'd been tricked. "Slate, no!" he said desperately. "I have to get into the castle. *Please!*"

Bryn shook his head. "Go back to the horses. That's an order, Bowie."

Bowie looked as furious as Aela had ever seen him. He glared up at Bryn, muttering a string of foul curses until Bryn placed the wooden cover back over the hole, blocking him out of sight.

They went through the kitchen, which was oddly deserted, creeping up a winding staircase and across a long hallway. There was no trace of soldiers on patrol, no servants. The hallway was lit only by slivers of windows, the rest of the building in total, oppressing darkness. This was nothing like the wide, bright halls of Saban's castle.

In the dim light, Aela caught a glimpse of Bryn's face as he glanced around. She wondered if he was thinking about his father too. When Saban had been crowned, he'd ordered all the windows widened and had demolished many of the outer halls' walls. He'd always said he didn't want to feel trapped and that he wanted to admire the world's beauty as much as possible.

Aela saw Bryn swallow hard. "Where is everyone?" he murmured.

As she looked furtively around the corner, Aela froze at the sound of voices and shoved Bryn back. "You had to ask," she hissed.

Ahead of them were four heavily armed soldiers. Aela's heart froze. She searched their uniforms for the Niellan symbol she knew well, King Marcus's gold flying eagle insignia. Their clothing was entirely free of markings, but it was familiar nonetheless, dark orange cloaks, same as Huntley's guard. In Dunwald, they had always worn helmets covering their faces, but these men took no such care, and now it was apparent why. They were Niellan, all of them, with the same unmistakable dark hair and blue eyes as Bowie.

"It's good to be home," one of the men said in Niellan. "Wish we didn't have to be away for so long."

"It won't be forever," said another. Their voices grew closer as they came down the hallway. Aela almost jumped a foot in the air as Bryn slid his hand into hers, pulling her back the way they'd come. "Just until the powers that be have their way."

Aela turned to Bryn. "We can take them," she whispered. "Get them to lead us to Huntley."

"No!" Bryn hissed back, pulling her away.

"The steward already has, if you ask me," another soldier said. "It's like King Saban never even existed."

Aela went rigid upon hearing Saban's name. Bryn desperately pulled at her hand, but she ignored him.

"That's the truth," a soldier said with a laugh. "You know, he hasn't even been buried. His body's rotting down in the crypt, probably covered in maggots. An appropriate end, if you ask me."

Fury obliterated rational thought, and Aela took a step forward, ready to burst out from behind the corner and kill the men in her path. A strong arm wrapped around her waist, pulling her backwards so that she collided with Bryn's solid, warm body.

"Calm down," he hissed. "It won't do any good."

"Get. Off. Me," she gritted out quietly.

Bryn's arm lingered at her waist. "Aela, breathe," he whispered.

His lips brushed her ear, and she shivered then remembered his instruction and drew in a deep, calming breath. Bryn's touch slid against her hip before he released her, only to take her hand again. He pulled her away, backing through a narrow door.

Someone behind them gasped, and they whirled together, reaching for their weapons. A wide-eyed boy of about fifteen looked up from where he knelt, scrubbing the floor. All the breath left Aela's body in a rush. Maybe she could pass as Niellan, but Bryn's distinctive blond hair stood out like a beacon.

The teenager opened his mouth, and Aela stepped forward, raising one hand in a quelling gesture and reaching back to Bryn with the other.

"Give me some coins, everything you've got," she said to him before turning to the boy and speaking in Niellan, "We won't hurt you. For your silence. Please."

Warily, the teenager rose from the floor. With a tentative step forward, he snatched the stack of coins from Aela's outstretched hand, turning one over in his fingers and examining it with a furrowed brow.

"Thank you," Aela sighed gratefully.

The teenager's blue eyes snapped up to meet Aela's. They were blazing with righteous defiance.

"You think I'd betray my king for the coins of a Dunwyan rat and a half-blood bitch?" He threw the coins away like they burned him, then cried, "Enemies! Enemies in the castle! Help!"

"Fuck!" Bryn grabbed Aela's hand again and tugged her towards the door. They burst out of it and around the corner, almost running headlong into one of the soldiers they'd just evaded.

Shock froze on the man's face as Aela ran him through, his expression sliding away as he dropped. She swept up her blade to meet another soldier striding forwards. He was tall, and a golden band on his arm denoted his status as the ranking soldier of the group.

"I don't think you want to do this," he told Aela in Dunwyan.

"You definitely don't want to do this," Bryn replied, moving to back her up.

"Bold talk for a dead man." Aela tensed at the new voice behind them. She and Bryn whirled to see another six of Huntley's soldiers moving in behind them. Aela froze as six crossbows levelled simultaneously on them. She closed her eyes in frustration, finding some solace in the fact that they hadn't been shot on sight. Whatever was about to happen to them, they had no choice but to let it play out.

The nearest soldier flipped the crossbow in his hands and struck Bryn hard. The blow connected with the side of his head, and he crumpled to the ground.

A moment later, Aela felt a blunt blow to the back of her head. Everything went black.

★★★

Aela's head was throbbing. The room wavered before her as she opened her eyes. A familiar tall, blond figure shuddered into view, crouching beside her.

Bryn raised his eyebrows. "We have to stop meeting like this, sweetheart."

Aela dizzily pushed herself up into a splayed sitting position. "Shut up."

"Shut up, *Your Highness*," Bryn corrected annoyingly.

Aela toyed with the idea of choking him but decided instead to take stock of her surroundings. They were in a large circular cage, the walls, ceiling and door were barred, coarse sawdust underfoot. Raised stands lined with plush seating cascaded on all sides towards their enclosure in the centre of the room. A fighting ring.

Aela had heard about this manner of Niellan entertainment. It was how they selected their finest fighters, pitting them against one another while an audience of nobles watched. It was how Nielle had determined which fighter should take on Aela in single combat during the war.

It wasn't uncommon for warriors to die in these fights. They were barbaric compared to Dunwyn's friendly melees, where soldiers used blunted weapons in lieu of real swords.

There was a sturdy wooden door beyond their cage in the far right corner of the room. It was shut.

"What is this?" she muttered.

Bryn shrugged, rising stiffly to his feet. "Not sure. I woke up right before you did."

Aela huffed out a frustrated breath, following suit and standing up unsteadily, trying to ignore the way the room spun, and nausea turned her stomach.

"Are you all right?" The tenderness in Bryn's voice was so intimate it felt invasive. She ignored the question and went to the barred door, shaking it experimentally. Bolted in place by a thick, heavy chunk of wood, it gave a hollow, metallic clang but didn't budge.

She was furious with herself. Slipping up with those three anarchists back at the Devil's Tongue had endangered her own life. This time, her poor judgment had risked Bryn too … and after she'd identified *him* as a potential threat to her. She hadn't believed for a moment that a Niellan serving boy would be so loyal to his king that he couldn't be bought.

Aela shifted her weight, bracing her shoulder against the door. She pulled until her arms trembled with the strain. And broke away.

"Damn it!" she growled, flopping onto the sawdust.

Her hands stung from gripping the bars repeatedly at different angles to get some kind of traction. Bryn was, of course, no help at all. He sat across the barred arena and watched her in silence, his long legs stretched out before him, ankles crossed. He almost looked entirely at ease, if not for the tension in his shoulders. He gathered a handful of sawdust and let it trickle through his fingers, reminding Aela of an hourglass. As their time ticked away inside this cage, she wondered grimly how long they'd have to wait to face whatever was coming.

"Bet you thought you'd be on the other side of the bars when I was captured," Bryn said.

Aela dropped her head, exhausted. It was her stupidity that had landed them in this cage. Bryn was right. If he was ever to be brought to justice, she'd wanted it to be on her terms. Not wanting to think about that, she distracted herself with a different question instead.

"How much money did you give Walter to buy Bowie out of his debt?"

Bryn's head jerked up. "What?"

For the first time, his expression was unguarded. Aela had

caught him by surprise, and he was desperately unused to it. She pressed her advantage. "At first I couldn't figure out why you did nothing to help him back in Dunwald, when he lied to Splinter about why we were in the warehouse that night. I thought it was because you didn't care if Splinter punished him. I thought you really did want Bowie to be kicked out into the street. And then Splinter did something that I found interesting. He burned my hand … to punish you."

Bryn still looked disconcerted. "Interesting? *That's* what that was for you?"

"If Splinter believed for a moment that you cared about Bowie, he'd target Bowie any time you stepped out of line." Aela drew in a long breath. Interrogation was something she had been trained to do in the army. "You fought those men who attacked me in the tavern. You didn't have to help me."

"I —"

"And you don't have to protect Bowie. Tell me, what were you going to do with that knife in your hand if Splinter had really tried to force Bowie into killing Araxa Leren's man back at the house? Gods, Bryn, you're only here because Bowie was determined to come to Eterre and you didn't trust me to look after him."

"That's —"

"Why didn't you kill them?"

Bryn blinked, overwhelmed. "Who?"

"Those men in the tavern, the ones who attacked me."

"Because I've never —" Bryn broke off suddenly, looking as disorientated as the soldier on grey dream in the forest.

The quality of the room changed. Aela was barely aware of their surroundings now. Her world had narrowed to this small space, which she and Bryn were inhabiting alone together.

"You've never killed anyone?" Aela said quietly. "Is your memory that poor?"

"I don't know what I'm saying," Bryn said furiously, pinching the bridge of his nose as if he had a headache. "Why are you asking me this?"

Unthinking, Aela reached into her jacket, running her finger over the familiar heavy gold design on the ring in her pocket. "Tell me about that night."

He stared at the bars blankly, as if her relentless questioning had sapped all of his energy. She could ascertain nothing further from his face, and it frustrated her. Usually, she was quite adept at getting a read on people. Bryn was good at this.

On the surface, he appeared perfectly calm, but surely he felt *something* for his father. It nudged at her, the desire to pull back his veneer and venture inside.

He's beautiful, but that won't make his side of the story any less ugly, Aela reminded herself. Bryn had been given leeway his entire life because he was the handsome son of a king. No matter what he looked like, he was still a murderer.

"I barely remember any of it. There was a feast, and I'd been drinking. A lot. When the king retired, I followed him." He looked up at Aela. He spoke quietly, but the beseeching desperation in his eyes was like a scream. "Like everyone else, I heard what happened afterwards. When the servants came to extinguish the candles in his rooms, the king was dead, his guard too. One of my daggers was sticking out of Saban's chest."

There was no emotion in his voice, but Bryn's carefully neutral tone hinted that he was holding back. Aela remained perfectly still, cautious not to disturb this moment. For the first time, Bryn was pulling back at least one of the layers that barricaded him from the rest of the world. She was no closer to discovering his motive though. Aela pulled the ring from her pocket, gripping it hard and trying to think of what Saban might say to his son if he was here.

Bryn said, "I remember small things, holding my dagger, looking down at him. I remember that my hands were soaked in blood. I remember panicking, running like a coward because I knew the king was dead. The next thing I remember is waking up in Underground."

"Why?" Aela's voice was raw.

Bryn shook his head and looked down at his hands. "Killing in battle, the way you have … they say that's honourable."

"It's not," Aela said. The only people who said that were those who'd never been to war.

He was still looking down. His hair fell across his face, and Aela was gripped by the desire to push back the golden strands.

"You think you're without honour? I can only imagine what you think of someone who takes the life of an unarmed man, his own *father*." He lowered his voice, like he was speaking to himself. "If we're going to die, I suppose it doesn't matter. Someone should know why I did what I did."

He looked up again, his eyes focussed on a point over Aela's shoulder. His voice was clear and hard. "You want to know why I killed him? The truth is that I can't remember. I never wanted him dead. I never even thought about it, not once before that night. All I know is that I did it. All I remember is that I looked down and there was blood on my hands."

Aela ducked her head. The golden king's insignia glinted in the light. Beneath it, her hands were calloused from holding a sword, from the years of training and fighting that had shaped her into the Reaper of Dunwyn, the lone soldier who had ended the war. She had done what Saban had asked of her. The country was at peace and thousands of lives had been saved … but she would give anything to be back in the rhythmic, brutal chaos of battle. She hated herself for it.

"There was blood on my hands," Bryn murmured again.

"I know what that's like," she told him.

Seventeen

With more aggression than was necessary, Aela jerked at the door.

There was no way her own force would be enough to open it, but she needed to give physical expression to what she was feeling. Bryn's confession had awakened something she hadn't expected — sympathy. There was something behind his expressionless mask, a feeling of helpless disbelief, as if he'd been describing the violence of a stranger. She kept trying to tell herself he was lying; he was a good liar. But what was the point of lying about his motive, while telling the truth about the act itself? If he was trying to protect someone, why bother to tell this story at all?

Instead of trying to make sense of all that, she was doing this.

Aela gave the door another aggressive tug.

"That won't work."

Aela tensed. She knew who it was, even before the tall, straight-backed woman weaved between the stands. She levelled her penetrating hazel gaze upon Aela and Bryn as she came to a stop outside the cage.

"Huntley," Aela said.

Bryn sucked in a shaky breath, scrambling to his feet.

Eighteen

"**L**et's go." Bowie gestured towards the flames demonstratively.

Aela stared at him in disbelief. Bryn grabbed her wrist, pulling her after Bowie.

"How did you get into the castle?" she asked him as they caught up.

"There's more than one way in, you know. Follow me." Bowie ducked into a narrow servants' corridor none of the evacuating courtiers were using.

Bryn and Aela followed Bowie as he led them confidently through the castle's winding halls. Bryn dropped back, matching his pace to Aela's.

"How bad is it?" His eyes were fixed straight ahead, but his jaw and shoulders were tight, tension that hadn't left him since they'd first woken up in the arena.

Aela passed a hand over her wounded side. It stung a little, no more than a superficial cut. "Don't worry about it."

"Why did you let me do that?" Bryn snapped harshly.

Aela shrugged. "We needed to stall for time, and they wanted a show. Besides, you'd cry like a baby if I landed a hit against you."

"Your Highness." Huntley's eyes were fixed on him. "Of all the places I was expecting to find you, Eterre was not one of them."

Bryn, who always had something to say, remained silent. A muscle slid in his jaw as he watched Huntley through tense dark eyes.

"Likewise," Aela said when it became clear that Bryn wasn't going to speak. "Dunwyn's steward, freely roaming the castle of an enemy nation?" She cocked her head inquisitively. "I've a feeling you know something we don't."

Huntley's expression was dismayed as her gaze shifted to meet Aela's. "Aela Rinn," she said. "After you murdered one of our own, I thought you could sink no lower. Yet here you are, throwing your lot in with the man who killed our king."

Aela scoffed, "You should have sent a better fighter after me if you wanted me dead, Your Excellency."

Huntley's posture and features remained entirely undisturbed, except for the slight narrowing of her eyes. "That is a very serious accusation."

"One I'm sure you won't mind me repeating at my trial back in Dunwald. Wait, apparently you don't believe in trials anymore."

Now, Huntley's expression turned cold. "You are anarchists, both of you. When you crossed that blue line in Dunwald, you forfeited your right to a trial."

"That's not what the law says," Aela persisted.

"Laws change."

"Apparently people do too," Bryn said, crossing the cage to stand at Aela's side. "What are you doing here, Huntley?"

"Diplomacy," Huntley said serenely.

The door behind her flew open, and dozens of men and

women, courtiers and well-dressed soldiers of high rank, filed inside, moving to sit on the benches around the cage.

Dread clawed up inside Aela's chest. "What is this?"

Huntley's eyes never left Bryn's. "King Saban's most celebrated warrior or his son, the prince. Let's see who's better."

Better? It hit her, a wave of cold dread. The audience, the cage. They were going to be forced to fight each other. She glanced at Bryn, who was appraising the audience tersely. Huntley smiled, pleased they'd both worked it out.

"You are trespassing in Eterre. This could have a serious impact on the outcome of my talks with Nielle, which is why I have agreed to a most creative form of … reparation. One thing I've always enjoyed about this country is that they know how to put on a show."

A soldier shoved a pair of blades through the bars. They dropped onto the sand. Aela stared at Huntley. "I'm not going to fight him."

Huntley opened her mouth to reply, but another calm voice cut across hers. "I think you will."

Aela's head whipped around as a young woman stepped in through the door.

"How well you fight will determine how slow and …" The newcomer smiled an unsettling smile. "… how *painful* your subsequent deaths will be."

"Bryn, Aela,'" Huntley said. "This is Alvine, the steward of Nielle."

It was like receiving a hammering blow to the gut. It had never occurred to Aela to wonder who had taken Marcus's throne in the event of his failing health. Huntley was gazing from Alvine to Bryn with superior amusement.

"I don't …" Bryn's voice was constricted. His face was pale as he took Alvine in. The young woman was not what Aela might have expected from a steward. She had to be a few years older than Aela, but she was stout and round-faced, as if she still hadn't outgrown her puppy fat. Her hair was long and silky, almost raven black, although streaks of lighter brown hinted at mixed heritage. Her light blue eyes were small, her features plain. She looked more like a dumpy schoolgirl than the warmongering mastermind Aela would have expected to succeed King Marcus.

"The king of Nielle was, in his time, a man of unparalleled intelligence," Huntley explained, "a trait he passed on to his daughter." Aela felt Bryn jerk backwards. "She understands that Dunwyn is weak after King Saban's death and that a strategic partnership will benefit both our countries."

"What *partnership*?" Aela asked. "What is the assignment that you gave Splinter in Anarchist Underground?"

Bryn, however, was staring at Alvine through the bars. "Marcus's *daughter*," he repeated breathlessly. "That can't be. I've never even –"

Alvine's voice was high and breathy, falsely cheery and feminine. "My poor father, losing his mind in his old age. After the tragic death of his son, there was no legitimate heir to the throne. I'm the last one left who can take his place."

Aela felt sick. It was too convenient. "I suppose you'd know nothing about the *tragic* death of Marcus's son," she said sarcastically. "Did you kill that boy yourself or hire someone else to do it for you?" She shifted her gaze to meet Huntley's. "That seems to be a popular method."

Alvine's smile widened, but Huntley remained stone-faced. She said aggressively, "Alvine is Nielle's rightful heir. That boy would still be a child, unfit to meet this moment. People need a leader. They need security, someone to rely on. And since you,

Prince Bryn," she said his name like it was a joke. "Have proven yourself unworthy and a traitor, Dunwyn must rely on me. The people will be grateful that I've found a way to protect them."

"*What have you promised her?*" Aela's voice trembled.

"You're not a worthy ruler," Huntley said derisively to Bryn, ignoring Aela. "The only thing you're good for is cheap entertainment. So fight." She gestured to the swords on the sand.

"I'm not picking that up," Bryn said.

"Then you'll watch as we eviscerate your friend, very slowly," Alvine replied sweetly.

Bryn's gaze flicked involuntarily to Aela. He swallowed. Seeming to come to a decision, he went forward and picked up the swords, passing one to Aela. She held it, tip down, resting in the sawdust.

"What are you doing?" Aela demanded in a low voice.

"Fight!" Huntley cried, and a cheer went up from the crowd of spectators.

Bryn adjusted the grip on his sword, looking anxious. "We have to," he said tersely. Advancing, he struck at her unguarded left side with an unexpected blow. Instinctively, Aela parried, and the crowd erupted in cheers.

"What are you *doing?*" Aela hissed again.

"Buying some time!" Bryn replied urgently. Again, he advanced. Aela parried, the blow shuddering through her shoulder.

Bryn struck again, hard, an attempt at veracity, and the spectators roared. As she raised her sword to block Bryn's blow, she saw the crowd reflected in the flat edge of the blade, a blur of eyes hungry for pain and death.

Aela's focus was shattered by a distracting flash of red

— someone's cloak in the audience. The vision mingled with blood-drenched sheets. The weapon driving towards her became the killing blow that had ended Saban's life. She looked into her opponent's eyes, and they were the eyes of her enemy, the eyes of Saban's killer. Reflexively, she drove him back, putting her full strength behind the blow.

She gained ground, injecting into every strike her fury and anguish. It was all she'd wanted to do since she had heard of Saban's death, meet his killer in a fight and bring him down. She was the Reaper of Dunwyn. She was death in steel, avenger of the king. She would have justice.

"Aela!" Bryn's breathless shock cut through the haze of her rage, crystallising it into horror.

She froze with her blade poised to make a killing blow. Bryn's face was pallid and sheened with sweat. He was looking at her like she was a stranger, moving to block her sword in desperation. At the last minute, he realised she had arrested her blow, and he swung wide to avoid wounding her. It wasn't wide enough. His blade sailed, unchecked, past her lowered guard. The sharp edge of the weapon clipped her side, and the cool sting of metal bit into her skin. If possible, Bryn's face grew even paler, and Aela realised that, as her attacks had increased in ferocity, Bryn had been putting a great deal of effort into deflecting without doing her harm.

Bryn flinched as another savage cheer rose up from the crowd, louder this time. His grip on his sword went slack. Clearly, he hadn't expected to be able to hurt her.

"Fight!" somebody called. "Kill her!"

Seeing the look in Bryn's eyes, Aela made herself advance, this time pulling her blows when they met Bryn's steel. Outwardly, it looked like a real fight. She might actually have enjoyed the exceptional swordsmanship if she couldn't sense Bryn's tangled up fear and remorse.

Ignoring that, he was an excellent fighter. He'd been trained by Dunwyn's finest sword masters. Unlike Aela's battle-hardened style, Bryn's skills had been cultivated for friendly melees, gentlemanly sparring matches in organised tournaments, where fancy flourishes pleased audiences and weren't a waste of time. There was evident sloppiness as well, natural ability overlaid by disinterest in technical training. A few surprisingly brutal swings, probably learned in Anarchist Underground, completed his repertoire.

Aela parried overhead, two-handed against Bryn's swing. He stepped in close, baring his strength down on her blade, coming near enough to whisper, "What the fuck do we do now?"

Because she didn't have an answer, she pressed a foot into his gut, shoving him away. She circled Bryn. Her eyes were on him, but her focus was all on finding an escape.

Think!

The audience's cries suddenly changed in quality, from bloodthirsty heckles to exclamations of surprise. Aela looked out into the stands and saw pandemonium. The spectators were descending quickly, almost trampling one another in their hurry to flee the room. Thick, dark smoke rose from the wooden seating. Aela saw Alvine and Huntley pushing people in their haste to escape as soldiers rushed towards the source of the smoke.

Aela shoved the sword through her belt, going to the barred cage door. Taking advantage of their captors' distraction, she tugged at it desperately. It didn't budge. "Help me!" she called to Bryn.

The room darkened with smoke. Aela's eyes watered, her

lungs congested. Bryn braced himself beside her, and they tugged at the door together. Nothing happened.

"Come on!" Aela said to him. "There has to be a way out."

They both looked around, cataloguing potential weaknesses in the structure. Bryn coughed. Aela pressed her sleeve down on her mouth and nose. Panic welled in her chest as the cries of spectators filled the room. Through the grey smoke, Aela saw the unmistakable flicker of flames. If the soldiers didn't douse the fire in time … if they couldn't get out of here…

They whirled towards the clang of the cage door at the same time. It slammed open. Poised to fight, Aela hesitated as a familiar dark head and deep blue eyes emerged through the darkness, a sleeve held over his mouth.

"Good fight," Bowie said.

Eighteen

"Let's go." Bowie gestured towards the flames demonstratively.

Aela stared at him in disbelief. Bryn grabbed her wrist, pulling her after Bowie.

"How did you get into the castle?" she asked him as they caught up.

"There's more than one way in, you know. Follow me." Bowie ducked into a narrow servants' corridor none of the evacuating courtiers were using.

Bryn and Aela followed Bowie as he led them confidently through the castle's winding halls. Bryn dropped back, matching his pace to Aela's.

"How bad is it?" His eyes were fixed straight ahead, but his jaw and shoulders were tight, tension that hadn't left him since they'd first woken up in the arena.

Aela passed a hand over her wounded side. It stung a little, no more than a superficial cut. "Don't worry about it."

"Why did you let me do that?" Bryn snapped harshly.

Aela shrugged. "We needed to stall for time, and they wanted a show. Besides, you'd cry like a baby if I landed a hit against you."

It was a joke, but Bryn apparently wasn't in the mood. "That's not funny," he gritted out. "I hurt you."

They had stopped, and Aela suddenly realised how close together they were standing. When they'd been close during their fight, she hadn't had time to think. Now, *all* she could think about was the way Bryn was looking at her, his hand reaching out. He pulled away before his strong fingers made contact with the hem of her shirt.

"Can I ..." He hesitated. Aela wasn't used to him being uncertain. "I want to see."

Normally, she would have refused. It was such an inconsequential wound, but there was something about the torment in Bryn's eyes that urged her to put his mind at ease. Gripped by the urge to stymie his self-flagellation, she pulled up the hem of her shirt, revealing the planes of her stomach, bronzed and lined with lean muscle from years of outdoor fighting drills.

Bryn gave a sharp gasp, his lips parting, and for a moment his dark eyes on her skin felt like the warmth of a touch, before she remembered that she'd almost killed him in the fighting ring, and why. She tensed as he reached out, and her skin buzzed with energy, anticipating his touch.

"Take your time. It's not like we're in a hurry." The moment shattered. Bowie watched them exasperatedly, a few feet away.

Bending down, he dug his fingers into the small gap between two wooden floorboards, prising one of the boards loose, then another, and another, until there was enough space for them to squeeze through. A sloped channel disappeared under the floor.

"Waste chute," Bowie said in answer to their questioning looks.

"Waste?" Bryn repeated, looking repulsed.

Bowie glared at him. "You want to be caught?"

He jumped in, sliding out of sight. Aela shrugged and followed, whooshing swiftly down through darkness, shooting out into daylight, her fall cushioned by something soft. Aela got out of the waste pile quickly, trying not to think about what she'd landed on. Moments later, Bryn tumbled out after her.

Outside the castle walls, they ran blindly through the trees. It felt like hours before they came to a stop in a small clearing, breathing hard. Bowie bent forward, hands on his knees, trying to catch his breath.

"All right?" Bryn asked him.

Bowie looked up, his eyes hard and cutting as a shard of glass. "Is it true?"

Bryn frowned. "What?"

"I heard them. They said you're King Saban's son." His voice quavered subtly. "You're the heir to the throne of Dunwyn?"

Bryn passed a hand over his face. "Bowie —"

"Is it *true*?" Bowie looked older than nine, his eyes narrowed, hostility and mistrust on every line of him. "Are you Prince Bryn?"

Bryn opened and closed his mouth. He glanced at Aela, as if she'd cut in and say everything he couldn't. "Listen, I ..." His stammered words were as good as an admission. "I need you to understand ..."

"You killed your father," Bowie interrupted with furious calmness.

"Bowie, you don't ..." Wounded, Bryn reached out a calming hand.

"What, I don't understand?" The boy's expression didn't change, nor did his coolly factual tone. "Really? I think *everyone* understands. You're a murderer. You killed your father."

Bryn's jaw clenched, tension settling across his broad shoulders. "Stop that. I know what you're doing and I'm not in the mood."

Bowie's eyes narrowed. His mouth twisted, furiously bitter. "You killed his guard too. Five people in one night. No wonder Splinter wanted you. You're such an overachiever."

"Bowie. Stop." Bryn was holding himself very still, his fists clenched, holding himself back with great effort.

"Did you do it because your father hated you? I can see why. He knew you'd never be good enough to rule Dunwyn. You weren't even good enough to lick the mud off his boots. Not that you can do that now anyway."

"I mean it. *Stop.*"

"I wonder what he thought right before you stabbed him in the heart in his own bed. Do you think he thought you were a coward? Doesn't matter what he thinks now, does it? He's a rotting corpse. He's *nothing*, just like you."

Bryn's hand shot out, grabbing Bowie's jacket. "I said shut the *fuck* up about my father!"

Bowie tensed, closing his eyes as if bracing for Bryn to strike him. It was the first time Aela had seen Bryn put his hands on Bowie, and Bryn seemed to realise his mistake immediately. Horrified, he released Bowie as though burned, his hands dropping to his sides.

"Bowie, I wasn't going to …"

Bowie stumbled backwards, staring up at Bryn like he was a stranger. Bowie was ordinarily the first to defend Bryn's character. Four days ago, he'd been absolutely convinced that Bryn had never killed anyone, and Aela didn't think his opinion was so easily swayed. Meticulously observant and intentionally cruel, Bowie's effort to hurt Bryn pinpointed a weakness guaranteed to spur him into an unthinking rage, but there was no victory in it.

As if the exchange had drained all the energy from his body, Bowie slumped onto the ground. He turned and flopped down, curling in on himself protectively, like he wanted the day to be over.

Aela and Bryn worked in silence to gather what meagre supply of berries were still hanging onto the trees against the cold.

Bowie's breath had slowed with the rhythm of sleep. Bryn stopped to lean against a tree, watching him. His hand shook when he pushed the tangled gold wisps of hair off his face. "He's right," Bryn whispered as Aela came towards him. "I'm a monster who killed my father in cold blood. Everyone knows it."

"He was trying to hurt you, Bryn," Aela replied wearily. "He trusts you, and you lied to him. He's just a kid who doesn't know how else to cope besides lashing out." She sighed. "This is a problem now."

"What do you mean?"

Aela gave him a cutting look. "Splinter's been hired to kill you. If he doesn't know yet who you really are, and Bowie gets back to Dunwald and tells him …"

She didn't need to say anything else. Bryn shook his head. "No. No, he'd never do that." Bryn gripped his hair, his hands balling into fists. "This is *exactly* why I didn't want him to find out. I don't want him to have to lie for me."

"Bryn, he might *not* lie for you. He's angry and upset."

Bryn looked up, exhausted but certain. "He will. I know him."

Aela shut her eyes hard. Confronting Bryn about this was a

delicate matter. "I know you don't want to hear this, but he's nine, and he's Niellan. Do you really believe that if someone was beating the truth out of him, he wouldn't betray you?"

"Yes," Bryn said without hesitation. "Because he knows that's what I would tell him to do. He knows I'm the only person in his life who would tell him to save himself. That's why he'd protect me."

"You're that confident," Aela said sceptically.

"Good people are difficult to come by, but I trust him with my life."

"Good people are difficult to come by when you live in Anarchist Underground," Aela shot back. She jerked her head at Bowie. "You need to watch your back."

Bryn was watching her, frowning. Silence settled around them. He didn't take his eyes off her.

"What's that look?" Aela asked.

He shook his head. "You don't let anyone in, do you?" His tone was melancholic. He had to be mocking her.

"After everything that's happened, I know better. You should too."

"Maybe you're right," Bryn said in an awful voice. "I trusted Huntley. I thought she was worthy of the throne. I really thought she'd do what was best for Dunwyn … but changing laws to prevent people from the right to a trial? Building an alliance with a woman who likely murdered the prince of Nielle?" He dropped his head into his hands again. "I can't handle this."

"You don't have a choice, Bryn," Aela said seriously. "You're the only other person with a claim to the Dunwyan throne. I don't know why Huntley's doing what she's doing, but I know she doesn't mean well to any of us. This *partnership* she's cultivating with Alvine could destroy our country."

"I already destroyed our country by killing the king," Bryn snapped. "I won't be able to do anything but make it worse."

He looked like he was about to throw up. His posture was hard, his expression unreachable. Bryn was like a statue inside a glass casing. Gripped with the sudden urge to shatter the barrier between them, she reached out, placing her hand lightly on the warm skin of his forearm. "This isn't about you," she told him firmly.

She felt the hard cords of muscle in his arm, shaped by years of training with a sword, and beneath it his racing pulse. She looked up to meet his molton brown eyes, and he swallowed convulsively.

"It's never been about you," she said. "This is about what's best for the people of Dunwyn. I wish you'd see that what you do for Bowie, the way you protect him, you're capable of doing that for all your people. But you have to *want* to."

"I want to," Bryn said. "I don't know *how* to. Ever since he died, I've felt … lost." He sounded unexpectedly young and vulnerable, as if he was about to cry.

Something changed in the quality of Bryn's touch; he brushed his thumb lightly across the back of her hand where it rested on his arm. Aela realised she'd moved closer to him without thinking. They stood too close, their chests almost pressed together. Her breathing went shallow. His gaze met hers as he leaned in. The sensation of his breath stirring her hair unlocked a self-destructive impulse buried in the depths of her heart.

Out here alone in the wilderness, if she tried hard enough, she could compartmentalise everything Bryn was, narrowing him into this singular moment. He could be anyone, a captivating stranger she'd met on the road with blazing brown eyes she couldn't look away from, golden hair she itched to sink her hands into, pulling him closer. She was lost in the fantasy of it, yearning for proximity. After everything she'd been through, the war, Huntley's betrayal, which had cost her home and her purpose, she deserved to be selfish. Some shattered part of her acknowledged that, after what happened in Eterre, maybe Bryn needed to be selfish too.

"You're not lost, Bryn," she whispered. "You're here. With me."

She closed her eyes, pulled towards Bryn like she was floating off the ground, caught up in some inevitable, undeniable force. His fingertips brushed lightly across her lips, and her resolve shattered. Catching Bryn's hand, she pulled him forward, knotting her other hand into his hair as she'd imagined. Bryn's lips parted and Aela's every thought shattered as he took her mouth with his.

Bryn traced a hand down her spine, gripped the curve of her hip and pulled her closer until their bodies fitted perfectly together. She shivered, breathless, mindless.

She hadn't allowed herself to imagine this. Now, she was consumed by the need to be closer, to take everything Bryn was willing to offer. He drew in a shuddering breath as her hands quested up beneath his shirt, spreading across the muscles at his back. She could feel the strength of his body against hers, and she closed her eyes, allowing the kiss to deepen …

A sudden, terrible memory flashed in her mind. All she could see was blood-drenched sheets. The hands that were tracing her body became bloody, stained with death. Aela jerked away, but not before meeting Bryn's gaze. His expression was a terrible mix of hurt and horror, as if he could tell what she had seen.

"I'm sorry," Aela whispered.

Bryn dropped his head. "*You're* sorry? I can't even remember the last thing I said to him."

With more sincerity than she felt, Aela said, "The end isn't what matters. It's all of the other times —"

"The times I disappointed him? The times I insulted him and shamed our family?" Bryn's voice was so soft that Aela could barely hear it. "I murdered him. My betrayal was the last thing he ever saw."

"You can still make him proud," Aela persisted.

Bryn shook his head. The intimate moment between them had passed. He looked a million miles away. "I'll never make him proud," he replied flatly. "He's dead."

✝

Nineteen

They set a slow, unsteady pace through the inhospitably thick vegetation that stretched along Nielle's eastern border, walking from daybreak to dusk. Bowie maintained a stony silence, rarely acknowledging Aela's presence and not acknowledging Bryn's at all. He stomped ahead of them, disappearing into the forest and stopping to rest in silence until Bryn and Aela caught up before pushing on again. Bryn was clearly growing frustrated.

"What am I supposed to do about this?" he asked Aela on the morning of their fifth day on foot, drawing a puzzled glance. "I haven't had a lot of experience with people … disagreeing with me."

Aela smirked. "People might not disagree with you to your face, *Your Highness*, but they all talk a whole lot of shit about you behind your back."

"Helpful. Thank you."

A few days ago, she couldn't have imagined teasing him like this, but the kiss had opened up an odd new dynamic between them. It was as if, now that a few of his defenses had cracked, Bryn no longer had the energy or will to completely rebuild his arrogant veneer. On the other hand, neither of them had spoken about the kiss, and Aela was beginning to wonder if it had been nothing more than a weak moment for Bryn. Maybe he'd sought comfort from Aela simply because she was there.

Even if Bryn *was* infatuated with her, he had a famously short attention span. Her memory flashed on the pretty blonde woman on Bryn's lap back at Walter's inn and she told herself it was good she'd pulled away first. She shouldn't be obsessing over how Bryn felt about her, or if he was comparing her to other women. He was a king-killer. And now she'd satisfied her curiosity and kissed him. She didn't need to do it again.

Still, it was too easy now to picture Bryn as a young man like any other, vulnerable and alone, the kind of person she'd always been driven by instinct to help. She was almost angry with him for it. Too much had been revealed between them. Before, with his guard up, it was uncomplicated. Bryn was an arrogant and abrasive enemy she was keeping alive out of necessity. Now, things were blurry. Bryn was … an ally … her future king? Fighting in the Border War, where the sides were clear, had given her no template for this, the idea that installing Saban's killer on the throne might be better than the alternative.

She needed to stop teasing him and keep a careful distance. Otherwise, it was too tempting to try and uncomplicate things further, to be friends or … *something*. But it was impossible to cultivate any kind of relationship with Bryn without acknowledging the reality of what he'd done. Facing the truth was too raw. Better to be a soldier, a professional. She needed to get them back to Dunwald so they could do what they needed to do.

Bryn made a face at her. "The king was the only person who properly argued with me, and he didn't even do it that often. I think you and Bowie are the first people aside from him who know who I am and actually get angry with me."

His eyes seemed to glaze over whenever he spoke of his father. His face softened, becoming younger and more open.

Be a professional.

"Can I ask you a question?" she said against her better judgment. He didn't reply, but he hadn't exactly told her she *couldn't* ask either. "Why do you always call him 'the king'?"

Bryn showed no outward signs of tension, except perhaps that his jaw was clenched tighter than usual. A little too lightly, he said, "He was fed up with the way I was acting. The drinking and fighting and … other things."

He trailed off awkwardly. Aela knew he was referring to all of the women. In a burst of fantasy, her mind replayed the moment her lips had met his, and she caught herself imagining what it would be like if Bryn was simply a man she met in a tavern or at a marketplace.

What would it be like between them if he wasn't a killer?

"He told me I wouldn't be his son unless I started behaving as a prince should. He said it at the feast, because I didn't want to be there, and I made certain everybody knew it. He was furious with me. When I think about that, I feel like I shouldn't …"

Aela dropped her head. She'd never known her parents. Instead, her mind latched onto Saban and how she'd always thought there would be more time with him, until one day there wasn't. Her last memory of Saban was his arms around her, bidding her farewell before she left for the front lines of war. The last memory Bryn had of his father was a fight.

"It doesn't mean anything," she said softly. "He loved you. You were everything to him."

"I'm not like him. He was born to rule, and I'm … I don't *like* being a leader. I can't imagine making choices that will affect the lives and livelihoods of everyone in the country. I always thought that if I ever succeeded my father's reign, I would only be his unready son, thrust onto the throne as a poor second-best. I'll only let everyone down. The people of Dunwyn deserve someone who's capable and smart and responsible, someone who will make the right choices and improve their lives."

Cautiously, Aela said, "Bryn. You can't be so afraid of making the wrong choice for your people that you make no choices at all. You're only twenty-three. No person is born a fully-fledged leader. I think you can grow into it with time and experience and perspective. I believe your father knew you'd be a great king one day. That's why he always expected more from you, because he always knew that you would prove yourself worthy."

Bryn gave her a long look. "You want me to take the throne."

"No," Aela said. It wasn't that simple. It *couldn't* be that simple. "I'm not going to try and convince you to take the throne if you truly don't want it." Besides that, there was the not inconsiderable matter of how the Dunwyan people would react if Bryn tried to rule in Saban's stead after what he'd done. "But when your father ... died, responsibility for the people of Dunwyn passed to you. I want you to go back and figure out what game Huntley's playing. Whatever happens after that, we'll figure it out."

Bryn drew in a long slow breath, steeling himself. Even before he opened his mouth, Aela knew he'd made a decision. She knew this about Bryn, he didn't allow himself to walk away from a problem, even when it was dangerous. *Especially* when it was dangerous. Resolutely, he said, "I'll take you and Bowie somewhere safe first."

Aela shook her head. "Just Bowie. I'll help you."

Bryn gave a bitter laugh. "You don't have to do my father's bidding anymore. He's not here." There was something insecure in his tone.

"I'm not doing it for your father," she said.

Surprise flashed fleetingly on his face. He opened his mouth, closed it, and looked ahead a little awkwardly. Bowie had disappeared into the trees again.

"Bowie? Come here." No answer. Bryn pinched the bridge of his nose. "Pain in my ass," he muttered, starting forward through the undergrowth. "What did I say? Don't get too far …"

He came to an abrupt halt. Aela also skidded to a stop, stumbling as Bryn shoved her protectively back, his body in front of hers and his hand on her wrist.

They'd found Bowie.

He was standing stock still a few yards away, rooted to the spot with his mouth shut and a crossbow bolt pointed at his face. Bryn's hand tensed on Aela's wrist.

A heavily armed group of five grubby men with pockmarked faces and yellowed teeth blocked their way forward. A tall, pallid man with oily black hair levelled the crossbow at Bowie. Aela instinctively reached for her blade.

"That would be a very bad idea," the bowman drawled in Niellan.

Bowie didn't move, not even to glance back at Bryn and Aela. "You're miles from the border," he observed factually. "Not many villages to raid in this part of the forest."

Only Bowie would make small talk with a deadly weapon held inches from his face.

"We rarely do that anymore," the man replied. "Our other enterprise has really taken off. We're supplying year-round now. Interesting you hadn't heard. Then again, if you had, I'd wager you wouldn't have come through the forest on foot at this time of year. You wouldn't have come through the forest at all if you'd had a choice would you, Bowie?"

Bryn couldn't understand the Niellan language, but he jolted at the shock of hearing Bowie's name. "Bowie," he said slowly. "Friends of yours?"

The bowman, who apparently knew enough of Dunwyn's language to translate this, laughed aloud, his companions echoing the sound. Aela jumped at the sound of laughter behind her. There weren't five men. There were at least twelve circling them. They were outnumbered with no way out.

"Your friends don't know who you are," the man said to Bowie. "What, you never told them who raised you?"

"*Raised* you?" Aela repeated, stunned. Growing up, she'd lived in fear of men like these, mercenaries who preyed on her village, cutting down anyone who was too weak to fight back. These men, with their well-forged weapons and King Marcus's clandestine support, were the snarling faces behind the strategic, brutal raids on the Borderlands.

"I suppose they'll die not knowing." The bowman waved his free hand casually at Aela and Bryn. "Kill them."

"Talon, *no*." Two men grabbed Bowie. His face was desperate as he looked back at Bryn and Aela. He tried to tear his shoulders from their grasp as they tied his hands behind his back. "No. Talon! Talon, *please* —"

They shoved a gag into his mouth. Aela's head was wrenched backwards by a rough hand gripping her hair. The cool tip of a blade bit into the vulnerable skin at her throat. Bryn hissed in a breath beside her as a sword hovered at his own neck.

"Stop," a commanding voice rang out through the trees.

With her head pulled back, Aela couldn't see who had spoken, but the voice sounded disconcertingly familiar. Dry leaves crunched under slow footfalls. Someone new was approaching.

"Boss." Talon's voice. "Look who's come home."

"Well, this is joyful." It was a female voice, low and raspy, speaking Niellan with a hint of amusement.

The man holding Aela released her hair, and she laid eyes on the person who had stayed Talon's blade.

Any sense of relief vanished.

Araxa Leren's presence had a clear and immediate effect on the rest of the group. They had lowered their weapons, watching her with hungry anticipation. She was the only one who looked Dunwyan. The rest, all men, bore a mixture of Niellan and Borderland features.

Having watched the exchange between Bowie and Araxa from the balcony of Walter's inn, it was the first time Aela had seen Araxa up close. Although her dark, southern colouring bore no resemblance to Bowie's Niellan appearance, Aela could see something of him in Araxa's expression. The same analytical intelligence that was occasionally unnerving in Bowie was downright terrifying in this grown woman. She cocked her head like a raptor as she looked thoughtfully at Bryn and Aela.

"I'm not sensitive, but I'd be lying if I said it didn't hurt my feelings that Bowie clearly likes you more than he's ever liked me."

"You must get that a bit," replied Aela.

Araxa's lip quirked. Abruptly, she turned and advanced on Bowie, gagged and in the hard grip of two mercenaries. Unable to move or speak, he flinched as Araxa's grip closed over the dagger at his hip. For a moment, she paused, watching him.

"So, here you are. In my forest, where Splinter can't protect you." Araxa sighed, feigning disappointment. "Now you see the hazards of overconfidence."

Araxa pulled the dagger from its sheath, examining it for a moment before carefully extending the deadly sharp point and using it to tuck one of Bowie's dark curls delicately behind his ear. Bowie made a small, frightened sound, jerking his head back slightly, eliciting a rumbling laugh from a few of the men surrounding them. Aela felt sick.

"Didn't I tell you that you would find yourself in a bind one day?" Araxa said softly.

Tucking the dagger into her own belt, Araxa reached out and brushed her fingers across the light skin under Bowie's jaw. There was a pronounced tremor in Bowie's body now. Bryn, who couldn't understand Niellan, understood this well enough.

"Get the fuck away from him," he said, his voice low and dangerous.

Araxa looked up, almost surprised, as if she'd forgotten Bryn and Aela were there. Her shrewd gaze skimmed over Aela's face then Bryn's.

"Compatriots from Dunwyn!" Araxa switched to speak Dunwyan, her eyes lingering on Bryn. "What a compelling development. You know, I could tell the two of you some things about your boy here that would curl your hair. What do you think, Bowie? Should we tell your friends a couple of stories around the campfire?"

Aela glanced at Bowie, who dropped his head, denying her a view of his face.

"We should kill them," Talon said impatiently. His finger was ready on the crossbow. There were a few murmurs of assent. Araxa looked around at the men with mild disbelief.

"Gentlemen, please," she said good-naturedly. "Show some

hospitality. These are Bowie's friends. It would be rude not to invite them back to our camp … for a drink." More laughter reverberated around the group. "Come on. We're moving out."

A pair of men corded Aela and Bryn's hands behind their backs and shoved them forcefully through the forest. With every step she took, Aela felt the need to escape becoming more dire. Out here, amongst this kind of company, she didn't know whether it would be worse for Bryn to be revealed and alive, or anonymous and dead. Either way, she was certain there was no scenario in which Araxa would allow them to walk away.

Bryn, rendered doubly powerless by his poor grasp of the Niellan language, murmured, "What did they say?"

Aela closed her eyes for a moment, steeling herself. "That's Araxa Leren."

"What? I thought Araxa was a man."

"And I thought Bowie grew up on the streets of Nielle. Apparently, we were both wrong. These people raised him."

Bryn stared at Aela. "*This* is where Bowie's from? How could he have been raised by Araxa? He's terrified of her."

Sometimes, the supreme privilege of Bryn's birth into a loving and sheltered home was almost painful. Aela didn't say that out loud.

"Probably because he has a brain in his head." Trying to sound optimistic, she added, "We've got time to figure out an escape. I don't think they mean to kill us right away."

Persistent thoughts plagued her, though. What did Araxa want? In her mind, Aela pieced together a chronology based on what she'd learned since leaving Dunwald. Bowie had arrived in Walter's inn two years ago. From there, he'd joined Splinter. It seemed safe to assume Bowie had fled the gang he'd grown up in. But if Bowie knew too much about Araxa's operations, then why was he still alive? Why were they all still alive? She was missing something.

"Not entirely reassuring," Bryn whispered. "Don't do anything stupid like in the castle. I don't want to watch you get hurt again."

Aela strove desperately to find an opportunity for escape, but they were surrounded by mercenaries, too many to fight. Even if they could escape, they had Bowie's welfare to consider, and he was separated from them at the head of the group. Bryn was right. This was bad, and Aela had a feeling it was only going to get worse.

★★★

They walked for hours through the forest. It unsettled Aela that Araxa's gang was making no effort to conceal the route from their prisoners.

Eventually, the steep terrain began to level out, and they came upon the tree line. Beyond it, Aela glimpsed an imposing, sand-coloured wall crumbling in places and weather-worn from decades of abandon. Behind it were the dilapidated remains of a once-grand building with a partially collapsed roof, and plants growing out of the walls. The imposing double doors of the formal entryway were to the left, bolted shut and overgrown with vines, unopened for two centuries. Aela's breath caught.

These were the ruins of Hiver Castle. Home was excruciatingly close.

A shove in Aela's back forced her forwards.

Aela had never set foot inside the castle walls. People from her hometown didn't come here, afraid of disturbing the dead who had given their lives defending the One Kingdom in the battle for Niellan independence. Some said it was a haunted place, but as they approached, Aela realised the demons that stalked the ruins were very much alive.

Araxa's gang had clearly inhabited the castle for some time. The grass in the courtyard was trampled, littered with haphazard rows of tents. There were flaming barrels that yet more mercenaries gathered around, cooking and warming themselves. Between the group who'd ambushed them in the forest and those Aela could see in the yard, Araxa had at least forty men. Far too many for the three of them to fight, even if they managed to get free.

Araxa led them up a flight of cracked steps into the castle's great hall, disintegrating walls leaving the space open to the elements. Birds flew in and out of the large cavity in the roof, and the stone floor was overrun with grass. Enormous blocks fallen from the caved-in ceiling served as seating and tables. Liquor bottles and weapons were strewn across them. Sconces were mounted intermittently across the crumbling walls, and a large fire burned in the centre of the room.

The dais at the back of the room would once have held a throne, but now it served as storage for rows of barrels, some bearing Splinter's serpentine insignia. If all those containers were full of grey dream, there was enough of the drug here to make every man in this castle rich. A large crate filled with papers was set on top of a barrel. Very carefully, Aela met Bryn's gaze, tilting her head minutely towards the dais. Barely, Bryn nodded.

"You can untie the boy, Talon," Araxa said in Dunwyan. She strode forwards and clapped Bryn amicably on the shoulder. "I think Bowie will be on his very best behaviour with his friends here."

The gag was pulled from Bowie's mouth. Immediately, he said to Bryn and Aela, "Don't touch *anything* she gives you —"

Talon hammered his fist into Bowie's gut, and he collapsed onto his knees, gasping. He looked up at the man. There was hatred in his eyes and fear, as Talon brought his face close to Bowie's.

"Your disappearing act caused a lot of trouble for us," Talon said. "Lucky they have to increase the dose with every passing month, or we'd never have been paid." His expression changed as the colour drained from Bowie's face, and he seized hungrily on Bowie's horror. "You didn't know that, did you? The more he takes, the more he needs to keep him alive. Pity for him, but it's a boon for us. His little habit's making us rich."

"*Fuck* you," Bowie spat.

"You little —" Talon grabbed Bowie's collar, raising his closed fist.

"Don't touch him you fucking coward!" Bryn's eyes blazed with utter fury, and he attempted a threatening step forward, brought up short by the restraining grip of Araxa's men.

Desperately, Aela tried to wring her hands free of the rope that bound them, but someone grabbed her from behind. She cursed with frustrated desperation.

"Talon." Araxa's calm, commanding voice arrested Talon's punch mid-swing. She had moved across to one of the large stones near the fire and picked up a pair of wooden cups and a wooden carafe. "What will our guests think of us?"

Aela couldn't help laughing bitterly. "You think we don't already know exactly what you people are? I've watched you kill my friends and family all my life. You're monsters. That's all there is to know."

Araxa straightened up and walked slowly forward, her eyes wandering approvingly over Aela's body. She reached out to brush a strand of Aela's hair behind her ear. "Pretty Borderlander."

Bryn struggled at Aela's side. "Take your hand off her."

"What are you going to do about it?" Araxa's eyes slid away from Bryn and she trailed her fingertips down Aela's throat. "You think I care about your friends and family? I was starving on the streets before I made something of myself. My men and I do what we do because we must."

Her touch brushed across Aela's collarbone, down her chest. And stopped. "What's this?"

Araxa's hand closed around her jacket pocket, delved inside the fabric. She pulled out the purple and gold king's insignia, and Aela's breath left her body with staggering force. She cursed herself silently for her carelessness. Stupid, blind sentiment had stopped her from hiding the ring in a better location. She wrestled an impassive look onto her face.

"Don't get too excited. I picked that up in a market in Dunwald. They were selling them for a copper each after the king died." Aela gave a short laugh. "May His Highness rest in peace."

It was a feeble lie. Aela refused to meet Bryn's gaze, and she held her breath, watching as Araxa eyed the ring, testing its weight in her hand. Slowly, she looked up, still wearing that unsettling smile, her mirthless eyes boring into Aela's.

"Do you know what we do to liars here, Borderlander?" Araxa's rough hand snaked around Aela's throat, tightening. She drew close, her lips brushing Aela's cheek sickeningly. "We cut out their tongues."

Bryn took another impotent step forward, straining against the grasp of his guards. "Try it and see what fucking happens," he growled.

Araxa ignored him. "How did you two wind up pocketing King Saban's insignia?" she wondered reflectively.

Aela clenched her tied hands into fists until they shook. Araxa couldn't find out about Bryn. "It's mine."

It was the truth, but it wouldn't add up in Araxa's mind. Aela had the look of a Borderlander. Bryn was the one who looked like Dunwyan royalty. Araxa looked slowly from Bryn to Aela.

"No," she said quietly, "I think not." Terror clouded Aela's vision as Araxa turned from Bryn to Bowie. "Let's play a little game."

Grabbing Bowie's thin wrist, she tugged him forward, pinning his hand down on a shard of stone. Aela heard the boy's shaky gasp as Araxa pulled her knife, holding it at the base of his index finger, just above his knuckle.

"Don't you *dare!*" Bryn's eyes were savage as he fought the restraining grasp of his captors. Two more men had to dart forward and help their friends to hold him back.

"Stand still and keep your mouth shut, or I'll confiscate this one's finger," Araxa told him calmly.

Bryn froze. There was utter loathing on his face, but he did as he was told. Araxa looked down at Bowie.

"What's your friend's name?" she asked casually. "His *real* name."

Bowie was rigid with tension, all his attention on the knife pressed against his finger. It looked like he wasn't even breathing. "His name is Slate."

He didn't try to pull his hand away, but the subtle tremor in his voice betrayed his careful composure.

"It's harder to fight without all your fingers," Araxa warned with precise viciousness. "Tell me the truth."

"His name is Slate." Breathy panic rose in Bowie's voice. He believed Araxa would follow through on her threat. Aela fought the urge to look around at Bryn, recalling something she hadn't believed at the time. Now, it felt disturbingly true.

He might not lie for you.

He will. I know him.

Araxa's knuckles whitened as she drove pressure down onto the blade, and Bowie's skin broke. He squeezed his eyes shut. "I'll ask you one more time —"

"Wait, stop!"

"You know who I am, damn it!"

She and Bryn cried out at the same time. Still with an iron grasp on Bowie's wrist, Araxa straightened up triumphantly.

"You lose the game, Prince Bryn." She tapped the flat edge of her dagger against her chin, eyeing him thoughtfully. "Who would have thought so much royal blood would end up in our humble camp?" The men restraining Aela laughed, and panic iced her veins. "What are we going to do with you, Your Highness?"

Bryn said nothing to deny the truth of his identity. Of course he didn't. Bryn would never allow anyone to suffer in his place. Aela's restraint, however, was fracturing. Her restless desperation to escape was mounting. She had to get Bryn out of here.

"And you." Araxa turned slowly on Bowie, her expressionless eyes glittered as she savoured the way he trembled. "You think you can lie to me? I taught you better than that. I taught you how to fight, how to steal, how to survive. You grew up rough, but you *grew up*. Never forget, I was the one who *let you live*."

Admirably, Bowie raised his chin and replied sarcastically, "And there was nothing in it for you."

Araxa smiled.

"I'll tell you what's in it for me," she said, shoving Bowie at Talon. "A king's ransom, a new test subject, and an opportunity to teach you what happens when you don't keep your smart mouth shut. Talon, take the boy down to the pit."

Bowie's gaze snapped towards Aela, and the remaining colour drained from his face. "Araxa, you have enough people. You don't need her."

Araxa gave him a cursory look and waved her hand, signalling his dismissal. It wasn't pleasant. Bowie fought back, but Talon was stronger. He shoved the boy towards a doorway between the rows of barrels.

"Slate?" Bowie reached back for Bryn, who struggled to rip away from his captors.

"It's going to be all right," Bryn called to him, a feeble attempt at reassurance while tied up and surrounded. "It's going to be fine."

Bowie shook his head with terrible defeat. "No, it's not."

Talon pushed him through the door and out of sight. Aela felt a release of pressure as the rope that tied her hands was cut. Araxa pressed something into her palm, and she looked down. Suddenly, frighteningly, Bowie's earlier warning made sense.

"*No!*" Bryn stared at her in horror, then turned. His gaze darkening murderously on Araxa, he tried to burst forward, struggling furiously against the men who held him back. "If you do that to her I will kill you! You hear me? I will kill every one of you …"

Bryn's furious cries faded as Aela's focus narrowed to the wooden cup in her hands. Surrounded by armed men and with

Bryn and Bowie in danger, she had no choice but to do what Araxa wanted. And what Araxa wanted was for Aela to drink the silvery-green, foul-smelling substance in her hand. Aela realised with rising dread that, in the derelict remains of Hiver, surrounded by heavily armed mercenaries, she was about to get her first taste of grey dream.

Araxa wore a terrible grin and she stepped in close enough to whisper in Aela's ear, "Bottoms up."

★★★

The world dipped and tilted. The colours around Aela were too bright. The walls were melting, churning as she stared. There were sudden bursts of light, shooting towards her like arrows. She raised her arm protectively, expecting the light to burn as it made contact with her skin. Instead, it shimmered and faded away.

She could make out voices but couldn't place them. They sounded low and lethargic, as if time itself had slowed. There were faces too, but they weren't right. Skin bubbled and warped at odd angles, like insects were crawling under the surface.

Aela couldn't work out if she was spinning … or maybe everything else was. She reached up with both hands to grasp her pounding head, but her fingers lengthened, undulating like grass in the wind. Everything whirled and flashed, then blackness loomed and swallowed her.

Twenty

Aela thought that maybe she was on a ship, being rocked by a gentle tide.

"Aela."

The rocking was getting rougher. It wasn't particularly pleasant.

"*Aela!* Wake *up!*"

Aela's eyelids felt heavy as lead, but she forced them open, meeting the desperate, blue-eyed gaze of Bowie, shaking her awake. With a gargantuan effort, she flopped to one side, finding her face inches away from a cool, stone wall. She hauled herself up to slump against it, trying hard to order her thoughts.

Looking about, she found herself in a subterranean cavern about twenty feet wide. The only light came from a tiny window set in the high ceiling above. Opposite where she sat was a small staircase, leading up to a solid wood door that was shut fast. Horror hammered at her. Had the grey dream wrecked her body or destroyed her mind? Would she crave more?

Even worse thoughts followed. She had no idea how she had gotten here or how much time had passed since she'd taken the drug. She couldn't recall anything after putting that fucking cup to her lips.

Her hand shot out, grabbing the front Bowie's jacket. "What. Did. I. Do."

Bowie shook his head. "No. It wasn't —"

"*Tell me!*"

"Nothing." Bowie held his hands up defensively. "It wasn't … about that. Araxa hasn't stolen from Splinter before. She only wanted to make sure his grey dream wouldn't kill the person who took it. She didn't use the others because she … she wanted me to know that she could hurt you."

Others?

It took a moment for that to sink in, for Aela to realise that she and Bowie weren't alone. As her eyes adjusted to the dim light, writhing shapes came into focus, the silhouettes of a dozen figures sitting or lying about the prison. Some of them moved lethargically, and others moaned softly or spoke in quick, unintelligible mutters. It was unnerving, more still because their uniform jackets were unmistakably familiar.

They were Dunwyan soldiers.

It felt like an immense weight was crushing her chest. A fresh wave of vertigo threatened to drive her back to the ground. "This can't be. The Niellan army executed all the Dunwyan soldiers that were captured in the war."

Eyes fixed on Aela warily, as if he was unsure how she was going to react, Bowie shook his head. "Araxa needs them to make sure the drugs are safe."

"That doesn't make any sense. If she's going to sell grey dream on the street, why would she care if it's safe —"

One of the soldiers screamed, his cry echoing around the cavernous space. Bowie flinched, wrapping his thin arms around himself tightly. Aela wondered how long he'd been down here in the darkness, surrounded by drug-crazed yells. Guilt twisted her heart. He didn't deserve to be the punching bag for her helpless fury.

"She's not selling it on the street," Bowie said wearily. "It's for someone. And they don't want him to die. At least not yet."

The fog was clearing from Aela's mind. She scanned the room with a more discerning gaze. "Where's Bryn?"

"Upstairs, I think. I haven't seen him since yesterday afternoon. Talon brought you down here right after me."

Yesterday? An entire night had passed, and she couldn't remember any of it. A fresh spark of fear licked through her, compounded by the thought of Bryn, alone at Araxa's mercy for hours.

"Araxa won't kill him now that she knows who he is." Bowie's reassurance was cold comfort. The mercenaries could do a lot to Bryn without killing him.

Trying not to think about that, she asked, "Where are we?"

"The pit," Bowie said. "That's what they call it. They used to make me sleep here sometimes."

Aela looked at Bowie. "Are *you* all right?"

There were marks on his face, bruises that hadn't been there before. His dark curls fell in front of his face as he dropped his head. "You were drugged because of me." His voice was very soft.

Aela hadn't spent much time around children, but she was keenly aware that Bowie wasn't an average child. She reached for what she knew. When dealing with distressed soldiers, calm, firm reason was effective. "Bowie, that's ridiculous," she said sternly. "You know it is. Araxa gave me those drugs, and she did it because she's a bitch, not because of anything you did or didn't do. It doesn't matter anyway. It saved my life. Talon would've killed me."

From the look on Bowie's face, he wasn't listening at all. "I can't believe it worked," he whispered in awe. He reached into his jacket, producing a pair of small items.

"What is that?" Aela asked. "What worked?"

The two things clinked together as he turned them over in his hands. Glass vials that were oddly familiar.

"It made you better."

"Is that an antidote? For *grey dream*?"

Slowly, he nodded.

Clarity cut through her drug-induced stupor, bringing a revelation into sharp focus. "This is what you had Walter making for you back at the inn, isn't it? You didn't owe him money because he gave you a place to stay. You owed him for making *this*."

Bowie's head jerked up. "You followed me."

"If you hadn't given it to me, what were you going to do with it?"

"Nothing anymore," Bowie murmured, drawing himself up. "We have to get out of here. I'll work out a plan. I just need to think, and I *can't*."

He looked incredibly frustrated, dropping his head and grabbing fistfuls of his hair, tugging tightly. It must have hurt. Aela couldn't imagine being Bowie's age and pushing through exhaustion and fear to be the one responsible for all of their lives.

"This must have been a hard place to grow up," she said to him gently.

Bowie looked up, and his big eyes were wider than usual, as if he was surprised she'd noticed. "It was very lonely."

It felt like the first honest thing he'd said to her.

"I'm sorry," she told him. That was honest too. "Listen to me. This secretiveness from you is going to stop right now. You've been hiding things from Bryn and I since Dunwald, but it's not only your life at stake anymore. We need to get out of here, so I'm ordering you to tell me what's going on."

Bowie recoiled and Aela chided herself to soften her tone. She had seen enough of Bowie's terrible past now to understand that he wasn't keeping secrets to betray them but to protect himself.

She tried again. "Listen, you're not in trouble. I know you're used to doing things by yourself, but I can help you if you tell me what you know. Please."

Bowie watched her carefully then drew in a deep, shaky breath and nodded. Dropping his head to stare at his hands, he said, "I grew up in Araxa's gang. They used to make money by raiding towns across the border. Then Araxa and the others started bringing these barrels into the camp and carrying them out a few days later. They were stealing them from Anarchist Underground, taking them west. I wanted to know what was in them, and Araxa caught me looking. I thought she'd be angry, but instead she told me that it was grey dream and that she was getting paid a lot of money to smuggle it into Eterre. She said she wanted me to help."

"And so," Aela said, dread rising. "That's how you knew the secret passage into the castle."

She closed her eyes, remembering what Alvine had said.

My poor father, King Marcus, losing his mind in his old age.

Everyone had blamed Marcus's condition on other things, the death of his son, Aela's defeat of Nielle at the Border War. But those things weren't truly the cause. She remembered Bowie telling Araxa at the inn, "I know what you've done." His history with Araxa, along with his sharp mind, had led him to the truth.

She looked up at Bowie.

"Alvine's using grey dream to poison King Marcus so that he loses his mind. He's easier for her to control like this. It's how she's running Nielle, even though Marcus is still alive."

She wondered if Huntley knew. If she didn't, she'd been taken advantage of. If she did …

"I didn't know they were testing the drug," Bowie said pleadingly. "I didn't know about the soldiers from Dunwyn, not until we saw that man in the forest after leaving Walter's place. I suspected what Araxa was doing after that, but I didn't know for certain until Talon brought me down here and I saw…" His voice cracked, and he broke off with a ragged breath.

Aela swallowed hard. "I had no idea Nielle was keeping its prisoners of war alive." Her hands curled into fists. "This might be Araxa's dungeon, but Alvine did this." She looked at Bowie. "They only want the drug to incapacitate Marcus, not to kill him. That's why they're testing it first."

"It doesn't matter," Bowie said quietly. "It's killing him anyway. That's what Talon said upstairs. If you take enough of it, you need more and more … until you …"

"So, the vials you bought from Walter were for King Marcus."

"I didn't want to stay with Araxa," Bowie said, "so I ran away. That's when I met Walter. He's very smart. We started trying to make a cure for grey dream. I thought if I could get into the castle and give it to the king, maybe he could recover and stop Alvine."

"But we were captured." Aela thought about another part of Bowie's story. "So, when Splinter caught you picking his pocket, Walter was still trying to figure out how to make the antidote?"

"Splinter said I was *promising*. He said that if I didn't go with him to Dunwald, he'd burn Walter's place to the ground with everyone inside." Bowie's blue eyes were apologetic. "I *had* to go with him, even though Walter and I hadn't finished our plan."

Ever since he'd been taken in by Splinter, Bowie had been waiting for an opportunity to safely get out of Dunwald and see if Walter had developed a successful cure. But Bowie had been forced to use it on Aela, not Marcus.

"Bowie," Aela said, "none of this was your responsibility."

"I had to do something. I was the only person who knew."

Aela rose stiffly to her feet. Bowie did the same. "You're not the only person who knows anymore. We can do something about this. We need someone who can give evidence about what's happened here, a soldier, Araxa, or one of her men."

Bowie said thoughtfully, "Now that you're awake, we can at least get out of the pit."

Delving into the side of his boot, he pulled out a small piece of cloth, unwrapping a pair of long, metal rods. Lock picks.

Aela cocked a brow at him. Always so prepared, this one. It was probably very wrong that her first thought was what a great soldier he'd be when he grew up.

"Do you keep a whole armoury in there?" she asked.

Bowie headed for the door resolutely. "Lock picks and a knife."

Aela's heart leapt. "You've got a knife?"

"It's small."

"Better than nothing." Aela paused as they neared the top of the stairs, watching Bowie kneel in front of the door. "Don't your shoes get uncomfortable?"

"More uncomfortable to be locked up. Splinter made me learn how to do this. Araxa wouldn't have left me in here if she knew. I need a minute."

The lock clicked softly and Aela raised her eyebrows. It had been less than a minute. "Can you teach me how to do that?"

"If we live." Bowie hesitated, his hand on the door. "There are nearly fifty men outside. Even you can't fight them all."

Aela's skin prickled with dreadful anticipation. "Actually, I think I have a plan for that."

Twenty-One

Aela opened the door to their prison as much as she dared, peering out across the castle ruins. Judging by the nascent light, it was early morning, but the camp was already active. Araxa sat before a fire, eating with a few of her men. There was movement out in the courtyard as men emerged from tents to prepare their morning meals at the braziers.

Bowie gasped. Following the direction of his gaze, Aela found Bryn. He was curled up on his side a few feet away behind the stone where Araxa sat, discarded outside the perimeter of the fire's warmth. He was facing them, a bruise darkening his cheek and layers of crusted and fresh blood staining his brow, chin and the side of his face like a gruesome mask. More blood pooled on the dirty floor beneath his head. It looked like his hands were still tied behind his back. Aela barely caught Bowie in time before he moved to push open the door.

"Wait," she hissed.

"He's hurt!"

"He'll survive two more minutes while we figure out a plan that won't get us all killed," Aela said with more confidence than she felt.

Bryn's eyes were closed, either asleep or unconscious or …

She looked away from him, forcing herself not to go there. Instead, she regarded the barrels of grey dream linked up along the wall. "Do you remember what you told us about grey dream back in Dunwald? That it would explode if it was lit? How big of an explosion are we talking about?"

Bowie's breath caught. "Big," he whispered.

"Good. Now, I don't suppose Bryn taught you any magic tricks to make a fire?"

"We don't need one." Bowie nodded towards a sconce carrying a flaming torch mounted on the wall a few feet outside the door. "What about Slate?"

Aela released a long, slow breath. She was glad to have Bowie with her, depending on her. If she'd been alone, she was fairly sure anxiety would stop her from executing this plan.

"We're going to have to take a bit of a risk where he's concerned. How's your aim?"

"I threw wide on purpose that day in the training room. I can hit anything you want me to … but I don't want to kill anyone."

Bowie's big blue eyes were pleading and a little apologetic, as if he was worried Aela would be angry with him for that, but she'd already considered it. Ideally, she wouldn't entrust a nine-year-old with this kind of responsibility, but she'd picked up a blade to defend her village when she was his age. Sometimes, childhood had to wait.

"Not a problem," she told him. She inhaled again slowly, exhaled, steeling herself. "That'll be my job."

She leaned down and told him in a whisper what he had to do, then she threw open the door and stepped out into the open air.

The door slammed shut behind her, and Aela moved fast,

covering ground while Araxa and her men were scrambling to their feet. She grabbed the torch from the wall, holding it an inch from an open barrel of grey dream before anyone had time to pull a weapon. She almost stumbled in relief as Bryn opened his eyes and raised his head lethargically. His jaw went slack as he saw Aela.

Araxa's eyes narrowed. She stepped over the block she'd been sitting on and grabbed Bryn's jacket, pulling him to his feet, pressing her sword to his neck.

"Think carefully," Araxa cautioned. "I'll cut his throat before you blow those barrels. Then I'm going to kill you too."

"Like hell." Bryn twisted in Araxa's grasp. The tip of her knife cut a red line across his throat as he turned and rammed his shoulder into hers. With his hands tied, he kicked her in the gut, sending her sprawling onto the block behind them.

Shouts rose from the yard, dozens of mercenaries called forth by the fight.

"Bowie!" Aela yelled.

The door flew open again. A fraction of Aela's attention noted the knife flying from Bowie's hand, Bryn applying a booted foot to Araxa's throat. Hoping with everything she had that it wasn't a terrible mistake, she plunged the flaming torch into the open barrel, turned, and launched herself into the doorway to the pit.

She barely had time to cover her ears before the grey dream exploded.

The world rocked like an earthquake. With an enormous boom, the stone wall blew out beside them. Aela covered her head protectively against a storm of obliterated rock and wood.

Ears ringing, she lowered her arms and looked around. The explosion had blown a massive hole through the wall, and light streamed into the pit. Soldiers screamed in terror. She flinched as something brushed her shoulder. A bloom of papers rained down, the contents of the crate that had sat atop the grey dream barrels.

Huddled in the doorway beside her, Bowie looked up through wild blue eyes, rattled but unhurt.

"Whoa," he breathed shakily, looking around at the carnage.

Aela surveyed the mess of bodies amongst the destruction urgently. Foreboding gripped her briefly until she glimpsed a familiar tangle of golden hair rising from behind a block of detached wall. She met Bryn's dark eyes and every breath, every thought fled in a rush as his bloodied face broke into a grin.

"Why do all our plans involve setting things on fire?" he called out weakly.

Aela attempted to glare at him, but she couldn't keep her own grin from breaking through as she jogged to his side and pulled him to his feet. "Turn around for me."

Obediently, Bryn turned. Aela didn't have a knife, so she set her fingers to work on the rough bonds at his wrists, glad the task was mindless. Her ears rang from the explosion, but the real problem was this proximity. It was difficult to focus on anything beyond the warmth of Bryn's hands and wrists as her fingertips brushed his skin. He held himself very still. The ropes fell away, revealing harsh red and purple burns on his skin.

Bryn turned, and Aela's stomach lurched with delighted shock as his hands cupped her face. His touch was gentle, at odds with the fury in his eyes. "Are you all right?" he demanded urgently. "Are you hurt? I didn't know what was happening to you after they gave you that stuff. I thought … fuck, I thought …"

Caught in Bryn's panicked gaze, Aela couldn't pin down any

of the tangential thoughts floating aimlessly through her mind. She was lost to the infinite depth of his molton brown eyes, the touch of his warm fingers on her neck, his thumbs brushing her cheeks. For a moment, the whole world around them vanished. It was only the two of them.

"*Are you all right?*" Bryn's voice was far away, trembling. His assumption, too close to her own when she'd regained consciousness, sharpened her focus.

Gripped by the need to allay his fear, she said shakily, "You're the one who survived an explosion. I'm fine. Nothing happened." Relieved, Bryn dropped his head, resting his forehead against Aela's. She ran a light, teasing touch up his forearms and felt him shiver. "Bowie was there. He said they only wanted to make sure the drug wasn't fatal."

"Shit. Bowie," Bryn breathed, as if he too had remembered that the rest of the world existed. He pulled away reluctantly, his fingertips lingering on her throat for a moment. Bryn jogged over to the doorway, where the boy was still huddled against the wall, as if fearing a second explosion. "Bowie, are you —"

He froze as he reached the top of the stairs. Bryn turned back to Aela, rubbing his skin, his lips parted in vulnerable shock.

"Are those *Dunwyan soldiers*?"

"Later." They desperately needed to escape. Aela went to Bryn's side and looked down into the pit. "For now, we need to work out how to bring them with us."

"Aela." Bowie rose shakily. His tone was sad, and he wore a pitying expression that Aela hated. "We can't bring them. The drug —"

Aela rounded on him. "You said it wasn't meant to kill them!"

"A little bit won't kill anyone," Bowie replied, "but they've been here since the war. They've been taking a lot of it … for months."

Aela took Bowie by the shoulders. "What are you saying?" she asked desperately.

"Aela." Bryn gently pried her hands off Bowie, but his voice was firm. "Leave him be."

Bowie kept looking at her with that same deep sadness. "I'm sorry," he whispered. "Maybe if we can make enough of the antidote and get it back here, but until then …"

He didn't have to say anything else. Aela knew how little hope there was of these poor people hanging on much longer.

She was almost driven to her knees by despair. Under her command, these soldiers had been captured. What they had endured here for months was unimaginable. Now, she couldn't save them if she wanted to save herself and Dunwyn's crown prince. She was a failure for walking away from her soldiers when they needed her. Even if they were dying, it was impossible to imagine letting them die here rather than on Dunwyan soil.

Tears of remorse filled her eyes, and she had to look away. This was a moment of weakness she didn't want anyone to see. Aela closed her eyes, collecting her thoughts. Bryn was Saban's only heir, the only one who could save Dunwyn. Every soldier in the Dunwyan army had sworn to give their life for their country. She looked back down at the pathetic, huddled figures silhouetted in the dim light on the cavern floor. It wasn't a dignified death, but it was still an honourable one.

"All right," Aela said roughly. "We need to go."

***

The fallout from the explosion was grizzly in the courtyard, bloody head wounds, broken limbs, and large chunks of wood from the barrels protruding from men's bodies. Most of the injuries weren't fatal, but some of them were.

Bowie was back beside the fire, surrounded by a mess of papers and rubble and bodies. Rooted to the spot, his breathing was shallow as he stared down at a pile of debris. A single brown arm protruded from beneath it, and Araxa's blood trickled into the dust.

There was movement at the perimeter of the camp, mercenaries finding their feet, and their swords.

"Bowie!" Bryn called up to the boy, who was now crouched beside Araxa, busily doing something Aela couldn't see. Bryn looked at her, rolling his shoulders stiffly. "We'll have to fight our way out of here, which is the very last thing I feel like doing. *Bowie!*"

Four of the mercenaries had now gathered themselves, advancing menacingly as Bowie continued to dawdle by the fire.

"Go get him," Aela said, turning to face them.

Bryn stared at her, as if the suggestion was unbelievably foolish. "You're unarmed —"

"Please," Aela interrupted derisively.

Bryn hesitated a moment, glancing up at Bowie, then back at Aela, irresolute. "Don't be stupid."

"Go," Aela said.

Bryn ran up the stairs as Aela walked towards the mercenaries. She dodged the first blow, grabbing the man's arm as he overshot his target. He yelled out as she drove the palm of her hand hard into his elbow, hearing it crack painfully. His grip loosened on his blade, and she had a sword.

With one efficient stroke, she cut his throat, facing the other men as he fell. They hesitated a moment, intimidated by the decisiveness of her first victory, then descended simultaneously, two before her and one behind. She ducked the thrust of a blade, pivoted to grab the man behind her and drove him forward, a firm grip on his belt.

His companion's outstretched sword slid directly into his gut. She sliced her sword upwards, skewering the man before he could withdraw the blade from his friend's belly. The last man standing took a horrified step backwards, his sword going limp in his hand, evidently making the calculation that whatever Araxa had been paying him was not worth being skewered.

"Go," Aela barked at him.

He turned and ran without hesitation. Bryn arrived at Aela's side, leading Bowie by the arm. He raised his brows at her.

"How does it feel to have men flee before you?" Bryn asked.

"Like the world is as it should be," Aela told him.

They crashed through the trees, slipping on the rain-drenched leaves littering the ground. Aela was breathing hard by the time they reached a wide, fast-flowing river. It was impossible to cross. Over her frantic heartbeat, she heard the distant shouts of mercenaries pursuing them, growing louder with every moment they stood still.

Bryn yelled, "This way!"

As they sprinted downstream with the rush of the water, the terrain became rocky, descending gradually until the trees cleared. The edge was a sheer drop. The river plunged straight down, a crashing waterfall that pounded into a dark lake below. Aela stopped.

Beside her, the others skidded to a halt too. Pebbles toppled, falling for far too long before sprinkling into the water. Bowie's eyes were wide and wild, like a scared animal's. "Slate." Bryn's alias tumbled from his mouth. He couldn't seem to shake it.

Bryn turned. "*What?*"

The water was inky against the stormy sky. Bowie stared down, shaking his head. His face was white as death.

"Don't tell me you're afraid of heights!" Bryn said urgently.

Bowie shook his head again, and Aela understood. It wasn't the height that bothered him.

"Bowie," she said steadily, "can you swim?"

His chest heaved, his hand shaking where it rested at his throat. He looked on the verge of a panic attack. "I … I can't."

Bryn looked back the way they'd come desperately. At any moment, Araxa's mercenaries would burst through the trees. They had to disappear. This was the quickest way.

Aela leaned down, putting a hand on Bowie's shoulder. "Bowie," she said hurriedly, "you have to jump."

He shook his head more vigorously. Raindrops flew from his hair. "I can't. You go. I'll figure something else out."

Bryn set his jaw. "If you don't jump, you end up back with them." He jerked his head in the general direction of the mercenaries' shouts. More voices had joined them, bloodthirsty for vengeance.

"Fine," Bowie said. "I'll go back, find another way to get out."

Bryn huffed out an impatient breath. "Sorry, little man. That's not an option." He grabbed Bowie around the waist and launched off the rocks.

Aela drew in a deep breath and jumped too. Her stomach lurched, light as air, as if she'd left her gut behind while her body dropped. The rush of pure adrenaline ignited like fire in her veins. The fall felt like forever, a gloriously terrifying plummet, finally arrested when she slammed down hard into the water.

Time slowed. The lake was freezing, and Aela fought the urge to inhale, knowing she'd only pull in a lungful of water. She kicked her legs, straining up towards the muted daylight that shimmered beyond the broken surface. Finally, she burst through, drawing a huge, gasping breath into her starved lungs.

Wildly, she looked around for Bryn and Bowie, who hadn't come up for air. Alarmed, she sucked in another breath, preparing to duck underwater in search of the others. As she was about to go under, Bryn came rocketing to the surface, drawing in a huge, desperate breath. He struggled to stay afloat, holding Bowie in the crook of his arm. Bowie's gasp for air immediately descended into a violent coughing fit. Water pasted his usually curly hair flat across his face.

Bryn looked at Aela. The water had washed much of the blood off his face, leaving an awful bruise and a long cut across his hairline.

"You alive?" he asked hoarsely.

"Great plan," Aela grumbled.

Distant shouts from above cut across the stillness of the forest, and Bryn swore. They were vulnerable here, bobbing in the middle of the lake, unmissable to any passerby. Aela and Bryn saw it at the same time, the sheer cliff they'd jumped off was undercut where it met the water, curtained with long, thick vines, a cavernous hiding place carved out of their bare surroundings. They swam, Bryn moving awkwardly as he held Bowie, who was still coughing.

They pushed through the veil of greenery, and the mercenaries' shouts were drowned out by the thundering waterfall. Concealed by rocks and vines and rushing water, they couldn't see or hear anyone anymore, which was its own problem. They wouldn't know how long to hide for. The water was shallower here, barely. Aela stood on her toes to keep her head above water, while Bryn hoisted Bowie higher in his arms. Water dripped from the rocks into the water, the sound echoing off the low roof above them. Bowie's harsh, gasping breaths echoed too. It sounded deafeningly loud, every slight noise reverberating in the cavernous space. Thank the gods, Aela thought, that the thundering waterfall was drowning out the pounding of her heart.

She lost track of how long they hid for. Long enough that they were all shivering uncomfortably. Long enough that the rain had, if possible, grown heavier, and thunder began to rumble, low and resounding all around them, hopefully forcing the mercenaries back to their camp. A few pale slivers of sunlight had begun to cut determinedly through the pelting rain when they finally swam ashore and hauled themselves up onto the muddy bank.

Bryn deposited Bowie onto the ground and looked at Aela, his gaze skimming her face and body carefully. Her pulse jumped when his chilled fingertips brushed her forearm, trailing down her hand, her fingertips.

"Are you hurt?" he asked. Mutely, she shook her head, all the breath knocked from her. "What about you? Let me see those bruises." Bryn reached out to cup a hand under Bowie's chin, but Bowie batted it away, turned, and began picking his way through the storm, leaving Bryn to shoot Aela a distressed look.

"He'll be fine. Let's keep moving," Aela said reassuringly. "Araxa might be dead, but it's still wise to put as much ground between us and the rest of them as possible." Aela could see hurt in the tense line of Bryn's jaw. She added gently, "He doesn't hate you, Bryn. He's a boy who doesn't know how he feels."

"He does," Bryn said bitterly. "Everyone knows exactly how

they feel about the prince of Dunwyn."

Twenty-Two

The flat, verdant terrain began to rise up into the dusty Borderland hills that Aela remembered from her childhood. The feeble streams of sunlight vanished behind more heavy clouds, and the pelting rain reduced the ground to mud that squelched and slid beneath her feet. Huge rocks littered the hillside. They had been entertaining climbing obstacles when she was young, but now the rainwater rushing downhill transformed them into a treacherous waterfall.

Aela made it to the top of the hill first, looking out over a familiar sight. Once carpeted with grass, the valley floor had been trampled into a muddy wasteland by months of thundering hooves and fierce fighting. The field was called Bayeau, and it was where Aela and her soldiers had spent eight months surrounded by the Niellan army, until Aela's victory in single combat had liberated them.

Every tree, every trampled blade of grass and patch of dirt had borne witness to the Border War. It had played out here, in the shadow of Hiver castle's decaying skeleton, the last relic of a long-dead unity between Nielle and Dunwyn. On the light breeze, Aela heard the clash of steel, the cries of the wounded, the dying. She felt the impact and resistance of driving her blade up through the Niellan champion's ribcage, piercing his heart. The hot spray of blood spattered her face all over again …

"It happens to me too sometimes." Bowie appeared beside her, watching her expression. "Seeing the bad things that have happened come back to life."

Aela looked down at him. The top of his dark curls barely reached her waist. "What bad things have happened to you?" she asked.

Predictably, Bowie ignored the question. "This is Bayeau," he said quietly, "isn't it?"

Aela nodded. She didn't have to ask him if he knew the significance of the name. She had spent enough time with Bowie now to know that he was unusually well-educated about the state of affairs between Nielle and Dunwyn.

Bowie didn't say anything for a moment but looked up at Aela with an unreadable expression. "You said you don't hate Niellans, but the war made you angry at *someone*," he said softly. "You always want to fight."

It was simplistic and childlike, such a soft summary for all that she felt. Still, the way he said it, with such profound sadness, made Aela's throat constrict.

"Just because I want to fight, doesn't mean I'm angry," she said defensively.

Bowie's gaze held steady, giving her a challenging look. "You told me to tell the truth. Why are *you* still lying?"

Aela's heart hurt. Bryn was right. Bowie was a pain in the ass with his inconveniently canny observational skills. She sighed as she looked down upon Bayeau. The battlefield seemed smaller from this angle. It had felt like the entire world while she was trapped there.

"All that death to appease one man's grievance," she mused.

"And that whole time, he was being lied to. All he wanted was to avenge the death of the son he loved more than anything else in the world, but his daughter was pulling the strings in the background." She laughed bitterly. "I suppose he found out the hard way that you really can't trust anyone."

"I don't think that's all he wanted."

Aela looked down in surprise at Bowie. He didn't say anything else, and together they stared out at the field. Aela wondered what he was thinking about. She didn't expect him to elaborate. He always seemed to say as little as possible, carefully guarding all he knew, so she was surprised when he spoke again in a whisper.

"And I don't think he loved his son the most." He shook his head, as if trying to erase some errant thought from his mind. Then he pulled something from his pocket. "Here. I took this from Araxa before we ran."

His small, cold hand was jarring in Aela's palm for the briefest moment before he pulled away, leaving a glinting, heavy trinket behind.

Aela's breath caught, and she closed her hand tightly around the king's insignia. She thought she'd never see it again. She looked down at Bowie, feeling a sudden surge of affection. Impressively capable as he was, there was a reason Splinter hadn't been able to force him to kill. His capacity for kindness was as sweet as it was incongruous with his thorny, defensive armour that guarded him from the harshness of Anarchist Underground.

"Thank you," she said, moved.

"Aela?" Bryn crested the hill.

He'd dropped further and further behind as they'd walked. Looking at him more closely, she realised beads of sweat glistened at his hairline. His face was ghostly, almost grey. He swayed, his eyelids fluttering dangerously.

Aela grabbed him before he fell, steadying him with firm hands that gripped his arms more tightly than she'd intended.

"Bryn?" Her voice came out brittle. "What's wrong with you?"

"Nothing," he slurred. "We need to keep moving."

"Bryn," she said again sharply. She'd seen that look on the faces of many soldiers and it terrified her every time.

"Fine. It's not even that bad." Bryn set his gaze on something far away and turned, pulling up his jacket and shirt to reveal his muscular body beneath it.

Aela couldn't stifle her gasp. The fabric on his outer layers was torn. The piece of wood that protruded from the delicate skin above Bryn's left hip bone was as long as a knife, surrounded by grizzly tendrils of blood. Trails of red inched outwards from the wound like string. Bryn clenched his jaw, still looking determinedly away.

"Why didn't you say anything?" Aela demanded.

She was angry that Bryn was hurt. Furious, actually. The fact that the explosion had been her idea and that it had done this … monstrosity. Aela felt sick. Left untreated for too long, the wound could go septic. If his blood became infected, he could die. Aela's anger flared again, this time inexplicably at Bryn. He wasn't being brave by hiding the injury — he was being stupid. His secrecy mixed with horror at the sight of the blood creeping from his wound was too close to what she'd seen on the battlefield during the war. Beneath her anger, another feeling clawed its way to the surface, a horrible, creeping fear for Bryn that was so profound it was almost painful.

I don't want to watch you get hurt.

Aela's hand twitched, reaching reflexively for him. She wanted to smooth her hand over the wound and make it disappear.

"Doesn't hurt," Bryn replied. He staggered and groaned impatiently as if frustrated that he had a weakness he couldn't conquer.

"Slate?" Bowie's voice was barely more than a whisper. He looked at Bryn with an expression of absolute horror. Even after days without sleep, enduring torment and terror, he still managed to hold himself back from tears, although it appeared to be not without considerable effort.

Bryn rolled his eyes. "Don't look at me like that, kid. I'm not *dying*."

"Maybe not yet," Aela said as evenly as she could. "But that thing's been lodged in your side for half a day. If you keep going like this, you *will* keel over eventually."

She bent down, examining the wound more closely. She had the basic rudiments of a healer's work, enough knowledge to clean and bind a wound until it could be tended by an actual physician. This was beyond her. She wasn't certain if pulling the shard from Bryn's side would cause a flood of bleeding that couldn't be stopped. Even if it was safe to remove the wood, she had no alcohol or clean bandages. They were all covered in mud, so using clothing wasn't an option.

She bit her lip. They were moving in the right direction for a detour, following increasingly familiar terrain. Aela had intended to lead Araxa's mercenaries away from civilisation, not towards it. Looking at Bryn though, it was urgently clear that they had to risk it. He was clearly calling upon a considerable amount of willpower simply to remain on his feet.

"All right," she said, drawing herself up. "We're a few hours away. Can you make it?"

"Away from where?" Bryn asked.

Aela sighed, running a filthy hand through her hair. "Hiver. My home."

Twenty-Three

Deadly-sharp steel drove towards Aela's head.

In the training arena at Dunwald, she ducked, dodging hard to the right, sending sawdust flying up from beneath her boots. She turned in time to parry a relentless barrage of strikes, all her focus on keeping Huntley Bartome from gaining ground.

It was difficult to believe this high-born woman, who spent more time in diplomatic discussions with Nielle than she did with a blade in her hand, had the stamina to continue this fight for a full half hour. Aela's own limbs were aching and heavy, her whole body drenched in sweat, but she pushed herself to draw out the fight. Her blood was singing. After months of taking down indecisive and untrained recruits in lacklustre and short-lived matches, she finally felt alive.

Their blades met, their eyes met, and approval glittered in Huntley's hazel gaze. "Come on, soldier. Make me work for it!"

Calling hard on her shaking muscles, Aela shoved Huntley backwards. The ambassador stumbled and looked up, a new, wary quality in her gaze. Aela attacked, breathing hard, driving her weapon towards the older woman's shoulder. She knocked Aela's blade away, swinging left. Aela moved to parry, but before her mind could make sense of what was happening, Huntley's blade was gone. Dodging right, Huntley spun inside Aela's guard, and for the first time in weeks Aela's blade went flying from her fingers, soaring across the field into the sawdust. She staggered back as Huntley brought the tip of her blade to kiss Aela's throat.

Aela's heart soared. Huntley's skills were wasted in diplomacy. She was the best fighter Aela had faced in her life.

"For a moment there, I thought I'd met my match," Huntley said approvingly.

Slow applause echoed about the arena, punctuated by excited murmurs. Aela looked up in time to see the entire arena go to its knees. Aela knelt too as King Saban of Dunwyn descended the stairs to stand before her on the sawdust.

"That was something to behold," he said. Through soft golden-brown eyes, he appraised her with interest and slight amusement. He bent down and in a low voice spoke just to Aela. "Soldiers have to be eighteen years old to join my army. Are you sure you should be here?"

Scarcely able to believe her own boldness, she replied, "Do I fight like I should be here, Your Highness?"

The king gave a quiet chuckle.

"You remind me of my son. He has a similarly … flexible approach to the rules. What's your name?"

Aela opened her mouth to reply, but it was Huntley who spoke first. She was the only person in the arena besides the king who wasn't kneeling. The loftiness of her station allowed her to look him in the eye after rising from a deep bow.

"Her name is Aela Rinn."

★★★

"**W**hat are you thinking about?"

Aela looked over at Bryn. He watched her with interest as they walked through the muddy Borderland forest. His eyes momentarily captured her full attention. They were the same colour as his father's. "Fighting."

Bryn laughed weakly. "Not one day after taking out the infamous Araxa Leren and fifty of her mercenaries, you're dreaming about throwing down again? Doesn't the Reaper of Dunwyn ever get tired?"

Aela gave him a wry smile. "I don't think it was quite fifty."

She kept her hand resting on her dagger, still convinced that the mercenaries who'd survived the explosion at Hiver Castle would appear from the trees behind them at any moment. They wouldn't be safe until they finally reached the village … not even then. It was hard to read the sky for the time with this much cloud cover, but it had to be at least midday. The rain had eased somewhat but hadn't ceased, giving them no time to dry off after throwing themselves off the waterfall after dawn.

Bryn's foot slid in slick mud as they traversed a particularly steep section of slope. Rainwater mingled with beads of sweat on his face, and the slight clumsiness of his movements made it clear he was fighting to ignore the pain in his side. Regaining his footing, he muttered a curse, kicking steps into the ground to improve his purchase.

"This place is a jungle. I can't believe all this land was part of a city once," he said breathlessly.

"Hiver was connected all the way from the ruined castle to the town we're headed for," Aela confirmed, indulging his effort to distract himself. "You know, tens of thousands of people used to live here, which is mad when you consider that Hiver's population is only about a hundred now."

"Not as mad as the fact that Nielle and Dunwyn actually used to be one country."

"Tell me about it. Must have been nice to live here and not have Niellan state-sponsored scumbags like Araxa raiding your home every other week —"

Aela and Bryn both turned at a painful-sounding splat. Bowie had slipped at the same place on the slope as Bryn. He braced on his hands and knees in the mud, his expression fell painfully between furious frustration and unshed tears. Aela was surprised he hadn't face-planted into the ground hours ago, given how exhausted he surely was. His iron will seemed to be the only thing keeping him moving at this point.

Bryn sighed. Carefully turning to pick his way back down, he extended a hand to Bowie.

"All right. Come here, you."

Bowie's cool blue eyes narrowed at Bryn, and he pointedly pushed himself to his feet. Bryn dropped his hand and turned away. He was hiding it, but Aela suspected Bowie's icy demeanour hurt as much as the piece of wood sticking out of his side.

"Thank the gods for some flat ground," Aela said as they reached the top of the hill. She gave Bryn a small, reassuring grin. Her attention caught on his captivating golden-brown eyes, and she was momentarily distracted by the beauty of his returning smile.

Bowie's sudden, desperate cry yanked Aela back to reality. The ground shifted, the earth dropped away, and Aela fell.

Ripping her knife from her belt on instinct, she drove it into the slick soil. She slid then jerked as her knife caught against a tightly-packed tangle of tree roots. At her left, Bryn gave a yell. Gripping a root with one hand, he reached out desperately with the other to catch Bowie by the forearm as the boy hurtled downwards. Bowie clawed frantically at Bryn's sleeve, his hands slippery with mud.

"What the *hell* is this?" Bryn demanded wildly.

Now that she wasn't falling, Aela looked around to take stock of exactly what *this* was. The roots that had arrested her fall were about six inches above the abyss where the earth dropped away, becoming undercut. She, Bryn and Bowie dangled in space over a wide rectangular pit that had been dug into the earth. About six feet below them, row upon row of tightly packed, wickedly-sharp wooden spikes pointed threateningly upwards. Aela's gut lurched sickly.

"Araxa," Bowie said, breathlessly incoherent. "Traps in the forest."

The strain on his frightened face wracked Aela's nerves. Even with that strong will, he'd only be able to hold on for so long.

"This one's …" Bowie's Dunwyan sounded more heavily accented than usual, harder to understand through his frantic straining. "From after I left … Didn't notice it early enough … Stupid … I'm sorry."

Bryn swore, and Aela glanced at him, her anxiety deepening. Bowie wasn't the only one who couldn't hold on for long. Where Bryn's jacket parted, Aela glimpsed blood staining his dirty white shirt. The dagger-sized piece of wood lodged in his right side was weakening the arm that held Bowie off the deadly spears.

She looked up. Years of training with a sword had honed

her upper body strength, and she was grateful for the hundreds of pull-up drills she'd logged over the years. A path of roots protruded from the earth, bridging the three-foot gap to the surface. If she was careful, she'd make it.

"I think I can climb out," she said. "But it'll take me a few minutes."

Bryn muttered another curse. His face was red with strain, beads of sweat already dripping down his face. He looked over at Aela. "I can't hold him much longer. Not with this fucking thing in my side."

She made a split-second decision. "Give him to me."

"Can you hold him?"

Aela wasn't sure, but Bryn looked as if he was a few precarious seconds away from falling into the hole and taking Bowie with him. She'd figure it out. "I'll be fine."

Bryn grunted as he shifted his weight to look down. "Bowie, I'm going to pass you over to Aela. Grab her hand."

"What? Why?" The panic in Bowie's voice was barely contained.

"Do as I say. Grab her hand." Gritting his teeth, he swung Bowie sideways, and Aela caught one of his arms. Bowie's hands latched tightly around her wrist. His weight jerked her down and a fresh wave of fear crested in her chest. Bowie was small and thin, but now that they were free-hanging over certain death, he was heavier than he looked.

"Are you strong enough to climb out?" Aela asked Bryn.

He swore again. "I don't know, I —"

Bowie's mud-slick hands slipped against Aela's, and he cried out. She tightened her grip desperately. "Bryn! Climb! *Now*! I don't care if it hurts. Do it!"

"Don't let go," Bryn said.

With a pained groan, he hoisted himself up, his right hand grasping a slightly higher tree root. Now, he had to pull up on his injured side. He cried out again as he swung up for the next root, barely catching it. His cheeks puffed with exertion. Above them, Aela heard a yell not far off, and her insides went cold.

Araxa's men had found them. Bryn was steadily traversing up through the roots, but it didn't matter. If he got to the top, he'd be killed by the mercenaries. If he stayed down here, they'd all fall to their deaths.

"Aela?" Bowie called up. His face was ashen. "If they find us, I think we should let go."

"Stop that!" Aela yelled back at him, refusing to believe that was the only option. "I have a plan … half a plan. Maybe."

It was a lie. She had no idea what to do. There was no way to think or fight out of this one.

"Holy shit! *Aela?*"

Aela's head jerked up, and she thought wildly that perhaps she'd already died and made it to the afterlife, because there was no way this was real. More yelling from the surface, and in the next moment something coarse hit Aela in the face. A rope, stretching from above.

"Climb up!" a familiar voice called.

"Bowie, grab hold!" she called down.

When her hand was free, she gripped the rope and pulled herself up. A few more pulls and her feet found the soaked earth. She crawled over the edge, a strong pair of hands hauling her to safety. Bryn's hands. He held her desperately for a heartbeat before the urgency of the situation caught up to them. Together, they hoisted the rope. Bryn reached down and caught Bowie's arms. Ignoring the grizzly wound at his side, he pulled Bowie in against his chest.

"Gods! You three must be the luckiest people alive!" A very tall, broad man pulled the sweaty strands of his dark-blond hair back into a tail then leaned down to untie the rope from a tree. He gestured at the smaller blond man beside him carrying a crossbow. "First time we've come this way on a hunt in a week, and we were about five minutes away from recovering your dead bodies." He shook his head. Disbelief and irritation mingled on his familiar face. "You know, things like this wouldn't happen if you'd become a healer."

"Good to see you too, Amory." Aela met Bryn's gaze over Bowie's head and saw her own relief reflected in his eyes. "Slate, I'd like you to meet my family."

Twenty-Four

"**G**ood to have you home, kid." Amory wrapped his arms around Aela, picking her up and spinning her round as he'd done when they were younger.

Amory was still young, only thirty-eight. He'd been a teenager when Aela had come into his care, but he'd never made Aela feel like an inconvenience. He set her down and leaned over to kiss the top of her head.

As a little girl, Aela had believed Amory when he'd told her that he was part-giant. He towered over all of them. Out of the corner of her eye, Aela noticed that Bowie shrank back against Bryn, eyeing Amory's imposing physicality. Amory was handy enough in a fight, but his bulging muscles had been developed through years spent rebuilding Hiver after endless catastrophic raids.

"Aela? I can't believe it's you!" Ewan grinned as he joined them. Aela embraced them together, reaching up for Amory and down for Ewan, who was a full foot shorter than his husband. In the simple, familiar presence of her family, everything she'd been through in Nielle, the danger she and the others were still in, momentarily melted away.

Amory pulled back and cupped her face in his hands,

examining her through concerned blue eyes. "You look like death," he muttered.

"Thanks."

He gave a quick laugh, bending down to kiss her forehead again. Amory was like Saban, like most other people from Dunwyn — openly demonstrative with affection. It was a custom Aela had never felt entirely comfortable with, but she weathered it now.

"Sorry," Amory said, "I wasn't expecting to find you out here, especially not … like this."

Aela had given little thought to her appearance until now. Their exploits in Eterre and at Hiver Castle had left her looking rather haggard. Bryn and Bowie looked worse. There was concern on Amory and Ewan's faces as they took in the bruises on Bowie's young face.

"Is this a new assignment?" Amory asked. "Something for the army?"

"I don't have time to explain." She nodded at Bryn. "My friend … Slate … He's wounded. And you should know there are Niellan mercenaries after us. They might have followed us here."

"We can deal with all of that," Ewan said steadily. "Let's get you back to town."

Comprising only two dozen houses, the town of Hiver was unimpressive, a collection of thatched roofs stretching down a single, muddy road with a town hall building at one end. The surrounding terrain was hilly, thick with trees and small, ambling waterways.

Aela stood on the hillside, looking down at the familiar sight.

Home. It was beautiful. And daunting.

There were so many memories here, running barefoot

through town with Tamas trailing behind her, sparring with Amory and Ewan. Sitting under a tree and sewing her first dress, pulling it on over her clothes and spinning so that the skirt floated out around her. It was the first time she'd felt beautiful.

She remembered screams and the pungent smell of smoke, the blinding, terrifying light of flames engulfing homes. The sound of mercenaries laughing as they looted the town while its residents cowered in fear.

She remembered stopping here after the Border War, sleeping in her tiny, comforting childhood bed in Amory and Ewan's home. She could almost feel the pressure of Tamas's body covering hers, that terrible night when she'd betrayed her oldest friend, seeking comfort and sensation from him that she didn't deserve.

It all roiled into some confusing reel that vacillated between happy and terrible, gradually coalescing until one feeling couldn't be differentiated from another.

The people of Hiver were hypervigilant, their eyes always trained on the border, monitoring for hostile arrivals, so by the time she and the others reached the foot of the hill at the edge of town, quite a crowd had gathered to greet them. There were, as Aela stepped into the road with the others, plenty of gasps and murmurs. A young man pushed through the gathering, handsome, bronzed, and clean-shaven with glittering blue eyes and long, dark lashes.

"Aela Rinn."

Despite her fears about Bryn, about the mercenaries, and about whether she could ever repair her oldest friendship after the terrible thing she'd done, she couldn't fight the urge to smile.

"Hello, Tamas."

Tamas Ashton stepped forward without hesitation, closing the distance between them and pulling her into a strong embrace. He'd cut his mousey hair since last time Aela saw him. It was shaven close to his head, emphasising his strong jawline. Years of chopping wood, hunting and helping with repairs had given him a build that resembled a soldier's more than it did a physician's. Aela could feel the strength in his broad shoulders and muscular arms and chest as he held her. It should have felt natural, after so many years of friendship, but she could still feel his lips on her skin. At the time, she'd needed to feel *something*, but she'd ignored the warning signs, the look in his eyes that told her how much it meant to him.

She went still in his arms as guilt tightened like a vice around her heart. Stepping away hastily, she cleared her throat. Her face felt hot, and she tried not to notice the flush creeping across Tamas's cheeks. She turned her body to include Bryn, suddenly, keenly aware that he was right there, watching her wrapped up in the arms of a very handsome young man.

The crowd was thinning. A few of Hiver's residents greeted Aela briefly then moved off, leaving her with nothing else to do but meet the Tamas's gaze. "My friend Slate needs your help."

Tamas looked Bryn over. If his thoughts lingered on their night together, he hid it well. He frowned with concern as Bryn pulled his shirt up to reveal the piece of wood lodged in his side. Tamas hissed in a sympathetic breath. "Not the most desirable circumstances in which to meet a new friend, Slate, but nonetheless it's good to meet you." His eyes flicked to Bowie. "And who is this?"

Bryn gave Tamas a cold look. "Perhaps you might save the small talk for after you get this thing out of me," he suggested icily.

Tamas raised his eyebrows, and Aela flushed. Tamas was accustomed to gratitude and politeness from his patients, two characteristics he would consistently fail to find in Bryn. Aela wasn't sure if Bryn was being more abrasive than usual because he was in pain or because he could sense the tension strung taut in the air. Tamas looked at her.

"Do you suppose the anger is a symptom of the injury or a pre-existing ailment?" he asked, mildly curious.

Bryn's eyes narrowed, as if he was about to show Tamas what real anger looked like. Thankfully, Ewan's arrival eclipsed the awkward moment. "Tamas, go get your bag," he said, all business. "We'll make them comfortable at our place."

Ewan took Bryn's shoulder, steering him towards the modest wooden home he and Amory shared. It was two storeys, cobbled together over some years, with additions made whenever they acquired the time, money, and supplies.

The ground floor was a single room. A fire crackled tantalisingly in the far corner, and Bryn lowered himself stiffly down onto a bench seat at the small table in the centre of the space, grimacing. Aela dropped down on the bench across the table, watching Ewan push his light hair off his face and sweep about the room. He gathered up a plate of bread and cheese from the kitchen and set it down before Bryn, who groaned with delight and reached for the food.

"None of that for you," Tamas said as he and Amory entered the house, arms laden with medical bags. "You might be sick when we pull that out."

"Well, I wouldn't want to waste it," Bryn said irritably, dropping his head into his hand. "Bowie, come here and eat something."

Bowie stood at the window, anxiously looking outside,

probably cataloguing escape routes, threats and viable weapons while simultaneously trying to battle his exhaustion. He was compulsively scratching his throat in what Aela was coming to understand was a nervous habit. At Bryn's order, he crossed the room, handing Aela a slice of bread and cheese, watching her take a bite before practically inhaling a slice of his own. Tangentially, Aela noted that Bowie's etiquette was impeccable for someone who'd grown up in the rough company of criminals in the forest. He always waited for Aela and Bryn to eat before starting his own food. It was a traditional custom in the west — elders ate first.

"Ewan, can you please take the boy out of here?" Tamas said. "This might become bloody."

Aela bit down on the urge to inform Tamas that it was a good day for Bowie if the bloodiest thing he saw was a physician patching up a non-fatal wound. But Bryn spoke up, "The boy has a name," he snapped. "And he can decide for himself."

Tamas, deftly unpacking his equipment, paused and looked at Bryn curiously. "Is he your …" Bryn and Bowie weren't blood relations, which was immediately apparent from their foreign appearances, but Aela understood why Tamas might wonder. Bryn was uniquely gifted at being a prick to everyone in his radius then turning around and doting on Bowie.

"He's my responsibility," Bryn replied quietly. He glanced at Bowie. "I'm assuming you want to stay and confirm I haven't died?"

Bowie nodded, his mouth full of bread.

"Then I hope for his sake that you're not going to scream bloody murder when I do this," Tamas told Bryn grimly. "Take off your shirt."

Wincing, Bryn obeyed, revealing the taut plane of his

sun-darkened stomach, which rose and fell shallowly as he fought the pain of the injury.

Tamas thoughtfully eyed the wound. "It's not lodged in there so deep that you'll bleed to death when I pull it out, but it's going to be painful."

"Of course it fucking is. Why would anything today be easy?" Bryn muttered tersely.

Carefully, Tamas wrapped a piece of cloth around the wood shard, braced both hands against it, and pulled. Aela looked away as Bryn cried out in pain, stifling the sound with a hand against his mouth. When she looked back, the bloodied wood was in Tamas's hand, and he pressed a piece of bunched-up fabric against the wound in Bryn's side.

Bryn gave another pained grunt. "You *bastard*."

"You mispronounced *thank you*," Tamas said cheerfully, switching out the bloodied cloth for a fresh one that Ewan had drenched in an odd-smelling liquid.

Tamas's mild disposition appeared to be increasingly irritating to Bryn, who wasn't used to having his adversarial jabs gently stymied by politeness. It would be almost comical if Aela's nervous system wasn't so tightly wound by the absurd discomfort of Bryn and Tamas sharing the same space.

"I'll stitch this up, and you'll be good as new," Tamas told Bryn.

Bryn looked around at Bowie, giving him a quick grin. "Told you I wasn't going to die. I'm impossible to kill."

Bowie's posture sagged. "Like a cockroach," he replied, but the tremor in his voice blunted the jibe.

"Perhaps now you can go and get cleaned up," Ewan suggested to Bowie. "We have enough water that you can bathe. There's a washroom upstairs, and Amory's gone out to heat some water for you." He looked at Aela and Bryn. "We have some spare clothes that should fit the two of you. This one on the other hand …" Ewan looked at Bowie intently, measuring him with his eyes. "One of the boys down the road might have something. I'll go and ask. Ah, here's Amory to take you upstairs."

Bowie hesitated, finding Bryn's gaze. Bryn dropped him a small, reassuring nod and the boy followed Amory, who hefted a bucket of steaming water towards the second floor.

Aela looked back to Bryn, whose teeth were gritted as Tamas tugged on a needle and thread, stitching the wound. The muscles of his torso flexed against the pain. He had the bulky physique of a fighter, muscle cording his abdomen and arms. Short, light hair dusted his chest, and a trail of it disappeared down beneath the line of his belt …

"See something you like?"

Aela's head snapped up. Bryn grinned wickedly as he watched her ogling him. He gave her a suggestive wink, and her face burned feverishly hot. "You should get some food in you."

It was more than a day since they'd eaten. Aela hadn't had a chance to think on it much. Now, she couldn't ignore the hunger pangs. Bryn was surely starving as well, but after what he'd been through, he didn't look thrilled by the idea of a meal.

"Run me through the town's defences," Bryn said to Tamas imperiously.

Aela dropped her head. Bryn said it like an order, even though he was meant to be one commoner casually addressing another. This was where his prior disinterest in Dunwyn's affairs did him a disservice. Bryn had no idea how people lived outside of the capital. Tamas looked up from his work in surprise.

"Got a sword?" he said. "Then you're it."

Aela explained, "The army was stationed here for a week after the war, until the steward sent for us all to return to the city."

"The steward?" Tamas repeated. "But isn't the king the one who —"

"The king's dead," Bryn snapped. If there was anything Tamas could have said to endear himself to Bryn even less, that was it.

Tamas stiffened. His eyes flicked to Aela, and he reached across the table to grasp her hand. "Aela, I'm so sorry," he told her softly.

Bryn looked down at their joined hands. "Are you going to finish stitching me up, or shall I do it myself?"

"That would be quite a talent," Tamas mused, still maddeningly unruffled by Bryn's attitude.

"What happened to you three?" Ewan asked, bustling back into the room with some spare clothes.

Bryn was gritting his teeth through the last of Tamas's stitches, so Aela replied. "Mercenaries. I meant what I said before. They might have followed us here."

"And I meant what *I* said," Ewan said calmly. "If they have, we'll take care of it."

Aela shook her head. "No, we need to leave as soon as possible. The last thing I want is to bring you any trouble."

"Nonsense," Ewan snapped. He jerked his head upstairs. "That little boy is starving and injured, and you all look as if you haven't slept in days. Take care of yourselves, for pity's sake."

"Ewan's right," Tamas said. "You should at least give Slate some time to recover from this injury."

Aela sighed, scrubbing her forehead with a grimy hand. They were right, of course. She didn't like it, but Bryn needed time. Bowie too. If she was honest with herself, it wasn't only the threat of danger that made the idea of staying in Hiver so unappealing. Milling around here listlessly struck her with more fear than the thought of fighting Araxa's gang.

Hiver was monotony, normalcy, everything she'd fled when she'd gone to Dunwald to join the army. It nudged at her, persistently needful, the urge to fight, to feel violence in her veins.

"You look awful," Ewan said. He put a gentle hand on her shoulder. "Go and wash up. You'll feel better."

"I'll bathe in the lake," Aela said. She needed time alone. Glancing at Bryn, she grabbed a bundle of clean clothes from Ewan. "See you soon."

It was still drizzling outside. A footfall landed lightly in the mud behind her. Tamas stepped over the threshold, following her into the street.

"Must feel odd being home again," he said, falling into step with her. His tone was so light that it was irritating. Anticipation jangled Aela's nerves. She'd been desperate to get this conversation over with, but now that they were here, she wished to be anywhere else.

"That's an understatement," she replied.

Silence drew out between them, compounding the strangeness. Aela felt awkward, and that in itself was exceedingly unusual. She'd never felt awkward around Tamas before their night together.

"What's between you and Slate?" Tamas blurted out, like he couldn't stop himself. Aela bristled. She'd been avoiding trying to figure that out for herself. She sure as hell wasn't ready to discuss it with Tamas.

"Why do you care?" she demanded defensively.

"You know why," Tamas replied quietly.

Aela shifted her feet. When she was mean to Tamas, she could hurt him more than anybody else could. She reminded herself to take a steadying breath.

"Tamas., I'm so sorry. I need you to know that what happened between us that night was —"

"Don't say it was a mistake, Aela," Tamas interrupted. "It wasn't a mistake for me. I knew exactly what it was for you at the time. I don't regret it, and I don't resent you for the way you feel. You've never once led me to believe you wanted anything more than friendship."

The stab of fury Aela felt went inwards this time. Tamas's steady, sincere tone made her feel worse than before. Damn his logical mind, his compassionate heart. Damn her for not being able to coax herself into making a smart choice. Loving Tamas would be so easy. He was handsome and smart, and he'd known her his whole life.

He'd also never murdered anyone.

Aela's heart hurt. It was more complicated than not feeling what Tamas felt. He represented a future that was entirely at odds with what Aela needed.

"You're my friend, and I'll always care about you. In another place, at another time, maybe things would be different between us. But this life in Hiver … it's what *you* want. It's not for me."

Tamas's gaze was filled with longing, but he kept a proper distance between them. "You won't ever come home for good, will you?" he said, resigned. Aela didn't reply. He already knew the answer. "What, you're a city girl now? Can't handle it here?"

"Shut up, funny man." Aela punched him in the arm. "I'm going to go bathe."

As she turned from Tamas, she glanced back at Amory and Ewan's house, where a figure ducked away from the window.

Twenty-Five

The sun dipped low in the sky as Aela slowly walked uphill and away from the village, taking the path back towards Bayeau. The rain had ceased for the moment. Beneath her feet, the muddy soil was a deep, healthy red. Aela couldn't remember if it had always been that colour. Maybe so much blood had been spilled on this land that it had seeped in, forever part of the earth.

She crouched down, digging her fingers into the muddy ground. In her mind's eye, she saw thousands of boots pounding into the dust, bodies falling, and the flare off a blade as steel caught the sunlight. Slashing axes, spears, and swords were all around. Everything moved so quickly that it was nearly impossible to distinguish friend from foe. She heard cries, shouted orders, pained screams. She was back there, standing on that battlefield, knowing what she had to do to end it.

The image changed. She walked across the field at Bayeau alone, Dunwyn's army at her back. Nielle's champion fighter stood before her. A shockwave rumbled through the lines of the Niellan army when she cut him down…

Just because I want to fight, doesn't mean I'm angry.

Why are you still lying?

Opening her eyes, Aela looked down at her shaking hand. Slick red soil stained her skin.

A splash nearby made her jolt. She stood and went down the other side of the hill.

Summer Lake was aptly named, warm year-round. Not hot like a spring but a pleasant tepidness. Aela used to swim here with Tamas, teasing him and laughing with abandon, neither of them giving any thought to the enemies beyond the hills.

The water was clear, glittering, the cloud-muted sunset casting golden rays across the surface. Emerging from the water was a shirtless figure with a distractingly muscular torso.

She must have been wandering, lost in thought, for a long time. Bryn had gone to the lake to bathe and was now standing waist-deep in the water, smoothing his wet hair back off his face. Muscles rippled across his bronzed arms and back. He looked like a fighter. If he hadn't killed Saban, the path Bryn would have taken was clear. A man with his own set of values, different from his father's, not better or worse. It was evident in the way he looked out for Bowie, in the way he strategised with Aela, even in the way he'd abdicated his responsibilities to Huntley, believing her capable of giving Dunwyans a better life than he could. He was a burgeoning leader, capable of taking on small challenges but not yet ready to face larger ones.

I would fight for him.

The thought startled Aela and saddened her. If things were different, Bryn might have made a good king, but there was no path forward for him as a leader.

He would always be an anarchist.

"I'm about to get out," Bryn called. "You can watch if you want to, but don't swoon and hit your head on something."

The playfulness in his voice sent warmth tingling through her lower back, the pleasant feeling chased by sudden, startled guilt at her voyeurism. Hastily, she stepped behind a nearby tree, pressing her back against the rough bark and chastising herself silently for leering at Bryn like a deviant. More quiet splashes. Bryn was probably stepping out of the lake to get dressed … What was he *wearing* right now? Her mind wandered into dangerous territory again.

She could turn around. He'd never actually said he didn't want her to…

Aela shook her head and tried to tell herself rationally that in the army she'd seen plenty of men in various states of undress … But Bryn was the prince … And he was *Bryn*.

"You know, back at the house you were looking me up and down like I was a whore in a harem. Now you're loitering in the shadows while I bathe? Anyone would think you're trying to take advantage of my virtue."

Bryn wiggled his eyebrows annoyingly as he appeared beside her shirtless, trousers undone, trailing laces. Droplets of water from his darkened and drenched hair dripped onto his tanned shoulders. The puckered skin around the stitched wound at his side was still red but no longer bleeding. Bryn brushed beads of water off his chest with the bunched-up shirt in his hand.

"What virtue?" Aela tried to focus on anything but the shape of his upper body. She cleared her throat. "You shouldn't be out here alone. Araxa's men could still be looking for us."

He folded his arms over his chest, his lip curling, probably because he knew exactly what that did to his biceps. "If I'm in danger out here, then so are you. We were beginning to worry. You were gone for ages."

"Amory told you to come out here?"

"Ewan did. He said he was worried about you, but if I'm

honest, I think it was a ruse to make me bathe. I doubt he's ever had so much mud in his house before."

Aela grinned. "Probably not."

Bryn slung his shirt over his shoulder. Aela had to concentrate very hard to keep her eyes on his face. He nodded at the lake. "Your turn."

"We've talked about this. It's not a spectator sport." Aela sat down beside the water and pulled off her boots. She pulled off her fabric headband and combed her fingers through her hair, shaking the sun-streaked waves loose about her face … and looked up.

Bryn stood frozen, staring at her.

His lips were slightly parted, and the intensity of his gaze quieted everything. The intimacy of his eyes on her was like being back in the cave behind the waterfall, hidden away from the rest of the world. "Gods," he whispered. "You can't do that while I'm watching. I'll lose my mind."

"Does that work on the other girls?" The joke was meant to put distance between her and Bryn to make Aela feel grounded again, but it was the wrong thing to say. A tiny, wounded crease appeared between Bryn's brows, and he looked away.

Avoiding eye contact, he lowered himself down beside her, wincing slightly. His shoulder brushed hers, and Aela's fingers jerked unsteadily as she unbuckled her weapons belt.

"How's the wound?" she asked more casually than she felt.

"Better, since your lover stitched me up." Maybe Bryn was trying a little too hard to sound casual as well.

Aela tossed her boots aside with a little more force than was necessary. "I saw you spying on us, back in town."

He snorted. "Spying? You weren't exactly subtle out there in the middle of the street."

"We were talking." She mentally kicked herself for being so defensive.

"You're in love with him."

Aela turned, irritated that he would presume to identify feelings that she'd struggled to name for years. "Tamas is my friend."

"I don't like him."

Aela feigned surprise. "But you were so sweet to him!"

"Very funny."

"You're being ridiculous." Aela jerked to her feet. "What's between Tamas and I is none of your business."

"It is," Bryn retorted, rising to look her in the eye.

"Oh?" Aela folded her arms across her chest, giving Bryn a challenging look. "How's that?"

"I'm not going to lose my army's commander because she wants to run off and get married to some country boy."

"*Your* army's commander?" The miniscule part of her that wasn't infuriated noted that Bryn had never taken ownership of the kingship like this before.

Bryn, perhaps startled by the gravity of what he'd said, cleared his throat awkwardly. "I know I don't deserve the throne," he admitted slowly. "I don't know what the people will have to say about being ruled by … someone like me. I want to do what's right. For once."

Aela's body slackened with relief. Hearing him submit to the responsibility of his bloodline ignited a spark of hope she'd once believed doused. Still …

"It isn't going to be easy," she warned.

Silence stretched between them. In it was everything that Aela couldn't say. Even if Huntley's partnership with Nielle could be stopped, would Dunwyn ever accept Bryn as the rightful king after what he'd done?

"I know." Bryn broke away from Aela's gaze, looking over at the lake. "Are you going in?"

Aela frowned. She went to the lake's edge, leaning down to run her fingers through the clear water. It was as beautiful as she'd remembered. Next minute, she was toppling, fully-clothed, into Summer Lake. Surfacing, she pushed at the strands of sopping hair that had fallen across her face and saw Bryn sniggering at her.

"Sorry," he said. "You were really dirty."

"And you're really dead!" Aela reared up out of the water, wrapping her fingers around Bryn's wrist and exerting a tug. Bryn toppled in after her. Surfacing, he shook his long hair like a wet dog, flicking Aela with a shower of droplets. He wore that young, mischievous grin that wasn't soaked with malice or sarcasm. The smile that had first taken her breath away when it had transformed his face, lighting his eyes.

Aela was suddenly conscious that she was still holding onto Bryn's wrist underwater, becoming hyper aware of how his skin felt in all the places it touched hers. Hot, smooth, right.

She should let go, but it felt too good. The quality of her grip changed, their fingers becoming intertwined. Bryn's expression was changing too. He didn't look away from her.

"What?" Aela asked, trying to keep her tone light.

"What's it like?" he said quietly. "Coming home."

"Like?" she repeated, unsure she'd caught his meaning.

He looked up at the hills that surrounded them. "You grew up here. You know these hills, the town, this lake." He drew his free hand lightly over the water, ripples dancing across the surface. "There must be memories everywhere."

Aela understood. "There's nothing to be feared in memories.

They help us to learn so that we do better next time."

Bryn shook his head, abandoning pretence. "I'm not sure the people will see it that way."

"You're their prince," Aela said quietly as much to convince herself as Bryn. She drew their joined hands out of the water, brushing her thumb lightly across his knuckles. He shivered. "Eventually, they'll come to know that you're a good person. They'll trust you to make the right decisions with everything that's important."

Bryn sighed, stirring the thin strands of hair around his face so that Aela caught a momentary glimpse of the cut on his head, the exhaustion in his eyes. Even worn out and battered, he was beautiful. They had moved closer together in the water. Close enough that she could read his expression, less guarded than usual. He said, "*I* don't even know if I'm a good person. And I sure as hell don't trust myself to make the right decisions. How can I, after —"

"Is that why you agreed to join Splinter? So you didn't have to give orders, only follow them?"

Bryn shrugged, staring down at their joined hands. "One of the reasons. But Splinter makes a lot of bad calls."

"He makes some good ones too," Aela said fairly. Splinter's orders weren't honourable, but they were necessary to keep a band of outlaws profitable and away from each other's throats.

"Bryn, you know that your father would want you to live in a way that makes you happy. But you can't keep going as you have been. You can't continue to shirk the responsibility of your bloodline because you're afraid. I've seen the way you look after Bowie. I've seen the way you fight, with both courage and mercy. You care about people's lives, even the lives of your enemies. You make the right decisions more often than you give yourself credit for. You need to trust yourself."

"Like you do? Launching yourself into danger without a second thought?" There was a hint of amusement in Bryn's voice, but he still didn't look up.

"I know what I'm capable of," she said defensively.

Now, he did meet her gaze, and there was fiery disbelief in his eyes. "That's bullshit, Aela, and you know it."

She drew back, caught off guard by the sharpness in his tone. She tried to pull her hand away from his, but he held on, kept his fingers interlocked with hers.

"I meant what I said back in Dunwald," he went on. "I remember what you were like in training. You weren't the best because of how you could use a blade. You were the best because of how you could *think*. You haven't been fighting like that recently. You're not fighting to win. You're fighting because you're angry."

"I'm not ..."

Bryn scoffed. "Come on. I don't care if you lie to me about it, but don't lie to yourself. You deserve better than that."

Aela couldn't take anymore. Wringing herself loose of Bryn's hand, she ducked under the water, welcoming the silence, allowing it to drown out the clamouring, incessant thoughts that prevailed when her head was above the surface. But there were hands on her arms, pulling her upwards, smoothing the soaking strands of hair off her face. She opened her eyes, and her heart stopped. Bryn's face was inches from hers. His hands trailed down her cheeks, his fingertips gently lifting her chin so she'd meet his gaze, as if she could look anywhere else.

"Tell the truth," he whispered.

Spellbound in the depths of Bryn's dark eyes and lost in his touch, something inside her that she'd believed immovable rattled loose. Suddenly she was speaking, unchecked.

"Fine. I'm angry." It was inexplicably easier to breathe. "At Bayeau, I was so angry with King Marcus. Every moment, I was furious with him. I could barely think about anything else. It was the force that drove my hand, every time I struck someone down in battle. Even as I was killing them, I blamed *Marcus* for sacrificing their lives to get vengeance for his son. But since I've come home, all I can think about is fighting."

Now that she was talking, she couldn't stop herself. For the first time, she could see her feelings clearly, as if giving voice to them was translating them into a language she understood.

She went on, "What I did in the war wasn't *noble*. I wasn't thinking about doing things that were right or good. I fought on that field every day because I love to fight. I cut down Nielle's champion and celebrated his death. I became the Reaper of Dunwyn because the thing I'm best at in the world is death. I'm a killer. I'm like him. I hate the way that I am, like I hate King Marcus."

Bryn shook his head. Behind the sadness in his eyes was powerful certainty. "Aela, no. You're not like him. When you volunteered for single combat in the war, you did it to save the lives of thousands of soldiers, Dunwyans and Niellans both. Without you, imagine what would have happened. Bayeau would still be a battleground to this day." Bryn's thumb slid across Aela's damp cheek. "That wasn't the act of someone whose only goal is death. You know your purpose. It's one of the things I —"

"People have paid in blood for my fucking *purpose.*"

"I know how you feel. Believe me, I *know*. But you're trying to do the right thing; you're allowed to forgive yourself for making mistakes. Everyone makes mistakes." Bryn was looking at her as if she was the only person in the world. The energy that buzzed around them was supercharged. He leaned in, and Aela could feel heat and desire pulsing from him in equal, tantalising measure. "In fact," he breathed. "I think I'm about to make one right now."

"No." Aela shook her head as she closed the remaining distance between them. "I don't think you are."

The kiss was an explosion of sensation. Their lips met, and Bryn drew his fingertips down her arms then wrapped his own arms around her waist, pulling her close. The bare skin of his torso slid against hers where her shirt rode up in the water. She knew, somewhere in the back of her mind, that the cut at her side was stinging and that Bryn's own wound was probably hurting him too, but the pain was blunt and distant.

Her pulse thrummed as Bryn's lips pressed harder against hers, their kiss deepening. His hands travelled over the curve of her hips, smoothing away the bitterness that had cloaked her body and dug in like fingernails beneath her skin. Bryn's fingers gripped her desperately. In his touch was a hunger to eliminate any space between them, for as much of their bodies to touch as possible. Aela gasped into his mouth, wrapping her legs around his waist as he lifted her up. She cupped her hand around the back of his neck, knotting her fingers into his hair …

She gripped the Niellan champion's coarse hair, wrenching his head back to expose his throat. As the Dunwyan army roared, she drew her blade clean through his neck and took the full weight of his head in her hand. He was dead.

Other images barreled into her mind, crashing into the first like a tidal wave, roiling together. King Saban embracing her before she'd departed for war … Her hands brushing over the bloodstain on his mattress … Pressing her palms against a soldier's gaping wound futilely on the battlefield at Bayeau.

"Aela?" the soldier called.

Panic and childlike confusion drenched his voice, honorifics abandoned in his final moments. Her name was his last word. Blood poured from his body, soaking her skin …

Had Bryn's hands been soaked in blood when he'd killed his father?

"Aela?"

She jerked backwards. Bryn's expression was dazed as he looked down at her. He tried to lean in again, but she flinched away, unwrapping her legs and taking an unsteady step back on the uneven bed of the lake. Pain chased the confusion from Bryn's face.

She didn't need to tell him. They both knew. Saban was dead and there was no reason behind it. If the king was alive, Aela would still be a soldier, and Huntley would never have had the opportunity to take the throne. She couldn't say any of that. Instead, she turned away.

"It's getting dark. You shouldn't be out in the forest. It's dangerous." She got out of the water as Bryn stood frozen. "I'll see you back at the house."

Twenty-Six

A fresh torrent of rain rolled in as Aela took the long route back to town, walking slowly across the muddy hills as the sky darkened, in an attempt to clear her head. She couldn't stop reliving the kiss. The pressure of Bryn's lips lingered on hers. It felt like his warm, wonderful hands were still exploring her body.

It had been pure and perfect and so, so right. But those same calloused hands that had been gentle on her body had driven a dagger into Saban's heart, stealing the life from him. For a few wild moments, she'd been able to separate the Bryn who was tender and handsome and sweet from the Bryn who had killed his father.

But when the haze of attraction cleared, there was no separating them.

Her heart ached, because there was a treacherous part of her wanted nothing more than to kiss him again, and for the kiss to deepen, to transform into more. But there was undeniably another part of her that yearned for revenge, to cut down the man who had taken the life of her king, the only father figure she'd ever known.

She paused outside the door to Amory and Ewan's home,

a hand on the doorknob, gathering herself to face Bryn. He would never forgive himself for what he'd done to Saban, she knew that. She doubted she could hate him more than he hated himself.

Steeling herself, she softly pushed open the door and stepped inside.

It was quiet, and the small, simple space felt cosy, protected from the cold, wet weather outside. A fire crackled in the corner, and beside it were two figures. Bowie sat on the floor amidst a tangle of blankets. He wore clean clothes, and his hair was mussed, his eyes wild, as if he'd been startled awake. Bryn, cross-legged before him, reached out and smoothed down Bowie's unruly curls.

"You're all right," Bryn said quietly. "It was only a bad dream."

Bowie's eyes focused on Bryn. "Did I ... call out for you?"

Bryn gave him a small smile. "Yeah."

Bowie flushed. "Sorry."

"I don't mind. That was an impressive throw, back at the castle." A teasing edge crept into Bryn's voice. "Did you think about hitting me instead?"

Bowie tensed. "Shut up. I wouldn't."

"I know. I know you." Bryn paused, then he gently said, "Do you understand why I didn't tell you? About me?" A nod. Bryn sighed. "I'm sorry for lying to you. I thought I was doing the right thing, but that doesn't matter. I hurt you, and you're angry with me."

"I'm not allowed to be angry with you," Bowie mumbled, avoiding Bryn's gaze. "You're going to be the king."

"That's not how it works." Bryn shifted restlessly on the floor. "I don't get a say about when you'll forgive me, or if you will.

If someone has ordered you in the past to change the way you feel, they were being unfair."

"A king can make any order he wants."

"No," Bryn said firmly. "No one can tell you how to feel."

There was another long silence. Bowie looked down at his hands awkwardly, frowning as if Bryn had posed him a weighty existential question.

Bryn drew in a slow breath and said, "I'm going to figure this out and take back the throne." The declaration came slowly, as if he was trying it out. "When I do, I want you to come and live with me in the castle."

The colour drained from Bowie's face. "You wouldn't want that."

"Why not? You think I'll find out how annoying you are? Believe me, little man, that ship's sailed."

Bowie didn't laugh. His head was down, his dark hair falling across his face. "I don't think it's a good idea."

Bryn looked a little hurt. "Why not? You'll have anything you want. You can study properly with a tutor. I know that court will be different from anywhere else you've lived, but you don't need to be scared."

"I'm not scared of living at court."

"Then what? You're not going back to live with Splinter."

Bowie looked up at Bryn, and Aela tried to read the expression on his face. It was conflicted, concerned, perhaps even afraid. The quality of the air felt fragile, as if one wrong word would cause the whole room to shatter like glass.

"I have to tell you something," Bowie whispered.

Another painful silence followed. Eventually, Bryn said, "Bowie, what?"

Bowie looked away again. He swallowed hard then shook his

head. "When you go back to the city to take the throne, I want to help."

"No," Bryn replied immediately.

Moodily, Bowie jerked his head at the front door. "*She* gets to go."

Aela sighed. Of course he'd noticed her. She shut the door as Bryn met her gaze for a heartbeat, then looked away.

She said, "It's my fight too, Bowie. It isn't yours."

Bryn looked conflicted. He rose from the floor, coming to Aela's side. Unsaid words thrummed between them. Aela felt the ghost touch of his bare skin against hers as she'd wrapped her legs around him. She shivered.

Ducking his head, Bryn whispered, "What are we going to do with him? He can't go back to Splinter, and we can't leave him here. What if Araxa's gang comes looking for him?"

"We can leave him with Walter," Aela suggested.

"That barman?"

"I believe he cares about Bowie. If we … if things don't go the way we want them to, he'll give Bowie a home."

Bryn gave Aela a long look. "Then that's the best place for him. Until I can get Huntley off the throne, anyone who's with me will be considered a traitor, and I'm sure you've gathered that criminals aren't treated as mercifully in the steward's court as they were in my father's."

There was something pleading in his tone, and Aela heard what he didn't say. She would be killed if she was caught helping him.

"Don't send me away. I can help you!" Bowie scrambled to his feet, his deep blue eyes brimming with desperation.

Bryn's gaze softened. Bowie only had to turn that sweet, pleading look on him for a moment, and he melted like butter.

"Go back to sleep, Bowie," Aela cut in before Bryn could waver.

"But you don't *know* everything —"

"It can wait."

Muttering a Niellan curse under his breath, Bowie turned his back on them and stormed to his makeshift bed by the fire. He pulled something from underneath the blankets, a stack of folded, limp papers that were clearly waterlogged. He stalked to the table, sitting down and delicately opening the papers, smoothing them out one by one.

"You're supposed to be sleeping," Bryn told him irritably.

Bowie glared. "Don't talk to me like I'm a stupid kid."

"You're not stupid," Bryn said wearily, sitting down opposite Bowie. "But you *are* a kid."

"But *you're* the ones who don't know what's going on," Bowie protested. "Look."

"What am I looking at?" Aela said, dropping down beside Bryn. He tensed when their shoulders brushed.

There were numbers on the pages, an order of twelve barrels of grey dream. All of the papers strewn across the table bore similar figures. On each one, Araxa's name was scrawled in smudged ink. There were two more signatures beside hers, a large set of initials so big they took up almost a third of each page: A.B.

"Alvine? And ..."

The other horribly familiar mark made Aela's stomach drop. She reached out and traced the steward's insignia, made by the ring Huntley wore on her finger.

"She knew about the soldiers," Bryn breathed.

Aela shook her head. "She didn't just know. She was part of it. She helped Alvine pay for the drugs."

Looking stricken, Bowie pulled a final page from the bottom of the stack. On this one, there were no numbers. Silence fell as they read the page. Aela's heart sank.

Bryn said, "This is a bilateral treaty between Nielle and Dunwyn. It signs Dunwyn's entire territory over to Nielle. Huntley can't *do* this. A steward doesn't have the right —"

"She's not dividing the land between citizens of Dunwyn, Bryn. She's surrendering it to another nation, and technically she's got every right to do that. Her job exists specifically to keep the peace, protect the people of Dunwyn. Remember what she said in Eterre about her partnership with Alvine? She's justifying this agreement with Nielle as an effort to make peace."

Bryn scoffed. "Except there's no fucking way this will be peaceful. Dunwyans won't sit by while their lands are signed over to Nielle and they're forced to bow to an invader ... Not that a civilian uprising would stand any chance without the army to back them."

"Some soldiers would fight," Aela murmured, thinking of Mason, Chase, and Landon.

But with no resources, no infrastructure to back them, there was only one way it would end. Aela's blood turned cold.

Bryn sifted through the pages again. "Why would Araxa have this?"

"I'd bet anything she stole it from Huntley and Alvine. They have armies at their disposal, all the resources of two kingdoms," Aela said. "Araxa would have wanted to make sure she was protected. Besides, it's not like she needed to cover her tracks. Everyone already knows she's a criminal." Aela exhaled slowly as the weight of the plot sank in. "Alvine and Huntley must've been planning this for years." Her mind flashed back to

Huntley's desperate, sudden arrival in Dunwald years ago, and her gut roiled. She met Bryn's disconcerted gaze. "Huntley was in Eterre when the Niellan prince went missing."

Bryn shook his head. "She was my father's closest ally. You really think she would have conspired to murder a little boy?"

Aela looked back down at the steward's insignia on the brittle page. "Bryn, I don't think your father knew her at all." She let her finger slide over the initials: A.B. "I still don't understand though. Huntley isn't the type to shy away from power, and she has to know the Dunwyan people would rather have her rule than swallow this manner of *peace treaty*. Why would she go through all of this to obtain the throne only to immediately relinquish control to Alvine?"

Bowie was watching her steadily. "You haven't worked it out yet? She doesn't care about taking power for herself, as long as —"

A terrible scream cut through the night. Aela froze then went and yanked open the door, seeking the source of the commotion.

Furious red and orange flames rose from a home on the far side of the town. The fire illuminated the hillside, where dozens of shadowy figures ran or rode on horseback down towards the town. Other figures flooded the streets, fleeing amid panicked cries. With all her attention outside on the terrified townspeople, sudden movement at Aela's side made her jump. Bowie stared out, his hand braced on the door frame. His face was white.

"It's them," he murmured.

Amory came sprinting downstairs, a blade in his hand. "Aela, you need to go."

Aela eyed his weapon, remembering what Tamas said earlier.

You've got a sword? You're it.

"What are you going to do with that?" she asked him, a foolish question. A sword only had one use.

"Aela." Bryn grabbed the bag Amory handed him and shoved their things inside. He took hold of Bowie's wrist and pulled him to the door. Amory stood aside to let them pass. "Come on."

Aela dithered. Guilt slashed through her at the thought of leaving her friends and family in trouble. Outside, the flames were getting closer, the screaming and the clashes of steel were louder. With her village burning before her eyes, it was no choice at all. She grabbed Ewan's weapon from where it hung near the door and shoved outside, taking off down the street.

Behind her, Bryn yelled her name, then his voice faded, and chaos swallowed her.

The sensory overload was the same as she remembered. The heat from the burning houses, the cries of distress, armed fighters bursting from the smoke to attack her neighbours, the indecisive frustration of not knowing who to help first. Blindly through the dark haze of burning wood, she raced to Tamas's home.

A scream ahead called her to fight. Armed with a sword and dagger, Tamas stood outside his house, his mother wide-eyed on the threshold as he stared one of Araxa's mercenaries down. The roof was on fire, and embers dripped onto the ground around him. He staggered back as the man swiped his axe, narrowly missing Tamas's belly. Aela aimed and launched her sword, overarm, at the mercenary. Her weapon speared straight through his throat, glistening where the bloodied blade protruded from his skin. Tamas's head whipped around, his mouth gaping in silent shock.

Aela pulled her weapon from the dead mercenary's throat.

"Go!" she called to Tamas.

Tamas started towards the hills with his mother. Behind them, she saw silhouetted in black, backlit by flames, a woman fall to her knees beside a small body. Chest aching, she moved forward.

A yell close behind Aela made her whirl. Bryn had followed her, unarmed, into the flames and fighting. He collided bodily with a mercenary, grabbing the man's raised arm and arresting the swing of his sword. Two more steps and he would have run her through. Even without a weapon, Bryn was a formidable fighter, taking the mercenary down with non-lethal precision, disarming him and driving his boot into the side of the man's head to knock him unconscious. He looked up at her, wild-eyed.

"Gods, Aela!" he said breathlessly. "That was too close. We need to go."

"No!" Aela said. "I won't leave them to fight without me!"

"*Aela*," he said again urgently. "Fighting right now is a quick fix. If we stop Huntley, we can end this properly."

Trapped in Bryn's dark, pleading gaze, her resolve shattered. She let him take her hand and lead the way. They both froze at the sound of a fresh cry that Aela knew too well.

"*Amory! Aela!*" It was Ewan.

Aela's heart twisted. She pulled her hand from Bryn's and turned back towards her home. The roof was burning, flames arcing up into the blackness of the sky. A mercenary stood outside, lighting sticks from a torch, throwing them up onto the roof, through the windows. Another advanced on Ewan and Bowie.

"Come here, boy," he growled at Bowie. "Don't let these

poor people suffer in your place."

He fell as Aela and Bryn approached, an unlikely weapon embedded between his eyes. Ewan was unarmed besides a handful of kitchen knives. Bowie turned towards Aela and Bryn. His eyes snapped wide, and he let a knife of his own fly. It sailed between Aela and Bryn into the leg of an approaching mercenary, who Aela dispatched efficiently before turning back to her home.

Her grip on her weapon went slack. The entire house was engulfed, burning out of control. The screams around her were drowned out by her own sharp breaths. Her eyes stung, not only from the smoke. She had lived her entire childhood within those walls, the last relic of her innocence.

Amory came barrelling past Aela, running without hesitation into the burning house. Screaming his name, Aela launched after him, but Bryn grabbed her waist.

"Don't!" he said. His lips brushed her hair as he held onto her desperately. "Aela, please."

Amory burst outside, the orange glow of flames behind him, weapon in one hand and a new object in the other.

"Here, take this. Don't open it now."

He pressed something towards Aela. The warm, hard contours of a wooden box sank into her palm. Plain except for a raised carving of her name on top, it was sealed shut with red wax.

"It's from your father. I'm sorry, I should have given it to you sooner, but when I saw you after Bayeau I thought it would have been …" He gripped her shoulders. "You need to go."

Aela sagged in his grasp. The heat of their burning home leaped outwards, searing her face. There was no ignoring the screams. Years ago, the best option was to stand and fight, but Bryn was right, damn him. The mercenaries would keep coming unless someone cut off the head of the snake.

Ewan took off in the direction of fresh screams. Bryn grabbed Bowie, leading him off into the darkness. Aela turned back to Amory imploringly.

"Please," she begged. "Come with us."

Amory drew her to him, pressing his lips to her forehead. "Open that box when you're safe … and in private."

Aela drew in an unsteady breath. How did you say goodbye to someone you'd known your whole life? How did you thank someone for a lifetime of sacrifices? It could be the last time she ever saw Amory and Ewan. Despair welled painfully in her chest, threatening to overcome her completely. She wrapped her arms around Amory, and he squeezed her tightly in return.

"I'd tell you to be strong, Aela, but you've never needed anyone to tell you that. It's in your blood."

As she pulled away, she tried to fix him with the same firm look she used to give her soldiers. "Don't do anything stupid."

Feigning affront, Amory replied, "Me?"

He squeezed her hand, and she mapped the familiar calluses on his palm one more time. Tucking the box into her pocket, she turned her back on her burning village and fled after Bryn and Bowie.

Twenty-Seven

Aela wasn't in the mood to talk. Her emotions were stormy, wracked with guilt. Her thoughts lingered in Hiver, on a fight that was unwinnable for a handful of Borderlanders.

She shouldn't have left them. Amory and Ewan were two of the strongest fighters in the village, but she knew, painfully, that they couldn't hold out in battle against the ruthlessness of mercenaries with a single, deadly purpose. She'd left them to be slaughtered.

Bryn had adeptly taken stock of her mood, allowing her to march out in front of them as they fled through the night. As dawn broke, they stole a pair of horses from a secluded farm and rode in silence, Bowie asleep against Bryn's chest.

Making camp in the nights that followed was habitual and silent. Bowie collected firewood then tended to the horses. Aela lit the fire. Bryn ned rabbits the way Aela had taught him – their usual, meagre meal.

Aela's dark mood lingered for a week, but as she slotted more sticks into the fire on their fifth night, she finally broke her silence.

"This is all well and good, you want to return and take the throne, but do you have any idea how you're going to prove Huntley's treachery?"

Bryn paused with his knife raised over the rabbit and huffed out a breath, looking sheepish.

"That I haven't quite figured out yet."

"We can't exactly extract a written confession from Huntley."

"That was very far down on my list of options."

Aela fixed him with an unamused look. Bryn's smart-mouthing was unhelpful. It was a reminder of exactly why it would be difficult to convince the Dunwyan council of nobles that he was more than the rogue Huntley had made him out to be. He had a lifetime's worth of bad behaviour to contend with.

He looked over his shoulder. Bowie had taken the horses to drink at a stream, but Bryn still lowered his voice.

"She doesn't know that we know everything," Bryn offered. "We may not be killed on sight."

"She knows we've seen her swanning around Eterre with the Niellan steward like our countries weren't just at war. And Alvine all but confessed to us that she murdered the Niellan prince. You'd better believe that every anarchist in Underground will be waiting to kill us." She prodded the fire impatiently. "We need proof beyond a piece of paper. We need ..." They needed something to corroborate the story. Something to force a misstep from Huntley, to trap her into admitting her treachery. Someone who knew what she'd done ... "We need to talk to Splinter."

Bryn gave Aela a look of disbelief and set his knife back to the rabbit carcass, vigorously giving physical expression to his frustration. "What the hell do I have to offer that'll stop him from skewering me on the point of his sword at the first opportunity?"

"I actually have an idea about that. You're going to hate it."

Bryn snorted. "I always hate your plans."

They fell back into a silence that reminded Aela of the uncomfortable tension that had existed between them during those first tentative days of travel together. She hated it, but she had no idea what to say to fix it.

"Are we going to talk about it?' Bryn asked quietly.

Aela looked up. Bowie was still off with the horses. "About what?" she asked, as if she didn't already know.

"I need to know," Bryn said urgently, his eyes pleading over the fire. "If things don't go the way we want them to, if we can't win this fight, I have to know that *you* at least can —" He swallowed hard, gesturing at Aela. "Even when you were in Anarchist Underground, you carried the king's ring. I know he was like a father to you. You think I don't? You were everything to him that I should have been."

"Bryn, I can't —"

"You can't talk about it now or you can't forgive me?" Bryn interrupted. "Aela, I need to know if you'll ever see me as anything but a murderer."

"I know I said it wasn't, but what happened between us at Hiver was a mistake," she said before she could stop herself. He looked like she'd slammed a door shut in his face, startled, hurt, and confused.

"A mistake," Bryn repeated. "I'm sorry. If I was presumptuous, or if I did anything to make you feel like ..."

Aela averted her gaze. "No. Bryn, it wasn't that. After everything that's happened ... I can't, all right?"

"Everything that's happened." Bryn's tone was dull. He

understood, and his hopelessness was worse than if he'd been angry or sad. The expression on his face was that of a man facing the inevitable. "I understand." Depressingly resigned, he stared for a moment at the knife in his hand, shifted his grip, and let it thud to the earth. "I wish I could at least tell you *why*, but I can't. I *can't*. All I can say is that I regret it. You have no idea how much I regret it."

"I know," Aela whispered. "I wish …" She couldn't wish away Saban's death or the blood on Bryn's hands, neither of them could. There was no point pretending otherwise.

★★★

"**B**ack so soon!"

Walter's imposing form had been visible at the inn's front door for a full five minutes before they drew up to the dingy building. He looked thrilled as he greeted them out in the road, the spiderweb tattoo on his cheek distorted by the enormous grin on his meaty face. The sun was still high in the sky, but Aela felt utterly exhausted. She was ready to eat a hearty meal of Walter's surprisingly good stew and fall into bed.

Taking the reins of Bryn's horse, Walter glanced up at Bowie, who looked as if he was about to topple from the horse and fall asleep in the dust. "Have you allowed the boy to sleep recently?" Walter asked Bryn, his eyes narrowed disapprovingly. He examined the fading bruises on Bowie's face. "Who've you been scrapping with?"

"Best you don't ask," Bryn replied grimly.

Walter shook his head. "Bloody troublemakers, the lot of you. Get inside and I'll make you some food. My assistant will take care of the horses."

"Assistant?" Bowie said warily.

"A new hire," Walter said. "Actually, he arrived here right after you left. Bit of a troubled fellow, but then I've always had a soft spot for that sort." Walter winked at Bowie, put his fingers to his lips and trilled a loud, sharp whistle. "Aran!"

A figure emerged from the stable. It took Aela a moment to recall where she'd seen the man before, as he was considerably cleaner now, beard trimmed and hair cut neatly. It was only when he smiled, revealing a row of jagged rotten teeth, and Aela heard Bowie's startled gasp that she realised.

Aela's heart ached for the rest of the Dunwyan soldiers who had been confined at Hiver. Aran was the only one who had gotten out with his life. Aela resisted the impulse to run and embrace him, relieved that at least one of Araxa's victims had escaped that hell, fearing what he'd say when he found out. The others were dead. Aela had failed.

"Woah," Bryn murmured, sliding from the saddle as he stared at Aran. "It can't be."

"It is," Bowie said as he dismounted beside Bryn. The boy stared up at Walter, eyes wide. "You made more?"

Walter held up his hands. "I know you said I shouldn't tell anyone, but there was a life at stake." He chuckled heartily and clapped Bowie on the back so hard he staggered. "It works, kid! It actually works!"

Bowie was still staring open-mouthed at Aran, who had gone still at the sight of them. Aran's visceral fear of Bowie in the forest, his reaction to a Niellan, hadn't made sense then. Aela swung herself down from her horse and went towards him.

"Do you know who I am?" she asked in a low voice.

Aran's gaze snapped to Aela. He looked guilty, as if they were back at training and she'd caught him daydreaming when he should have been paying attention. He swallowed, inclining his head. "Commander," he said, "I need you to know, whatever I said and did before, it was only because …"

"I understand," Aela said. It was difficult to speak through the tightness in her throat. "I went to Hiver. I saw —"

Aran's eyes went wide. "Did they … did the others make it out?"

Aela forced herself to hold Aran's gaze. "No," she replied honestly. "I'm sorry, soldier."

Aran nodded. He knew. "There wouldn't have been any hope for me if not for Walter. I think they only let me go from Hiver because they thought I was too far gone. But with these brews, I'm starting to feel well again, like myself." Aran glanced at Walter, who approached with Bowie and Bryn, leading the horses. "Walter's a great man."

Walter snorted. "Don't know if I'd go that far. Let's get you three inside. I'll see if I can rustle up some clean clothes. You'll need to wash up before you eat or you'll scare away all my customers. And that's saying something, considering they're all derelicts."

As it transpired, the discarded clothing that Walter had managed to fish out of the depths of his trunk for Aela was a dress. It was in the current popular style, a sand-coloured garment with short, puffed sleeves that fell off her shoulders, a light underskirt and a brown leather belt to cinch her waist. It was standard fare for most Dunwyan women, who wore an iteration of the style every day of their lives. Aela, on the other hand, cast her mind back and decided that she hadn't worn a dress since she'd joined the army at sixteen.

It wasn't that she didn't like dresses; actually, she loved the way she looked in the garment. It gave her an air of femininity that was impossible to achieve in military attire or the functional fighting gear she'd donned since moving into Splinter's manor. She even untied the fabric restraining the wispy curls from her face, allowing them to fall loose. Her short brown waves were a little matted since she didn't have a brush, but freeing them felt good.

Feeling sensible, she tarnished the aesthetic by buckling a sword belt around her waist, grateful that Walter had given them free reign to select from his disturbingly large stash of confiscated weapons. Before handing her pile of filthy clothing off to Aran for a wash, she rummaged through the rags, pulling out the box that Amory had given her and tucking it into her skirt. Something rattled inside.

She slipped out of the washroom and into the bedroom that Walter had offered them. After Bowie had bathed, he'd disappeared off somewhere with his characteristic lack of communication. If he was any other child, Aela would have assumed he was asleep somewhere. Instead, she figured he was probably leaning over a flame in the kitchen obsessing about the grey dream antidote with Walter.

That left her alone in the room with Bryn. Sitting on the bed, he looked up as she entered. His lips parted slightly with clear shock, and a flush crept across his face, all the way down beneath the collar of his shirt.

"Will you be angry if I comment on your appearance?" Bryn asked, and there was no disguising the husky desire in his voice.

"Not if you give me a compliment," Aela replied, feeling self-indulgent.

Bryn rose, stopping a careful distance away as if with great effort. "You look…" His voice was like a soft touch. "You look the way you always look. Beautiful. And I bet you could still fight better than anyone. You'd probably find a way to strangle your opponent with your skirt. I'm sure you've thought about all the ways it could be used as a weapon."

It wasn't the compliment Aela had been expecting. She couldn't help smiling. "The belt's better for strangulation," she told him. "I've thought about it."

It was meant to be a joke, but her voice came out shaky with adrenaline. She was suddenly aware of the proximity between them. It was the first time they'd been alone together since Summer Lake. She'd told Bryn that was a mistake, but when it was just the two of them in the quiet, intimate solitude of this room, it was difficult to focus on the reasons why. Bryn took a slow step closer. He could reach out and touch her if he wanted to, but he didn't.

"Aran got out," he said softly. "He's going to live."

Aela looked away hurriedly. Her throat hurt as she tried to push down the sudden urge to weep. Beneath her grief was a strangely tangled sensation, anger mixed with warmth at Bryn's ability to see into the darkest depths of her mind. His voice wrapped around the aching shards of her heart like an embrace she felt guilty for craving.

"Don't do that," Bryn ordered gently. "Don't push down all of the terrible things. Denying what you feel won't make you stronger. And I can't keep watching you put yourself in danger just so you'll feel something other than pain. It's breaking you, and you know it. The rush you feel when you risk yourself is a distraction, nothing more. You need to let someone in. It's the only way you'll heal."

Aela still couldn't look at Bryn. It took all her power not to break down. Beneath it all, she was still angry, but she was fearful too. Bryn didn't understand. She hadn't needed anyone to carry her burdens for her through the war. She couldn't remember needing anyone since leaving home at sixteen.

Except maybe that wasn't true. She couldn't believe she'd ever thought Bryn was without feeling. He had a way of holding a mirror up to her heart, reflecting the truth. And the truth was that she *had* needed someone but hadn't allowed herself to reach out. She *couldn't* reach out. After all she'd seen, all she'd *done*, if she asked for comfort, she feared she'd break down in a debilitating flood of anguish, never capable of standing on her own again.

Her whole body jolted with shock as Bryn's fingers wandered lightly across her cheek, brushing her hair behind her ear. His lips parted in adoring wonder, as if he couldn't believe she was permitting the intimacy of the touch.

"I'm afraid of what we're going to do in Dunwald," he said with shattering honesty. "You're the strongest person I've ever met, but I know you're afraid too. I know you don't trust anyone. I know you said us being together is a mistake, and I understand why, after what I took from you … but I'm still hoping like a fool that you'll trust me. As long as you believe I'm worthy of you, I can handle losing this fight. I can handle losing anything, Aela, except you." He took a step forward, standing so close to her now that their bodies were touching. "Let me in. It won't make you weak. You could never be weak."

Her focus narrowed to the man before her. In this shattering moment, she didn't care what he'd done or where they were or what was about to happen — she needed this. She needed Bryn. She wound her arms around his neck, pulling him close. He gasped as his mouth met hers, matching the urgency of her touch.

She ached to give physical expression to feelings she couldn't begin to name. Gripping the hem of his shirt, Aela broke away, standing on her toes to pull it over his head so his hair was mussed and his eyes were dazed. He fumbled slightly with her belt buckle, his capable hands rushing clumsily. Aela distantly heard her sword clatter to the floor. Her senses were obliterated. This wasn't as it had been with Tamas, desperately, mindlessly searching to escape herself. Now, she wanted nothing more than to be exactly who she was, in this moment with this man. There was nothing in the world but Bryn.

Their lips met again, and Aela traced her fingers up the soft skin at Bryn's back, feeling his hard muscles flex. Blood pounded in her ears as she drew her fingers along the waistband of his pants, feeling the circumference of his body, his hip bones, the puckering of the stitched wound at his side. She began pulling at the laces, and the hard-planed muscles of his stomach contracted. His trousers slipped lower, and he was undone before her.

Wanting nothing between them, Aela shrugged the dress off her shoulders. Bryn groaned quietly. The last remnants of his reserve seemed to shatter and he closed the space between them, sliding the fabric down her arms. His touch was softer than silk. Eyes dark with desire, he met her gaze and his breath caught sharply as he let the dress fall away, pooling at her feet. His eyes roved hungrily over her exposed breasts and heat coiled in Aela's stomach. She couldn't believe that it could be like this with Bryn, so tender, so intimate, his eyes filled with a needful wonder that seemed so … innocent.

But there was nothing innocent about the practised way he raked his fingers through her hair, cupping her face so he could capture her mouth with his. Bryn's tongue swept through her mouth briefly, a hint of the urgent passion he was holding back. She leaned into him, craving his taste. He bit down on her bottom lip, the burst of pleasure and pain wringing from her a shuddering gasp. Bryn pulled back with a wicked grin.

"Like that, do you? I'm dying to find out what sounds I can coax from that pretty mouth of yours."

Aela reached out, her fingers searching for Bryn's unlaced trousers, but Bryn caught her wrists, pressing them above her head, pinning her against the wall. It was the desire burning in Bryn's golden eyes, not his restraining hands, that held her trapped in place.

"Not yet," he said. "I've wanted to get on my knees for you ever since you held that knife to my throat in Underground. Don't move, sweetheart."

His hands left her wrists, and she felt his calluses, pleasurably rough against her skin when his fingertips ran down her arms to her chest. Her breath reached a crescendo as his middle finger circled her nipple. Her eyes fluttered closed. There was pressure at her waist. Bryn's fingers dug in and he leaned forward, tracing glancing kisses across the sensitive skin at her throat, unbearably, tantalisingly sensual. This wasn't enough – she needed more, needed all of him.

"Bryn," she gasped.

His lips left her throat and her breath hitched again as his tongue circled her nipple. Arms still trapped above her head by Bryn's command, she arched her body, desperate for more, and Bryn took her breast with his mouth. When he pulled away, his hot, wet kisses travelled downwards and her gut clenched with wild anticipation, watching him drop, with his eyes on hers, to his knees.

As if from a great distance, her mind acknowledged how

incongruous it was, Bryn Ryland, the arrogant, selfish, spoiled son of King Saban, on his knees for her. But this was the truth of him; exposed, vulnerable, giving. This was the part of Bryn no one else got to see. She desperately, possessively hoped no one else would ever see Bryn this way. She shuddered as his lips travelled across her hip, then lower, his fingers circling the most sensitive part of her, light, teasing.

"Gods, Bryn," she gasped. "More."

Instead, he pulled away, licking his lips and looking up at her. "You have no idea what it does to me, hearing you beg like that. I've never wanted anyone the way I want you, Aela Rinn. I'll give you more. I'll give you everything."

Her whole body jolted as his tongue roved over her again. She brought one of her hands off the wall to cover the whimper that escaped her lips when he slid one finger inside her, then another, her body tightening around the place he was giving his attention. Her pulse pounded in her ears.

Fuck, he was good with his hands. Aela stifled another gasp as Bryn curled his fingers inside. His tongue stroked her, pulsing in time with his fingers and her skin tingled. Aela's hips rolled, pushing towards him, desperate to feel more of his mouth as he drove her wild. His movements quickened. He was going to drive her over the edge; her mind was numb, pleasure shooting through her body, so deep she felt it in her heart. She gave a frustrated moan when Bryn's tongue left her, his fingers pulling out. Her world tilted as the pleasure ebbed. Bryn stood, grabbing her waist and swinging her around, pushing her towards the bed. Her back hit the mattress and he stood over her. His fiery gaze was like a touch, the same pleasure. She allowed herself the indulgence of watching the last remnants of his clothing drop to the floor, until he was standing exposed before her, his arousal rising from golden curls.

When he came forward, she pushed herself up, desperate to meet his mouth again. Bryn braced one knee on the mattress beside her and his thumb brushed wickedly over the supercharged skin just beneath her nipple, turning her breathing ragged. Needing more of him, she reached down and took his cock in her hand, running her thumb over the slit, already slick with precome. He moaned, his eyes flying wide as if shocked she could make him feel so good. Aela stroked down Bryn's length and his body convulsed, arcing forward. Gasping into her mouth, he kissed her slow and deep, and his weight bore down, pushing her back onto the mattress.

"I need you," Aela breathed against Bryn's lips. "Now, Bryn."

He drew back slightly, and beneath the undeniable want in his eyes, Aela saw a flicker of uncertainty. His voice was husky with arousal. "There's no going back from this, Aela. You know who I am, what I've done and I …"

He'd killed the king, he wanted to take the Dunwyan throne. Perhaps she should heed the low warning and pull away, but instead his voice hooked into her soul, dragging her closer to him.

"I want you to fuck me." Aela knotted her fingers in Bryn's hair, pulling him down for another kiss.

"Yes," he breathed between kisses. "Anything you want."

He groaned as she bit his lip, pulling at it with her teeth. His hands slid back to her breasts, and his eager, massaging touch was more like a caress than ownership. It was a reflex to bite down on at the skin of Bryn's neck, his shoulder. Aela pushed her body up towards him. The warm, wet head of his cock slid against her, agonisingly close to where she needed him. She took it in her hand, hot, slick and hard, guiding it towards the entrance of her body, and her thoughts shattered as he gently pushed inside. His size was overwhelming, an adjustment as he began to move slowly against her.

Bryn drove his hips down, forward, and she matched his rhythm, pushing up towards him, digging her fingers into his skin to feel the flex of his muscular thighs. The tension of building pleasure was overwhelming. She felt his hands on her wrists again and he was pulling them up, pushing them into the mattress beside her head. Thrusting deeper into her, his entire length was inside, and this time when he took the hard peak of her nipple in his mouth, she cried out. Aela writhed against his restraining hands, the unbearable pleasure of his mouth, the rhythmic pounding of his cock inside her. Fire infused her blood and her pulse quickened. It was too much and not enough.

"Gods, Aela." Bryn pushed her knee towards her chest, taking her deeper, and the entire world narrowed down to the two of them. Pleasure deafening her, she heard his words from a distance. "I've never felt this way before. I can't have this only once. I want …"

His hand travelled downwards and her body jerked. His thumb stroked the sensitive place between her legs, torturously gentle against the hard pounding of his body against hers. Needing to be closer, she pushed herself up, felt Bryn's strong, calloused hands guiding her, pulling her against him. Her thighs tightened as she wrapped her legs around him, feeling his muscles flex as he lifted her off the bed. The breath was knocked momentarily from her when her back collided with the wall. One of Bryn's arms was propping her up, and the other hand returned lower, his thumb circling faster, heat and pleasure building. Aela sank her hands into his hair, guiding his lips to hers in a fierce kiss.

It was like being in battle, the same thrill, her heartbeat reaching a crescendo, her body falling into rhythm with another. Bryn broke away, tracing kisses across her shoulder, and every movement, every sensation felt vivid and real and overwhelmingly bright. But this was tender, insulated from the horrors of the world.

For once, Aela stopped thinking about fighting. Each breathless sound Bryn made imprinted on her heart. His every movement suffused her body with hot, heady pleasure. The tension inside her exploded, stars bursting across her vision, brightening, then darkening. She cried out Bryn's name and heard him answer, and together they hurtled into a fierce, wonderful oblivion.

★★★

Downstairs, the tavern was crowded with patrons eating lunch. Aela shot Bryn a quizzical look. "This place is in the middle of nowhere, but somehow business is always booming. I'd love to know how Walter does it."

"I'd imagine he puts a pot of stew on the stove every day at lunch and criminals simply manifest out of thin air," Bryn said.

They grinned at each other, and warmth flared in the pit of Aela's stomach, tingling across her lower back and chasing away an impending onslaught of self flagellation. She'd fucked Bryn, the wanted king-killer, but it was becoming disconcertingly easy to separate the man before her from the one who had done that terrible deed, especially now. The passionate inferno that had burned between them upstairs had simmered into something steadier, something that felt sustainable. Something teasing, light, and … sweet.

Across the room, a raised voice grabbed Aela's attention, knocking her fresh wave of desire for Bryn off-kilter. They both turned towards the ruckus at the same time.

At a table by the window, Bowie sat alone, shovelling an unrealistically large spoonful of stew into his mouth. All his focus was on the full bowl before him, so he jumped when a patron slammed a tankard down hard on the table in front of him.

The man had eastern features, tanned with a blond mohawk. He was stocky, almost as broad as Walter despite being half Walter's height. He wore brown leather cuffs on his wrists and an expression of pure disgust as he looked down at Bowie.

"I said, get up, Niellan rat," he snapped. "Go and eat outside in the dirt where you belong."

"For fuck's sake," Bryn muttered irritably. He strode across the room with Aela at his heels and casually leaned against the table. His hand rested lightly on his sword at his belt as he regarded the blond man. "Do we have a problem?"

"Not unless you're content to breathe the same air as Niellan scum," Mohawk sneered. "Here, kid, let me show you to your new seat."

He reached over the table and grabbed Bowie's bowl, flinging it out the window. Stew splattered into the dirt. This time, Bowie didn't flinch, but Aela had spent enough time around him to know that his sharpened, unblinking expression was a sign of danger.

"Now," Mohawk said, pointing at Bowie, "get up and move your ass outside."

Aela knew what was going to happen before it did. Bryn

seemed to as well, because he snorted exasperatedly and looked up at the ceiling, as if silently beseeching the gods for a shred of patience. Bowie crossed his arms on the table and stared up at the man with a blue-eyed gaze that was as unyielding as it was sweet, a clear refusal.

Incensed by Bowie's confident disregard, the man slammed his hands down on the table. "I said move!"

With his usual terrifying speed, Bowie stood up and stabbed one of his knives into the table with perfect accuracy and impressive force.

Thud.

The sharpened tip deliberately missed flesh but sheared straight into the leather cuff at the man's wrist, pinning him to the table. The man swore.

"*You* move," Bowie retorted. He cocked his head, examining the dagger trapping the man's hand. "If you can."

"Bowie ..." Bryn began, frustrated.

Roaring furiously, Mohawk grabbed the knife, jerking it free from the leather. He lunged across the table, and Bryn spun to deflect the blade stabbing towards Bowie.

"You had to pull a weapon," Bryn snapped at Bowie. He jerked his head towards Walter's back room as the man turned his murderous gaze on Bryn. "Go!"

Bowie took a step back but didn't retreat. He pulled another knife and traded a dirty look with Mohawk, who glanced at Bryn and Aela incredulously.

"You're siding with that little *animal*? You have no idea what war with Nielle was like!"

The flurry had resulted in a number of yells from the tavern's patrons, petty thieves who scattered at the first hint of violence. Bryn shoved the man backwards and glanced at Aela with a pained look, as if the effort of holding back laughter was causing him physical discomfort.

"If only one of us knew what the war was like," he said sarcastically.

Pulling her own weapon, Aela said tiredly, "Get out of here before I run you through."

"Not if I kill you first!" Their opponent raised his blade again, driving it towards Aela's unprotected body. Bryn moved to parry at the same time Aela did.

But someone else was faster.

The furious look on Mohawk's face froze as a blade drove clean through his chest, spraying Aela and Bryn with blood. The blade withdrew, and the man fell to his knees. Aela gasped.

A figure stood behind him, calmly wiping clean his bloodied blade. Entirely unbothered by the chaos erupting around him in the tavern, he looked down indifferently at the dead body before his grey-blue eyes rose to meet Aela's.

"The only one who gets to kill my people," Splinter said smoothly, "is me."

Twenty-Eight

It was odd seeing Splinter again after what felt like a lifetime. In reality, it had been less than three weeks, but everything that had happened in that time had caused Aela to deprioritise Splinter as a threat in her mind. Now she remembered that he was not to be underestimated. His presence, imposing as it was, signalled danger. He was ready to fight, his grey-streaked hair pulled back. His hands, calloused from decades of cutting men down with emotionless precision, were ready on his broadsword.

Aela swept her own sword up defensively, forming a barrier between Bryn and Splinter. The tension in the air seemed to crystalise into solid form. Aela felt as if she could cut through it with her blade.

"You know you can't beat me in a fight," she warned Splinter.

"If I wanted to attack you, I wouldn't have announced myself by killing that degenerate. You do surprise me, Commander Rinn," Splinter said, sparing a glance at the dead man on the floor. His voice didn't match the pandemonium around them. It was calm and quiet, an unsettling signal that everything was going how he wanted it to.

"What are you doing here?" she asked him.

The tavern had all but emptied out. Aela was hyper-aware that Bryn and Bowie were behind her. In the silence of the room, she and Splinter held each other's gazes. Aela felt it was fair to assume that Splinter hadn't come all the way to Walter's inn on a leisure trip. She flexed her grip minutely on her blade, ready.

"Did you really expect I was going to allow three of my people to vanish?" Splinter asked.

"I expect you to select your battles carefully," Aela warned him. "You'd be wise to consider allowing us to go our separate ways."

"And *you* would be wise to consider what I've told you before: nothing happens in Dunwyn that I don't know about. Not even the disappearance of a certain Prince Bryn, most wanted fugitive of the steward of Dunwyn."

Aela's stomach lurched. She took a step forward and flicked her blade up to the base of Splinter's throat. "You're on dangerous ground," she told him darkly.

"Am I?" Splinter asked pleasantly. His gaze flicked back to Bryn. "I think *Slate* might be in a decidedly more perilous position, wouldn't you say, boy?"

Aela drove her weapon slowly forwards. A bead of blood welled where the tip of her blade pierced his skin. Splinter didn't flinch.

Bryn moved closer. "How long have you known?" he asked.

A slow, predatory smile slid across Splinter's face. "I knew at my house when you woke up chained to the bed," he said evenly. "I knew in the castle, when I slipped grey dream into your drink." Aela's whole body went cold. It felt as if the room was closing in around them. "I knew in the hallway, when I found you alone and directed you to your father's chambers. I knew when I watched you drive your knife into his heart." He gestured casually at Bryn, whose breath had gone uneven. His chest was rising and falling, increasingly fast. "Grey dream is *very* effective. A few orders from me were more than enough to transform you into a killer."

Bryn lunged for Splinter. Aela stepped between the two men, pushing Bryn back. She couldn't breathe. The world tilted around her, reframing Bryn in her mind. She put herself back in Saban's room with his bloodied sheets and saw what had truly happened, the atrocity Splinter had done to Bryn. The way Splinter had turned Bryn into a murderer against his will, forcing him to take the life of his own father.

The distraught fury on Bryn's face felt like destruction. All the times she'd pulled away from him, the times she'd thought of *killing* him, because of what he'd done, through no fault, no *choice* of his own.

In addition to stealing Saban from both of them, Splinter had stolen Aela and Bryn from each other. She didn't know how they could come back from hating Bryn for a murder he hadn't willingly committed.

Bryn stared at Splinter with violence in his eyes. His expression was a shot through Aela's heart. She wondered if he was trying again desperately to grapple for the memories that slipped like smoke through his fingers every time he tried to recall the events of that night. Worst of all was the possibility that he might be thinking about how Aela had doubted him. Despite everything she knew of Bryn — his kindness, his good heart — she'd let people convince her that he was nothing more than a killer.

Splinter's grip had loosened on his weapon, and he was infuriatingly relaxed. "What are you going to do? You're not a killer. We both know you would never have raised that knife against your father without me. What I did was business. If you're upset about getting set up, take it up with Huntley Bartome. She's the one who tasked me with killing you while she sat pretty inside the castle, spreading rumours, casting aspersions." Splinter scoffed. "And they say anarchists have no consciences."

"Business? He was *my father!*"

Bryn started forward again as Splinter spread his arms, an invitation.

"You want to fight, then let's fight. You'll lose though. And for what? Attacking me won't bring him back."

Aela looked from Bryn's unyielding expression to Splinter's arrogant smirk. Splinter was a good fighter, but Aela didn't know if he was better than Bryn. And even if Bryn managed to kill Splinter, then what? Aela's heart went cold at the thought of Dunwyn at Huntley and Alvine's mercy.

"Bryn, stop," she commanded.

His head jerked up, as if he'd been ripped from a nightmare. "What?"

Aela almost flinched away from the deep betrayal and hurt in his eyes. Wracked with guilt, she moved towards him instead, lightly brushing her fingertips over his in a gesture so subtle she hoped Splinter wouldn't notice. Bryn shivered at the touch.

"Splinter's word will corroborate our evidence against Huntley. We can't kill him."

"*He killed my father,*" Bryn said, roiling fury and heartbreak twisting in his voice.

"Yes," Aela murmured, "you lost him. You can't lose your country too. Not for revenge."

Splinter was still smiling that horrible smile. "You need to understand, Bryn, the only thing that kept you alive for the eight months you were under my roof is that I knew your death would eventually become profitable. I'm expecting a *very* persuasive offer in exchange for your lives."

Aela raised her eyebrows. "Bold words with my sword at your throat."

Splinter clicked his tongue. "Oh, come on," he said. "You don't really think I came alone."

Aela closed her eyes in dread. She glanced back in time to see Dagny press the cold tip of a blade to Bryn's throat. In a swift move, Bryn grabbed Dagny's arm, twisting it brutally until Dagny dropped his weapon. Stumbling backwards, Dagny reached for another blade at his belt, drew it, and froze. His weapon was met with a pair of swords at the hands of Bryn and Bowie.

"You keep showing up like a bad smell," Bryn said to Dagny irritably. "Or mould. Or syphilis."

Splinter's eyes narrowed at Bryn. "You should be grateful you've lived this long. You know my rules. No one leaves the house without my permission. Even without the bounty on your head, you disobeyed me."

Bryn's dark gaze was icy as he looked at Splinter, his blade still steadily trained on Dagny. "*I* should be grateful? You should be on your *knees* begging me for mercy. You conspired with your friend the steward of Dunwyn to orchestrate a coup. Against me. I'm the prince of Dunwyn, and I'm going to be the king."

Splinter's eyes widened slightly and Aela wondered if Bryn was trying to sound like his father. He was using the same measured, confident tone she'd heard from Saban during fierce negotiations. She heard the resemblance between Bryn and Saban but couldn't see it. Bryn held himself differently, more formidably, daring Splinter for a fight. Saban had never been confrontational like that, but Aela knew Bryn enjoyed a fight more than his father. At some point over the past few weeks, his boyish petulance had transformed into self-assured strength, the kind of strength that made a man like Splinter take notice. He was a worthy opponent, and Splinter knew it.

Unlike Araxa, whose expressions were consistently impenetrable, Splinter used his feelings like a weapon, expressing them clearly, daring those around him to make him feel the full extent of his fury, disappointment, or sadistic amusement.

"Oh, the steward and I aren't friends," Splinter said. "But we are colleagues. We understand that sometimes you have to call a ceasefire, especially when there's a mutually beneficial business opportunity on the table."

"This might have been a *business opportunity* for you, but it's personal for me." Bryn's voice cracked. He took a slow breath before continuing. "This is what happens now. You agree to my terms, or I will make sure you're hunted for the rest of your miserable life."

He took a step forward. Aela watched him, impressed by his composure. For the first time, she was getting a glimpse of Bryn as the statesman he could be, calm, measured, articulate.

"What you did was treason. I could have you sentenced to life in prison, but instead I'm choosing to negotiate. I want you to come with me to Dunwald. I want you to expose the truth to Dunwyn's council about your partnership with Huntley. And then I want you to do what you do best, disappear without a trace. You won't be imprisoned. You won't be executed. You won't even be tried for your crimes. If you help me take the throne from Huntley, I'll make sure your work in Anarchist

Underground continues uninterrupted. Dunwyn will never seek to control you. That's my promise."

Aela closed her eyes as Bryn forced out the vow, against everything his father had wanted. Saban had let the anarchists be, but he'd always dreamed of finding a way to end them.

Splinter was still smiling. "Do you think the steward has not approached me with an offer of her own? I already have a pardon for my crimes, as long as Huntley remains on the throne."

"Then tell me what you want."

"You have transgressions to answer for," Splinter said.

Aela laughed. Displeasure flickered across Splinter's face, and it only made her laugh harder. "For someone who's usually so strategic, your plan here is remarkably short-sighted," she said. "Bryn is the prince of Dunwyn."

"He is a murderer and a fugitive," Dagny spat.

Aela drew her blade away from Splinter's throat. "Not for much longer. Help us, and I promise you won't regret it."

Splinter raised his chin. "You want to negotiate? Very well. Let's negotiate."

Twenty-Nine

Aela never imagined Bryn's first diplomatic endeavour as king of Dunwyn would be with the boss of Anarchist Underground, but it undeniably felt akin to a peace parley between two heads of state. If you ignored Splinter's boots crossed on the table before them, the same tension hung in the air. The stakes were the same, an agreement or mutual destruction.

"You can start by handing over Bowie," Splinter said smoothly.

"No." Bryn's voice was hard. "I'm not going to bargain with his life."

"He comes back to Dunwald with me," Splinter persisted.

"No." Bowie spoke up, voice trembling, from his place at the table between Aela and Bryn. "I'm not going to Dunwald. I'm staying here with Walter. I have work to do."

Aela looked at Bowie in surprise. The table was an inadequate barrier to separate him from Splinter. Her concern rose as she remembered Bowie refusing Splinter's order back at the house in Dunwald, knowing what it had almost cost him. But Bowie looked determined. His blue eyes were fixed, not on Splinter but on Bryn, as if he was trying to communicate something, perhaps an apology for staying behind while Bryn went on to Dunwald.

Splinter's eyes narrowed with dark delight, as if he'd been hoping Bowie would defy him. "It seems there's nothing you can offer me then," he told Bryn. "Perhaps you should have walked into this negotiation better prepared."

"We're not done," Bryn said. "There's something else I can give you. Something *only* I can give you."

"And what is that?"

Bryn swallowed hard, and Aela braced herself for him to execute the plan she knew he hated. "Statehood," he said. "When I return to the throne, I won't just let you go. I'll give you land to run as you see fit, by your own laws. You'll have an independent realm inside Dunwyn. Only the king may divide the country between its citizens. Help me, and there'll be no more hiding in the shadows, no more working around the law." He looked steadily at Splinter. "Help me, and you'll have more power than you ever imagined."

Now, Splinter was surprised. He traded a long look with Dagny, sitting at his side. Silence stretched out between them. "You know," he said after a considered moment. "The word of an anarchist may not be particularly reliable to members of the Dunwyan Council."

Bryn eyed him steadily. "It will be, if there's proof."

"For example …" Aela reached into her pocket, producing the signed paper Bowie had retrieved from the explosion at Hiver and held it up.

"The deal I'm promising you is a good one." Bryn's tone was measured. "Alvine and Huntley are deceivers, and you know it. Whatever they've offered you, can you really guarantee they won't overreach into your affairs in the future? I'll personally secure you a pardon for your part in this, and if you help me, no one from Dunwyn will ever come after you again."

"A compelling offer," Splinter replied.

Aela tried to keep her shoulders relaxed as Bryn held the anarchist's gaze.

"One more thing," he said evenly, "I need you to confess to the king's murder." Aela's head whipped to Bryn, who gave her an apologetic look. "It's the only way, Aela. I've thought about it. I know you have too."

She closed her eyes, trying not to think about Saban. Would he approve of the lie? Saban had always believed in transparency with his people, but Bryn was right. The circumstances of how he'd killed his father didn't matter. There wasn't a way forward for Bryn in Dunwyn if anyone knew he'd used that knife on the king.

Splinter gave a knowing smile that made Aela's skin crawl. He looked almost proud. "Why, Your Highness," he said, "building your entire reign upon a lie. How very … me of you."

Bryn's stare didn't waver. "Do you agree or not?"

Slowly, Splinter lowered his blade, watching Bryn steadily as he considered. Finally, in an amused tone he said, "Hail King Bryn of Dunwyn."

★★★

Bowie stood at the door of the inn the next morning, Walter behind him, a miserable farewell party for Aela and Bryn's journey back to Dunwald with Splinter and Dagny. Aela imagined the next two days on the road were going to be awkward at best and fatally violent at worst. She wasn't sure she'd have the willpower to hold Bryn back from attacking Splinter a second time.

She crouched down beside Bowie. "If even half of my soldiers were as brave as you, the war would've been over in a week."

Bowie rolled his eyes, but he didn't say anything, a telltale sign despite the look on his face.

Aela said in Niellan, "I know you're staying here to create more of the antidote. I want you to know, whether it cures King Marcus or not, you should be proud of yourself for what you're doing, what you've done. I'm very proud of you. I know Bryn is too."

"Glory to Nielle and no other," Bowie muttered, a quiet refutation.

It was a traditional phrase Aela had heard Niellan soldiers utter to diminish personal triumphs on the battlefield. Niellans were supposed to prize humility, which seemed an oxymoron to Aela, who'd spent her life witnessing Marcus's ego-driven conquest to expand his country's border. Despite his modesty, a pleased flush crept over Bowie's pale face. When was the last time anyone had said they were proud of him?

"Will you look after him?" Bowie asked, looking very young, his blue eyes wide and imploring.

"I promise," Aela replied.

She found herself riding alongside Bryn. In the hours since they'd departed Walter's , they hadn't spoken a word to each other, and Aela's anxiety was getting the better of her. She had no idea how to broach a discussion about the terrible pain of what Bryn had been forced to do or how to bring up her own clawing remorse for believing he could ever have killed Saban of his own volition.

Before leaving the inn, she'd dismally traded the pretty dress for something more practical. She'd made a point of being absent when Bowie had bade Bryn farewell. It wasn't an easy choice for Bowie to stay behind in Walter's inn without Bryn. Bowie didn't like being vulnerable; he wouldn't have wanted anyone witnessing that goodbye.

As if he was thinking about that too, Bryn said in a sudden, quiet voice, "Bowie's not wrong very often, but he was wrong about one thing."

Aela glanced at him. "What's that?"

Bryn gave a short, sharp laugh. "He thought I wasn't a killer."

Aela's heart seized. She was coming to understand that savage, bitter aggression was Bryn's way of getting what he thought he deserved, hatred and disgust from everyone around him.

"Bryn," she said softly, conscious of Splinter and Dagny riding behind them, "you're not —"

"Don't bullshit me, Aela," Bryn interrupted sharply. "I used the knife."

"It's not that simple. You know it isn't. It wasn't a *choice*." She looked hard at him. "I know you wish you could take it back. You can't, but what you *can* do is protect your people from what's about to happen."

"I'm intrigued," Splinter announced, catching up, and Aela's frustration crested at the interruption. She was already dangerously close to running her blade through his throat. "What do you think is about to happen?"

Aela turned in the saddle to glare at him. "Please. You know full well that we're riding to Dunwald to clean up the mess you made when you allied with Huntley."

Splinter gave her a withering look. "I do business with a lot of people, Commander Rinn. Getting paid by Huntley to provide a service is very different from *forming an alliance* with her. If you want to know what an alliance looks like, why don't you ask the steward's little friend in Nielle?"

"You mean Alvine," Aela said disdainfully. "King Marcus's bastard?"

Splinter's lip curled. "You really don't know anything, do you?"

Aela raised an eyebrow at Splinter dangerously. "Say what you want to say."

"You're so fixated on the fact that King Marcus is Alvine's father. Did it ever occur to you to consider who her *mother* might be?"

Bryn looked at him like he was an idiot. "Ives was her mother. Marcus's *wife*."

A slow smile slid across Splinter's handsome, weathered face. There was a long, heavy silence, during which Aela remembered the initials on the grey dream contract they had taken from Hiver.

A.B.

"Alvine ... *Bartome?*" she whispered.

Another silence dragged out. It suddenly made sense, the allegiance, and what Bowie said at Amory and Ewan's house.

Why do you think Huntley is doing all of this?

It felt like a full minute before Bryn broke the tension. "Well," he said, sounding bewildered. "I suppose now we know what Huntley was doing on all those *diplomatic* visits to Nielle. King Marcus was really *penetrating* the Dunwyan culture, if you know what I mean. Ow!" He flinched from Aela's hard punch to his arm.

"Do you think you could handle this like an adult?" she demanded irritably. "This is a big problem! Alvine's claim to the Niellan crown is true. She might be a bastard, but she's Marcus's *only* living heir. There's no one who can remove Alvine from the Niellan throne and now we know Huntley's allegiance to Alvine was forged by blood. Her desire to secure power for her daughter is stronger than her love for Dunwyn. We need to get her off Dunwyn's throne before she signs our country over to Nielle without Alvine ever having to raise a sword!"

Bryn paled. He turned on Splinter. "You knew about this?"

"I found out after I had completed my business agreement with Huntley," Splinter said icily. "A Niellan invasion is bad business for Anarchist Underground if it sparks an all-out uprising from the Dunwyan people ... which it will. I would never have agreed to our deal if I'd known."

"What do you know, we've finally found one line you won't cross," Bryn said sarcastically. He reached out again to press the slightest touch of his fingers against Aela's, as if the contact grounded him. "If we're all in agreement that we need to protect this country, then let's get to Dunwald and do something about it."

It felt to Aela as if Anarchist Underground should be entirely changed. So much had happened to her in the past three weeks, but in the city everything was the same. Addicts still huddled in doorways and in the corners of alleyways. Merchants shouted about illicit wares, the sounds combining with yells and shattering glass from some nearby bar fight to form a grim symphony. If Huntley had put out word that there was a price on Aela and Bryn's heads, no other anarchists acted on it as Splinter led them through the streets of Underground. Aela didn't care if it was out of deference or fear — they were safe with Splinter, as long as their agreement remained in place.

Splinter's house, outwardly dilapidated but grand and pristine on the inside, seemed the one place of order amidst the chaos.

As they entered, Aela glanced at Bryn. They needed to talk, desperately. Her desire to beg his forgiveness for not believing in him was stymied by the urgency of what they were doing here. She shoved her frustration down, willing herself not to lose focus.

Something wasn't right about the manor. Splinter had left Laz and Nula behind, but the entrance hall was dark, the house utterly silent, as if the whole place had been shut up, its residents long absent. They should have been greeted, but no one was here. Splinter's posture was stiffer than usual, his knuckles white on the hilt of his blade.

"Would they have gone somewhere?" Bryn asked, sharing their unease.

"No," Splinter said shortly.

Their voices echoed in the hall, which seemed more cavernous than usual. In a reflex born of hyper-awareness and suspicion, Aela's hand found the blade at her belt.

"So you think they're here?" Dagny's hand also rested on his sword as he walked towards the stairs to the training room.

"*Someone's* here," Splinter said, his voice harsh.

Aela followed the direction of his gaze. At the foot of the stairs was a mark on the wall that hadn't been there before, a dark smear. Even in the dim light, Aela didn't need to be told what it was. She knew blood when she saw it. She drew her blade.

"I wouldn't bother with that." The voice rang out above them was horribly familiar. The last time Aela had heard it, she'd been surrounded by the tumbledown ruins of Hiver castle. Araxa Leren looked down from the second floor landing. "You're very much outnumbered," she said with a mirthless smile.

Aela glanced behind with a sinking feeling; men filed out of the training room below, carrying weapons from Splinter's armoury. More emerged from the dining room, the kitchen, and from upstairs, flanking Araxa as she descended the stairs into the hall. Her face was mottled with cuts and bruises, and blood-flecked fabric bound an injury at her shoulder. Some of the others bore bandages too, and Aela realised with mingled horror and relief that the majority of Araxa's gang had survived the blast at Hiver. There were more than thirty men inside Splinter's home, too many to fight.

"Thought we'd killed you," Bryn said, looking at Araxa with absolute hatred.

"I bet you did," Araxa replied smoothly. She looked at Splinter. "I suppose that would have been a neat way for you to eliminate the competition."

Splinter smirked. "You flatter yourself. You're not my competition. Your skills extend only as far as the thievery of other people's work."

Araxa's eyes narrowed. "Your work was destroyed by your little protégés there. I was to deliver a dozen barrels of grey dream to Eterre, and I didn't. Someone has to answer for that." Her gaze moved slowly, brushing across Aela then Bryn. "And someone will."

Rising dread told Aela exactly what Araxa planned to do, and even though she knew they were outnumbered, the urge to fight rose up within her. At her side, Bryn wrapped his fingers around her wrist, his touch the only thing keeping her from launching at Araxa in a desperate bid to stop what was coming next.

"Take them to the steward," Araxa ordered.

Thirty

Aela braced herself as the heavy double doors opened, revealing the dark expanse of the great hall. Huntley sat on the dais. The image of her there, as she had been the day Aela returned after the Border War, called Aela's mind back to the moment she'd learned of Saban's death. A remnant of the agony that had threatened to drive her to her knees that day shuddered through her body. But this time it was overpowered by fury as she recalled Huntley's crocodile tears. The steward had pretended to weep and grieve for Saban, but now there was no pretending. His blood was on her hands.

Today, Huntley didn't look exhausted or grieved. There was something in the line of her body that seemed wholly too casual for the lofty position in which she sat. Her ankles were stretched out and crossed before her, and her head rested lazily upon her hand, her elbow perched on the arm of the throne. She was, of course, unsurprised to see them. Huntley said nothing as they approached, Aela and Bryn held fast in the grips of Araxa's men.

"Steward." Araxa's husky voice boomed across the great hall. "We've succeeded where you failed. Here is the fugitive prince you've been searching for." She gestured to Aela, Splinter, and Dagny. "With his accomplices for good measure."

Slowly, Huntley raised her head, appraising Bryn with disinterest. He shot her a venomous glare in return. Huntley said calmly, "So, you consider four criminals a fair exchange for twelve barrels of grey dream."

Detecting a brewing conflict, Aela shifted into a slight defensive stance. Bryn's eyes flicked to Aela's briefly, understanding passing between them. He shifted his weight slightly too, preparing for a fight.

"Steward, I'm sure you can appreciate that these aren't just any criminals," Araxa said, not quite matching Huntley's calm tone. Violent indignation unfurling in her voice. "The problem with our most recent supply of grey dream is … unfortunate." She inclined her head towards the group. "But I clean up my messes. *They* destroyed your supply, and they did it because they *know*."

Huntley's nonchalant posture disappeared, and she snapped to her feet. Araxa was not a small woman, but Huntley towered over her on the dais. Her figure cast a long, looming shadow down the stairs, over Araxa and her men.

"What did you say?" Huntley said softly.

"I said they *know*," Araxa replied. "So I've brought them here to be dealt with. You see? I don't leave loose ends."

A slow smile crept across Huntley's face as she descended the stairs with the grace of a fighter. The sharp, rhythmic footsteps of her boots hitting the marble floor echoed off the walls. Huntley had a commanding presence that was impossible to look away from, yet a creeping threat nudged at Aela. She tore her eyes away from the steward to glance around the room. Almost in time with Huntley, as if their bodies and minds were connected to hers by an invisible string, her orange-cloaked Niellan guards were moving from the periphery of the room, closing in on Araxa and her men. They stopped when Huntley stopped, directly in front of Araxa.

"Then we have something in common, Araxa Leren," Huntley said, in the same soft, sad tone she'd used when telling Aela that King Saban was dead. "I don't leave loose ends either."

Blood spattered across Aela as Araxa fell. More bodies hit the ground around her. It happened so quickly that Aela's mind didn't piece it together until she saw Huntley's raised arm, the blood-drenched dagger in her hand. The steward watched expressionlessly as the life inched from Araxa's prone body, surrounded by her dead mercenaries.

Droplets of blood pattered onto the white stone as Huntley dropped her hand. It was only then that her eyes met Aela's then slid to Bryn's.

"They outlived their usefulness," she said. "You, on the other hand, might have more to offer."

"I'll show you what I have to offer," Bryn said, raising his middle finger with intent before one of Huntley's guards caught hold of his arms and jerked them hard behind his back.

Huntley offered Bryn the same sort of look one might give a particularly putrid breed of rodent. "At noon tomorrow, you will be executed publicly. A just end to this sordid chapter in Dunwyn's history, and a clear path for this country to move towards a future brighter than anything Saban could ever have dreamed of."

Bryn scoffed. "You really think you can execute me without a trial? It goes against everything my father believed in. The council would never allow it."

"Your father is dead. And you will forever be remembered as a heartless king-killer. That is how your bloodline will end."

Bryn spat at her feet. "We know what you're doing. The

people of Dunwyn will never be ruled by Nielle."

"The people of Dunwyn are sick of wars and fighting. I'm going to offer them peace. For that, my daughter will be loved more than Saban ever was."

Bryn reeled back slightly. It was worse to hear the truth straight from Huntley's own mouth.

"You don't want peace," Aela cut in. "You want to destroy Dunwyn."

Huntley's eyes blazed with furious conviction for a moment when she turned her gaze on Aela, then her expression softened.

"Aela," she said gently. "Commander Rinn. I remember the first time I fought you. You were the most gifted soldier I'd ever seen. You don't have to hang with these anarchists tomorrow." She gestured callously at Splinter and Dagny. "You have always been loyal to Dunwyn. Let that loyalty live on. I'm scheduled to meet with the council early tomorrow morning. Tell them of the horrors you witnessed in Anarchist Underground. Tell them of Bryn's crimes. I'm begging you to be on the right side of history. Help me lead Dunwyn into the future."

A furious pain surged inside Aela's chest, threatening to tear her open. She remembered that moment, years ago, when she and Huntley had fought in the training arena.

Aela remembered lying in the sawdust, defeated, watching Huntley pass off her sword and walk away. Aela hadn't felt angry or disappointed in herself in that moment. All she'd felt was deep admiration, a desire to walk in Huntley's footsteps, to also become great.

That memory gave way to another, walking with Saban in the garden the night before she had departed for the war. She could almost feel the ghost of his touch, where he had taken her face in his hands and reminded her what she was fighting for, freedom, goodness, light. Dunwyn's values. Saban's values. She slipped her hand into her pocket, letting the golden king's insignia encircle her finger, its familiar weight grounding her, reminding her of her path.

"That would have meant something to me once," she said to Huntley. "Before I could see you for what you really are. You're wrong. I'm not loyal to you. I'm your enemy, and I'll die before I let you betray Dunwyn."

Huntley nodded as if she had been expecting this answer. She looked triumphant. "Then you'll get your wish," she said. "Lock them all up."

Thirty-One

"Must you keep pacing like that?" Bryn asked irritably.

Aela paused to grip the bars in frustration and looked back at him. Through the barred window above his head, the golden-blue glow of morning light tinged the sky. With every excruciating hour that had passed in captivity overnight, Aela's anxiety grew, while Bryn's energy appeared to be ebbing away. Hunched against the wall of their cell, he kneaded his forehead with his fist. There was an implacable feeling between them, something unsettling that reminded her of the way he had been when they'd first met at Splinter's house — deliberately abrasive, firmly establishing a barrier between himself and the rest of the world. Those walls were up again, and there was nothing Aela could do about it. She felt confined, not just by the bars but by the fact that she didn't know how or when to make this right. She didn't even know if she'd live long enough to try. She fought the urge to scream.

"One of us has to have some sense of urgency!" she snapped back at him. "Every moment we sit here, Huntley and Alvine get closer to destroying Dunwyn. We know what needs to be done, but until we get out of this damn cell, we can't do it! Forgive me if I'm a little agitated."

"Pacing isn't going to get us out of here, Commander," Splinter drawled.

He was reclining on the filthy mattress in the cell next door, looking totally at ease.

Aela folded her arms. "By all means, if you have a better idea, now would be an excellent time to share it."

"Can you pick locks?" Bryn asked.

His unhelpfulness nettled Aela, who hated to think that he might be giving up. She gestured at the huge wooden bolt, slid into place inside a hole of rectangular metal. "There's no keyhole, genius."

"Then how do you propose we get out of here?" Bryn asked.

"Perhaps," Splinter said drily, "you should simply accept that your neck is going to find its way to a noose. If you ask me, it's little more than you deserve."

"Couldn't agree with you more," Bryn replied, leaning his head back against the bars and closing his eyes. "But if you really feel that way, why'd you bother taking me into Underground after I murdered my father, instead of just killing me? It would've been neater for you, and you'd have collected a nice pile of gold from Huntley."

"I thought you were smarter than that," Splinter said. "The only remaining heir to the Dunwyan throne and the only person who stood between the steward and her objective was worth far more alive than dead."

Bryn's eyes flicked open. "You were going to hold me for ransom?"

"I wondered how much the steward would inflate the price on your head to get what she wanted."

Bryn snorted, gesturing around the cell. "Job well done."

Fed up, Aela crossed the cell in two brisk steps and kicked

him hard in his side.

"Ow!" Bryn exclaimed. "Did you just kick your prince?"

"I don't know," she shot back. "Did I? Because you can't have it both ways, Bryn. If you want to be treated as a prince, then you damn well better start acting like one. Do you want your country back or not?"

Bryn threw his hands up in frustration. "I don't want to be locked up in here, but what hope do we have of getting out? And even if we do escape, we'd need an army to take on Huntley and Alvine. Do you see one anywhere?"

Aela had nothing to say to that. She dropped her head, defeated. Maybe this was it. Maybe their lives were destined to come to an abrupt, unsatisfying end, all evidence of Huntley's treachery dying with them. It was an ironic way for a war hero's story to finish.

"Don't tell me that the Reaper of Dunwyn needs us mere mortals to save her ass!"

Aela's head jerked up. She knew that voice. She pressed her face against the bars and saw a trio of shadows approaching from the corridor. "*Chase?*"

Sure enough, Chase Fenner swaggered up to the bars, grinning. "What do you know, for once she's not making us all look bad."

Behind him, Landon stared into the cell at Bryn with his mouth agape, and Mason shook her head in disbelief. "Holy shit. The kid was telling the truth."

"What kid?" Bryn rose to his feet.

Another shadow appeared in the dark corridor, smaller this time, emerging slowly into the lamplight, blue eyes glittering triumphantly.

"Did someone call for an army?" Bowie asked.

***

"I thought the whole idea of letting you escape was that you wouldn't end up in here, Commander," Mason said drily as she yanked the cell door open and clasped Aela's forearm.

Aela rolled her eyes. "Yes, thank you, Captain Tanner. This wasn't exactly the plan. It's a long story."

"One that might be best discussed later," Bryn said, pushing past Aela and kneeling to take hold of Bowie's narrow shoulders. "What are you doing here?"

Bowie craned his neck to look past Bryn. "Saving your ass. And looking for Walter. Where is he?"

Aela turned. "What are you talking about? He was with you."

"I know that." Bowie snapped. "But after you left, Huntley's soldiers rode in. Walter told me to hide, and then they came in and said he was under arrest. They didn't tell him what for, they just took him away. I came back to the city to find you, but when I got to Splinter's house, no one was there. I figured you'd all been arrested too. I thought that if I found some of your soldiers, Aela, they'd help."

"I won't lie, Commander, when the kid found me in the tavern and told me you were with the prince, I didn't believe it!" Mason said.

"Believe it, Captain." Bryn straightened up.

Mason's hand dropped lifelessly from Aela's grasp as she stared at Bryn. Chase and Landon were staring too, not even attempting to hide their shock. Aela knew what they were seeing. Bryn's defiant smirk, the glittering mischief in his brown eyes, and his strong swordsman's build, paired with the backdrop of the prison certainly weren't helping them to see him as anything other than the man who had murdered the king.

"Prince Bryn?" Mason said, her dark eyes wide.

"Actually," Aela said wryly, "I think it's *King* Bryn."

"But he …" Landon began, and Bryn looked up, raising his eyebrows, as if daring Landon to continue.

"No," Aela interrupted. She didn't feel guilty. It was barely a lie. "He didn't. Huntley is the one who planned the king's murder. She paid the anarchists to kill him. These men will confess it before the council, if we release them."

She gestured to Splinter and Dagny, still confined in their cell.

"Commander, you can't be serious!" Chase said. "You've struck a deal with anarchists?"

Resigned, Aela looked back at Chase. "My friend, until we can get Huntley off the throne, we're all anarchists."

"Then what do we do?" Landon asked quietly. He looked unsettled. The thought of breaking the law, even if it was the law of a traitor, didn't sit right with him. The fact that he was here, despite that, filled Aela with gratitude. She looked at the three soldiers, drawing strength from their presence. If she was going to fight, she felt better about doing it with them on her side.

"It's time to finish this," Aela told them. "I need you to be ready. If what Bryn and I are about to do works out, Dunwyn will need all of its soldiers back at their posts. Chase, Landon, I want you to get out of the castle and find any soldiers left in the city who are loyal to the king. Assemble them at Splinter's manor in Anarchist Underground. Tell them to prepare to return to their posts when I send word. Bowie and Dagny know the way. Mason, Splinter, you're with Bryn and I."

That triggered immediate protestations. "Commander, no. Whatever you and the king are about to do, let us be there to protect you!" said Chase.

"Our place is *here*!" Landon agreed. "Watching your back."

Aela opened her mouth to reply, but Bryn spoke first. "You need to trust us to do this alone. Do your duty as soldiers and prepare to defend the castle. Even if we stop Huntley, we may face resistance. You swore an oath to protect your country. I don't care if you do this for me, for my father, or for some other reason. All I need to know is that you'll answer our call when the time comes."

Mason, Chase, and Landon stared at Bryn as if they didn't recognise him. Evidently, he wasn't what they'd expected. He was a leader worthy of respect. They would follow him. Aela was certain of it.

Mason breathed deeply. "I'll answer, Your Highness," she said gravely.

"I will too." Landon stepped forward.

A heavy pause filled the room. "Chase?" Aela prompted eventually.

His head listed in surrender. "Ugh, fine! But if we win, I'd better be showered with glory."

Aela grinned at him. "You'll still need to fix your personality if you want to get laid."

"You don't need a good personality when you look like this." Chase smoothed back his perfectly styled hair haughtily. "Don't get yourself killed, Commander. You either, Your Highness."

Aela's lip twitched. "Don't worry. I plan to continue making you look bad well into the future."

The soldiers turned to leave, Dagny at their heels. Aela's gaze, and Bryn's, turned to Splinter, who leaned, ankles crossed, against the barred side of the cell he'd been sprung from. He towered over Bowie, whose blue eyes were fixed on him. The boy was clearly uncomfortable, his arms folded protectively over his chest, but he spoke to Splinter in a quiet voice. Splinter was listening intently, nodding. He moved away as Bryn approached and crouched down in front of Bowie.

"What was that about?" Bryn asked. Bowie shrugged evasively, and Bryn, apparently knowing better at this point than to expect Bowie to be forthcoming, sighed in resignation. "All right. Go with Chase and Landon out of the castle," he said quietly. "Then go straight to Splinter's house. I'll call for you when it's safe."

Bowie looked up at him solemnly. "I wanted to tell you … about Alvine and Huntley, but so much has been happening and I —"

"I'm not angry," Bryn said. "I'd forgive you for anything. You know that."

"Anything?" Bowie's expression was an odd mixture of uncertainty and yearning. "You promise?"

Bryn straightened up and clapped him on the shoulder. "Promise. Now, get out of here. I'll send for you."

Bowie was still wearing that strange expression, but he nodded and made off down the passageway after Dagny and the soldiers.

When they were gone, Aela drew in a slow breath. She looked at Splinter, who was watching them with his arms folded, still lounging against the barred wall.

"Remember what's been promised to you," she said. "It will only be yours if you hold to our agreement."

Splinter cocked a brow. "The steward went behind my back and made an agreement that put my business in jeopardy. She's no friend of mine."

Satisfied that that was as close as Splinter would get to pledging his allegiance, Aela fell into step with Mason, hurriedly outlining their plan. When she finished, Mason said quietly, "All right. Want to tell me what's between you and the prince?"

"He's the king now," Aela replied evasively.

Mason jostled Aela with her shoulder. "Right. So you might have finally found a worthy match … barely."

I don't know. I think I might have ruined everything.

Because it was easier than saying that, Aela elbowed her back then followed Bryn up the passageway, lowering her voice as she spoke to him. "We'd better get up there in time for the council meeting. Are you ready?"

Bryn gave her a long look. "Are *you*? I don't want you to do anything stupid, not on my account."

Aela met his eyes. Her nerves were mounting as they approached the great hall, but beneath them she could feel something else, a dark undercurrent too painful to acknowledge.

"I don't know what you're talking about," she said innocently.

Apparently, Bryn wasn't afraid to acknowledge it. "We've spent the last three weeks together, Aela. And before that I watched you."

"You *watched* me? I did find you in my washroom that one time."

"Stop making jokes," Bryn snapped. "You take risks you know you shouldn't. You let your anger get you into trouble. Splinter saw it immediately. It's what he *liked* about you, that you don't care about your life."

"Bryn –"

"No. Listen, Aela." Bryn reached out, and for an exhilarating moment she thought that he was going to take her hand. Then, with a frustrated grunt, he withdrew. "I don't want you to take risks for me. I don't want your blood on my hands. We have a plan, and we're going to stick to it." He raised his voice then, including Splinter and Mason in the conversation. "Fighting is the last option. For all of us."

At the end of the passageway out of the cells was a fork, with one route leading downwards via a set of stairs to the courtyard, allowing prisoners to be brought into the cells directly. That was the path the soldiers had taken with Bowie and Dagny. With a brief nod, Mason also made off down the same route with considerable haste.

Aela, Bryn, and Splinter took the second, short passage, leading up a set of stairs to a door. Aela wondered if the guards posted outside would be Huntley's Niellan troops or Dunwyan soldiers who Huntley had kept on to serve in low-level positions. She'd never thought she might be an enemy to her own people.

Bryn glanced at her then looked closer. In the shadow of the dark passageway, his brow furrowed. "All right?" he murmured.

She threw him a disbelieving look in response, and they came to a halt at the door. She took a breath and opened it, all but running into two of her own men standing guard. Their eyes went wide as they recognised their commander emerging from the depths of the castle, still covered in Araxa's dried blood.

Bryn stepped in front of Aela and Splinter wordlessly and the soldiers started, hands jumping to the swords at their belts. Aela didn't blame them. They'd been told Bryn was a murderer, accused of patricide, and that Aela was a killer and a deserter, accused of treason. She knew how it looked, showing up here with an armed, intimidating stranger. It was as good as proof that every word Huntley had said against both of them was true.

The guard at their right hesitated then reluctantly grabbed Bryn's arm, calling to his comrades in the guard room ahead as the man at their left took hold of Aela. At the point of swords, they were pushed along the familiar route towards the great hall. It wasn't the ideal way she would have liked to re-enter the room, but it was at least better than a trip to the gallows. She exchanged a look with Bryn, her heart pounding furiously. This was their one chance to take on Huntley, and being marched right into her stronghold by armed guards struck Aela as a wilder gambit than she'd originally thought.

Huntley was on the throne, a dozen of her Niellan guards lining the wall behind her. Before her, seated at the room's perimeter, were Dunwyn's six royal councillors. Jaws dropped as she, Bryn, and Splinter were shoved forward. All eyes were on Bryn. Many of the councillors, Aela saw with some satisfaction, looked more than a little mortified at seeing the crown prince escorted into their presence by heavily-armed guards. It was far easier to call King Saban's son a traitor in his absence than to do it to his face.

The councillor sitting closest to Huntley rose slowly to his feet. About Huntley's age, Clemens Farland had a balding head, piercing dark eyes, and a resting expression of disapproval. Aela narrowed her eyes. She didn't trust him as far as she could throw his sweaty, rotund body. He'd always been too quick to praise the king or anyone the king had favoured and equally as swift to condemn anyone who had disagreed with the king's politics, however diplomatically they'd done so. Aela had wondered more than once if Saban kept him on the council simply to guarantee himself at least one favourable vote in meetings.

"Prince Bryn!" Clemens exclaimed. He didn't throw himself to his knees the way he would have for Bryn's father. Aela frowned. So did Bryn.

He said, "Actually, I think you'll find it's *King* Bryn. I'm so glad you're all here to bear witness as I claim my throne."

Clemens fidgeted awkwardly with the gold buttons on his jacket. Around the room, a few of the councillors shifted in their seats. Aela wondered what they had been expecting. Maybe they'd thought Bryn had come to hack off their heads. Or maybe they had believed he was surrendering himself. Either way, it was glaringly obvious they didn't know the first thing about their prince.

Huntley didn't rise. Lounging on the throne comfortably, she looked Bryn up and down. Aela knew that look, that triumphant appraisal, daring them to challenge her. They hadn't managed to outplay her before, but they would now.

"Prince Bryn –" Huntley began.

"King," Bryn interrupted. "King Bryn."

Huntley gave him a narrow look. "That remains to be seen. You're accused of a grievous crime, and you fled before you could be convicted."

"Before I could be *exonerated*, actually," Bryn corrected again smoothly. He sounded impressively confident. "I understand that, so soon after the Border War, you've had other priorities that far supersede the need to uncover the truth about who killed my father the king." His tone was dry and cutting. Aela remembered his proclivity for this kind of talk from the early days in Splinter's manor. "That's why I've done your job for you," he said.

He raised a hand, inviting Splinter forward. Splinter looked totally at ease despite being in an environment that was not only foreign but indisputably risky. His unnerving air of calm, mixed with his threatening size was clearly unsettling the councillors in the room, who eyed him with varying degrees of fear and distaste. He looked back at them with an expression of supremely aloof amusement, like he was watching a kitten attempt to scratch him with tiny claws. Now, Huntley rose from the throne, eyes on Splinter. There was tension in her shoulders.

"You dare bring him here? An anarchist? These *people*." She gestured at Splinter in disgust, as if he were some abhorrent scuttling vermin, rather than a recent business partner. "Want to see our country in ruin!"

Calmly, Splinter tilted his head to one side, his eyes fixed on Huntley with quiet appraisal. "On the contrary, Your Excellency, I'm thriving in this city. My business has never been better."

Thanks to your ineptitude. The sentiment was implicit in his condescension.

"And yet he wants more!" Huntley said, looking around grandly at the councillors, as Splinter had corroborated a theory she'd previously shared.

"Her Excellency is right. These anarchists will take more and more from us. They will corrupt our good people, as they've corrupted our prince and Commander Rinn," Clemens agreed.

Aela stepped forward. "This is it?" she said to Huntley. "*This* is the lie you've chosen to tell? You say that the anarchists want to take over this country, that they're the reason the king is dead?" She gave Huntley a look of utter scorn. "How convenient for you that the anarchists have corrupted our prince and murdered our king. Now there's no one else but you who can take the throne."

Huntley's eyes narrowed at Aela. "It sounds, Commander Rinn," she said smoothly, "as if you're making an accusation."

"How perceptive," Aela replied. She turned her eyes to the council. She had expected hesitancy from them, but Clemens's haste to back Huntley in the absence of a formal trial against Bryn was unnerving. "Do you all really believe King Saban wouldn't have put up a fight when he was attacked? He was drugged before the murder. With grey dream."

Muttered exclamations rippled through the councillors. Clemens went to Huntley's side. "Grey dream?" he repeated. "The drug the prince took before he murdered his father."

"Somebody slipped me that drug!" Bryn said in a low, trembling voice. "I have *never* taken it by choice."

"You'll forgive us if we don't believe you, Prince Bryn," Clemens said coolly. "Not with your history."

Bryn looked as if he was holding himself back with great effort. Aela recognised the subtle signs, the tightening in his jaw, his face paling, his hands twitching as he resisted the urge to clench them into fists.

"We thought you wouldn't believe him," she said. "So we've brought proof." She looked around at the councillors. "Do you want to know what really happened the night His Highness died? Someone slipped grey dream into Bryn's drink, as well as into the king's. The drug altered the prince's mind. It's true that he went to his father's chambers, but he was set up. The real killer is someone else."

"Really. And who might that be?" Huntley asked scornfully.

Splinter's eyes were glittering as he watched the steward steadily. "Me," he said calmly.

There was a ripple of startled gasps and murmurs from the

council.

Huntley had to raise her voice slightly to speak over it. "That would be an interesting story, if only it were true." She looked around again at the councillors, her expression lamenting. "Commander Rinn has fallen victim to anarchist propaganda. How could that man kill the king and then vanish into thin air?"

"He couldn't," Aela allowed. "He was aided by someone in the castle. Someone who didn't want to get her hands dirty. I have proof. Actually." She turned and nodded to Splinter. "*He* has proof."

Huntley's composure wavered, a flash of uncertainty, and she shot a quick, expectant glance at Clemens.

He said, "This council does not have time for anarchist lies —"

"Let the man speak, Clemens." A tall, older woman who Aela recognised as a noble named Renia Mailand rose, looking at Splinter through piercing dark-brown eyes. Huntley's jaw clenched even tighter as Reinia prompted Splinter, "Well?"

Splinter stepped up to Aela's side, reaching into his pocket. "I've told you before, Steward," he said softly. "I've been running my business for a very long time. Your problem is that you're an outsider, and you cannot outwit us if you do not know our rules." He pulled something out of his pocket. A piece of paper that he calmly unfolded. "You claim never to leave loose ends, but you left a trail of evidence leading right back to Anarchist Underground." His voice, low and dangerous, held utter contempt. "You cannot believe that a pile of coins would buy my unquestioning loyalty while you went behind my back to destroy my business. You were working with another anarchist faction to facilitate a Niellan invasion of Dunwyn. Truly, did you think you would conceal it from me by confining your scheming to a different corner of Anarchist Underground? I *am* Anarchist Underground."

He held up the unfolded paper. It was a confirmation of payment for grey dream … and for Splinter's services in the castle. On the left was the word "seller," and above it, plainly, was Splinter's symbol. And on the right was written, "buyer." Above it, the steward's insignia, manifested in red wax.

"There's only one ring anywhere that can make that symbol," Bryn said, breaking his silence, gesturing at the page. "And right now, *Steward*, it's on your finger."

He pointed toward Huntley's right hand where, sure enough, the silver steward's insignia glinted.

Clemens strode up and snatched the paper from Splinter's hand. His head whipped from the paper to Huntley and back, his eyes widening in horror. "B-but you said —"

He slammed his mouth shut, clearly thinking better of whatever he was about to say. Reinia glided across the room, perusing the paper over Clemens's taut shoulders. She looked up.

"Huntley Bartome, you will be placed under arrest," she commanded. Then, faltering, she looked to Bryn and gave a long, low bow. "That is, if it pleases you, Prince Bryn."

Bryn's gaze turned to Huntley. He gave her a long, slow look. He didn't smile, but his eyes were alight with cold victory. "It's *King* Bryn," he said, with an echo of Huntley's own simpering smile. "And it pleases me."

Huntley whirled around to her guards. "Kill them all!" she barked.

Mason burst in through the double doors, brandishing the bow she'd retrieved from the armoury in the barracks. She let an arrow fly and it sailed straight into the throat of one of Huntley's

Niellan guards. He fell to the floor, the impact knocking his helmet loose. It rolled off, revealing light skin, dark hair, and wide ocean blue eyes.

"*Niellans!*" Renia yelled, and pandemonium erupted.

Mason pressed a blade into Aela's hands, and beside her Bryn swept up a weapon of his own. They fell into a precise rhythm, striking the Niellans down, the lighter red of the armour in contrast with the darkness of the blood that pooled on the floor.

When it was over, Huntley didn't kick or scream or protest. She surrendered in silence, back straight, composure intact as Mason led her out of the great hall to the cells. Her gaze fell chillingly on Aela, and her lips twitched into a calculating smile. Unnerved, Aela moved surreptitiously to Bryn's side.

"I don't think this is over," she murmured.

Bryn nodded and turned to Splinter. "Go. Before anybody gets any ideas about locking you up too."

Splinter didn't move. "Our deal."

"You have my word," Bryn said. "Once this is over, I'll deliver."

Splinter stepped in close to Bryn, lowering his voice. "You'd better, boy. Never forget that I know something about you. If you don't hold to your end of the bargain, *everyone* will find out what you did to your father."

Bryn held Splinter's gaze, unrattled. "I understand."

As Splinter swept from the room, Bryn turned to Mason. "Send a team to assist Chase and Landon in tracking down any soldiers left in the city. If they want their jobs back, they can have them. We need as many fighters as possible at their posts immediately." He turned to Aela. "Alvine's still out there. You're right — this isn't over."

✝

Thirty-Two

I t was as if nothing had changed. The late morning sun beat down on Dunwyn's soldiers as they resumed their regular posts. Aela ached for the soldiers who had left the city or declined to return to their posts, disengaged after Huntley's sudden decision to disband the army. Their force of almost six thousand would have to do. And thanks to their years of regimented training, it was as if their last few weeks spent drinking and idling had barely occurred.

Having spent the past two hours giving orders and taking reports, Aela watched with satisfaction from the vantage point of a bastion overlooking the Great Ocean to the east. If she didn't think about all that had happened, she could almost picture Saban walking along the ramparts to receive her morning report.

She shoved her hand into her pocket and wooden ridges scratched her skin. She pulled out Amory's box, turning it over in her hands. He'd said to open it when she was safe. Things didn't exactly feel *safe*, but it was at least a quiet moment. Slowly, carefully, she slid a dagger under the wax-sealed lid of the box, levering one side open. Her fingers slid along the rich velvet lining inside, meeting the cold, hard surface of a metallic object.

Frowning, Aela pulled on the metal, working it out until she held it in her hand. She set the box on the wall and examined the gold chain curled in her palm. At the end of the chain was a golden pendant. It was heavy when she lifted it.

A jolt of recognition pulsed through Aela. The symbol was a golden eagle, wings spread elegantly. She'd seen this symbol on hundreds of banners, on armour, on tents and saddles during the Border War. This was King Marcus's insignia, forged in gold, which meant it belonged to a member of the royal family.

How had something like this ended up in a tiny Dunwyan village?

"Aela."

She jumped, grabbing the box off the wall she shoved the pendant inside and stowed safely it back in her pocket, whirling to face Bryn. He'd excused himself earlier, and Aela had assumed he'd gone to get cleaned up, but he wore the same bloodstained clothes. There were bruise-like circles beneath his eyes, which were red and swollen. Aela wondered if he'd spent the past few hours in the lonely vaults beneath the castle, where Saban's body was entombed.

"You did it," he said, looking out over the soldiers on the ramparts with relief.

"No, you did. These women and men are loyal to you. You shouldn't have doubted that."

Bryn shook his head. "I never doubted them. Only me." He let out a breath that was almost a laugh. "I still do. I'm … glad you're here."

He looked up at her with uncharacteristic timidity, and Aela saw shame in his eyes. Instinct propelled her forward. Desire to drive the hurt from his expression made her reach out, brushing the tips of her fingers down his arm, to his hand. She was expecting him to grip her fingers with his, but instead his hand fell limply away. Painfully, Aela swallowed the lump in her throat. Maybe she couldn't be … this … for Bryn, not after everything that had happened between them. But she could still give him her loyalty.

In time, the ache in her chest would heal, and she'd be able to stand a professional distance from Bryn. They would talk strategy, and she'd watch on from afar as he courted other women and one day married his queen, while she deservedly remained locked out of the fortress he'd built around his heart. One day, she'd be capable of enduring the warmth of his presence without feeling on the verge of breaking down over what her foolish distrust had cost her. She would make herself capable of it. She owed that to Bryn.

She opened her mouth to tell him that he wasn't alone …

"Your Highness!"

She and Bryn whirled at the same time as Chase and Landon hurried towards the bastion. Their faces were drawn and pale, set with the steady focus that Aela recognised as the calm before a fight. She took a tentative step towards them. "What's the matter?"

Landon looked to Chase. As the ranking soldier, it was his place to speak. Aela could tell from the look on Chase's face that he wished it wasn't. Steeling himself, he stepped forward and dropped to one knee before Bryn. "Your Highness, we've received word from a scout. The Niellan army's moving towards the valley. They'll be at the walls in a matter of hours."

Bryn took off across the ramparts. They all followed him, circling the castle until they were looking out over the vast greenery of the valley and the forest beyond. At the edge of the tree line, Aela could see banners, flickering red and gold like flames, emerging from the wall of verdant life. Banners bearing the soaring eagle symbol she'd just held in her hand.

"How many soldiers?" she asked Chase.

"Ten thousand, at our scout's estimate. A woman who calls herself Nielle's steward released her with a message."

"Ten thousand," Aela said faintly.

Even Dunwyn's full force would have been outnumbered, depleted by the Border War. They were depleted further in the absence of those who'd failed or refused to return to their posts. She felt, once again, Huntley's guiding hand, pushing the country towards destruction.

Bryn leaned towards Aela, lowering his voice. "Alvine must've mobilised right after we escaped Eterre."

"Your Highness," Landon said, "word's spreading fast. The city's emptying. People are seeking refuge inside the castle."

Bryn passed a hand over his face. "The Niellan army made it across the entire country undetected. How come no one raised the alarm before they got this close to the city?"

Aela clenched her fists. "There are no patrols on the border, no scouts on the roads. If Nielle met any resistance on the way here, it would have been cut down before anyone could get a message to us."

Her mind reeled with terrible thoughts. Who knew how many towns had been destroyed when this tide of thousands-strong warriors swept across the land they'd fought to protect? She called on all her self-restraint to hold back from marching down to the cells and running Huntley through with her sword.

By her side, Bryn swore. "You were right. Alvine's coming for Huntley. What was the scout's message?"

Chase cleared his throat uneasily. Aela braced herself. He was a seasoned soldier. If the Niellans had done something to take him by surprise, she was sure she wasn't going to like it.

"She wants to meet with you. She demands that the steward be present."

Bryn ran a hand across his mouth. After a long silence, he looked up at Chase. "Fetch Huntley from the cells."

When the soldiers were gone, Aela turned to him gravely and told him what he already knew. "Alvine's not coming for her mother. She's coming for Dunwyn."

Thirty-Three

“You seem to have settled nicely onto the throne.” The steward's ring had been taken from Huntley, but she didn't kneel before Bryn, nor did she avert her eyes to the floor as a sign of respect. She stood before Bryn's throne in the great hall with her hands chained, her posture as authoritative as ever, as if she was still in total control.

Bryn set his elbows on the arms of the throne, palms pressed together, watching Huntley calmly over his joined hands. “I have,” he replied evenly. “Thank you.”

Unease washed over Aela like a constant, relentless tide. She stood to the right of Bryn's throne, hands clasped behind her back, watching Huntley carefully. When she'd been retrieved from the cells, she'd been unsurprised, as if all of this was going exactly as it should.

“Enjoy it while it lasts, *Your Highness*,” Huntley simpered.

The door slammed open, but it wasn't Alvine who appeared on the threshold. Bowie's eyes were wild with panic as he scanned the room.

"Someone showed them —" he began.

“What the hell are you doing here?” Bryn interrupted, rising to his feet.

Bowie didn't appear to hear him. He froze as his piercing blue eyes landed on Huntley, darkening murderously. Yanking a dagger from his belt, he advanced on her resolutely. Huntley's jaw fell open as Bowie moved towards her, weapon raised. For the first time today, she looked genuinely shocked.

Aela moved, but Bryn was faster, launching off the throne and down the steps of the dais, placing a hand on Bowie's chest, forcing him back.

"Bowie!" Bryn snapped. "Hey, stop!"

He wrapped his hand around the boy's wrist. Bowie tried to raise the dagger again, and Bryn wrested it from his hand.

"Bowie!" Bryn cupped a hand around the back of Bowie's neck, forcing Bowie's gaze to meet his. "What are you *doing*? Step back."

Bowie struggled in Bryn's grip. His gaze hadn't broken away from Huntley, and his expression was intent and deadly. "You're killing him! You're killing him! *I'll kill you!*"

"Step back, Bowie," Bryn barked. "Now! That's an order from your king!"

"His *king*." Huntley laughed, smirking at Bowie. "They really don't know anything, do they?"

Bryn's hand tightened on Bowie's shoulder. "Don't speak to him again," he snapped at Huntley. He whirled on Bowie. "I told you to stay put at Splinter's house."

"They're coming in through Anarchist Underground!" Bowie's voice trembled, almost unintelligible as he rushed to speak. The desperation in his eyes was almost manic. "I don't know how they knew to do it. I don't know who told them –"

"Slow down. You're not making any sense," Bryn interrupted.

"You need to listen –"

He broke off as the door opened and a party of three swept inside. Alvine was flanked by a pair of Niellan soldiers, both of them carrying swords. One of them also carried a brown hessian bag. Pulling the red hood from her head, Alvine cut a sweeping gaze across the room through piggy, calculating eyes. Bowie's posture was very, very tense.

"I would like my mother returned to me," Alvine announced without preamble.

Huntley flashed a smile. Straightening up, Bryn squared his shoulders, facing Alvine. "I take it you're the one commanding the army of invaders at my gates?" he said.

Alvine gave him a courteous smile. "It is my army, yes."

"I thought it was King Marcus's army," Bryn said coolly.

"And I'm commanding it at the king's bidding."

"King Marcus didn't command you here." Bowie took a step forward, ignoring Bryn's furious warning look.

Alvine's eyes flew wide. Her expression mirrored Huntley's, absolute shock.

Huntley followed the direction of her daughter's gaze greedily. "Isn't he a pretty child, Alvine?"

The two women shared a weighty look. With a small, decisive nod, Alvine looked back to Bryn, unsettling triumph in her eyes.

"Yes indeed," she replied quietly, "no one could *ever* forget a face like his."

"You didn't come here to make small talk," Bryn growled.

Alvine's small blue eyes glittered with amusement. "Tell me why I came here then, Prince Bryn."

"It's King Bryn now." Bryn matched her cool tone. "And you came because you're under the mistaken impression that you can take my throne from me. I strongly suggest you stand your army down and go from my lands immediately. If you don't, we will cut you down."

Alvine sighed with exaggerated regret. "Alas, I cannot stand my army down, Prince Bryn. Not while you have a Niellan prisoner in your custody."

"A *what?*" Surely Bryn didn't mean for that to tumble from his mouth. He shot Aela a questioning look, but she shook her head. Huntley had been the only prisoner in the cells, and despite her traitorous affiliations, she wasn't Niellan.

"Huntley is a citizen of Dunwyn," Aela said icily. "We have no Niellan prisoners here."

Alvine's gaze shifted. At first, Aela thought she was looking at Bryn, then she followed the woman's eyeline and realised it was fixed elsewhere.

On Bowie.

"Tell them, Your Majesty," she said. "Don't be afraid. No harm will come to you here."

Aela heard Bryn's breath catch. Bowie looked sick, but he raised his chin and looked Alvine dead in the eye. "It's not what will happen here that I'm worried about," he said softly.

Bryn's head whipped around to stare at Bowie.

"You are holding the crown prince of Nielle against his will," Alvine said.

"The crown prince of Nielle is dead," Bryn snapped, still staring at Bowie. Uncertainty wavered in his voice.

Alvine's smile widened. "Why don't you check the chain around the boy's neck if you require proof?" She drew herself up. "He will be taken back to Nielle so that we can garner an understanding of how he was forced into a plot to poison his father, the king."

Dread rising, Aela looked at Bowie. All the remaining colour had drained from his face. When it became evident he was not going to speak, she said, "That's the pot calling the kettle black if ever I heard it."

Alvine raised an eyebrow. "Is that so? The architect of the plot might beg to differ. At least, his written confession might."

"What architect?" Aela replied scornfully. "What confession?"

Alvine raised a hand, and her guard handed over the hessian sack. Alvine pulled something out and tossed it across the room so that it landed and rolled, bumping gently against Bowie's scuffed boots, leaving a dark-red trail of blood and gore across the pristine white marble.

The object was so out of place in the great hall that Aela didn't immediately register what it was. Then Bowie gasped and stumbled backwards, pressing his hand to his mouth, and recognition plummeted through Aela's gut. There was a spiderweb tattoo below the right eye, the mouth hung open. On his face was etched an unchanging expression of shock and fear. The tender skin at his neck was gruesomely jagged, where a blade had sheared through flesh and bone.

Walter was dead.

Entirely undisturbed by the gruesome sight, Alvine said breezily, "If you do not return the prince and my mother to me, I will have no choice but to reclaim them by force. Is that what you want? You have an hour. Decide quickly."

She turned and strode from the room, the Niellan soldiers hurrying in her wake.

Bryn remained deadly still, his eyes fixed on the door, as Huntley was escorted back to the cells. It wasn't until the room had emptied that he turned to Bowie, who stood frozen, staring at Walter's severed head.

"Prince … The prince of Nielle died." Bryn shook his head, as if furious with himself for missing something. "It was a lie."

Bowie closed his eyes with the air of someone who had been punched repeatedly and was preparing for the final, knockout blow. He looked up at Bryn, and the expression on his face was adult, a clear-eyed admission of wrongdoing in the face of a betrayed friend. It would be better, Aela thought, if Bowie behaved like the child he was, if he cried or argued with juvenile petulance. It might not feel so calculated.

Bryn stalked over to Bowie, who flinched as Bryn reached under his collar and pulled out the chain that was always concealed beneath his shirt. On the end of it was a silver pendant. Aela saw with a sickening jolt the flying eagle, King Marcus of Nielle's insignia, a near-perfect twin of the one in her pocket.

Bryn made a strangled sound, inadequate to express what he was surely feeling. But Aela understood completely. Everything she knew was crumbling like rotting wood, intact on the outside but broken and dead beneath. Little Bowie, the boy from the streets who could pick pockets and scrap and swear like a sailor was of royal blood. The only legitimate heir to Nielle's throne.

"Captain Tanner!" Bryn called. Mason stepped inside the great hall, and he shoved Bowie towards her. "Put him in my chambers. Guard the doors. Don't let him out until I say so."

Bowie took a jolting step backwards, as if he was about to turn and run. Mason clamped a hand down on his shoulder. "Wait, please," Bowie gasped. "You can't send me back there. *Bryn*, please."

It was the first time Bowie had used Bryn's real name, and it was like pouring liquor onto an open flame. Bryn's fury exploded.

"My people are about to be killed because of you! I can't keep the heir to the Niellan throne here in Dunwald." He passed a hand over his face as if suddenly exhausted. When he spoke again, his voice was colourless. "And you should *never* have manipulated me into doing so. I can't put the welfare of one Niellan, prince or not, over the lives of my own people. All those things you said to me in the forest, the way you treated me when you discovered who *I* am ... And you were hiding *this*?" He looked at Mason. "Get him out of my sight."

Bowie dropped his head. Fighting back tears, he set his jaw and said nothing, allowing Mason to steer him towards the door and out of the great hall. The door slammed shut.

"You're not really going to hand him over to Alvine, are you?" Aela demanded.

Bryn made a helpless gesture. "He's Nielle's *crown prince*. You think any Niellan in that army outside our walls would believe Marcus's nine-year-old son *chose* to come into the enemy's capital? With Bowie here, they have every right to attack us."

"I know that, but Bowie's right about Alvine. *She* wants the throne. If you give her the chance, she'll kill him, and you'll spend your entire reign fighting to push back a Niellan invasion at the border."

Bryn flinched. "What if he has some part in this?"

Aela stared. "Who, *Bowie*?"

Bryn clenched his fists. "What if this is a plan to turn my people against me further? Imagine how it'll look if I put the welfare of one Niellan above the lives of every Dunwyan in this city."

Aela pointed at Walter's severed head, lying on the floor. "Bryn, Alvine *killed* Walter, the man Bowie was working with to save Marcus's life."

"He manipulated me into helping him."

"That's not fair. He didn't know who you were when he met you. All he knew was that you were kind to him. Why do you think he reacted the way he did when he discovered *your* true identity? He probably thought you'd want him dead. Don't confirm his worst fears by placing him in the hands of those who would do him harm!"

Bryn turned away. "I wouldn't," he murmured. "Of course I wouldn't. But if I don't give him over to Alvine, *thousands* of people in this city are going to die." He jammed his fingers into his hair. "Gods, I shouldn't have gotten angry with him. I'm *still* angry! Why the *fuck* didn't he say anything? I thought he trusted me."

"He doesn't trust anyone," Aela said sadly.

"With good fucking reason, after what I just did. He's afraid of me." Bryn's voice cracked. "If I go speak to him now, we won't get anywhere."

"I'll go," Aela said.

Thirty-Four

T he grandeur of Bryn's chambers was impersonal and cold. It was immediately clear that nobody had lived here since he'd fled on the night of Saban's death. Eight months of dust coated the floor and surfaces. The bed was unmade, one of the curtains half shut. A pool of light spilled across the floor, which was littered with expensive casual clothing, probably the outfit Bryn had discarded in favour of the formal suit he'd worn to his father's feast.

Naturally, Aela had never set foot in Bryn's rooms before. Entering now should have been acutely personal, but instead she felt oddly detached. There were no signs of the Bryn she knew, no weapons, no personal trinkets, even the black clothes heaped on the floor didn't suit him, too dark. Bryn looked better in brown, to match his eyes.

Bowie sat in the parlour, perched on the window alcove with his head on his knees. He looked smaller than usual. Ever vigilant, he looked up with a jolt at the sound of her light footsteps, his attention catching on her. He hugged himself tighter.

"The king sent me," she told him.

Bowie shook his head. "I need to speak to *him*. It's important!

He doesn't understand —"

"My questions first, then your excuses." Aela took advantage of his silence. "You knew Araxa Leren. She said she raised you. But if you're the prince, how is that possible?"

Bowie swallowed hard, not looking at Aela. "You already know the story. I was kidnapped."

"Your father lied about that."

"*No*." Bowie's blue eyes blazed furiously. "He didn't lie. He *wouldn't* lie, not about that. He was betrayed by Huntley. She paid Araxa to take me from the castle so that the prince would be gone for Alvine. Huntley was visiting Eterre from Dunwald. She made sure Araxa could get into the castle and then Araxa took me into the forest and put a knife to my throat."

He raised his chin, revealing a thin white scar that marred his pale skin. Angry red marks slashed through it, lingering signs of Bowie's compulsive scratching. He drew in a shaky breath. His fists were clenched so tightly that his knuckles whitened. Aela knew what trying not to cry looked like.

She moved years around in her head. The prince of Nielle had been nearing his sixth birthday when he'd gone missing. Bowie was the right age. He was so small now, would've been even smaller then. He looked away out the window at the endless expanse of the Great Ocean.

"I couldn't fight, couldn't defend myself. I was useless back then." Bowie's expression was as distant as the swells mounting on the horizon. "But Araxa decided she didn't want to kill me. She said I was worth more alive."

"She blackmailed Huntley," Aela guessed.

Bowie nodded. "She brought me to meet with Huntley in the forest and said that she was going to keep me alive and that everyone would find out what Huntley had done. She promised to keep me hidden if Huntley paid for her silence. Huntley paid Araxa for years until she found out I'd run away."

Aela thought back to Walter's inn, when Araxa had spoken with Bowie.

They still want you, you know.

"I never wanted to leave Walter. I just … *liked* him." Bowie sounded painfully bewildered. "But Splinter made me go, and the inn was on Araxa's route to Dunwald anyway. I was always scared I'd get Walter killed." His voice cracked and he closed his eyes, drawing in a few deep breaths before continuing. "I thought if I was worth something to Splinter, he'd protect me from Araxa … and Huntley. She came to Splinter's house the day after we fought Araxa's men in the Devil's Tongue. Do you remember?"

That day was drilled painfully into her memory, the moment she began to pull at the thread, unravelling the truth of what Huntley really was.

I was told that you are in possession of something that belongs to me.

"She was looking for *you*," Aela whispered. "She's the reason Nielle attacked our border four years ago. Marcus thought he *had* to fight us. He really believed you'd been killed, and that it was an act of war by Dunwyn. She set him up."

Aela saw Bowie's small hands clench into shaking fists. He looked up at her. "*I* started the fighting again. *I'm* the reason so many people died in the Border War. I'm the reason your soldiers got drugged at Hiver."

Aela pressed her eyes closed. Terrible realisation settled over her, an imposing weight crushing her body. "The war was never the point, only a byproduct of the plan to install Alvine into power in Nielle and Dunwyn."

"But it all happened because of me. The grey dream that's poisoning King Marcus. What Bryn did, killing his father. He was my *friend,* and it happened because of me." The calm expression on his face shattered and he looked away determinedly. "I didn't want to do this. I didn't want to fight or lie or hurt anybody." He lowered his voice to a whisper. "I don't want to do any of it anymore."

"Bowie," Aela said gently, "you're not Bryn's enemy. You are not your father, and Bryn is not his. You two can take your thrones and change all of this."

Bowie looked back from the window, shaking his head. His eyes were red with unshed tears. "Bryn's in danger."

"What do you mean?"

"Dunwyans won't accept a Niellan queen, especially not while Bryn's still alive. There's only one thing she can do."

Dread sank into Aela, chilling her to the bone. "She's going to attack anyway. She's coming after Bryn."

A sudden commotion rang out far below. Aela and Bowie scrambled off the alcove, bursting into the hallway, looking out the window over the sprawling expanse of Anarchist Underground. A soldier toppled from the ramparts, arrows protruding from his gut and chest. Far below, Aela saw a flood of red flowing out of the slums. Soldiers in Nielle's military uniform.

She gasped, turning to Bowie, whose gaze was grim and steady as the enemy surrounded the castle walls. More shouts, and the drawbridge was raised hastily over the chasm.

"That's why I came back to the castle. I wanted to tell you," Bowie said urgently. "They came in through Anarchist Underground. Someone showed them the way."

Thirty-Five

"Let *go* of me!" Bowie tried to tug his wrist free of Aela's grip. She tightened her hold and led him around a corner towards the walls.

"Bowie!" Aela said, as the boy exerted another pull. "It's *Bryn.* He's not going to hurt you."

Bowie stared up at her, his blue eyes accusing. "No, he'll let Alvine do that."

Aela shoved open a door, and they emerged into blinding daylight atop the ramparts. An arrow whipped past Aela's shoulder, and she ducked behind the wall's protective barrier, pulling Bowie down with her.

Bryn was a few yards away, standing in the shelter of a guard tower, issuing orders.

"… aim for Anarchist Underground. Get anyone who's fled the city into the castle. Make sure no one has weapons on them. Keep them under guard. Aela!" He pushed his hair off his face. "How the hell did they get into the city?"

Aela shook her head. "That's what Bowie was trying to warn us about. Someone on the inside showed them a way in through Underground —"

Bryn lunged forward, grabbing Aela and Bowie's arms and

jerking them into the shelter of the tower as another volley of arrows soared over the wall. "He's supposed to be upstairs." He gestured at Bowie without looking at him.

"You need to leave," Aela said. "Both of you."

"You know that's not happening."

"Bryn, if the Niellans break through these walls, they'll be coming for you and Bowie. This may be a fortress, but we can't outlast them forever. Let me do my job. Yours is to survive."

"I'm not going to run!" Bryn barked at her.

"Bryn," Aela said. "Your people are defenceless inside the castle. You need to get them down into the sanctuary. They can hide in the cavern under the castle until low tide then skirt around the army across the rocks and into the forest. We'll send a contingent of soldiers, anyone we can spare."

Bryn pinched the bridge of his nose. "Anyone we can spare? Have you *seen* the size of Alvine's army?"

They looked out on the sea of Niellan fighters moving through the city, red banners flooding the streets right down to the gates. She shared a dark look with Bryn. "We need time to get everyone out."

"The coin trick." Bowie stared out at the Niellan army. *His* army.

"What?" Bryn said.

"That trick you taught me," Bowie explained as if it was obvious. "You said it's about making people look somewhere else."

Bryn, still furious at Bowie, surely didn't want to look as impressed as he did. "I'm going to hate this plan, aren't I?"

Bowie was still staring out at the flood of soldiers below. "You're only going to do what they want."

***

"Commander, I'd like to restate that I oppose this plan." Mason's face was grim as she fastened Bowie into body armour that was too big for him. Aela and Bryn watched on as she secured the lacings with more force than was necessary. "We're playing into the hands of the enemy."

Bowie flinched as the hard metal bit into his tender skin, but he didn't say anything. They'd returned to Bryn's chambers, where Bowie had explained what they needed to do. Then he'd fallen into silence, staring fixedly at the floor.

"That's the point, Mason," Aela replied. "Their focus will be on getting what they want from us, not on the people fleeing into the sanctuary."

Mason shook her head, muttering an oath under her breath. If it had been anyone else, Aela might have reprimanded them for it, but Mason had been doing this a long time. She knew a reckless plan when she saw it, but she was loyal and would follow Aela's orders, even if she hated them. The least Aela could do was allow her to curse about it.

"He's ready." Mason pressed Bowie forward. He stumbled, his arms weighed down by the thick armour. He still didn't say anything. His expression was carefully shuttered, but he swallowed convulsively. He was scared. Bryn looked at him for a moment, as if he might say something, then he turned his eyes on Aela and dropped her a nod, communicating with one look all that he couldn't articulate aloud. He would see her later. They would all make it to the end of this safely.

Then he was gone.

Mason slipped out of the room, and then it was Aela and Bowie alone. Bowie stood with his arms slightly outstretched, awkward in the bulky armour.

Aela knelt before him. "I never understood why you cared so much about King Marcus, but I do now."

Bowie shook his head. His gaze and voice were distant. "You don't understand anything."

At a loss, Aela rose. The box dropped from her pocket, landing face down on the floor with a heavy smack.

Bowie jumped at the sound. He glared down at the box … and froze.

The lid cracked and the golden pendant inside clinked onto the floor. Bowie reeled back, looking up at Aela, his expression twisting into a complex combination of recognition, horror and something like … worship?

Frowning, Aela bent down and hastily gathered the items off the floor. When she straightened, the boy was still frozen.

"Bowie?" she said.

He could have been made of marble, he was so still. In Niellan, in a voice so soft it was barely a breath, he murmured a single word.

"*No.*"

Thirty-Six

Aela stood in the courtyard, staring up at the gate. Through the thick wood, the sound of arrows hitting steel had subsided, as had the cries of wounded soldiers. The drawbridge creaked as it lowered over the chasm.

From the walls above, the raised voice of a herald announced the ceasefire's commencement, notifying Alvine of their intention to surrender Bowie and Huntley to Nielle. Aela glanced left at Mason, stone-faced beside her, a hand gripping Huntley's arm. Bowie was on her right, fidgeting with the armour plating his chest. By now, word of his identity could have travelled through the Dunwyan army lining the wall above them. When she called down the volley of arrows, Aela didn't want any strays, accidental or otherwise, to hit him. Desperately, she hoped that this ridiculous plan would buy enough time for Bryn to lead the people down through the cavernous sanctuary and into the safety of the forest.

"Open the gates," she called.

The doors opened, the portcullis lifted, and Aela blinked as sunlight drenched the shaded courtyard. She raised a hand to shield her eyes and saw Alvine and a guard of six Niellan soldiers crossing the drawbridge. Steering Bowie forward, Aela went to meet them.

She stopped at the centre of the bridge. Alvine and her soldiers halted a few feet away. "Prince Bryn isn't joining us?" Alvine asked, brows raised.

"The *king*," Aela said firmly, "is on his throne, where he'll remain, despite your best efforts. Apparently time works differently in Nielle. The hour you offered for us to deliberate your terms really flew by."

Alvine shrugged delicately. "I assumed your answer was plain."

"You assumed incorrectly."

Alvine's hostile gaze came to rest on Bowie. "You'll return the prince to Nielle?"

"Dunwyn won't acquiesce to your demands unless there's something in it for us."

"You'd strike a bargain with me? With your prince absent?"

"My *king*," Aela stressed a second time, "has delivered to me his terms. If we give you what you want, you'll leave Dunwyn and never return."

"Never return to Dunwyn?" Alvine pretended to think about it. "I'm not sure that suits me. If you want another fight, Commander Rinn, I'd be happy to oblige." Slowly, Alvine's gaze turned back on Bowie. "What a shame, so much death. Bryn's father and so many soldiers who were simply following orders. If only there was something somebody could do to stop it. But since there isn't…"

She shrugged, turning her back.

"I can." Bowie moved forward, closing the distance between Alvine and her soldiers. Alvine stopped but didn't turn. Bowie said it again, "I can do something."

Slowly, Alvine turned, her expression coloured with surprise.

The first threatening tendrils of foreboding bloomed in Aela's chest. The only thing that had surprised Alvine before this moment was seeing Bowie in the great hall. Aela had a feeling she wasn't truly surprised now.

"You know," Alvine said to Bowie softly.

"He told you, didn't he? You could actually do it right this time," Bowie took another steady step forward.

Self-doubt nudged at Aela, who didn't understand what was passing between Alvine and Bowie. Control was slipping through her fingers. Had enough time passed to allow the people to safely escape? She wasn't sure, but she was beginning to feel as if it didn't matter. It felt like their plan was a small deviation from a much bigger strategy, entirely orchestrated by Alvine and Huntley. The power balance was shifting in her enemy's favour. Aela's hand twitched, an almost imperceptible signal to anyone who wasn't watching for it.

In the towers, her archers were watching. The order sounded, and a moment later arrows rained down around them.

"Bowie, get back!" Aela called. He was in the midst of the descending storm of arrows, Nielle's soldiers advancing towards him.

Abandoning Huntley, Mason reached Bowie first, grabbing his arm to haul him away. She staggered, dropping to one knee. Aela lurched forward, instinct driving her. She glimpsed the dagger protruding from Mason's gut, thrown by one of Alvine's guards, advancing towards them over the bridge.

"Mason, get inside!" Aela called, placing herself in front of the captain and Bowie.

The first clash of steel sent a shudder up Aela's arm. Fighting multiple opponents was one of her strengths, but she usually didn't have to worry about protecting an unarmed child, vulnerable in the middle of the fight. In Aela's peripheral vision, she saw Mason struggle to her feet, one hand pressed against the bloody wound in her abdomen, the other reaching for Bowie, who was still staring at Alvine, standing safely behind her soldiers. Instead of retreating to safety, he seemed caught in Alvine's gaze, trapped like an insect in amber.

Aela felt the fighting change in quality around her, lighter but still consuming her attention. Two soldiers had dropped away from the fight. With splintered attention, Aela scanned the bridge, found them advancing on Mason. One kicked her, the booted foot landing on the dagger sticking out of her stomach, sending her sprawling backwards, perilously close to the edge of the bridge and the sheer drop beyond.

Bowie grabbed Mason's sword, but fighting a soldier three times his age while wearing heavy armour and carrying a weapon made for a grown woman … Aela knew what was going to happen.

Her opponents were tiring, but it was still four on one. She shoved one of them with her foot, and he toppled from the bridge, hurtling into the rocky crevasse. Three soldiers left, clearly Alvine's best fighters. Above the relentless barrage of steel against steel came the unmistakable sound of Bowie's sword clattering onto the bridge. Aela staggered back in time to see the hilt of a Niellan soldier's blade come down hard on Bowie's head. Beyond his crumpled body, Huntley was unguarded and raced towards Alvine. A Niellan soldier scooped Bowie up as Mason tried desperately to pull herself up through a haze of pain. The soldier kicked Mason again and this time she went over, her fingertips latching frantically into a gap in the bridge's wooden floor, barely keeping her from plummeting.

"Aela!" she cried.

Dunwyn's volley of arrows had stopped. Aela and Mason were too close to the enemy for the archers on the wall to get a clear shot. Alvine's guard backed off at some unheard command, and the order to fire rose from the castle walls again.

In a panic, Aela whirled. "No!"

One of Alvine's soldiers had Bowie, unconscious, slung over his shoulder, directly in the trajectory of the arrows. She froze, irresolute. The soldier carrying Bowie was retreating towards a line of advancing Niellan soldiers. Mason was barely holding onto the bridge. Aela made her choice, skidding to the ground beside Mason, grabbing her friend's forearms and exerting all her strength to pull her to safety.

"Get back inside!" she ordered Mason.

On her feet again, she started after Bowie, but the Niellan army was closing in, moving closer across the bridge. Alvine walked calmly away as her soldiers advanced. Looking back, she smiled victoriously at Aela, then disappeared within a sea of Niellan fighters.

All Aela could do was turn her back on Bowie, fleeing inside the walls of the city.

They staggered into the great hall, and Mason collapsed onto a wooden bench by the wall. Ashen-faced, she pulled the dagger from the wound with a grunt and pressed her hand there as it leaked blood. Mason rattled off a string of curses under her breath, punctuated by sharp, shallow breaths. Her forehead was pricked with sweat, but Aela knew she wasn't swearing because of the pain.

Distant yells and an almighty crash signalled the Niellans breaking through the portcullis. Steel clashed, and there were more yells as fighting erupted in the citadel. She straightened up.

"We need to get out of here," she told Mason hurriedly. "We're outnumbered. The army needs to retreat to the sanctuary."

She took a step towards the corridor to go and give the order. At the far end of the room, the door thudded open. Sweat-drenched and dishevelled, Bryn appeared in the doorway.

"They're gone. The people made it down –"

He strode forward, concerned as he saw Mason's wound. He looked to Aela as he moved, relaxing slightly, realising she was unhurt. Then his gaze moved away, flicking about the room, searching, confusion turning to fear as he failed to find the third face he sought.

"Aela, where is he?"

She opened her mouth to reply but was cut off by a small, pained groan as Mason lifted herself off the bench. Stiffly, she went to her knees.

"Forgive me, Your Highness," she said solemnly. "I should have protected him."

Bryn went white. He looked back at Aela, his eyes begging for an explanation. Chest tight, she shook her head.

"He's not …" Bryn's voice was quiet, raw and adamant.

She shook her head. "He was alive. But he's with Alvine … and Huntley."

"Then we have to go after him."

"And do what?" Aela asked. She felt like she was falling. "Fight Alvine's entire army? Bryn, we need to *run*. We're outnumbered. Alvine already has Dunwald."

"If we leave him, he's *dead*!" Bryn shouted. He looked around helplessly, his breaths coming quickly. Then he passed a hand over his face and turned, yanking the door open. With a harsh crack, it slammed back against the wall as he punched it violently on his way out.

Aela's mind buzzed. She couldn't think, except about Bowie. This had been his plan, and as always they'd trusted it, trusted Bowie and his brilliant mind. Now, she couldn't believe they had. Aela was Dunwyn's commander; *she* was the one who was supposed to have the answers. She'd failed, and now a little boy was going to lose his life.

She sent a herald with the order for all the remaining soldiers to abandon the fight and flee into the sanctuary. Then she watched in silence as Landon came to sling one of Mason's arms across his shoulders, leaving Aela alone in the great hall as the castle emptied out.

She shoved her hands hard into her pockets. Her fingers collided with the sharp-angled edges the box Amory had given her. Its corner barely left a scratch, but breaking the skin allowed everything else to break loose too, grief and fury and frustration at her failure. Fear and helplessness, knowing that Dunwald was overrun and that Alvine and Huntley would claim both Dunwyn and Nielle. They'd lost.

Saban had always known how to respond to complicated situations. Aela felt useless and slow and stupid in contrast. She grabbed the box from her pocket and threw it across the room with a furious scream.

The Niellan royal insignia clattered to the ground, and with it the box, now in pieces. Something light and delicate floated down through the air, landing soundlessly on the ground beside the broken shards of wood.

Paper.

It must have been tucked beneath the lining of the box. Aela picked it up and unfolded the letter written in elegant, curved script.

My daughter Aela,

I named you Rinn, the Niellan word for survivor, *because that is what you are, the survivor who will secure the future of our country and our bloodline. The survivor who will protect and preside over Nielle, as our family has for two hundred years.*

My health is deteriorating. With each passing day, I feel myself becoming old and ill, and I've written this to you because I fear for my own life now, the way I have always feared for yours. You are my only heir. From the day you were born, I knew you would be under constant threat from our enemies. The only way to truly keep you safe was to convince the world you were dead, to send you away from Eterre so you could grow up in peace.

To this day, I have lingering doubts about my decision. When your escorts took you across the border into Dunwyn, I lost contact with them and you never arrived at your final destination.

Some years after your disappearance, your mother passed while giving birth to a son. He would have been your younger brother, but he was stillborn. I took in another infant to pose as him. He wears an insignia identical to this one, but in silver. I hope that the focus of our enemies will remain on him.

Those who are in my confidence say you are lost, but my faith is stronger than my fear. My agents have searched for you for years, and their search will continue, ceaselessly, until you are found. I have to believe that when you receive this message, you will return home, for your true name is not Aela Rinn. It is Aela of Nielle. Our princess. Our future queen.

I never stopped loving you.

Your father,

King Marcus of Nielle

The bottom of the letter was stamped with a familiar seal, a flying eagle.

Aela staggered as if she'd been punched.

Queen?

She couldn't be the queen of Nielle.

She had fought for Dunwyn, given her *blood* for Dunwyn. Amory and Ewan, Dunwyans, had raised her. Her mother was Dunwyan.

But her father …

Her whole body trembled as realisation shuddered through her. She was a Borderlander and she'd always known half of her was Niellan. She'd just never considered … King Marcus's wife had been Dunwyan. Their offspring would produce a child who looked like a traditional Borderlander, a child who looked like Aela.

All the breath left Aela's lungs with the force of a galewind, her mind jumping back to Bowie. He wasn't the heir to Nielle's throne, but a decoy. And the way he had reacted when he'd seen Aela's gold pendant, the resemblance it bore to the silver eagle around his neck …

Bowie knew who Aela really was.

He'd known when he faced Huntley and Alvine in the great hall and on the drawbridge. He had stood before Alvine and the entire Niellan army, pretending the heir he'd been raised to protect was not standing right beside him.

King Marcus of Nielle was Aela's father. And he had raised Bowie to deflect danger from Aela, except …

He told you, didn't he?

Aela's whole body was cold. Alvine and Huntley must have ascertained from King Marcus in his drug-addled state that

Bowie was not the true heir. They knew he was the only person living, and with a lucid mind, who might have the identity of the real heir to the Niellan throne.

Alvine needed Bowie. Alive but not unharmed. She felt sick.

Alvine and Huntley had Dunwald. They had everything they wanted … almost.

Aela remembered Bowie standing before Araxa Leren at Hiver, under the blade of a knife, denying this truth of Bryn's identity with his characteristic unshakeable determination. Unknowingly, she'd observed Bowie doing exactly what he'd been trained to do. But Aela didn't know how long Bowie could hold out against Alvine and Huntley. Days? Weeks, perhaps, because of the sheer force of his impossible will, his unshakeable loyalty to his king. His whole life, he'd been raised for this, to protect the Niellan throne. And Bowie didn't like to fail.

Nor do I. Aela scooped the golden insignia off the floor.

"Commander!" Chase staggered into the great hall. There were three soldiers with him, all bleeding, their uniforms tattered. "The courtyard's overrun, the front walls too. We can't get anyone else out. We have to move!"

Aela shoved the letter and pendant into her pocket. "How many of ours are still out there?"

Chase shook his head. "I don't know. More than half maybe."

Aela's vision tilted. More than three thousand Dunwyan soldiers trapped as Nielle overran the castle. Blindly, she pulled her sword and tried to push past Chase. He caught her arms.

"Aela, stop! You can't go back out there. You'll only be killed along with them!"

Aela shoved him away, barely biting down on the sob of despair that rose in her throat. Leaving her soldiers was like driving a blade through her heart, but Bowie's face flashed before her, and she remembered the expression on his face as he'd walked towards Alvine and the Niellans, ready to give himself up. His sacrifice, that of her soldiers, meant nothing if she gambled it away by acting rashly. Trying to block out the sounds of the clamouring fight outside, Aela turned and followed Chase towards the sanctuary.

Thirty-Seven

The roiling waves were loud and constant. Just above sea level, the sanctuary was an enormous cavern of hollowed-out dark rock. A yawning hole in the wall formed a jagged frame around the vast blue mass of the Great Ocean, which seemed to stretch forever, vanishing into the horizon.

Aela weaved through the line of retreating soldiers picking their way across rocks slick with sea spray, skirting the coastline towards the forest. The tide hadn't gone out yet; the water still lapped high enough to make the path treacherous, but Bryn had ordered the people to traverse into the forest anyway. Only top-ranking soldiers and members of the royal family knew about the sanctuary and the route to the forest. Given Huntley had been in Saban's inner circle for decades, there was every chance their escape would be cut off by soldiers by the time the tide went out.

She looked up at the castle, which towered overhead at the top of the sheer sea cliff. Its enormity usually inspired her, but now the structure felt forbidding and dangerous. Saban had given her command of the army on the border because she had experience fighting in the terrain. Here in Dunwald, she had no blueprint for a fight to reclaim the castle. She'd never given a single thought to the possibility that anyone, let alone Huntley Bartome, would take down the capital from the inside. Saban had always believed anarchists were the greatest threat to the city.

A flash of light fabric against the dark rock snatched her attention. Aela climbed up towards the lone figure, apart from the throng of retreating soldiers. Bryn sat with his knees drawn up to his chest, an eerie doubling — Bowie had sat in the same huddled position little more than two hours earlier, before Aela had discovered who either of them really were.

She'd intended to explain everything to Bryn, to leave nothing out, but the expression on his face gave her pause. He looked up at her the way a drowning man would in his final moments battling a current, like he'd lost all hope of fighting back, without even the strength to call for help.

Her lack of faith in Bryn had already poisoned the feelings growing between them. He might never get past the discovery that her blood made them enemies. The truth of her identity would surely be enough to sever the tenuous connection left between them forever.

She told herself she wanted to spare him the pain a little longer. But in reality, she was terrified of Bryn seeing her as anyone other than just Aela. Once he knew the truth, he couldn't unknow it. There would be no going back. Would he look at her differently? Would he look at her at all? Maybe he'd cast her out of his country for good, drawing out the bitter enmity between Nielle and Dunwyn for another generation.

Carefully, she said, "Your father first told me about the sanctuary when he made me commander. He told me you used to sneak down here at night to swim when the ocean was calm."

Bryn gave a breathy laugh. "He said I was misusing sensitive information. When I was about twelve, he found out I'd been coming down here and he got so angry he tried to send me to my room for a full day without any meals. He gave in after an hour, had a servant bring me some food. He was too gentle with me. I was so naïve. I thought every man was like him."

He turned away as Aela sat down beside him.

"The first time I met Bowie was when I woke up chained to a bed in Splinter's house. You remember how it goes."

"You stayed," Aela ventured, an unspoken question. "You could've run."

"He unchained me. I was worried he'd get in trouble so I ordered him not to, but when has he ever listened to my orders? I never asked him why he did it. All I know is that he was going to help me escape."

"Splinter caught him." Aela didn't need to hear the end of the story. Bryn shook his head, as if trying to erase a memory.

"After … what I saw, I couldn't leave him there, but he said that if I left, he wouldn't come with me. He was adamant. Always so fucking stubborn." Bryn gave a breathless laugh. "I thought it was because he was afraid of Splinter. I should've known there was something else going on. Everything he does is strategic. But it didn't matter, I stayed. I thought that, even if I was a murderer and my life was over, I could still do right by *someone*."

Aela closed her eyes for a steadying moment. "We can save him."

Bryn didn't look up. "Don't kid yourself," he said hopelessly. "If they haven't already …" He drew in a ragged breath.

"They'll keep him alive," Aela said. And she told him what she knew about Bowie's past, carefully omitting her own part in the story.

When she finished, Bryn's face was, if possible, even paler than it had been. He looked as if he was about to be sick. "How can you be sure?" he whispered.

"You said it yourself. Everything Bowie does is strategic. If he really was the prince, he would never have suggested facing Alvine, leaving himself vulnerable for capture. I think he's *playing* them, Bryn. He's buying time."

Bryn shook his head in disbelief. "If you're right, why did he let us think he's the prince? Why didn't he tell us the truth, ask for our help?"

Aela scoffed. "It's Bowie. He *never* asks for help. Besides, he didn't know what we'd do with such sensitive information. You're the king of an enemy nation."

"He knew." Bryn's voice was soft. "He was always going to give himself up so we could find a way to fight back. He let us send him out there to those fucking *people*."

Aela's throat constricted as she thought about Bowie, standing before his own country's army, making the decision to surrender himself to Alvine and Huntley. For Bryn … and for her.

She said gently, "Bowie knows you'll be a good king. He knows you want to stop Alvine and Huntley. He wanted to protect you. That's always been his job, to protect royalty."

Bryn jerked to his feet, his eyes blazing. "What kind of a king, what kind of a *man*, puts a boy in that kind of danger? He's *nine*! When this began, he was *five*! Marcus let Huntley —"

"He didn't know that Huntley would betray him."

"But he believed *someone* would! He threw Bowie into a killer's path to save his own flesh and blood." Bryn pinched the bridge of his nose for a long moment. Then he looked up at her. "I don't know if I believe you're right or if I just want you to be right, but we have to do something. I can't let him think I've abandoned him like Marcus did."

He looked around as a voice rose up over the relentless crashing of waves. Chase ran across the slippery stones, precariously close to the drop into the roiling sea, moving against the crowd of people evacuating to the forest. His shirt was soaked through, a mixture of sweat and sea spray.

"Your Highness," he said breathlessly. "Commander. You should come and see this."

They followed Chase, traversing the coastline until the rocks were swallowed up by forest. Wading through the overgrown scrub to a clearing ahead, Aela almost tripped over a rogue tree root as she recognised the rabble of people gathered there.

They were a mess of men and women on foot or astride horses. They carried weapons, though they weren't gathered in any formation, and Aela couldn't identify any distinct traces of armour or livery. Most of them wore simple riding leathers. Standing before the group was a familiar imposing figure with grey-streaked hair and steel-blue eyes.

"Splinter," Bryn said icily.

He turned and gave a smooth smile. He didn't kneel. "At your command, King Bryn. Or perhaps it's more accurate to say that I'm here at the prince of Nielle's command."

"*What?*" Bryn's tension gave way to utter disbelief and a hint of hope. "You've seen Bowie?"

"Not since he broke us out of the cells," Splinter replied. "He informed me that, should the Niellan army occupy the city, I'd be compensated if I assembled the anarchists to fight. Every willing and able fighter stands before you. We left the city as the Niellans arrived through Underground. They believe we've abandoned Dunwald." He looked at Bryn with amusement. "I'll need capital if I'm to build a new country from the ground up with the land you're giving me. And a larger population. I'm taking any Niellan soldiers who are captured when we fight."

Bryn folded his arms across his chest. "So I'm to believe you had nothing to do with the Niellans breaking in through Underground."

Splinter's eyes narrowed. "This is my city too."

Aela remembered Bowie and Splinter speaking in hushed tones at the cells and supposed she shouldn't be surprised that Bowie had sized the anarchists up as a potential mercenary force. She still wasn't used to the way his mind worked, how far in advance he had planned for Dunwyn's invasion, for his own capture. Aela tapped her fingers against the hilt of her blade, jittery tension rising inside of her. She itched to set her strategic skills loose in urban warfare against Nielle.

"All right," she said briskly to Splinter. "How many fighters can we expect from you?"

"None," Splinter replied lightly. "Until the prince of Nielle is standing before me."

Bryn kneaded his forehead with a closed fist. Aela suspected he would have preferred to drive it into Splinter's face. "Bowie is a prisoner in the castle, Splinter, and every minute we waste out here allows them more time to ... We need to *do something*, damn it."

Splinter folded his arms with the slow leisure of a man under absolutely no time pressure whatsoever. "The terms Bowie and I agreed upon are that the anarchists will attack once we have proof he's alive. Dead bodies don't pay, King Bryn, and I don't work for free."

"For fuck's sake," Bryn muttered furiously, turning to Aela. "Bowie's going to try and escape."

"He'll never make it out. The castle's crawling with Niellan soldiers," Aela said. "Besides, he barely knows his way around up there, and there are only two exits, the sanctuary and the main gate."

Bryn raised his eyebrows. "There's another way, but he'll need help." He looked at Chase. "Make the people safe in the forest and have the army ready when I return. If I'm not back by dawn tomorrow, get everyone as far away from Dunwald as possible."

Chase shot Aela an alarmed look. Aela didn't blame him. "Bryn, you are *not* going back into the castle alone!" she snapped. "Your life's too important."

Bryn whirled on her. "My father believed you could beat Nielle in the Border War because you didn't think like a Dunwyan soldier, you thought like a Borderlander."

"What's your point?"

"To beat Nielle, maybe I need to stop thinking like a king and start thinking more like an anarchist."

Of course.

Splinter didn't need an army. He achieved his ends by operating covertly with a small, dangerously capable team. Bryn had grown up in the castle. He knew it better than anyone, even Huntley. He looked at Aela intently and she was captivated by his singular, determined focus. The confidence in his golden-brown eyes was impossibly contagious, cutting through her despair at losing the city, diminishing her desolation at her impending loss of Bryn. That look charged her with the same vigorous energy that had crackled through her body back at Bayeau, when she'd stood victorious at the end of the war, unbeatable, unstoppable.

She wasn't just the Reaper of Dunwyn. She was the queen

of Nielle. She never turned her back on a fight, and this fight wasn't over.

"Not even an anarchist can do whatever they want, Bryn," she said. "If you're going into that castle, I'm going with you."

Thirty-Eight

"This is a ridiculous plan."

Soaking wet, Aela stared up at the sheer wall, black rock at the base, lighter brown where it was too high for the ocean spray to reach, the white marble of the castle high above. She swallowed hard, her palms pricking with sweat, her heart thundering with exhilarated, terrified anticipation.

By now, Niellan soldiers had emerged along the rocks, so they'd had to swim from the forest's pebbled shores back to the castle. Bryn had led the way to a small alcove where the water was calmer, and they'd scrambled up slippery boulders to the base of the towering wall. On the opposite side of the castle from the sanctuary, they were hidden for the moment, but it wasn't smart to linger here, in case the soldiers took it upon themselves to venture off the known escape route out of the castle.

Not that their route out of here was particularly smart either. She looked at Bryn, who was wiping his palms uselessly on his wet pants. "You've definitely done this before," she clarified.

"I told you I used to sneak out. It's easier than it looks. See that first window?" He pointed almost directly upwards, indicating a small opening at the base of the white marble. "It's a storeroom for the kitchens. We can get in there. The castle walls are too smooth to climb further up."

"And getting back out?" Aela wasn't sure she wanted to know the answer.

Bryn gave her a grim smile. "You know, one day when I'm the king and you're commanding Dunwyn's army, we're going to look back on this and laugh."

This time, Aela's gut clenched with guilt rather than fear. *If they made it out of this alive, she'd only command the army in one last fight before leaving Dunwyn for good.* Wiping her own hands resolutely on her shirt, Aela advanced towards the rocks after Bryn, braced herself, and began to climb.

The rock was slick with seawater that mingled with the nervous sweat on Aela's hands. It was brittle from exposure to the elements. Every time she pushed down on a foothold, the stone disintegrated beneath her boots. The wind whipped her short hair across her face, battered the fabric of her shirt and jacket, adding to the heady exposure of the forbidding cliff line stretching out under her feet. There was nothing between her and death.

She tried not to look down beyond sighting holds for her feet, but looking up was sickening also. The sheer face seemed intimidatingly blank.

A fresh gust of wind whipped past Aela, who cried out as it pushed her weight to the side. When she readjusted her foot, the hold beneath it crumbled, and she tightened her hands on the rock until her forearms ached.

Swearing under her breath, she repositioned herself onto solid holds, pausing to shake out her arms, one at a time. Caught between the need to concentrate and the urge to distract herself, she glanced at Bryn, about a foot away, watching her through wide brown eyes.

"You all right?"

"I'm definitely not going to look back on this and laugh, Bryn."

He didn't look amused. His jaw was set, consternation clear on his face.

"He's going to be fine," she told him.

He reached for his next hold. "I sent him out there. I used him, like Marcus did."

"He'll forgive you."

Bryn gave a slight shake of his head. "He's a boy. Huntley and Alvine are —"

"We'll get him," Aela said firmly.

"What if …" The terrible silence that followed was filled with unspoken fears.

"Bryn," Aela said gently. "Bowie adores you. He would forgive you for anything. When we find him, you'll see."

Aela had never been more grateful to feel flat ground beneath her feet. The storeroom was dark as they climbed through the only window. Stacked pots, bags of grain, and bushels of dried herbs lined the walls. She wished she had a chance to collapse onto one of the grain bags and savour the familiar, invigorating pounding of her heart, but the adrenaline wasn't welcome now.

It had been a little over three hours since the Niellans had overrun the castle. Bracing themselves against the storeroom door and listening for passing soldiers outside, neither Aela nor Bryn mentioned what might be happening to Bowie. It didn't need to be said.

"Where do you think he'll be?" Aela murmured. "The cells?"

"It's a start."

Aela opened the door a crack, but Bryn hauled her back into the room. His hand circling her wrist, Bryn braced against the door as boots thundered along the corridor outside. Raised Niellan voices permeated the storeroom.

" … guard was unconscious!"

"He picked the damn lock!"

"Search every inch of the castle! Find the prisoner!"

"What are they saying?" Bryn whispered.

"Bowie's escaped."

Pressed up against Bryn, she felt the tension in his body slacken slightly. There was a new expression on his face, burgeoning pride.

"Well done, kid," he murmured.

Moving through the castle was difficult, with the footsteps of soldiers searching for their runaway prisoner following them through the halls, rising up from around every corner. It took over an hour to scour the ground floor of the castle undetected, and every time they passed a window, fading light was an urgent reminder that time wasn't on their side. If they didn't get out by dawn, the Dunwyan army would leave them here alone, but there was no way to speed up their search.

Their pace as they combed the corridors was stilted, as they were constantly forced to duck suddenly into narrow doorways along the dark passageways, not knowing if they faced yet more soldiers on the other side. Aela's concern for Bowie grew.

She could sense Bryn's fear and frustration growing as they ascended a windowless spiralling private staircase near the king's garden. Aela had passed this staircase many times to meet outside with Saban, although she'd used it only twice.

"There's no way he could've gotten outside. The exits are too well-guarded," Bryn whispered agitatedly. "He'll be in the castle. Somewhere."

"He's not stupid. He would've headed somewhere he knows."

"He's only been on the ground floor. Mason and the others got him into the cells, and then he was with us in the great hall until —"

Aela realised it at the same moment as Bryn. He gripped her wrist, pulling her along as he quickened his pace up the stairs. They were breathless by the time they passed the first floor. They needed to get higher and started upwards again, but a door slammed open above them. Footsteps echoed jarringly down the rounded stairwell.

Bryn rattled off a string of curses, tugging Aela back down to the door on the first floor, and yanking it open. A long, wide hallway opened up in front of them, with a door at the far end and a staircase opposite. Instead of moving straight ahead, Bryn hesitated, drawing in a steadying breath before dodging to the left, ramming the wall with his shoulder until part of the wall dislodged.

It wasn't a wall at all. A wooden door behind the stone facade shifted and swung inwards, a secret opening leading into a darkened room that Aela had only set foot in once before. It still felt wrong to be here, like she was breaking a sacred rule, encroaching on some private territory that she had no right to see.

In the dim light across the room, the bloodstain on Saban's mattress was black as night.

Aela held herself carefully still, not wanting to disturb the fragile silence as Bryn walked slowly forward. The only sound was his shaky breath. He stopped between the canopy of half-open curtains that shrouded the bed. This was where he had killed his father.

At the foot of the bed, Bryn reached out, splaying his hand across the blood. Aela tore her eyes away, pain rising in her throat as she looked around, wondering where Splinter had stood when he'd given Bryn the order.

The stillness of the room shattered, a sudden flurry of movement bursting from behind the curtain at Bryn's right. Aela saw the glint of a blade as a figure launched at Bryn. She reached for her own weapon, but Bryn reacted quickly, catching his attacker's wrist, staying the knife before it found its mark. Bryn gasped sharply as the low light caught the face of the assailant.

Bowie stared wide-eyed up at Bryn, his chest rising and falling convulsively. He looked terrible. Blood oozed down the side of his face from a cut at his hairline. His raven curls were pasted together with more crusted blood. There was a bruise on his jaw, and his lip was bleeding. The neck of his shirt was torn, and beneath the shredded fabric was a trio of angry red blisters, burns oozing clear liquid.

There were tear tracks down his grimy face. More tears welled in his red, swollen eyes.

"Bowie." Bryn's voice cracked.

The boy jerked his wrist from Bryn's grasp and took an unsteady step backwards. His knuckles were white where he gripped the knife. Bryn's eyes flicked down to it. He held out his hand to take the weapon, but Bowie took another step backwards, clutching it even tighter.

"Hey, it's me." Bryn stepped forward carefully with his hands outstretched, palms open, the posture of someone trying not to startle a wild animal. Bowie's posture relaxed minutely, and Bryn took another step, gently pulling the dagger from the boy's fingers. "You don't need this now. I'm here."

Bowie drew a shaky breath, and tears spilled from his eyes. He turned his head, trying hastily to hide his face as he wiped them away, but more fell, and he was, for the first time since Aela had met him, unable to rein himself back under control. His chest heaved, and he gulped in a great, gasping breath, then another, his small body trembling.

"I'm sorry," he blurted out in Niellan through violent, terrible sobs.

"Bowie." Bryn went to his knees and pulled the boy against him. Bowie buried his face in Bryn's shirt, fisting his hands in the fabric.

Aela's heart seized painfully. Bowie was ordinarily so closed off that she'd never imagined she would see him cry, even though he'd been through more than enough.

She moved hesitantly towards him. His face was pressed against Bryn's shoulder, hiding his tears. "Bowie, we know you're not the heir."

Bowie buckled, collapsing into Bryn, who smoothed a tender hand over his curls. "It's all right," he murmured softly. "You're not in trouble."

"No," Aela agreed, "but we know now. I know *everything.*" She hoped Bowie would understand what she couldn't say aloud in front of Bryn. "Did you tell Alvine and Huntley who the heir is?"

Bryn shot her a hard look. Bowie shook his head against Bryn's shirt.

"You didn't tell her?" Aela pressed.

"No." Bowie's small voice was muffled against Bryn's shirt. "That's why they ..."

"They're not going to hurt you again," Bryn interrupted firmly. "But we need to stop them. Can you help us?"

Bowie pulled back and rubbed his eyes. When he looked up, Aela saw a shadow of characteristic determination in his blue eyes. "Yes," he said.

Thirty-Nine

"We have to kill Alvine and Huntley," Bowie said quietly. No trace of emotion flickered in his eyes. He sat at the foot of Saban's bed, a careful distance from the bloodstain, head resting on Bryn's shoulder, gripping his sleeve like a lifeline.

Aela leaned against the door frame, half listening for any sounds of Niellan soldiers outside. Watching Bryn from across the room, she saw him clenched his jaw. He didn't relish the idea of killing anyone, but Alvine and Huntley had done more than enough.

"I'd imagine Splinter will be more than happy to oblige once we get you out of here." He gave Bowie's wrist a squeeze.

Bowie brightened a little, pulling back to look at Bryn. "Splinter's going to fight?"

"Not for free," Aela said wryly. "It was a smart strategy, Bowie. Well done."

Bowie gulped nervously. "I know it wasn't my place. It's not my money and …" He looked up through tangled strands of hair, his eyes deliberate on Aela's. "I might be punished when the heir finds out."

Bryn snorted. "If the heir's got any sense, they'll understand why you did it. And if they don't, fine. I'll pay them back myself."

Bowie slumped against his side again.

Aela crossed the room to look out the window. The ocean was a glittering silver in the light of the setting sun. It occurred to Aela as she eyed the vertical drop down to the rocks that the tide was going to start coming in again soon. That was probably the least of their worries. She was certain Huntley would have Niellan soldiers patrolling the rocks outside the sanctuary as night fell to prevent an attack from beneath the castle.

"Our first priority is getting out of here." She looked at Bryn. "You claim this is your area of expertise?"

Bryn scrubbed the back of his head with the arm Bowie wasn't holding. "The bad news is that we're all about to launch off the side of a vertical drop again. But the good news is that the descent will be much slower than last time." He gave a quick grin, not quite reaching an approximation of his usual brashness. "Finally, I get to take you to my bedroom."

Aela pulled the door open a crack …

And immediately shut it again, as a group of soldiers ran past, shouting.

"Any ideas?" she asked the other two.

"Maybe," Bowie ventured, looking nervous. "Should we split up?"

"No." Bryn's voice was hard. He disentangled himself from Bowie's grasp and gave the boy a stern look, then he turned and glared at Aela. "No. You and I fight together. Not you, Bowie."

"But —"

"That's an order."

"Two daggers," Bowie wheedled.

"I don't think you understand what an order is."

"Bryn, I can fight."

"I know. You've been fighting. That's all you've been doing. The conversation's over." He stood up, pulling his sword from his belt, fixing his burning golden-brown gaze on Aela. "One flight of stairs and we're out of here. Open the door."

Aela flung it open and assessed the odds. Better than expected. Eight soldiers stopped in their tracks at the end of the corridor, turning ominously towards her.

"Perhaps we can talk about this?" Bryn suggested lightly, coming out to stand beside Aela.

Aela adjusted her grip on her blade, but her resolve was unsteady. These Niellan soldiers were her responsibility, misguided and under orders from people who didn't mean any better to Nielle than they did to Dunwyn. People who were killing their king. One after another, the Niellans' blades hissed from their sheaths.

"What a shame your career as a diplomat is over before it began," she quipped to Bryn. "Bowie, go!"

Even injured, Bowie moved fast. He dashed out of the door and down the hallway towards the private staircase. Then the soldiers were on them. Bryn grabbed one and slammed him hard into the wall. Swearing, Aela shoved her blade back into her belt, eyeing the two soldiers advancing on her. She dropped, sweeping her leg out and driving them both to the floor, aiming a debilitating kick at the first one's ribs and one to the second soldier's face. Fighting with her fists never satisfied Aela like a sword did, but now it felt like the only right way.

As bodies dropped around her, bleeding but not dying, she felt for the first time a victory in failing to kill her enemies. She and Bryn turned and ran after Bowie towards the staircase.

Bryn called out, "You didn't kill them."

"No," Aela replied. "How are we getting out of the castle?"

Ahead of them, Bowie yanked open the door at the top of the stairs, taking a hard turn into Bryn's rooms. Bryn ushered Aela in after him and slammed the door.

"Aela, we need to barricade the door," Bryn said. "Bowie, look under the bed. There's a rope. Pull it out."

"A rope?" Aela repeated as she and Bryn pushed a massive hardwood cabinet in front of the door. "Damn it, Bryn."

Bang.

Pounding on the other side of the door made Aela jump. Shouts rose from outside. Bryn swore.

"Pass me that." He strode over to Bowie, who was frozen, staring at the door fearfully. "Quick, Bowie. We need to move."

Bryn deftly tied an end of the rope around the bed, first one foot and then the other. By the time Aela had finished shoving every piece of loose furniture available in front of the door, he'd crossed to the window and thrust it open. Wind whipped about the room, ruffling the curtains violently. Aela's head spun as she tracked the tail end of the rope flying from the window and slapping onto the rocks far below.

"Take this." Bryn passed Aela the rope. "Wrap it around your leg, over your hip and up across the opposite shoulder. Let the rope out slowly in your hand."

Stepping down out of the window was stepping out into an abyss. Her arms shook with the effort of holding the rope taut as she lowered herself cautiously down the castle wall. When she was back on the slick rocky ledge, Bryn set forth from the top with Bowie clinging to his back.

The light was almost lost by the time they reached the ground. Bryn placed Bowie on the ground, straightened, and looked up at Aela. He was impossibly beautiful, his determined dark eyes glittering in the rising moonlight. His blond hair whipped in the wind.

"We've got a war to win," he said.

Forty

Staying low amidst the greenery, they followed the faint sounds of voices and the metallic clangs of weapons to the perimeter of the anarchists' camp. Splinter leaned against a tree, holding a sword in one hand and a hatchet in the other. He whirled as they emerged out of the rustling bushes, and Aela stepped in front of Bryn and Bowie. "Only us," she said.

"You wanted to see him?" Bryn snapped at Splinter, a hand on Bowie's shoulder. "You've seen him." After a last dirty look at Splinter, Bryn led Bowie away through the trees. Having, predictably, hated being towed by Bryn back through the waves in the growing darkness, Bowie leaned heavily against Bryn like all the exhaustion and fear had been wrung from him. His face was blank.

"We'll ride to the city at daybreak." Aela folded her arms and examined the weapons in Splinter's hands. "Who would ever have thought you'd fight a war on the same side as the king of Dunwyn. I shudder to think how much Bowie offered to pay you for this."

Splinter shrugged. "If you're good at something, never do it for free."

"You know, if you'd taken a different path in life, you would have been an excellent soldier."

"Soldier?" Splinter repeated. "I would've been an excellent *commander*, Aela Rinn."

Aela choked back a laugh. Then, sobering, she said, "Alvine and her people snuck into Dunwyn through Anarchist Underground."

"I'm aware. And I told you that I don't want these people in my city any more than you do." Splinter sounded genuine, but that meant nothing. He was an expert at deception.

Aela narrowed her eyes at him. "Are you with us?" she asked. "Is this a real allegiance? Because if it's not, if you intend to harm Bryn, I swear I'll make you regret it."

Splinter's steel-blue gaze sparkled with barely suppressed amusement. "Look who finally decided to be a soldier. Or is there another reason you might be so protective of the king?"

Aela looked away from Splinter, knowing better than to give his postulations any sort of affirmation. She went to move off, stalled by Splinter's hand gripping her arm.

"I'll keep my word," he said in a low voice that Aela felt in her bones. "Unless your king breaks his. Then you'll have good reason to question my loyalty."

★★★

A herald was sent ahead to the city. Aela rode alongside Bryn as they left the forest in the grey morning light, Splinter, Dagny, Mason, Chase, and Landon following, a makeshift army of Dunwyan soldiers and anarchists at their backs. Last night had been a flurry of giving orders, receiving reports, and making preparations. She'd barely had a chance to say two words to Bryn.

She felt a renewed need to tell him the truth of her identity, stymied by the urgency of what they were about to do. "Where's Bowie?" she asked, because that was easier.

"I left him in the forest with some of Splinter's men. I won't have him in this fight."

Aela frowned. "Do you think that's wise?" she asked. "Leaving him with the anarchists?"

"They think he's the prince of Nielle," Bryn reminded her. "Splinter's not going to let us send him anywhere else until he gets paid. They won't dare hurt him while this is playing out, so it's the safest he's going to be until the fighting's over."

The city loomed large across the field. Aela's horse tossed his head in agitation. She had seen horses behave this way before. They always knew when a fight was coming. She felt it too, the prickle beneath her own skin, the barely contained violent energy that crackled like lightning in the air around them.

She didn't like it. It was the feeling she'd been chasing since the war, but now she found herself wishing she was anywhere else. Because if she was going to fight, then so was Bryn.

"Are you all right?" They pulled up before the walls. Bryn watched her closely, his golden eyes flickering with concern. He cleared his throat, looking a little uncomfortable. "This is your first real battle since … If you're not ready, there's no shame in staying back."

"I'm not staying back," Aela said firmly. There was no way Bryn was going into battle without her.

If she could help it, there was no way he was going into battle at all.

A flood of red surged out from within the city walls. Ahead

of them, Niellan soldiers emerged from inside Dunwald's walls, riding across the grass. Alvine and Huntley rode together at the head of them. Aela couldn't take her eyes off Alvine. She knew now that they were sisters – by half, at least. It was something she couldn't fathom. Never in her life had she expected to come face-to-face with any blood relative.

As a child, Aela had secretly dreamed of having a sibling, a blood relative to confide in and love. But if Alvine found out the truth, she wouldn't want Aela as her family. She would want her dead.

Aela tugged on her reins a little too hard as they came to a stop, her white mount tossing its head in protest. Thirty feet of space stretched out between them and the Niellans, but Bryn's commanding voice carried.

"Alvine and Huntley Bartome, you are occupying my country," he said. "You have killed my people. You paid an anarchist to murder my father. Now you will relinquish control of Dunwyn and step down from the seat of power in Nielle, or you will fall to the might of the very people you sought to form an allegiance with. The anarchists fight with me now."

Alvine was watching him steadily. Aela didn't like the look on her face. It was too calm.

"Do you really expect their loyalty to hold?" Alvine inquired lightly, her voice barely carrying through the air. "The anarchists defected to form their own community long ago, to escape the authority of rulers like you. Don't be naïve, Prince Bryn. Once they see their friends falling around them, they will flee. Half your army is dead or imprisoned. You don't have the numbers to defeat us."

Aela's skin prickled with adrenaline. She had planned for this. It had occurred to her too that even with the incentive of gold, the anarchists were not soldiers. There was no telling if their loyalty would hold when the fighting began. Besides, facing the Niellan army was different this time. This time, she knew that her countrymen stood on both sides of the field. There was only one way to protect all of them.

Steeling herself, she turned to Bryn. "Do you trust me?"

He nodded, slightly puzzled. "With my life."

Satisfied, she dug her heels into her horse and rode forward, closing the distance between herself and Alvine's army. "They're not going to fight," she said calmly. She knew Bryn could hear her. "Alvine Bartome, as commander of Dunwyn's army, I challenge you to single combat. The losing party will relinquish control of their kingdom to the victor."

Surprise flickered across Alvine's face. Everyone knew this was how Aela had sealed Dunwyn's victory in the Border War. According to Aela's reputation, she was unbeatable. Except she *had* been beaten. By the tall, blonde woman beside Alvine, whose ominously triumphant smile grew as she watched Aela through glittering hazel eyes. Aela had known this would be the likely outcome of a challenge, but she still trembled as Huntley leaned in and murmured something in Alvine's ear. The confidence in Alvine's simpering smile echoed her mother's.

Alvine raised her voice. "If you intend to fight on behalf of your king, then I'm permitted to choose a champion of my own. I accept your terms. And my mother will meet you on the battlefield."

Forty-One

"No. I don't like it." Mason glared at Aela, eyes blazing. They'd retreated back into a forest clearing. Chase and Landon stood beside Mason, looking equally furious. Bryn leaned against a tree, arms folded across his chest, wearing an unreadable expression.

Aela strapped on the unfamiliar anarchist leathers Splinter had supplied. It was different from the armour she'd worn during the war, light and flexible, easier to move in but not nearly as protective. She shrugged. "Too late to object. I've already made the agreement."

Mason swore under her breath. "If I'd known what you were going to do, I would *never* have let you go out there. Huntley's a good fighter!"

"I'll try not to take that personally, Captain. *I'm* a good fighter." Although a voice in the back of Aela's mind told her that *good* didn't guarantee she was better than Huntley. She'd only fought Huntley once, and she'd lost. Pushing the thought down, she faced her soldiers. "I need you three to do me a favour. Take everyone who got out of the city, and get them as far from here as possible."

Chase baulked. "With all due respect, Commander, fuck you.

We're staying here."

"This is not the time to argue, soldier," Aela snapped. "If I lose this fight, the people cannot be found here, and they'll need a force to defend them."

"And so you'll go out there with no army at your back," Mason said dubiously. "Chase is right. We need to stay."

"I've got an army," Aela argued.

"An army of anarchists," Mason shot back derisively. "With allegiances that are fucking questionable at best —"

"Stop." Bryn cut through the argument firmly. "If this is Commander Rinn's plan, then this is what we'll do. She says she's going to fight, so she'll fight. She says to take the people away from here. Take the people away."

"Your Highness —" Landon started.

"Landon, please," Aela implored. She looked around at the others. "I'm asking as your friend."

Mason closed her eyes for a moment. When she opened them, she moved forward, placing a hand on Aela's shoulder. "Fine. As a soldier, I'm obligated to follow orders, but as your friend, I want you to know that if you live, I'm going to kick your ass for this."

"That sounds like insubordination, Captain," Aela said.

Mason gave a sharp laugh. She squeezed Aela's shoulder then jerked her head at Chase and Landon. "Let's go."

Mason pulled away, and Chase lurched forward, pulling her into a quick, firm embrace. "Give her hell, Commander." His voice shook.

Landon reached out, squeezing her hand without a word, and then they were gone, disappearing into the trees, leaving Aela and Bryn alone and curtained from view by shrouds of thick greenery. Coming forward, Bryn lifted a leather gauntlet off the ground and pressed it against Aela's wrist. Gently, he began to tighten the fastenings.

"That's it?" Aela inquired. "I expected you to fight me on this."

Bryn kept his eyes fixed on the gauntlet's laces. "I was going to object," he said as he worked, his tone deliberately casual. "I don't like seeing you in danger. Do you know why I didn't?"

"No." Aela's throat felt suddenly tight.

"It's because I know that when Aela Rinn wants to win a fight, she never lets anyone beat her." He looked up, his eyes locking on hers, and the fiery confidence in his gaze was wildly, intoxicatingly empowering. Her heart flamed with unstoppable boldness fuelled by desire. Bryn said, "You don't stop fighting until you have what you want. Not ever. There's no one I trust more than you with the fate of this country."

There was no trace of his detached arrogance or teasing. This was all Bryn. It was the truth.

Swept up in the urge to give him something real in return, she blurted helplessly, "Bryn, I'm sorry."

He raised his eyebrows. "What for?"

For still wanting you, even though I'm lying to you.

She couldn't say that, so she selected her less grievous betrayal. "I believed you killed your father, even as I came to know you, even though I could see that you were a good man, that you would never …"

"Wait." Bryn held up his hands. He gave a harsh, disbelieving laugh. "Aela, I *did* kill my father."

Aela opened her mouth to protest, but Bryn held up a hand. "I'm not finished," he said. "You didn't let me down. And the way you —" He paused, pulling in a long, steady breath and exhaling slowly. "The way you served Dunwyn after my father's death, how unafraid you are of stepping up and being a leader, it made me want to be that too. It made me want to be everything to this country that I never thought I could be."

Unable to bear it, Aela looked away. She should welcome the fact that Bryn would rule in his father's stead. It was what Saban had always wanted. It was what Aela had wanted once too. But the closer he got to taking Dunwyn's throne, the further he and Aela would drift apart. By inspiring him to fulfill his duty, Aela had ensured they would never be together. It almost hurt, the tender concern on Bryn's face as his fingers brushed her chin, gently pulling her gaze to his.

"Hey, what is it?" He looked young and vulnerable. A flush crept across his cheeks, as if even this light touch was enough to set his senses alight.

"Nothing." Voice cracking, Aela caught herself on the cusp of breaking down. Even if she survived the fight with Huntley, this was goodbye. Caught in the magnetism of Bryn's dark, molten gaze, it took a few long moments to compose herself enough to speak. "You're going to be a great king."

"And you're going to win this fight," Bryn said quietly with absolute confidence. "I do have one favour to ask first though."

He was still holding her wrist. Unthinking, they had moved closer, heat and energy thrumming between them.

"What's that?" she whispered.

Bryn's voice was rough with needful heat. "Kiss me again."

Aela felt swept away in a wave of helpless desire. She couldn't have Bryn for the rest of her life, and she shouldn't have him now, not with the truth of who she was unspoken between them. But selfishly, desperately, she yearned to give everything to this one last moment. Her resolve cracked like glass, and she stepped in, wound a hand through the soft waves at the back of his neck, pulling his lips to hers, savouring the warm, firm pressure of his body.

Bryn let out a groan of satisfaction, pressing his fingers to her waist. Delicate at first, the kiss turned hungry and eager, shifting desperately as Bryn took control, walking her backwards until they collided with the coarse bark of a tree. His trembling hands searched for the skin beneath her shirt, then travelled further down her body.

"Wait." She pulled away.

Bryn's hands tightening possessively at her hips did nothing to strengthen her resolve. "Are you trying to make me lose my mind?" he muttered impatiently.

"Shut up. There's something you need to know." Aela took Bryn's face in her hands. Capturing Bryn's gaze with hers, she said what she'd been longing to say. "I know what you did, Bryn. And I want you to know it's all right. I don't want some fantasy version of you. I didn't fall for a perfect man. I fell for a very good man who does his best for the people he cares about. No matter what anyone else thinks, that's enough for me. It should be enough for you too."

"Aela." Bryn leaned in, and their foreheads pressed together. Aela shivered as he spoke, his lips brushing hers. "I don't know if I'm a good man or not. But I will be. I will do everything I can to be the man you see when you look at me, the man you believe in. I will be worthy of you, Aela, I swear it. The way I feel about you … I've never felt this for anyone. I only want to feel this way for you."

Her heart was pounding, her body shaking with adrenaline as Bryn drew her into another kiss. His searching hands quested up under her shirt and she gasped into his mouth as his thumbs traced across her nipples. A shiver of arousal passed through her body. Bryn's breath caressed the sensitive skin at the column of her throat a moment before he pressed his lips there, punctuating delicate kisses with swift, sharp bites. She tilted her head back against the tree, moaning softly without restraint. With each tender touch, want clenched tighter in Aela's gut. He was still tracing torturously light, teasing circles over her nipples with his thumbs.

Needing his attention elsewhere, she snagged one of his wrists, guiding his hand downward. He didn't stop kissing her throat as he unlaced her trousers with a practised hand, his fingers delving down. Her breaths ripped from her raggedly as his thumb circled the most responsive part of her body, lingering there.

His tongue quested into her mouth, consuming her in a long, languorous kiss that she would remember for the rest of her life. She'd never have Bryn like this again. It was a gilded knife through her heart, a soaring arrow piercing her soul, as he slid two fingers inside, delving deeper. Each time, he stroked her until she was breathless. The rhythm of his fingers quickened just as he nipped at her throat again, the two sensations coalescing into one flare of arousal so overpowering she cried out in pleasure.

She reached the knife's edge of climax and his rhythm inside her slowed. Her thoughts scattered. Frustration crested and she groaned. The maddening, leisurely circles Bryn was making with his thumb on her sensitive skin didn't stop, but he laughed against her neck. "You're going to have to stay quiet, unless you want an audience. Cover your mouth."

Aela obeyed, gasping into her hand when Bryn knelt to pull off her boots. He grabbed the fabric at the waist of her trousers and pulled them down.

"I want you on my cock." His voice was husky with barely-contained arousal.

He reached up and gripped her hips hard, pulling her down. She barely managed to stifle a startled cry with her palm, bracing the other hand on Bryn's shoulder as she straddled his hips. Her body buzzing from the interrupted orgasm, Aela fumbled with the lacing on Bryn's pants, his hands travelled back down, strong calloused palms stroking up her thighs, parting her legs. She drew out his rigid cock and shuffled backwards on her knees to suck lightly on the tip, massaging the slit with her tongue.

"Oh, *fuck!*" Bryn's body jerked. He hissed in a breath as she took him in her mouth, sliding down his length. "Aela. Look at me."

Aela slid back up to circle her tongue around the head of his cock, meeting his pleasure-darkened gaze, and precome pulsed into her mouth.

"I – I need to be inside you," he said raggedly.

As she straightened up, he grabbed her backside, dragging her forward. Aela took his cock in her hand, aligning it to where she needed him. He slid inside and she began, slowly, to grind against him. With one hand on her waist to guide her movement, Bryn brought his other hand up to her face, his thumb tracing across her lips, her cheekbone. He didn't take his eyes off her and she was trapped in his gaze. The world softened, and their bodies moved together in perfect harmony. Bryn's hand moved from her waist, returning between her legs, and her body arced towards him as he began to trace faster, harder circles and she rode him towards climax.

"Aela." There was shattering honesty in Bryn's voice, and she felt in her heart everything they couldn't say to each other.

She'd never thought anything else could feel like fighting, but this did. Only, replacing the threat of death was exhilarating pleasure, and beneath it was the looming terror of loss.

Aela tried to make herself remember each moment, the ragged sound of Bryn's breath as she fucked him harder, the soft, unthinking sounds he made as his cock pulsed and he pulled her against him, thrusting through his own orgasm. Her every nerve felt supercharged as she called his name and shuddering pleasure electrified her body against the fiery heat of his skin.

Some distant part of her that wasn't consumed by the heady bliss of Bryn's touch quietly urged her to preserve this memory. It was all she'd have.

★★★

Aela walked alone into the forest. Her lips felt swollen from kisses. The buzz of pleasure lingered in her body. During the war, she hadn't had the luxury of being alone before a fight. She'd had troops to command, strategy to discuss with Mason. She liked the idea of having a moment to gather her thoughts, to smile as she thought about making love to Bryn, drawing strength from the memory.

She came to a small copse of low bushes, pushing through the greenery towards a tiny figure, standing alone in the centre of the clearing. Bowie's dark curls fell over his face as he fiddled with the silver Niellan insignia that hung around his neck.

"You know now," he said without looking up at her.

"You're impossible to sneak up on," Aela remarked. "Yes. I know."

Bowie dropped to his knees. Quickly, Aela closed the space

between them, catching Bowie's arm. "Please," she said firmly, pulling him upright, "you don't need to bow to me. I'm … We're friends."

Bowie's lips parted in speechless shock and Aela wondered for the first time what Bowie's relationship had been like with King Marcus. His detail-oriented mind clearly had no template for this manner of conversation with Niellan royalty.

"I thought you'd be angry," he admitted. "I knew who you were, and I didn't tell you."

"I'm not angry."

Bowie dropped his head, his messy curls shrouding his face. "King Marcus would say it's not my place to make decisions for my queen."

The honorific was utterly jarring. Bryn's face flashed in her mind, painfully reminding her again of what she was about to lose.

"You're going to fight," Bowie concluded softly, watching her.

Aela nodded. "Alvine's not fit to rule. Nielle is my kingdom."

"It's not your job to die for Nielle. That's why you have people to serve you."

It was painful to hear Bowie give voice to the purpose he'd lived his entire life for.

"I'm not my father," Aela said firmly. Calling him that felt strange when habitual, bitter malevolence for the king of Nielle still hummed in her veins. After all these years, it was practically a part of her. "Ordering people to the border to start a war that he would never fight. Dunwyn doesn't belong to Nielle, and Nielle doesn't belong to Alvine. If it's my kingdom, I'll be the one to defend it."

"They're saying you can easily beat Huntley." Bowie's eyes

were intent on Aela, assessing her expression.

She sighed. Attempting to deceive Bowie was perpetually pointless. "You know better than anyone that people can lie for good reasons."

"Like His Highness did," Bowie said, nodding.

Saban, Aela thought automatically, but that wasn't who Bowie meant. "Yes," she replied. "Bryn lied about who he was. If he hadn't done that, he might not be here now."

There was sadness in the endless blue of Bowie's eyes. "I'm sorry."

Aela frowned. "I said you don't need to –"

"No," Bowie interrupted. "I mean, I'm sorry about you and His Highness. How will you be together now?"

Aela felt her face grow hot. Bowie said it like a fact, unabashedly honest and completely oblivious to her discomfort. "I … and what about you?"

"Your Majesty?"

It didn't sit right in her mind, hearing the formal Niellan address spoken in Dunwyan. It was even stranger having it directed at her.

"If this falls out the way we want it to, then your job is done. You can do whatever you want."

Bowie lifted his hand absently to grasp his silver pendant. "It's my duty to serve King Marcus."

"After all you've done, he should be indebted to you! I am!"

Bowie shrugged. "I'll obey his decision. He's my king." It sounded hollow, like a recitation.

"What do you want?" she asked him.

Bowie looked up, genuine surprise flitting across his face. It wasn't often he was caught off-guard. "That's not —"

"If you were free to decide, what would you do?" she

explained. "Don't tell me you haven't thought about it. I know you think about everything."

His mind was clearly whirling with possibilities and answers, and the consequences of those answers.

She said, "Don't think, just tell me."

Bowie's face flushed. "At Hiver, His Highness said that … maybe I could go with him to Dunwyn. But I don't know if he still wants that," he added hastily. "A lot's happened."

Aela placed a hand on Bowie's bony shoulder. He flushed again, and Aela saw herself, years ago, the first time Saban had touched her with affection, the same admiration and eagerness to please. "I think he'd love that."

Hopefulness flickered in Bowie's eyes. Concern chased it away. "But Bryn's Dunwyan. And King Marcus –"

"Bowie, the old codger's just going to have to live with it," Aela said impatiently.

Bowie choked, his eyes flying wide. It took a moment for him to compose himself. Then, he spoke shyly. "You don't think you're going to beat Huntley," he told her. "But you will." His steady blue gaze was fixed on Aela, and in his eyes was a tangled mess of feelings — fear, hope, adulation, all in equal measure. "For Nielle."

Forty-Two

The Niellan army gathered in full force outside the city gates to watch the fight. Alvine was at the head of them, astride a war horse the colour of onyx. Huntley was beside her, strapped into steel armour with a sword in one hand and a dagger in the other. Clad only in leathers and wielding a single sword, Aela felt rather less protected than her opponent. Self-doubt teased at the edge of her mind. Maybe she couldn't do this.

"Are you ready?" Bryn appeared beside her, his eyes also on Huntley.

"The last time I fought Huntley, I lost."

"You're not going to lose," Bryn said confidently.

He was a good liar. Aela forced herself to reach out and squeeze his fingers reassuringly. Then she walked forward to meet Huntley on the grassy field before the walls of Dunwald.

Huntley moved with deliberate carelessness, like she was meeting Aela for a casual conversation, not a fight to the death. Mind games, Aela thought. This woman was a master manipulator, deceiving Saban into two decades of false friendship.

"Aela Rinn," Huntley said smoothly. "I remember when

you first came to Dunwald. You were only eighteen and you fought me two months into your training. You've always been overconfident."

Aela arched her brows at Huntley. "It's not overconfidence if you're good. And I wasn't eighteen when I lost to you. I was sixteen. I wasn't better than you then, but I am now."

"Perhaps instead of flapping your tongue," Huntley said smoothly, "you should prove it."

Huntley lunged first, her effortless fighting style was as Aela remembered, the light footwork as she advanced, forcing Aela to give ground. Aela parried Huntley's blow to her head, shoved the blade away, sending Huntley stumbling backwards three steps.

Aela circled her with a cocky smile. "So?"

Huntley eyed her carefully. "You may wish to check that attitude, soldier."

"I don't think so."

This time, Aela advanced first, but Huntley was ready. She shoved her blade into the grass, freeing her hands. She grabbed Aela's arm, one hand at her wrist, the other above the elbow. With a quick, brutal twist, there was an unnatural crack. White hot pain lanced up Aela's arm, and she bit down on the cry that threatened to escape. Her sword dropped to the ground.

Aela stumbled backwards, her right hand hanging uselessly at her side. She barely leaped back in time to evade Huntley's blade – retrieved from where she'd skewered it in the grass – swiping at Aela's stomach. It grazed the leather at her belly, scarring the material. Unarmed now, Aela backed away as Huntley advanced on her, stepping over Aela's discarded sword as if it was a piece of the landscape.

"It's as I told you years ago, Commander Rinn," she said with a mild smile. "I thought I'd met my match. But the truth is that you can't fight like I can. And Bryn? What makes him a better ruler than my daughter? He's no king. He's not even a prince. He's an ungrateful, entitled vagrant who had the good fortune of being born into royalty. The chain needs to be broken. It's time a new leader is crowned to rule."

"Alvine's no leader," Aela told her. "And you're a coward, disguising your hunger for power as a mother's love. But you're right about one thing. I'm not your match. I'm better."

Aela launched a flying leap at Huntley. Her broken arm screamed in pain as she jammed her fist into the woman's jaw. She rolled onto her knees and lunged for her blade, ignoring the nauseating way her arm throbbed.

Pain is temporary. Jerking to her feet, she whirled and struck out at Huntley's right side then her left, driving her opponent back with all she had. Huntley swung wildly at her head. Aela ducked, slashing through the skin below Huntley's knee. The woman made a pained sound, stumbling, and Aela flipped her sword, catching the sharp edge of the blade in her uninjured hand, swinging it so the pommel caught the back of Huntley's leg. She buckled, sprawling onto the grass.

Aela held her broken arm gingerly. Underneath the adrenaline, the strengthening tendrils of a pulsing ache wound up into her shoulder. She looked back at Huntley, who was still down, reaching weakly for her sword.

"I don't want to kill you."

"That's why you'll lose," Huntley growled. She dragged herself up, knuckles whitening around the hilt of the weapon, but she didn't make it farther than a few steps before something whipped past Aela, stirring the air at her side, landing with a sickening, heavy *thump* in Huntley's chest.

Time slowed. Aela stared frozen in shock at the crossbow bolt protruding with terrible finality from Huntley's flesh. The steward's eyes flew wide and then her shock cracked, replaced by a look of deep betrayal that was so profound it tugged at Aela's heart. Clawing at the arrow in her chest, Huntley staggered, turning back towards the sea of red Niellan soldiers. From a distance, Alvine's short, dark-haired form was barely distinguishable at the head of the group. Huntley's head whipped back to look at Aela and a single tear inched down her cheek.

"Hail Queen Alvine of Nielle," she whispered and collapsed onto the grass.

Aela whirled in time to see Splinter's blade sing from its sheath, slashing across Dagny's throat. Blood spattered. The crossbow Dagny had fired clattered to the ground as he fell. Splinter paused, meeting Aela's eyes across the field. She knew what was going to happen before it did.

A cry rose up from the Niellan army loud as thunder, together as one. "*Treachery!*"

It was like a wall of water bursting from a dam, the crowd of Niellans erupting into a terrible cacophony of battle cries, thirsting for blood. In the middle of it all stood Alvine, and even at this distance Aela could see the horrible, satisfied smile creeping across her face.

She swore and sprinted towards the anarchists. She was breathless as she reached them, fetching up before Splinter and Bryn. Looking down at Dagny's dead body, she remembered the hushed conversation he and Huntley had shared outside Splinter's house, Alvine accessing Dunwald through Anarchist Underground.

"He was Alvine's man."

"I didn't know." Splinter's eyes blazed with white hot fury.

Aela believed him. Splinter wouldn't have allowed Dagny to split his allegiance.

"She had her own mother killed," Bryn whispered in horrified disbelief.

Alvine's voice boomed across the field as she rode towards them with three soldiers flanking her, a dozen more riding behind.

"You've broken the oath of single combat!" She pulled her horse to a halt in front of them. "Nielle won't let this stand."

A shadow flew overhead. Something thudded to the ground between them and Alvine, then another, and another, odd objects that Aela didn't recognise at first. With detached confusion, she noted hair, blood, eyes that were sightless in death. Realisation took far too long, her stomach plummeting like a stone through a bottomless pit.

Heads. They were severed heads.

Bryn swore, his voice shaking. "The anarchists ... Bowie's guards."

Alvine swung herself out of her saddle, swaggered towards them, her eyes on Bryn. "King Bryn, I don't need to fight you to get what I want."

She raised a hand, and Aela turned towards the sound of hooves, thundering out of the forest. An anarchist Aela didn't recognise rode through the crowd, past Aela and Bryn and coming to halt on the grass before the Niellans. Aela's heart sank. Mason had been right to question the anarchists' loyalties.

"It seems," Alvine said to Splinter sweetly, "that in this matter, you don't speak for all of Anarchist Underground."

The anarchist threw Bowie off the horse, and he landed painfully on one shoulder at Alvine's feet, pushing himself up unsteadily with his hands tied in front of him. Blood gushed from his nose and down his chin and neck. More trickled from a cut above his eye.

Aela stepped forward, but Bryn caught her uninjured wrist and shook his head. His eyes were on Alvine, who was in turn watching him in amusement. She grabbed Bowie and dragged him to his feet.

"It wasn't Huntley's plan, was it?" Bowie said with some difficulty, his words thick through the blood. "It was *your* idea to use grey dream. You're the one who's killing King Marcus!"

Alvine glanced down at Bowie with malicious delight. "Very bright, aren't you? I can see why my father liked having you as his little pet." Her tone darkened as she looked up. "Be a good boy now, Bryn, and step forward for me." Alvine moved her grip to Bowie's neck, tightening her fingers around the delicate skin there until he choked. "I don't think you want to find out how far I'm willing to go to get what I want."

"Stop. Don't hurt him." Raising his hands in surrender, Bryn walked forward, allowing one of Alvine's soldiers to grab his arms.

"Tell them to retreat," Alvine ordered, jerking her head at the anarchists. Her eyes flicked to Splinter's ready posture. "I understand your hesitation," she said sweetly. "Bowie may be the only person in the world who knows who the heir to Nielle's throne is."

Splinter froze, his expression darkening. "He *is* the heir to Nielle's throne."

Araxa gave a high, girlish laugh. "Is that what they told you? Oh dear, I hope you didn't hinge your loyalty on it. If you walk away now, I'll double whatever payment they offered."

Aela's heart sank as Splinter turned to her. "Bryn's the king of Dunwyn. You'll still be rewarded," she assured him hastily. "Everything that was promised will be yours –"

She broke off, dismay chipping at her confidence, as Splinter turned and signalled his people to move out. In a thunder of hooves, a flurry of yells, and a cloud of kicked-up dust, they rode back into the forest. Splinter spared Aela a final cold look before stepping over Dagny's dead body and leaving them alone. Alvine watched them go with satisfaction then shifted to look at Aela, who felt it suddenly - the magnitude of what was happening. Bryn had surrendered to Nielle's custody. Aela faced Alvine and her soldiers alone with no one at her back.

"'You're not leaving?" Alvine asked Aela without much interest.

"I think I'll stay," Aela replied. "I might need to kill you."

Alvine's eyes glittered. "Dare to dream, Commander Rinn. You're the one who is going to die today. You and this little vermin who calls himself a king."

She doubled over as Bowie elbowed her in the gut. It wasn't enough to pull from her grip, but he squirmed as Alvine loosened her hold, so that he turned to face her. His head snapped back when she slapped him across the face.

"Stop!" Bryn tried to jerk free of the man holding him, and a second man stepped in to restrain him.

A third stepped forward and grabbed Aela, sending a fresh eruption of pain up her broken right arm. She felt a dagger pressed to her throat.

"You don't like seeing him hurt," Alvine observed, watching Bryn with interest.

"Yeah, no shit," Bryn spat.

Alvine's hand returned to Bowie's throat. "Tell me, Bryn, do you love him?" She cocked her head to one side thoughtfully.

"Let's see how much he loves *you*."

With a nod from Alvine, one of the soldiers holding Bryn jerked his head back by his hair, pressing the tip of a knife to the base of his throat. Bryn sucked in a pained breath.

"*No!* No, stop!" Bowie tried to lunge forward, brought up short by Alvine's restraining hand.

"You can *make* it stop." She brought her lips close to Bowie's ear, as if she was going to press a gentle kiss to his cheek. "Tell me who the heir is, and he'll live. You'll *both* live."

"Bowie, *no* –" Bryn's terse warning was cut off prematurely as the blade pressed harder against his skin. Rivulets of blood beaded and trickled down his neck.

Bowie's lip trembled, and Aela's heart ached. Bryn had no idea who Nielle's heir was, but still he was valiantly trying to fix things between their countries, even if it cost him his life. But it was Bowie who had to choose. A choice between Bryn, as dear to him as a brother … and Aela, the queen he'd been raised to protect with his life.

"I…" Conflicted, tears welling in his wide eyes, he shook his head. "Bryn?"

Alvine shook him hard. "*I am not playing games with you!*" She looked to the soldier holding Bryn. "Kill him."

"*No!*" Bowie grabbed the front of Alvine's shirt. "Please, *please!*"

"Then *tell* me –"

"If you were a little smarter," Aela said, shoving at the guard who held her. "You might have figured out the truth yourself, rather than having to coerce it from a nine-year-old."

Bryn's face went white as she stepped towards Alvine.

"You don't have to die," Alvine said to Aela, supremely calm. "You have been Dunwyn's best fighter. You can be still. At my side."

Aela gave her a cutting smile. "I don't intend to command Dunwyn's army. I intend to sit on Nielle's throne."

Alvine's lips parted, eyes widening, before she brought her expression under hard control. "Prove it," she hissed.

Aela couldn't look at Bryn. At the corner of her vision, he reacted bodily to her words, as to a physical blow. She levelled a steady gaze on Alvine. "I have nothing to prove to you."

"It's not her!" Bowie struggled, his eyes desperate. "She's not the heir. She's trying to …"

"To what? Save *your* worthless, common life?"

She shoved Bowie into the grip of the nearest soldier and strolled up to Aela at a leisurely pace. She didn't try to stop Alvine from reaching out, let her trail cool fingers down Aela's neck, beneath the fabric of her shirt, wrapping around the chain she wore and tugging it out. The gold Niellan eagle insignia glinted in Alvine's hand. Alvine caught her breath. She looked up at Aela.

"*You!*"

Murmurs rippled through the soldiers at Alvine's back. One man wheeled his horse and galloped back to the rest of the troop before Alvine could stop him. Maybe the word that Marcus's legitimate heir was on the field would be enough to stay a few blades, but Aela wasn't about to bet on it.

"Yes," she said softly. "Me. Let Bowie go. Bryn and I will give you what you want."

Alvine beamed. She turned back to the soldier holding Bowie. "Kill him."

"*No!*" Bryn pulled against the men holding him with a burst of such sheer brute force that he hauled them forwards. Two more of Alvine's guards had to leap in to restrain him.

Aela started forward too, but more hands clamped down on her, too many to fight with her good arm broken. With another violent yell, Bryn broke free of his captors, pulling the sword from his belt. He whirled on Alvine with his blade at her throat, looking at the soldier who held Bowie. The soldier shoved Bowie away, rounding on Bryn. Alvine held up one restraining hand, holding her fighters back.

"Wait." Her posture as she faced Bryn was not at all fearful. She looked … hungry, smiling gleefully. "Are you going to fight me, Bryn? Are you going to *kill* me?"

Bryn's sword wavered, his hand trembling. Aela saw fear in his eyes, warring with the desire to kill. It wasn't strong enough to push over into action. Bryn clenched his jaw with furious frustration.

"Come on, Bryn," Alvine taunted. "I know you can do it. You killed your father."

Bryn's grip tightened on the blade. He pressed it against Alvine's throat, and the first traces of red bubbled up as the sharp edge pricked her skin. Tears welling in his eyes, he let out a furious cry. Pulling the blade from Alvine's neck, he rammed it with full force into the ground.

Triumphantly, she laughed. "Oh dear, looks like you're not a killer after all."

The smile on Alvine's face froze. The corners of her mouth curved upwards, even as her eyes flew wide and a sickening gurgle broke from her lips. The tip of a blade, drenched and dripping with blood gruesomely burst through the front of Alvine's throat and she fell to her knees.

"But I am."

Bowie's face was almost unrecognisable, stained with a torrent of Alvine's blood. His expression was utterly blank.

Someone who didn't know him might think he was too young to understand what he'd done. Aela knew better. The small dagger in his tied hands had Alvine's initials on it. The sheath at her belt was empty. Aela remembered him spinning in Alvine's grip, keeping her attention on his face.

You have to make your audience look somewhere else.

He'd planned this, knowing it would haunt him, that it would horribly and irreversibly change him. After fiercely fighting his deadly talents for so long, Bowie finally had the motivation to kill.

He watched Alvine's lifeless body wilt to the ground. Her blood inched like spilled paint, running in tiny rivers across the grass. He didn't even blink.

"Bowie," Bryn murmured with dismay and his voice seemed to cut through the boy's stricken trance.

The dagger fell from his fingers and he looked up at Bryn, swaying dangerously. His pleading eyes were so blue in contrast to the deep red blood coating his face. He began to shake as he tried, clumsy with horror, to wipe it away with tied hands, smearing thick stripes of red across his cheeks like paint. He opened his mouth but nothing came out. When he tried a second time, his voice was barely audible. "Please don't hate me," he whispered. "I had to."

That seemed to drain the last of his remaining strength. Bryn was there in time, and Bowie collapsed into his arms.

★★★

I t was quiet.

The terrible, rotting funk of death hung heavy over the

field, mingling with the tang of vomit. Bowie sat with his head hanging between his knees. Bryn hadn't moved from his side since he'd woken up.

Tearing her eyes away from them, Aela took a couple of halting steps towards the Niellan army. The sea of red armour moved, a ripple becoming a wave as ten thousand soldiers dropped to their knees before her.

Forty-Three

In the dark, Aela turned up the collar of her jacket against the wind. The torches flickered on the ramparts, illuminating Mason's stocky figure, standing watch above the drawbridge.

The wind whipped Aela's face. The air outside was cold and fresh, a stark shock to her system after the comforting warmth outside Bryn's chambers. He'd met her gaze out on the field, his golden-brown eyes unreadable, his lips parted in shock.

"We need to talk," he'd said before scooping Bowie off the ground and turning towards the city. Then she'd been pulled in dozens of different directions, calling the soldiers and people back from the depths of the forest, freeing the soldiers captured in the castle, viewing the dead and cataloguing injuries, and making arrangements for the Niellan army to surrender their weapons and camp outside the city. By the time she'd had a moment to breathe, the night was deep and Bryn had retreated to his chambers.

When Aela had gone to see him, peering tentatively inside the door, she'd seen Bowie curled up at the foot of the bed, his small body convulsing with violent sobs. Bryn had pulled Bowie into his lap, holding him like a child of four instead of nine and speaking in gentle, comforting murmurs. It was too much. Aela's heart was as brittle as fractured glass. Like this, she couldn't mend Bowie's heartbreak or atone for denying Bryn the truth.

Instead, she was out here on the wall, hiding like a coward. She told herself she was doing it this way because she couldn't afford to wait, because it might be days, weeks even, before Bryn was free of his duties as a freshly-ascended monarch to have the conversation they needed to have. But truthfully this way was easier. She didn't have the fortitude to nurture her relationship with Bryn while her duty to Nielle loomed, foreboding, before her.

"Commander?" Mason approached along the wall. She gave a short laugh and shook her head in disbelief. "Guess I can't call you that anymore. Queen Aela."

Aela shook her head. It sounded ridiculous, especially coming from one of her closest friends. "Gods, don't call me that either. How's the wound?"

Mason lifted her shirt tails, revealing a blood-flecked bandage at her stomach. "The stitches smart a bit, but I'll live. How's the arm?"

Aela flexed her fingers gingerly in the sling a physician had tied this afternoon. "It's a good thing the fighting's over. Unless you intend to make good on your promise to kick my ass."

"The night is young." They stood side by side, staring out into the darkness. "What are you doing out here? Casing the joint for another Niellan assault?"

Aela gave a short laugh. "No way I'd risk it. I've heard Dunwyn's new commander is a stone-cold bitch." Mason gave another disbelieving grunt, and Aela took her friend's wrist with her uninjured hand. "I'm serious, Mason. I need you to take command of the army. Bryn will formalise the transition, probably tomorrow when he wakes up."

Mason's dark brows furrowed. "I suppose I know where you're going."

"I'm going to Eterre." Aela watched Mason's expression in silence as it sank in.

The older woman's dark eyes went wide, her lips parting in shock. Slowly, she turned to look up at Aela. "You're not coming back, are you?"

It was as if there was a hand around her throat, choking her speech. She shook her head.

"How the fuck am I supposed to break it to His Highness?" Mason breathed.

"I'll see him again." But it wouldn't be with Bryn as it had been before. They would have a coolly professional relationship, talks over tables, structured, soulless meetings, always under the appraising gaze of subordinates.

"You should take backup with you to Nielle," Mason warned. "You may be the rightful queen, but there could still be resistance."

Aela snorted. "Backup? You mean Dunwyan soldiers? Not a good look." She grinned with more bravado than she felt about travelling to Eterre with a troop of ten thousand Niellan soldiers. She reminded herself that they weren't her enemies. "I'll be fine."

"Be sure that you are." Mason looked hard at Aela. "No matter whose blood is in your veins, no matter what throne you sit on, you are my friend. You always will be."

Forty-Four

"What's the first thing you're going to do when you get home?" Aela cast a sidelong look at Commander Victoire Gage as they rode across the meadow outside Eterre. Ahead, soldiers filed into the city.

Tall and fair-skinned, Commander Gage had a hard-edged, slim face with narrow lips that always seemed to be pressed into a tight line. "Weapons inventory," she replied shortly.

"A fate worse than death," Aela mused. It didn't have the desired effect. Instead of laughter or a knowing grin, Commander Gage simply pursed her lips so tightly they went white.

Aela wondered if the Niellan army's top brass was always this surly, or if she was simply on edge about welcoming the half-Dunwyan former enemy soldier as her country's ascendant queen. Aela couldn't blame her for that. She supposed she should consider it a victory that she'd made it all the way to Eterre without anyone trying to knife her in the back. But respect for the royal bloodline wasn't the same as camaraderie. Aela had a fluent grasp of the Niellan language but still felt entirely foreign.

The thundering of hooves caught her attention. A small

group rode out at a pace from the city. Aela winced as she reached with her right hand reflexively for her sword. A week of travel had done little to improve her broken arm. A greying man in his late sixties dismounted as a relieved-looking Commander Gage took off towards the city. The man hobbled towards her and went stiffly to his knees.

"Your Majesty," he said in heavily-accented Dunwyan.

"I can speak Niellan," Aela replied awkwardly, dismounting. "Who are you?"

"Your Majesty," The man said again, and this time Aela heard disbelieving wonder in his voice. He rose slowly with the trepidation of one unsure of how his joints might take the exertion. "My name is Philippe Daubert. I received the herald's message that you and the army were on their way. Thank the gods. I told Lady Alvine that marching on Dunwyn was not advisable. I'm relieved we didn't take too many casualties. I'm also relieved that … you're here to take her place." Philippe gave another short bow. "I am King Marcus's primary councillor. I've served at his right hand for forty years and I swore to him that if you should ever return to Eterre, I would serve you too. If it pleases you."

Aela couldn't help asking, "Are you … surprised I'm here?"

Rather weakly, like he was grappling with the truth, Philippe said, "If I may speak freely, Your Majesty, this isn't a *surprise*, it's a miracle! With the king's health deteriorating, we had no choice but to put Nielle in the hands of Lady Alvine. She wasn't the true-born heir, but with your whereabouts unknown … The law of the land states that if any blood relative is living, the country must go to them. When your father was in better health, he was adamant that his agents would find you one day, although I must admit, I had my doubts. Sending you away was a gamble, but it was one His Majesty felt he had to make, to protect you." A fond quality crept into Philippe's voice and his brightening blue eyes made him look younger. "He always was uniquely gifted with wildly ambitious ideals."

Aela bit her tongue. Those *wildly ambitious ideals* weren't remembered so fondly across the border.

Instead, she said, "You knew he sent me away?"

Philippe gave a gracious bow. "Yes, of course. I was in your father's confidence. I aided him in leading everyone to believe you'd died at birth."

"Then you'd know about Bowie too?"

The old man's brow furrowed. "Who?"

"King Marcus pretended he was the heir after his last son passed."

"Oh. Yes." Philippe cleared his throat awkwardly. "It was … unfortunate, when he was taken, but as His Majesty always said, better him than you."

Aela felt a flash of fury as she remembered Bowie driving his blade into Alvine's throat. "*Better him than me?*" she gritted out.

"It's what he was raised to do," Philippe said matter-of-factly. "He understood his duty."

There was no refuting that, but the cavalier attitude was still infuriating. "I don't support the reckless endangerment of children to achieve political ends, Philippe. You should know that about me before we proceed."

Philippe raised his eyebrows, not angry, simply curious. "From what I've heard of your life in the Borderlands, I thought you'd understand quite well that desperate times call for … undesirable measures."

It wasn't the same, but there would be plenty of time to argue that point. Right now, there was something more pressing on

Aela's mind. "Speaking of which, I grew up in Dunwyn. I *killed* Niellans in the Border War. Do you think the people will easily forget that? How will they ever trust me?"

Unconcerned, Phillipe shrugged. "You are not Dunwyan, Your Majesty," he told her, as if the idea was ludicrous. "Niellan blood runs in your veins. Your father's blood. The people trust that. Besides, what you did at Bayeau is legendary."

"What, defeating the Niellan army?"

"Saving Niellan lives, Your Majesty," Philippe replied quietly. "Risking yourself to end four years of bloodshed."

Aela closed her eyes. She'd spared little thought for how her victory might be received this side of the border. All she knew was that Philippe was only half right. She was Niellan, but she was Dunwyan too. She didn't know how to turn her back on Dunwyn any more than she knew how to stop desperately missing the man who ruled it.

Everything happened in a mind-numbing flurry. Aela was shown to the queen's apartments, servants folding to the floor as she walked along the corridor – she tried to ignore that. It was harder to ignore the persistent thought that nudged at the back of her mind as she stood like a stranger in her enormous rooms. *My mother lived here.*

Philippe took her orders for the army and informed her that dinner would be brought to her. "Tomorrow morning, Your Majesty, I'll send an urgent summons to your councillors," he said. "They hold land across the country, so it will take some days for all of them to arrive, but it's important you meet with them. We have matters of diplomacy to discuss."

He bowed deeply again and left her alone in the expansive chambers. It had been weeks since she'd been by herself for more than a few minutes. Everything felt too quiet, too empty, and when the time came for her to sleep, she sent away the gushing servant who arrived to dress her in a ridiculous silk nightgown. Aela tried to curl up on the bed, still wearing her travel clothes and boots, but it felt too soft, like she was sinking through the sheets and being swallowed by the mattress.

She spent the night on the floor by the fire, staring up at the ceiling, wondering how this would ever feel ordinary.

Forty-Five

Aela woke at dawn as usual, an unbreakable habit after so many years of deeply-ingrained military training. She progressed through the morning routine she'd developed for herself over the past two weeks in Eterre. Push-ups followed sit-ups, then stretching, then staring up at the jagged mountains rising outside her window while she mulled over the political landscape of the Niellan court.

She'd always been comfortable in solitude, and if the guards posted outside her rooms and the servants poised to serve her breakfast had reason to believe she was a late sleeper, so much the better. It gave her several hours alone with her thoughts before her first engagements of the day, and gods did she need that time to mentally prepare herself.

Council meetings were becoming incrementally less awkward, though she still felt uneasy in a room with the four men who had given their allegiance to Alvine. At the beginning of the first meeting, Aela had definitively cut short an attempted interrogation from one of the more suspicious men by slamming the golden eagle pendant and her father's letter down onto the table and welcoming him to prove the items were inauthentic. That had shut everyone up.

So far, Philippe's assessment of how she would be received was proving accurate. Whether or not Philippe's analysis of sentiment for her victory at Bayeau was accurate, Niellans certainly had an impressive level of deference for Marcus and Ives's lost progeny. It reminded Aela of Bowie's unfailing loyalty to the throne. Niellans were more proud and patriotic than she'd ever given them credit for.

She shook her head to rip her mind away from thoughts of Bowie. Thinking about anyone in Dunwyn right now was dangerous. Her mind slid far too easily towards images of blond hair and golden-brown eyes, strong hands exploring her body, and unattainable fantasies of travelling alone through the wilderness, strategising by firelight.

Someone knocked at the door, shattering Aela's wistful imaginings. It was still too early for anyone to be here, which meant something was probably wrong.

Opening the door, she found Philippe, dressed haphazardly as if he'd moments ago rolled out of bed.

"What is it?" she asked him.

"Your Majesty." He looked rather harried. "The … erm … His Highness, King Bryn of Dunwyn is here. He requests an audience."

Aela froze. "*Here*? In the castle? Shouldn't he have been detected when he crossed the Niellan border?" The bewildered questions were sensible enough. Philippe didn't need to know they weren't motivated by security concerns so much as they were by the fact that she'd hoped to have more time to prepare, mentally and physically, before facing Bryn again.

Philippe flushed and cleared his throat awkwardly. "It appears he travelled covertly with a small guard. He advises that his own council does not know he's here. I gather they would have frowned upon this particular … excursion."

The old man's eyes glittered as he said that, his lip quirking slightly. Aela fought the urge to suppress a smile too. Despite herself, she rather liked Philippe.

It felt bizarre and disorienting, entering through the side door that brought her out onto the dais. When she walked into the great hall, she looked down upon four figures, and Aela realised that Philippe had understated when he'd described Bryn's guard as *small*. It was almost non-existent.

He was accompanied only by Chase and Landon … and, to Aela's surprise, Bowie, looking wan and wary as his eyes darted about the room, wearing clothing more expensive than anything in his wardrobe in Anarchist Underground. His eyes were tired, and his curly hair was dishevelled as ever. Aela descended the three steps to the floor, coming eye-level with them, looking directly at Bryn.

The sight of him hurt her heart. He too was wearing finer clothing than anything he'd donned in Underground, a deep purple jacket with gold buttons over a white shirt that looked cleaner than expected after a week of travel. His captivating eyes stood out beautifully against the fabric's dark colouring. There was a slight flush on his cheeks, possibly from the chill of the morning air … or, she thought hopefully, from seeing her again. Bryn's eyes were fixed on her, his lips slightly parted.

Aela also looked nothing like she had in Underground, wearing a dress of dark-red velvet with long sleeves, a tight bodice, and flowing skirt that trailed on the floor. Her caramel-streaked hair flowed loose about her face.

"So," she said, surprised to hear how steady her voice sounded, "within a fortnight of your reign as king, you've absconded from Dunwyn with an insufficient guard and crossed into a foreign country without first consulting your council. I'm intrigued as to the nature of this visit."

Bryn held her gaze. Aela couldn't read his expression. It was Chase who spoke.

"*Insufficient* guard?" His teasing tone was entirely at odds with where they were. "That's a little insulting, Your Majesty."

She couldn't help grinning at that, but her gut clenched with painful anxiety as Bryn continued to regard her silently. She wondered if, to him, she looked changed, if he was trying to see past the royal trappings, seeking a glimpse of the Aela he'd come to know on the road. They hadn't spoken before she'd left Dunwyn, not properly. Perhaps he was searching for any sign of a threat, any indication that Nielle was still his enemy.

His voice coiled deep into her core, spreading warmth through her body. "I'd like to propose a diplomatic meeting between Nielle and Dunwyn."

"When?" Aela asked.

Bryn's lip twitched. "Now."

Forty-Six

It wasn't the way things were done. Someone who didn't know Bryn might believe he simply lacked the decorum to send word in advance and formally schedule a visit through an envoy. His decision to engage in discussions without a single member of his council present might be considered reckless or impulsive … but Bryn was a better strategist than he let on. The impropriety was entirely the point. He was deliberately instigating a different way of doing things.

Aela's own impropriety was less premeditated. She always arrived with military punctuality to important meetings, which meant she was usually seated before her councillors arrived. It was a faux pas, but at least this morning she had the excuse that they were all still dragging themselves out of bed. And unlike at her other meetings, she wasn't the only attendee who was early.

Bryn sat silently beside Aela. A second chair had been moved to the head of the table so the two of them could sit together. He was flawless, even with bruise-like smudges beneath his eyes. She wondered what time they'd started riding today to get here so early.

Morning light, thrown across the table through a series

of windows that looked out upon the Jaws Range, scattered luminous gold through Bryn's light hair. Sunlight streaked across the strong lines of his body and reflected in his warm, dark eyes. He looked ethereal, unreachable, both because of his beauty and because he hadn't met her gaze since walking into the room. Suspenseful longing for a proper conversation crawled under her skin, desperate to break loose, stymied by the need to wait for Aela's council.

Bowie was at the door speaking to Chase, who would remain posted outside with Landon. The boy murmured something, and Chase laughed easily. Warmth flooded Aela's heart.

"Bowie seems to like Chase," she ventured, not daring to look at Bryn. Chase was easy to like, but Bowie was customarily taciturn, deeply untrusting of new people.

"He asked Bowie to teach him Niellan curses on the ride here." Bryn's lip curled, but he didn't look at her either. "A week later, the lesson continues. I don't think Chase was fully prepared for the vulgarity. Poor Landon certainly wasn't." Aela laughed softly. Bryn's eyes flicked to her then away. "I've appointed Chase as captain of my guard. I figured anyone with the respect of Aela Rinn must be excellent with a blade and loyal to a fault."

There was something in his voice that made Aela turn towards him, but before either of them could say anything further, a commotion rose outside the great hall, raised voices growing closer. Bowie backed up before the door opened violently, slamming back against the wall.

Four men entered, all with distinctly western looks, dressed in the regalia of Niellan nobility – long, deep-red robes bearing the golden Niellan eagle over tailored trousers and shiny boots. Philippe was flanked by two men about his age, one rotund and bald, and the other with greying hair pulled back in a tail. The fourth councillor was in his early thirties with a narrow face. His hair was as dark as Bowie's, his blue eyes lighter, cloudier.

Expectantly, Bryn leaned over to Bowie, who sank down in the chair at his left and muttered, "The one with no hair is called Edouard. I know him. He's served King Marcus almost as long as Philippe. Jorden is the other older one, lower nobility from the north. He was here before I left too." He frowned as he nodded subtly at the youngest of the four. "That one I don't know."

Aela leaned over. "His name is Gilles. He was appointed by Alvine."

Bryn raised his eyebrows. "And he's still here?"

"I figured his was a useful perspective, for now. It bothers me more that neither Marcus nor Alvine saw fit to appoint any women to the council, but I'm planning to expand it significantly … in time."

Gilles was red-faced, ranting in Niellan at the other men. "...absolutely *unacceptable* on such late notice! There are protocols to observe."

Aela cocked a brow. "He does lack charisma, doesn't he?"

Bowie pressed his lips together hard and dropped his head.

Aela rose to her feet. "Hey!" she called in Dunwyan over the ruckus. Gilles hesitated, suddenly looking horrified at the realisation that he had been yelling in the company of a king and queen. "If it's all right by you, King Bryn and I would quite like to commence."

There was an uncomfortable silence.

Philippe went to his knees, breaking the tension. "Hail to Her Majesty, Queen Aela of Nielle."

The routine words that commenced each council meeting

today seemed a little pointed. Slowly, the others knelt also, murmuring the phrase. Out of the corner of her eye, Aela saw Bowie move to do the same, but Bryn put a restraining hand on his arm, murmuring something in his ear.

"In the spirit of forging a new friendship between our two countries," Bryn said as the councillors sat, "Dunwyn brings an offering of peace and healing." He reached into his jacket. The handful of vials clinked softly as he placed them on the table. "I'm sure you know by now that your king has been poisoned for some years. This is an antidote for grey dream. It's a cure for King Marcus."

In the stunned silence that followed, Aela sympathised with the Niellan councillors, who had probably believed her sudden appearance would be the most surprising thing to happen to them this month. For Aela's part, she was ashamed to realise that, amidst her upheaval, she'd entirely forgotten about the grey dream cure.

"It works," she assured them. "I've seen it. I've … experienced it."

"King Bryn," Philippe stammered, "this is an incredible gift. Dunwyn is most generous."

"Dunwyn isn't responsible for creating the antidote," Bryn said quietly, inclining his head towards Bowie. "He is."

This silence dragged out longer than the last, as recognition and guilt, to varying extents, crossed the faces of the three older councillors. Bowie had said he knew them, and apparently they knew him too. Bald-headed Edouard rose from the table, clearing his throat.

"Well … thank the gods he's still alive."

"Not sure the gods had much to do with it," Bryn said snidely. "But perhaps more than you people."

Edourard valiantly managed to ignore this. "Queen Aela," he said.

She followed him with her eyes as he moved around the table. She and Bryn were probably the only ones to notice the tension thrumming in Bowie's body as the older man paused, placing his hands on the back of his chair.

"This boy has been a loyal servant indeed to His Majesty. If it pleases you, I'd like to see him rewarded." Edouard pulled his chair out from the table and nudged Bowie encouragingly. "Well? Stand up."

Aela saw Bryn frown. The tone Edouard took with Bowie was as a schoolmaster addressing a pupil who was slow at learning. Bowie rose, one hand creeping up to scratch the scar at his throat. His wounds and bruises had faded in the past fortnight, but the look in his eyes gave Aela pause, haunted, distant, like he'd retreated into himself.

"If it pleases Your Majesty, I'd like to offer him a position in your household," Edouard said, with the grand air of a man accomplishing an act of extreme generosity. "Any position, boy. Name it, and it's yours."

"I –" Bowie clearly hadn't expected to be singled out. He glanced pleadingly at Bryn, who looked up at Edouard. To an untrained eye, Bryn appeared perfectly at ease, lounging back casually in his chair, but Aela could see underlying aggravation in the tension of his shoulders.

"You're rewarding him with a servant's position?" Bryn enquired lightly. "Isn't that a little … inadequate?"

Across the table, Jorden looked puzzled. "He *is* a servant, King Bryn."

"No," Bryn answered shortly, "He respectfully declines your offer. He's coming with me back to Dunwyn to be part of my family."

A series of shocked exclamations from the Niellans filled the room. Gilles cleared his throat. "With respect, King Bryn, he's not yours to take. He belongs to King Marcus."

Bryn sat forward in his chair, the relaxed quality of his posture visibly shifting, changing the mood in the room. "He doesn't belong to anybody. He's a boy," Bryn said. "He's the reason Nielle's queen sits in this room right now ... And he's just saved your king's life."

"King Bryn," Gilles said coolly, glancing at the vials on the table, "*if* this cure works, then it is ... remarkable, to be sure. But with respect, the boy was in King Marcus's confidence. I'm afraid we simply cannot allow the information in his head into your kingdom." His lip curled into an oily smile. "As ... a precaution, nothing more. You understand."

Aela pushed herself up from the table, and all eyes turned to her expectantly.

"For the first time in two centuries, Nielle and Dunwyn are in a room together, discussing not only an end to fighting but an actual friendship. I want Dunwyn to be our ally," she said. She looked pointedly at Gilles. "Anybody who does not share our vision for peace should stand up and leave this room now."

"We all want peace, Your Majesty," Jorden said awkwardly. "Of course. But –"

"Surely a nine-year-old boy is not a threat to our country's safety."

"Well, no, Your Majesty, but –"

"Then there's no harm in letting him go." She gave Bowie a little nod across the table. "If you want to go back to Dunwyn with Bryn, then go with my blessing."

Tension left Bowie in a rushed exhalation, and he slumped

down into his chair. His blue eyes brightened, happiness creeping onto his face. It was the first time Aela had ever seen him smile.

"Thank you," Bowie said softly.

They gave Bryn a room down the hall from Aela's after an hours-long conversation covering everything from territorial disputes to the boundaries of military patrols to potential trade agreements. Not a lot was resolved. It would be a long time before official agreements were firmed up. Diplomacy was far more gruelling than fighting on a battlefield.

It was late afternoon by the time Marcus's physician knocked on the door of Aela's chambers and informed her that the grey dream antidote was beginning to take effect. She was to be granted an audience with her father for the first time since her arrival in the city. She'd had high hopes after witnessing Aran's recovery, but the physician's prognosis was clear. Marcus had been given too much grey dream. More than four years had passed since his first dose. In his late stage of poisoning, there was only so much the remedy would do. She could expect him to be lucid but weak, deteriorating. It wouldn't save his life.

When Aela arrived outside Marcus's chambers an hour later, she stopped in surprise as she came face-to-face with Bryn, Bowie and Landon, loitering outside the door, which was guarded by a pair of soldiers attempting to studiously ignore their Dunwyan counterpart.

"They seem to think I'm here to assassinate the king of Nielle," Bryn said, looking amused.

"Your Majesty, that's not what was said —" one of the Niellan soldiers began, her blue eyes stricken, clearly fearing she'd sparked an international incident.

"I understand," Aela told her. She narrowed her eyes at Bryn, a silent admonition. "The king of Dunwyn has an unorthodox sense of humour."

Out of the corner of her eye, Aela caught Landon pressing a hand to his mouth to stifle a grin.

"I hope you'll forgive the intrusion," Bryn said to Aela, too formal as the Niellan soldier opened the door. "Bowie would never ask, but –"

" Of course he can see the king," Aela said.

One foot over the threshold, she halted, heart stumbling at the sensation of Bryn's warm, strong hand wrapping around her wrist. In a low voice, he said, "He's an infirm old man now, not the warmonger he used to be."

"You're telling me to be gentle?" Aela struggled to keep her voice light. Everything unsaid was still strung hard between them.

Bryn let go to shrug his shoulders, and she could breathe again. "I don't know. Personally, I'd quite like to punch the man in the face for what he did to you and Bowie … but he's still your father."

The curtains were flung open, and fading sunlight flooded the room. A cold, gentle breeze trailed in from the open windows, ruffling the drapes that were pinned back at the posts of the king's bed.

Marcus was propped up by a stack of pillows. Illuminated by the setting sun, his skin was faded, almost translucent, rivers of blue veins starkly clear. His frail flesh looked as if it would disintegrate under the lightest touch.

A flood of conflicting feelings thundered into Aela's heart, crashing over each other, impossible to process individually. This man was her father. The thought was distant and almost didn't make sense. He didn't look like anyone's father. Even before she'd known they shared blood, this fragile husk of a man had been one of the most important figures in her life. His raids on Hiver had forced her to mature far earlier than she should have. His actions on the border had driven her into life as a soldier, and into war. For so long, her hatred of him had obliterated her heart, degraded rational thought. She'd fantasised about what it would be like to face him one day, to rip his life away from him for all he'd done.

But the longer she looked at him, the less revenge seemed to matter. Like a receding tide, her anger ebbed away, leaving pity in its place. Marcus had lost his wife, his children. He'd given away his daughter. He'd sacrificed the adopted son who had grown up in his home, who still loved him unconditionally, despite the monstrous life Marcus had subjected him to. The greatest tragedy was that he had to live out his remaining days inside his own miserable head.

A violent, shaking breath cut through the turmoil of Aela's thoughts, and she looked around at Bowie, who stood behind her and Bryn. With his long dark hair falling across his face, she couldn't see his expression, but his fingers vigorously scratched at his throat. Bowie took an uncertain step and drew in another breath as if he was about to speak …

"Boniface?" King Marcus pushed himself up in his bed with a great effort, the cords in his neck straining. "Is that you?"

Aela didn't realise what was happening when Bowie bowed his head and moved forward. It was a painful, quiet moment before she pieced together what suddenly seemed as obvious as a slap in the face. Araxa and her gang would have thought a grand name like *Boniface* was ridiculous, not to mention indiscreet. Bryn closed his eyes, shaking his head, surely coming to his own realisation. Perhaps, like her, he was wondering if he'd been calling Bowie by a name he hated.

"Boniface?" Marcus's cloudy eyes lit up, as if for the first time he had the energy to feel something other than his illness. His mouth slid into a shaky smile. "They said you'd returned, but I couldn't believe it. Come here." With some trepidation, Bowie moved forward to stand beside the low bed, his eyes still fixed on the floor. Weakly, Marcus held out a hand to Bowie, gesturing stiffly to the bed. "Come."

Bowie climbed up to sit tentatively on the side of the mattress, a careful distance away from the king. Marcus's eyes roamed over Bowie, as if relearning him by heart. Reaching out, he ran a trembling finger over the thin scar that marred Bowie's throat. "And what happened here?"

Aela exchanged a glance with Bryn. Even with the antidote, the grey dream had affected Marcus's memory beyond repair. Everything Bowie had suffered had evaporated from the king's mind. Bowie seemed to realise it too, because he took a moment to monitor his words.

"I ... got in a fight, Your Majesty."

At the mention of a fight, Marcus's posture straightened and he leaned forward slightly with interest. For a painful, conflicting moment, Aela thought that maybe she understood this part of him.

Marcus's wheezing laugh dissolved into a fit of coughing. Flecks of blood flew from his mouth, staining the white sheets. "As boys do. Tell me, did you win?"

Bowie looked, fleetingly, back at Aela and Bryn, then returned his gaze to Marcus. "Yes, Your Majesty. It was close, but we won."

Bryn and Bowie left the room, shutting the door with a definitive snap, and Aela felt desperately alone, feet away from her only living relative. Slowly, she walked towards him. Closer, Aela could see his features more clearly. His eyes were blue like hers. Did they look alike? She couldn't tell. It was hard to see yourself in a stranger.

"Father?" she said, trying out the word. He looked drowsy, his eyelids drooping. "Father," she whispered again, and she was hit suddenly with the full force of powerful longing. To have seen this man whole and well, to know what had truly motivated his choices, to see in him the wisdom and heart that inspired such loyalty from his people. To understand him. "What do I need to do? How can I be a good queen?"

Marcus gave a soft, comfortable sigh, his chest rising and falling lethargically. Aela thought that perhaps he'd fallen asleep. Then, in a low, mumbling voice, he said, "You should do what I did not. Fight only when you must. Don't fight for glory. Fight for peace." He paused, drawing in a laboured breath. When he spoke again, Aela saw a small, sad smile on his face. "And perhaps also for love. Don't ever sacrifice someone you love."

Forty-Seven

The next night, there was a feast.

It wasn't a relaxing occasion. Aela was introduced to everyone of importance in the Niellan court that she hadn't already met. Many of them had travelled for days to Eterre upon receiving word that King Marcus's heir had returned. She was expecting hostility from some and to dislike many of them in return, but she routinely found the Niellans to be amicable, at least to her face, and eager to meet their lost queen. They all had one astounding similarity with the people of Dunwyn, unswerving loyalty to their king.

Aela had scarcely spoken to Bryn before dinner, caught up in countless conversations with Niellans clamouring for her attention and favour. When she finally collapsed into a chair to eat, he settled beside her silently at the head of the table. Aela steeled herself to talk to him — finally a proper conversation — when someone tapped on her shoulder. It was Philippe.

"Your Majesty, you have visitors from Dunwyn. This is … rather embarrassing. Usually, we don't have breaches like this, I can send more soldiers to the border."

"Who are they?"

"One of them says his name is Amory and that you'll know

who he is, but I can –"

Aela was already on her feet, running from the banquet hall out into the cold night.

There was indeed a small cluster of people in the courtyard. Their faces were familiar. Tamas, with his mother, frail but standing tall in the stronghold of the enemy. And Ewan, standing beside a man who towered over all the others. Aela hurtled down the stairs and threw herself into Amory's bulky, waiting arms. He squeezed her tightly, laughing.

"I heard we'd find you here," he said.

Aela pulled back. "Heard from who?"

"A messenger from King Bryn arrived earlier this week." He nudged Aela. "Your friend *Slate* bears a striking resemblance to His Highness."

"Oh." Aela's heart throbbed.

It was a painful reminder of Bryn as few people knew him. She realised it a little sadly, wondering if this was the last time his kindness would be extended to her in such a deeply personal way. Aela and Amory trailed the group as they were ushered inside.

"You knew, didn't you?" she said to him, a little wounded. "You knew who I was and never told me."

Amory's smile faltered. "I resealed the box. I couldn't help myself. This woman showed up in town with it asking questions, a few months after you left to join the army in Dunwald." He shook his head as if still in disbelief, years later. "Let me tell you, I was not expecting to discover I'd been harbouring the enemy's future queen. But you deserved a chance. Nielle deserved a chance. I don't regret what I did."

He was smiling, but guilt seized Aela's heart. "Amory, I'm so sorry," she whispered.

His face softened. "I am too. I was afraid to tell you. I didn't know how. But I should've reached out, should've called you back from Dunwald. Denying you the truth led you to the frontlines of a war against your own people."

Aela shook her head. "Marcus should never have restarted the war. I have no regrets about defending the border, only about how many lives I took before I ended it. And I hope I would feel that regardless of which side of the fight I was on."

"You're a good person, Aela. It's the only thing that's kept me from feeling like I failed you, seeing the woman you've become." He winked at her. "Perhaps Nielle should thank me for raising a worthy queen. Do you think they'd build a statue in my honour?"

"Not sure we've got enough stone to make a life-size statue," Aela teased. "They weren't really merchants, were they? The people who brought me to Hiver."

Amory shook his head. "They were passing through when the mercenaries attacked. I don't know where they intended to take you, all I know is that neither of them made it out the raid alive." He huffed a humourless laugh. "Marcus almost killed his own daughter in that attack without even realising it."

He stopped walking, turning to grasp her shoulders firmly. "Aela, the only reason I took you in was because you were alone. I didn't know the truth back then. All I ever cared about was raising you to be brave and kind and selfless." He reached out, touching her cheek. "I didn't care what you did with those gifts, so long as you had them. Can you forgive me? Are we still family?"

Aela nodded. "Of course." She pulled him into another embrace.

Squeezing her tightly, Amory whispered, "Maybe this is a

new start, Aela. Maybe one day there can be unity for Nielle and Dunwyn again."

By the time the night's jovial celebrations faded into sleepy, early morning silence, Aela's body was exhausted, but her mind was still active. She settled between the sheets in her grand chambers, beginning to feel the full weight of being queen of Nielle.

What Amory had said echoed in her head. *Unity for Nielle and Dunwyn.*

It was a prospect that had been playing in her mind since she'd first discovered the truth. But it required a conversation with the only person she hadn't properly spoken to tonight.

Closing her eyes, all she saw was Bryn, a collage of images, hard-edged sarcasm, occasionally blurred by hints of tenderness, the softness in his eyes when he looked at her right before they kissed. The professional tone he'd adopted since finding out who she really was, which occasionally morphed into something implacable.

Aela swung herself out of bed, dressed, and padded silently to the plush rooms down the hall.

Chase and a Niellan soldier stood guard at the door. Actually, *standing guard* was too generous. Aela knew her friend well enough to see his signature moves at work, the way Chase leaned in towards his attractive Niellan counterpart, gazing up through his eyelashes, casually brushing the dark-haired man's arm as they spoke.

"Are you behaving yourself, Chase?" Aela asked as she approached.

To his credit, the Niellan soldier reddened and took a hasty step away from Chase, who met Aela's gaze unabashedly.

"Are *you*, Your Majesty?" He inclined his head to Bryn's door and gave her a conspiratorial wink.

Aela rolled his eyes. Leaning in, she said in an undertone, "Does setting you loose on an entire foreign army's worth of new sexual prospects qualify as an act of war by Dunwyn?"

"Take it up with His Highness." Chase stepped aside, allowing her passage to Bryn's room.

Quietly, in case he was asleep, she rapped on the door.

"Come in."

Carefully, she pushed the door open and stopped. She'd expected Bryn to be alone. He wasn't. He was in bed on top of the covers, shirt unlaced at the collar, shoes kicked off. Beside him, sleeping soundly beneath a thick quilt, was Bowie. One of Bryn's arms was trapped where it cushioned Bowie's head, the boy's inky hair spilling over Bryn's white shirt. In his free hand, Bryn held a stack of papers. He looked up from them.

"Sorry," Aela whispered. "I thought you'd be by yourself." Bryn shook his head carefully. Aela nodded at Bowie. "Nightmares?"

"He sleeps better when he has company," Bryn replied, glancing down.

"He sleeps better when you're with him," Aela amended.

Bryn half-smiled. "The latest word from Dunwyn." He placed the papers down on the bed. "Before we left, I formally appointed Mason Tanner as commander. She's no Aela Rinn, but I'm cautiously optimistic we won't be fighting at the border again any time soon. What are you doing here?"

"I —" Aela suddenly wasn't sure about this. She paused, gathering her thoughts, then tried again. "You have a kingdom to run."

"Are you asking when I'm leaving?" The tremble in Bryn's voice was almost imperceptible. "Is Nielle's queen wary of allowing her enemy to stay behind her walls?"

"You're not my enemy."

"I'm going to leave." Even though it was the answer she'd expected, it caused a hollow ache in her chest. "But if you'll permit me, I'd like to remain in Nielle for at least the next fortnight." His voice softened and he inclined his head to Bowie, still fast asleep. "He wants to wait until Marcus …"

The silence was a sufficient implication.

Aela paused again and cleared her throat. "Will you take a walk with me?"

Bryn smiled. "I thought you'd never ask."

He pried his arm gently away from Bowie, who stirred, murmuring in his sleep but not waking.

The gardens were cold and still, illuminated only by the glow of the waning moon. A fine layer of snow dusted the bare branches of the rows of blossom trees that lined the path and more snow fell silently, clinging to Aela's hair. Their boots crunched quietly on the white pebbles underfoot, and for a while that was the only sound.

Aela stopped. "You came to Nielle."

Bryn's eyes fixed on a point over her shoulder. "Marcus needed the antidote."

"Is that the only reason?" When he said nothing, Aela felt desperation rise. "I'm no different. I want to figure out where we go from here. You and me. Bryn and Aela. Not a king and a queen."

"Oh," Bryn said.

Fuck. She wasn't saying this right. They were facing each other, standing close enough to touch, but the small distance between them was carefully imposed. Aela could feel each excruciating inch and strained with the physical effort of holding herself back from reaching out and pulling Bryn against her.

"We're allies," she said.

"Is that all?" Bryn's face was carefully without expression, and Aela ducked her head, unable to bear the thought of him closing off from her. She had believed she was prepared for this. It was the conversation she'd wanted to have, but now that she was looking into Bryn's eyes, her mind was blank.

"This whole talking about my feelings thing is not my strong suit," she admitted. She flicked her eyes up to gauge his reaction.

Bryn clutched his chest, feigning exaggerated shock. "Whatever do you mean?"

"Fuck off," she muttered, looking away again. "I'm trying to tell you. I need you to know. If I wasn't … who I am, I'd still be fighting for you."

With her eyes downcast, she only heard Bryn's quiet laugh, the familiar, self-assured amusement that made her pulse quicken and her blood heat. "I know that," he said. "If you'd asked me a couple of weeks ago, I would have said you'd be fighting for me because you need to fight, but that's not true now, is it?"

"I'm beginning to see that peace has its merits."

Aela looked up as Bryn gave another breathy laugh. The meticulously curated tension in his posture was trickling away. He was lowering his guard as he did with a select few people. It was exhilarating, knowing he might still trust her enough to show her this, his heart, his aching vulnerability. That was what made Bryn far more beautiful than his handsome face and strong body. She had always thought he'd been built to fight until he'd held her in his arms. Then she'd wondered if maybe he was actually built to do that, to fit his body perfectly against hers.

"We're going to miss you in Dunwyn," Bryn said.

Aela closed her eyes. It was too much. If this was goodbye, she should do it right. She reached into her pocket and squeezed the gold ring against the fabric.

"Speaking of Dunwyn." Tentatively, she caught Bryn's hand. It felt like a spark when their fingers touched, heat sizzling up her arm, travelling through her entire body like a fire igniting. Her touch lingered for a moment as she dropped the king's insignia into his hand. "I think your father would say you've earned this."

Bryn turned the ring over in his fingers, wonder in his dark eyes. Aela wished she could let herself be distracted by the delicate touch of his strong hands on the raised gold stars, but she couldn't stop thinking.

"I don't know if I can do this," she confessed desperately. Bryn was the only person she could admit it to. "I'm a commander of armies, not a queen."

Bryn gave her a knowing grin. "Back at Hiver, at the lake, you told me I had to trust myself."

Silence stretched out between them. That captivating smile always stole her breath and words.

"You came to Nielle," she said again quietly, because it was easier than asking for the truth.

Slowly, Bryn nodded. "Yeah, I came. I missed having you around to give me good counsel ... but if I'm honest, that isn't the real reason why I'm here. I came because I couldn't do it. I couldn't let you go with so much unsaid and undone between us."

He took her face in his hands. Aela felt the shock of the cool metal ring, encased in heat where his palm touched her cheek.

His golden-brown eyes blazed with desperation.

"We both have duties holding us apart," he said, "but I don't want diplomacy to be all that's between us. I think about seeing you only when the friendship between our countries brings us together and I can't breathe. You're the only person I've ever wanted to share everything with, the ugly, bitter, shameful parts of me, as well as all the good I've done and the good I'm going to do. I came to Nielle because I refuse to give up the fearless, unshakeable, selfless, beautiful fighter I met in Anarchist Underground. I don't care how hard it is. I'm falling in love with you, Aela Rinn, and if you're falling for me too then I don't want to know a future without you in it. Our kingdoms deserve to be happy, but so do we. "

Something released inside Aela that she hadn't realised was pulled taut until Bryn first began to unravel it on the road. The tension in her body rushed out as a short laugh. "Bryn Ryland, a man of action. Who knew?"

"You did. You saw what I could be for Dunwyn." His lips quirked into a softer version of the cocky smirk she remembered from those early days. "I can be something for you too, if that's what you want. Tell me what you want from me, Aela, and I'll give it to you."

"What I want." Aela breathed. It was overwhelming to consider. "I want to honour my blood. I want to do all I can on the throne to achieve lasting peace for Nielle. But I don't want to leave Dunwyn behind. My friends, my family. I don't want to let them go. I don't want to let *you* go. I thought fighting was the only thing that could make me feel alive, but it's this — it's thinking about everything I can build as the queen of Nielle, and everything you and I can achieve together. It's the endless possibilities that bring me to life. Bryn, I want us both to hold the heart of the One Kingdom. I want to rebuild the castle at Hiver and for it to belong to both Dunwyn and Nielle. I want it to stand as a reminder that we've been one nation before. Maybe we will be again."

Comprehension dawned on Bryn's face as it sank in, the gravity of what she was suggesting. "You and I, we both hold Hiver? Together?"

A smile crept across his face. Aela met his seeking gaze and saw again the trace of that unreadable emotion, except this time she could name it for what it was. Hope.

"Together," she said.

Epilogue
Six months later

"Did you know there are eight hundred and sixty-two thousand bricks in Hiver castle's wall?"

Aela glanced at Bryn in time to see him roll his eyes as they walked uphill towards the looming sandstone structure. Their pace was different from the last time they'd been here, unhurried. This was their place, and they could walk as slowly as they liked. You couldn't ride horses up here where the path was disintegrated, uneven, and the risk of laming was too high. Something would need to be done about that. Aela added it to her mental list.

"No, Bowie," Bryn said, fondly irritated. "No one in the world knows that but you."

"And Alexander," Bowie reminded him helpfully.

"His tutor," Bryn explained to Aela. "He taught me too."

"He says I'm a better student than Bryn," Bowie added. This new cheeky grin on his face made him look younger, even with the dark, exhausted smudges lingering beneath his eyes. Red scratch marks stood out, prominent against the pale scar on his neck.

"I think everyone in the world knows *that*," Aela quipped. She stopped and looked up. "Here we are."

Hiver was a sprawling enormity of turrets, stained glass and sandy brick. Even in ruin, it was magnificent. It had taken a month and dozens of soldiers with hatchets to hack a proper road into Hiver's courtyard so that Aela and Bryn and their respective entourages hadn't had to trek through the forest to sign the treaty.

Now, Hiver and its traditional territory, all the way to the dusty streets of Hiver town, where Amory and Ewan were rebuilding their burned home, belonged to both Nielle and Dunwyn. After another four weeks of work, the vines covering the castle's entryway had been completely cleared, and the doors stood wide open. Inside, Aela could see rubble, greenery, and a few birds.

"It's going to take years for this place to recover," Aela said to Bryn.

He winked at her. "In the meantime, I'll visit you for summers in Eterre, and you can spend winters in Dunwald. It doesn't sound so bad."

Bowie had wandered off to a corner of the courtyard, kneeling to examine something nobody else would have noticed.

"Is he still getting nightmares?" Aela asked Bryn quietly.

Bryn sighed, passing a hand over his face. He looked tired too. "Every night."

"He's tough," Aela said confidently.

"I know," Bryn agreed. "Look."

Across from the official entrance stood the old great hall, the dilapidated section of castle where Araxa Leren and her gang had once made their home. All traces of Araxa's anarchist legacy were long gone. Aela and Bryn had speculated more than once about where her remaining men might have disappeared to after hearing of the king of Dunwyn and queen of Nielle's plans to rebuild Hiver castle together.

Maybe they'd retreated to the mass of land in Dunwyn's southwest that Bryn had signed over to Splinter. A concern for another time.

Aela followed the line of Bryn's gaze. In front of the dais, where one day two thrones would sit side by side, were the first traces of work to rebuild the castle's interior. The grassy floor had been paved over with stones from the rubble of the room's back wall, which had caved in the last time Aela and Bryn had been here, *because* they'd been here. Etched on each stone was the name of a Dunwyan soldier who had died here, thirty-three in total. It had taken some time to identify them all, to find their families and offer answers and comfort.

"Ready?" Bryn held out his hand. Aela took it. Together, they walked up the stairs and into the castle.

The winter breeze whipped around the high ceiling. Leaves danced in the overgrown hall.

"We're the first king and queen through these doors in two hundred years," Aela whispered.

In silence, hands linked, they stood within the high walls of Hiver.

Raw adrenaline pumped through Aela's veins. She was exhilarated by the sheer size of the castle, the weight of its history, and the magnitude of the decision that had brought them here.

It felt like falling through the sky.

Hello from Nicole Rowles

From the bottom of my heart, thank you so much for reading Anarchist Underground! I love this world and I really hope you had as much fun living in it as I have over the years. I first wrote this story in 2017, and its release has been a long time coming. It means so much to finally be able to share Aela, Bryn and Bowie's adventures.

If you loved the story, spread the word! Reviews mean so much to me as an indie author. I would love to read your reviews on Goodreads and Amazon, as well as anywhere else you like to publish your book reviews.

Want to explore the world some more? Subscribe to my newsletter for exclusive deleted scenes and bonus content, giveaways, and upcoming news, offers and releases. Visit www.nicolerowles.com or my Goodreads blog for more information.

About the author

Nicole Rowles is an epic fantasy author. Her debut novel, Anarchist Underground, released in 2024.

Nicole writes stories she loves to read - immersive, character-driven and gritty fantasy novels with political intrigue, fast-paced action and adventure, and a touch of romance.

Based in Brisbane, Australia Nicole has lived many lives, having worked as a professional dancer, TV journalist and media and communications adviser. She balances her work as an author with a day job and a love of adventure sports like rock climbing, kayaking and canyoning. Basically, she wishes there were more hours in the day!

Sign up to Nicole's newsletter to discover deleted scenes and bonus content. Visit www.nicolerowles.com or Nicole's Goodreads blog for more information.

Follow Nicole on TikTok, Instagram @nicolerowles_writing and Facebook.

To my husband Andrew, thank you for your love, endless support and constant annoying hilarity. I first seriously considered working to publish Anarchist Underground while lying in our tent on a climbing expedition in the Dolomites. Back then, neither of us had any idea how much time and effort this journey would demand from me. Every step of the way, you've given me the space, understanding and encouragement I needed to shape this story into something I'm proud of. I love that we empower each other to pursue our big dreams from the safety of an equal partnership.

Anarchist Underground would not exist without the many hours spent with my dear friend Hannah Cliff in our mid-2010s writers club sessions, hashing out plot twists and getting to know these characters and this world inside-out. I love you. I couldn't have done it without you.

To Phil Ho, thank you for understanding this story and helping me make it stronger. Aside from me, you're the person who has spent the most time in this world. Every time you came back for more, it gave me the confidence to continue sharing my writing with others. And to Sam Gibson, thank you for giving Underground some much-needed tough love. Some of your insights totally crushed my soul, but they were absolutely necessary to create the finished product. I've learned so much from both of you during this process, but most of all I'm grateful that it has brought you into my life as friends.

The concept for the cover of Anarchist Underground was designed by my friend Bonny Nilsson, a talented artist and a positive, nurturing and endlessly supportive friend. I have no idea how you managed to juggle raising your beautiful boy with designing a piece of art that is stunning and so representative of this world and story. Your vision was better than anything I could have imagined!

Thank you to my sister, Monique, my editor, Jason, my dear friend and PR queen, Kat Orchard, and my friend and fellow writer, Lisa McNeil, for your guidance, insights, feedback and positivity. And thank you to my mum, Deb, an endlessly supportive beta reader and spelling and grammar wizard.

Finally, if you've gotten this far, I can only assume you've enjoyed the story, in which case … THANK YOU! I have more stories to tell and more worlds to explore, and I hope you'll join me on the journey.

www.ingramcontent.com/pod-product-compliance
Lightning Source LLC
Chambersburg PA
CBHW070522220726
48294CB00019B/90